WHAT HUNTS INSIDE THE SHADOWS

OF FLESH & BONE BOOK TWO

HARPER L. WOODS

ADELAIDE FORREST

Cover Design by Adelaide Forrest

Editing by Light Hand Editing

Chapter Headings & Scene Break Art by Etheric Designs

Map by Abigail M Hair

❋ Created with Vellum

For the ones who need the journey....

ABOUT WHAT HUNTS INSIDE THE SHADOWS

*Once, I fell in love with a man who decei*ved me.

For weeks, he stood by my side, twisting his words into pretty half-truths. He enraptured me with his smooth temptation, leaving no corner of my being untouched. He consumed my mind and my body, then finally claimed my heart for himself. But Caelum's true identity is terrifying enough to bring me to my knees.

Then, I discovered the truth of who he is.

Caldris is whispered in the Nothrek wind. The legend we only speak of with hushed words, in shuttered rooms, for fear of drawing his wrath once again. His intentions are a mystery, his desires impure, and he seeks to shackle me to his side for all eternity. With the Wild Hunt as our guard, he points us back to where it all began: the village of Mistfell and the boundary where the Veil once shimmered in the wind.

Now, another secret crouches, poised to change everything.

The Mist Guard have been sworn to keep us from crossing into Alfheimr, and from treading Faerie soil, even if innocents must pay with their lives. They have orders to resurrect Mistfell's shimmering barrier, but, once again, there's a greater cost than what has been revealed. Once, the people of Northrek blamed me when the Veil fell.

Soon, they'll want me to pay the price the magic requires.

Author's Note: This book is intended for readers who are 18 and older. It contains mature language, graphic violence, and explicit content with darker elements. This is book two in a series and ends in a cliffhanger.

TRIGGER/CONTENT WARNINGS

The Of Flesh & Bone series is set in a medieval style world where human women are subservient to their male counterparts. The world is a dark, dangerous place for women, particularly those who do not conform to societal standards and the purity culture that determines how they live. As such, some elements may be triggering to certain readers.

- Religious purity culture
- Verbal and physical abuse (NOT the male lead)
- References to grooming behavior & assault of a minor by an authority figure (NOT the male lead)
- Ritualistic Sacrifice
- Suicidal thoughts & ideation
- Graphic violence
- Graphic sexual content

GLOSSARY OF TERMS

Alfheimr: The Fae realm.

Calfalls: The Ruined City that was once a tribute to the God of the Dead before he destroyed it in the war between the Fae and humans.

High Priest/Priestess: The top Priest and Priestess who profess to commune with The Father and The Mother and pass along their messages.

Ineburn City: The capitol of the human realm, a gleaming city of gold.

Mistfell: The village at the edge of the Veil, where it is closest to Alfheimr. Serves as the access point between realms when the Veil does not block passage.

Mist Guard: A separate army with the sole purpose of protecting the Veil from harm and fighting the Fae should it ever fall.

New Gods: The Father and The Mother. Worshiped by humans after they discovered the truth that the Old Gods were truly Fae. The Father and The Mother make the choice of whether a soul goes to Valhalla, Folkvangr, or Helheim after the true death at the end of the thirteen-life cycle.

Nothrek: The human realm.

Old Gods: The Old Gods are the most powerful of the Fae race known as the Sidhe. Most commonly, these are the offspring of the Primordials.

Priest/Priestess: The men and women who lead the Temple in service of the New Gods and their wishes (The Father and The Mother).

Primordials: The first beings in all of creation. They do not have a human form by nature, though they can choose to take one for various reasons) and are simply the personification of what they represent.

Resistance, The: A secret society living in the tunnels of the Hollow Mountains (as well as elsewhere in Nothrek) that resist the rules of the Kingdom and live their lives as they please. They also resist the Fae and offer protection to the Fae Marked and other refugees from fleeing the Royal or Mist Guard.

Royal Guard: The army that works on behalf of the King of Nothrek, ensuring that the Kingdom remains peaceful and compliant with his wishes.

Sidhe: The human-like Fae who are *not* of the first generations and are less powerful than the Old Gods. Their magic exists, but is far more limited than their older counterparts.

Veil: The magical boundary that separates the human realm of Nothrek from the Fae realm of Alfheimr.

Viniculum: The physical symbol of the Fae Marked. Swirling ink in the color of the Fae's home court extending from the hand to the shoulder/chest.

Wild Hunt: The group of ghost-like Fae from the Shadow Court that are tasked with tracking down the Fae Marked to return them to their mates in Alfheimr, as well as hunting any who may be deemed enemies to the Fae.

Witches: Immortal beings with powers relating to the

elements and celestial bodies; i.e. the Shadow Witches, Lunar Witches, Natural Witches, Water Witches, etc.

HIERARCHY OF THE GODS & FAE
PRIMORDIALS

Khaos: The Primordial of the Void that existed before all creation.

Ilta: The Primordial of the Night

Edrus: The Primordial of Darkness

Zain: Primordial of the Sky

Diell: Primordial of the Day

Ubel: Primordial responsible for the prison of Tartarus

Bryn: Primordial of Nature

Oshun: Primordial of the Sea

Gerwyn: Primordial of Love

Aerwyna: Primordial of the Sea Creatures

Tempest: Primordial of Storms

Peri: Primordial of the Mountains

Sauda: Primordial of Poisons

Anke: Primordial of Compulsion

Marat: Primordial of Light

Eylam: Primordial of Time

The Fates: Primordial of Destiny

Ahimoth: Primordial of Impending Doom

Old Gods of Note:

Aderyn: Goddess of the Harvest & Queen of the Autumn Court.

Alastor: King of the Winter Court and husband to Twyla before his death.

Caldris: God of the Dead.

Jonab: God of Changing Seasons. Killed during the First Fae War.

Kahlo: God of Beasts & King of the Autumn Court.

Mab: Queen of the Shadow Court. Known mainly as the Queen of Air & Darkness. Sister to Rheaghan (King of the Summer Court).

Rheaghan: God of the Sun & King of the Summer Court. Rightful King of the Seelie.

Sephtis: God of the Underworld & King of the Shadow Court.

Shena: Goddess of Plant Life & Queen of the Spring Court.

Tiam: God of Youth & King of the Spring Court.

Twyla: Goddess of the Moon & Queen of the Winter Court. Rightful Queen of the Unseelie.

The Wild Hunt

Sidhe

PROLOGUE
CALDRIS

My soul had split. Half of it consumed by the panic coursing through my veins—the fear that I knew logically did not belong to me, but was hers. The other half of my very being, whom I had felt as the phantom whisper of a caress along my skin through torturous centuries of waiting.

Terror like she'd never known possessed her, driving her forward with every step. I couldn't see past the blinding fear that overwhelmed the bond, couldn't use it to track her down and offer her the sanctuary she needed. I spun in place, trying to anchor myself in her reality to get my bearings. All I could glean from her were flashes of trees and her scent lingering in the air surrounding me.

With the ghostly imagery of woods at the sides of my vision, I paused for a moment to search for any sign of her passage. To prepare for what might wait for me when I found my way to the mate who needed my protection.

The village of Mistfell hadn't changed for the better in our centuries apart. There had been no development beyond the improvement of both the looming structure of the Manor and the barracks that housed the Mist Guard. If anything, the village itself had fallen into disrepair in the centuries since I'd last crossed over the boundary, as if the income disparity between the wealthy allies of the crown and the destitute had grown ever worse in our absence.

I wished I could say it was a distinctly human custom to allow some to suffer in misery while others possessed riches beyond their needs, but that was a problem that united our races in misfortune. On another day, in another time, I might have felt sympathy for the people of Mistfell, but this village was where my mate had nearly died. A downtrodden hellhole with nothing to offer to the mate of a God—to the mate of a *prince* of Gods.

The mist bled out from the boundary, clinging to earth from which the humans had been formed and masking the filth they lived in. I walked across the stones lining the main street through town, moving away from the gardens where I felt the presence of my mate the strongest.

As a man stepped out of the shadows between buildings, a tang of iron hanging in the air as he thrust his sword toward my heart, all I could think was, this was such a waste of time.

I'd had centuries of time wasted by the Gods-damned Veil keeping us apart. My patience had worn thin.

I pinned the man to the side of one of the ramshackle buildings along the main street, my fingers wrapped around his throat. His sword clattered against the stone pathway as the noise echoed through the silence.

Most of the humans had retreated inside, abandoning the revelry that had clearly been meant to be a great feast. Long tables had been set up in the square by the fountain, awaiting the platters of food that would accompany their celebration. Samhain had come and gone, but the humans had likely long since abandoned the traditions they'd held so dear when we'd controlled the Kingdom of Nothrek.

Most of the Mist Guard had retreated to their iron-warded fortress, taking the new Lord of the village along with them. Leaving their people to die, abandoning them to the wrath of those Fae who'd been close enough to escape into Nothrek before Mab could gain control of the boundary.

We were angry. We were *ravenous*. We wanted what had been kept from us for centuries, and we would cut down any who stood in our way.

"Where is she?" I growled, leaning into my sword against his side. The man stuttered, reaching up to grasp at my wrists as if he could ever hope to remove them.

"Who?" His voice wheezed out of his throat, stretching between us as the battle raged on behind me. Humans fought, too stupid to understand it would take a single moment for me to slaughter them all if I so wished.

"The woman," I snarled, hating that I couldn't give a description, but could only speak of my mate in feelings. I could only speak of what existed within her, her very soul, and not the vessel that housed her. This man had likely seen my mate in passing every day. He knew the color of her eyes and the shape of her smile, where I had yet to lay eyes upon such blessings. "She was about to die when the Veil fell, but I know she still breathes. I can feel her light. *Where?*"

Fresh panic raced through the bond now, vibrating down the connection in a tangled mess. It overrode my focus, making it harder for me to pinpoint where she'd gone and how far she'd run in the time it had taken me to sail across the Mist.

At least she still drew breath.

"The Barlowe girl?" he asked, glancing toward where the Veil had once swayed in the breeze. The earth beneath it was scorched, the grass at the edges of the gardens blackened and stained with the magic I'd used to break through—to reach her in my desperation to spare her from death. "They were sacrificing her to the Veil when she fucking touched it and it all came down."

Barlowe.

I'd felt her on the other side, so close yet so far away. There might have been a deep channel of water between our realms, two halves of the Veil swaying on either side of it, but the magic of the boundary had made it feel as if she existed just beyond. As if I could reach through the curtain and grasp her hand in mine.

"Where has she gone?" I asked, feeling her in the distance. She was too far already, and I wondered for a brief moment if someone had taken her. If they'd loaded her onto a horse and tried to get as much distance from me as possible. I'd left Azra with Holt and the others of the Wild Hunt in my hurry to sail across, braving the channel in a rowboat so I wouldn't need to wait for the ship to be readied to set sail.

Fires burned at the end of the main street through town, wooden structures aflame in the midst of the fighting. I hadn't wanted this, hadn't wanted the war to renew.

"Enough!" I shouted, calling out to the Fae. As fiercely as the animosity between our peoples had burned in the decades of war that preceded the Veil, these humans hadn't been alive long enough to remember such things. All we would achieve through this violence was renewing a war that had been cut short centuries before.

"Yes, Caldris," one of the Fae murmured, dropping his torch to the ground. He stomped the flame out as I turned my attention back to the human I held pinned to the building.

"*Caldris?*" he wheezed, his eyes rounding in shock as he took in the crown gleaming upon my head, blending in with my silver hair before his gaze traveled down to my face and the swords strapped across my back.

"The woman is my mate," I said, tipping my head to the side as I gave him the truth not many would be privileged enough to know. My secret would die with him soon enough. "I think you can guess exactly how far I would go to find her."

The man swallowed as I pinned him with an icy glare, his bottom lip trembling as he realized just who held him trapped. Who held his life in his very hand. I slid my fingers across his skin, the sharp tip of a black nail cutting into the side of his neck in warning.

"She went into the woods," he finally gasped. "I don't know where she's gone from there."

"Was she followed?" I asked, squeezing his throat for good measure. His sword lay at his feet, discarded when I'd spun and pinned him after he dared to try to fight against the inevitable. There was a reason his ancestors had worshiped me as their God.

He was nothing more than a worm waiting to return to the dirt when compared to the lifespan and strength of the Fae.

"The Mist Guard went after her," he said.

"Fuck," I cursed, hanging my head as I released his throat. Shadows gathered at the edges of Nothrek, forming a void that I'd become too familiar with in my centuries at the Queen's side. I shifted my grip on my sword, plunging it into the man's side and quickly withdrawing it. He sputtered, dropping his hands to push on the wound as if he could apply enough pressure to keep his life from seeping out of his body into the stone walkway beneath our feet.

His body sagged, sliding down the wall as I released his throat. I stared down at him, at the betrayal he thought I'd committed written on his face.

"I told you what you wanted to know," he said, his head

dropping to the side as it became too heavy for him to support. "You really are the God of the Dead."

I crouched in front of him, meeting his stare and reaching up to pat his shoulder. "In death you will find peace that no longer exists in this place. In the Void, you will realize there are some fates worse than death itself," I said, watching as his eyes drifted closed.

The shadowy void at the edge of the gardens drew my eye as his soul left his body, leaving nothing but a husk. I slowly stood, turning back to where the Queen of Air and Darkness prepared to set foot upon the soil of the human realm for the first time in centuries.

The shadows opened, parting for Mab as she stepped through with all the lethal grace of a female who had grown up as royalty, practicing her cruelty and honing it into the sharpest blade over her countless centuries of life.

Her dress gathered at her throat above where the delicate fabric draped down her body, spreading into a keyhole at her chest and clinging to her waist until the cloth that was as dark as night shifted to deep red. As if she'd dipped the ends of it into the blood of her victims, letting the stain trail across the grass as she turned her watchful stare over the chaos of Mistfell.

She breathed in, smiling as the suffering around her strengthened her. Her deep red lips peeled back to reveal the gleaming white of her teeth as her dark eyes found mine across the gardens. She took a step forward, raising her hand to drape in front of her as she waited.

I stepped forward, calling to the shadows and letting them carry me to her. They wrapped around me, trapping me in their void as I disappeared from the village of Mistfell. The whispering hands of her servants trailed over my skin when I stepped through the Shadow Realm, emerging in front of her and lowering myself to my knees.

Reaching up as I bowed my head, I took her hand in mine before she could put it into position, touching my lips to the back of the ring on her center finger. A single stone lay in the center of it, the gleaming black tourmaline matching the stone pillars twisted into the gold base of her crown. In the center of it, resting directly above her forehead and nestled perfectly into her hair, the gem of darkness glittered.

The Cursed Crown. The stone that had twisted Mab from a daughter of the Summer Court into the Queen of Air and Darkness.

I wanted nothing more than to shatter it and drive the shards through her eyes.

"Rise, my child," she said, slowly pulling her hand from my grasp. I stood, forcing my hatred to abandon my face, so the mask of indifference could conceal me and shelter me from the cruelty she would use against me if she knew. If she thought she could gain a reaction to her hatred, to her bitterness and her pain, she would do far worse than treat me as a weapon.

"Yes, my Queen," I murmured, meeting her malevolent stare.

Her dark eyes glittered, hard and unforgiving as stone, as she reached out to condescendingly pat my cheek. "There is work to be done."

1

CALDRIS

$\mathcal{E}$strella's knees shook before her weight collapsed in on itself, her body sliding down the wall at her back until she sat upon the jagged stones beneath. Pulling her knees to her chest and leaning forward to touch her cheek to the tops of them, she stared at the carnage around me in shock, the gaze in her green eyes going distant. Studying the wreckage I had wrought to save her life, she ignored the motives to focus on the end result.

Making me the villain of her story, when all I wanted was to be her everything.

Her bronze skin paled against her inky-black hair as she took in the mangled bodies of the Mist Guard that rose the moment their corpses touched the ground. She stared into a hole where a heart should have been, her eyes glassy as her full bottom lip trembled. Something inside me cracked, seeing the grief rife on her face as she tried to process what stood in front of her.

She weighed my confessions and everything she hadn't seen, finding herself lacking for not acknowledging my deception before.

Her eyes traveled over the place where the dead surrounded the rest of the Fae Marked, allowing them to get comfortable in the circle as the fight trickled out of them.

Crouching down in front of her, I willed her to take a good look at me, instead of the aftermath of my fury, and see the male in front of her who would do anything to protect her. To finally see me beyond the illusion meant to keep her wandering in the dark.

Her eyes snapped back to mine suddenly as the bond arced between us. Nothing existed outside of the two of us, the world beyond our bond existing outside of the haven we created. Without my glamour to lessen it, the magic seemed to pulse through the air, the hands of the Fates and their threads working to connect us as we had always been destined to be.

From the moment I'd been created, from the very instant I'd come into this world and drawn my first breath, she'd been in the Void between life and death.

Waiting to be born. Waiting to be mine.

She tore her gaze away as sharply as she'd given it, the magic between us severing like a broken twig with the loss of her eyes upon mine. It was still there, still lurking and waiting for the moment when she would return to me, but there wasn't a doubt in my mind that my human mate had somehow found a way to keep her mind closed to me.

I took half a step closer to her, watching as she tried to shrink further back into the wall. Within me, the intent to give her the space she needed to come to terms with her new reality warred with my desire to simply draw her into my arms and show her she had nothing to fear from me.

She'd fallen in love with Caelum, and from the terror on her face, I knew she thought him dead and gone. Lost to the monster I'd revealed myself to be. "I'm still me, Little One," I said, holding out a hand for her once more.

I ached to pull her to her feet, to lift her from the ground that was stained with the death of an entire city centuries before she'd been born. To bring her to the palace that should have always been her home. To bathe her in the luxuries I had to offer.

"Is that supposed to comfort me? I don't even know you," she snapped, turning her head to the side. She refused to give me the blessing of her eyes, refused to look at me as best she could manage.

She knew as well as I did that what pulsed between us was undeniable; it would never again cease to exist or even be diminished. When she raked her eyes over the skeleton standing closest to her, I wondered if it was the first time my mate had seen such death and decay.

We'd both been fortunate that the corpses I'd left behind hadn't decayed in the same way a body would normally have decomposed in the centuries since I'd leveled Calfalls. As the God of the Dead, I needed bodies to reanimate, and so left corpses to litter the ground after a battle where I brought death upon my enemies. I needed mindless servants for my army, and as such, the bodies of my victims would remain preserved until I, too, was gone from this world.

"You know me as well as you know yourself, my star. The heart that beats inside your chest is mine. The soul that resides within your body has been mine for longer than you have existed," I said, keeping my voice soft and gentle as I took another half-step toward her. "Everything you have felt is real. Everything you will continue to feel for me is real. You were made to be mine."

Estrella dropped her eyes to my feet and the cautious path I carved through the distance she'd put between us in her frantic need to escape my truth. She watched them for only a moment, glaring when I ceased moving.

Her panic was tangible, her body twitching as if she were an animal trapped in the corner, in desperate need of escape. She scurried to her hands and knees suddenly, ducking between the leg bones of the closest skeleton and emerging on the other side of the protective circle they'd formed. It reached for her as she slipped past, its movements too sluggish to catch her.

"Estrella!" I shouted, leaping to my feet and following after her. Halting on her hands and knees in the middle of the road as soon as she was free, she struggled to find her bearings. She couldn't seem to get her legs under her. The shock of her discovery rendered her body sluggish as her brain fought to process all that she'd willfully ignored in her pursuit of the happiness she wanted so desperately. Someone like Estrella, or someone like me, who'd never known joy or even contentment, would do anything to preserve it when we discovered it.

We'd even ignore the half-truths.

Shoving one of the mangled skeletons out of the way, I prowled toward where she turned to face me. Scurrying backwards on her hands with her feet slipping in the blood that soaked the ground, she flinched back from me when I stood over her. I kept my face gentle as I stared down at her, making sure to channel all the love I felt for her in place of my fury over the rejection she showed me by running.

Her fear pulsed through the air anyway, striking me in the chest like a blow as she stared up at me. Her fingers curled into the dusty earth beneath her, her full bottom lip trembling in a way that made me want to soothe it with my own. I longed to give her the comfort a mate was destined for, if only she would accept me into her heart—if only she would allow me into her mind and recognize the other half of her soul.

"*Min asteren*," I said, the Old Tongue coming out instinctively. With nothing left to hide, I could speak her namesake in my native language, even if it wasn't one I used often.

"I am not your anything," she said, her top lip peeling back to reveal her teeth as she glared at me. All traces of the affection she'd grown to show me over our time spent together was gone, hatred hardening her gaze as she forced her quivering bottom lip to still. I inched closer, determined to prove to her, no matter where The Fates took us, she always had been and always would be mine.

Whether she was mine in the realm of the living or the afterlife, I would follow her wherever she went. Should the day come when she died her true death without me, I would accompany her to the Void to await the final judgment of The Father and The Mother. I would never return to a life without Estrella, without the warmth of her burning light shining around me.

Where she went, I would follow—immortality be damned.

I held out a hand, waiting for her to take it so I could help her up from the ground. My stubborn star ignored it, choosing to remain on the blood-soaked earth rather than accept anything from me. Her body twitched, tensing for the flight the predator in me recognized before she'd even made the conscious choice.

"Don't do it," I warned, knowing the outcome of my instinct to chase her wouldn't be one she'd enjoy while real fear coursed through her veins. There was no doubt in my mind that she'd come to enjoy such games one day—but not this day. "I mean it, Little One. I will not be held responsible for what I do if I have to hunt you down."

She scrambled to her feet anyway, turning and running with speed that she shouldn't have possessed. Even for a Fae Marked female, Estrella was unthinkably quick compared to what I'd seen of the others like her, centuries ago. She was stronger and more agile, her body seeming to struggle to adjust to the changes the mark had wrought on her, like a newborn fawn walking on new legs.

I moved, leaping forward. Tackling her to the ground, I rolled myself beneath her to take the brunt of the fall. My body struck the ruined ash and rock of Calfalls, Estrella landing on top of me as I wrapped my arms around her, holding her tightly to my chest.

"Let *go!*" she screamed, her hand moving quickly as I fought to restrain her. Grains of sand flew into my eyes as she flung them at my face, blinding me for a moment until I raised a hand to wipe them clean.

Estrella slipped free from the cage of my other arm, wriggling through my grasp like an eel and turning to straddle my thighs. She took the opening to punch my stomach three times in quick succession, knocking the wind from my lungs as a chuckle rose despite my better instincts.

Fuck.

My lungs heaved with my shocked laughter, my stomach cramping against the pain of the punches that she'd thrown her entire weight behind. She jumped to her feet, angling past me to try to escape down the ruined streets of Calfalls.

I turned onto my stomach, throwing out a hand and wrapping it around her ankle—dragging her to the ground alongside me and hoping her instinct would drive her to protect her face. She twisted as she fell, catching herself with palms that struck against the jagged stone with a loud slap as the side of her hip crashed to the ground. Curling her knee up with the momentum of that fall, she viciously aimed for my nose in the same motion with a vindictiveness that stole the breath from my lungs.

Flinching back from the strike of her knee so the fabric of her pants barely skimmed across my face, I kept my grip tight on her ankle as she fought to shake it off and pushed to her hands and knees.

I got up from my place sprawled on my stomach, crawling toward her and slipping my legs around her hips. To stop her from rising any farther when I finally released her ankle, I covered her with my weight and used it to trap her. I couldn't fight the amusement surging within the twisted part of me that found it greatly entertaining how this tiny slip of a human girl dared to fight a male many Fae ran from. "Are you finished?" I asked, chuckling lightly.

She slammed her head back so suddenly she caught me in the face. My nose cracked, pressing into my skull as my lip split beneath the force of it. She fell forward, hanging her head as if she were dazed as I lifted a hand and wiped it along the moisture under my nose.

My hand pulled away stained with red, and I sniffled back the remaining blood.

"Just so we are clear," she said, her breath coming in deep gasps as I quickly slid my hands beneath her body and flipped her to her back. Laying my upper body over hers, I pinned her beneath me and held her as still as I could. There was no telling what stunt she'd pull next in her desperation, and every strike like that would only risk greater injury to herself. "That was meant to fucking hurt."

She raised a fist, quickly jabbing for my temple in a move I had no doubt she'd intended to knock me out. I caught it out of the air, slamming her hand against the ground beside her head as I wrestled her other wrist into my grip and wrapped my fingers around it. Mirroring the posture on the other side, I pressed all my weight onto her wrists and shifted my weight forward, leaning over her.

Her blood thrummed in her veins beneath my grip, the sound a direct echo of my racing heartbeat. I shook my head, all traces of amusement disappearing as I wondered if she'd broken the skin on the back of her head—if even now her blood stained the stone beneath her. "I don't want to hurt you, Little One."

"You already have!" she shouted, lifting her upper back and neck off the ground as she struggled to get free. She knew as well as I did that it was pointless; with my legs straddling her hips, she didn't stand a chance of getting away.

"I never intended to hurt you," I said, trying to appeal to the part of her that had to know it was true.

The corners of her mouth tipped up into a grin, something sinister gleaming behind her green eyes for the briefest of moments as she prepared for the threat—the strike she meant to hurt me. "You say that like it will stop me from cutting out your heart the first chance I get," she snarled.

She shoved her hips upward, lifting my body as she forced her arms to slide across the ground toward her legs at the same time. My grip on her wrists followed, throwing off my balance and leaving me to release her in order to prevent my face from hitting the broken stones of the road. She moved quickly, the maneuver well-practiced in a way that made my teeth grind. Wrapping her arm around my elbow, she pressed her hand into the joint until it collapsed beneath me and she rolled me to my back.

Watching as she hurried to stand, I couldn't help the laughter that escaped me. "There's that tingle," I said, getting to my feet. She didn't run this time, facing me as if she were a conquering warrior, with her chin raised high. I took a single step toward her, feeling my nose shift to the side as it healed. Estrella stared at it in horror as I took another step. "Do you want to find out where I feel it, min asteren?"

"Fuck you," she snarled, taking a single step back. The

corpses behind her closed in, forming an impenetrable wall
and leaving her with nowhere to go.

"No objections on my part," I said, quirking a brow as I
stepped toward her. I didn't stop until her breasts pressed into
the black metal and leather armor on my stomach, making me
yearn for there to be nothing between us. I'd felt her body. Felt
her skin against the magic of my glamour, and wished all
along that I could feel her against my true form.

Her mouth twitched with the need to reply, to offer a
scathing remark, but as soon as it had appeared, all pretense
dropped from her face. Her eyes dropped low, avoiding my
gaze as she asked the question burning inside of her. "Why?"
It was barely a whisper between us, something the dead and
the Fae Marked watching us from a distance wouldn't have
even noticed, but for the movement of her lips.

I watched the heartbreak pass over her face, stealing her
features back from the rage that had contorted them. Her eyes
filled with the threat of tears, but Estrella never let them fall.
Sniffling them back to keep for herself, she shook her head
minutely as she shoved that vulnerable part of herself down.

I had my work cut out for me if I wanted my mate to love
me as she had before. "We knew of the Resistance before the
Veil was formed. Mab sent me here to infiltrate it and discover
if the witches might have hidden her daughter there. I
couldn't do that if I revealed myself to you as your mate, so I
gave you the opportunity to fall in love with me before you
learned the truth, instead," I said, reaching out a hand to
touch her cheek.

She lifted a hand between us, trembling fingers brushing
against the nose she had most definitely broken. The skin felt
tight where she touched it, newly formed as if she'd never
harmed me. She stared at it as if she couldn't quite believe
how quickly my body had healed the proof of her assault,

then let her hand fall away. I watched it tremble as it dropped from my view.

"You lied to me," she said, sinking her teeth into the corner of her mouth. Her chest heaved as she fought back the surge of rising emotion. In the wake of the ebbing rage and desolation that she couldn't escape me, there was nothing to distract her from feeling my betrayal burning between us, turning our love to ash.

"I never once lied, min asteren. I couldn't have even if I'd wanted to. I never said I wasn't your mate," I said, dropping my forehead to hers and staring down at her. "You saw what you wanted to see. I simply didn't correct your assumption. All you needed to do was ask."

2

ESTRELLA

"The Fae can't lie," I whispered to myself, thinking back to the legends I'd read in the books during our brief time with the Resistance. I'd assumed most of them to be grandiose versions of the truth; the human perception of the creatures that had always been larger than life.

"All the stories I told you about my life were true. Everything you have come to know about me and my history has been real. I've never once lied to you," he said, his jaw clenching as he considered the words.

"You told me a bunch of Fae half-truths in the place of something real. Just because you did not lie, doesn't mean you were honest, either." Running my tongue over the backs of my teeth, I fought back the surge of nausea in my gut. He stared down at me as if nothing had changed and he was still the man I'd fallen completely in love with, but he was the reason I'd lost everything.

He was the reason my mother was alone in a brutal village that had no use for her any longer; the reason my brother's body floated in the sea somewhere. If Caldris didn't exist, I'd be...dead, but at least my family would be unchanged.

"I simply never told you I was Fae. Can you really blame me when you've proven exactly why that was necessary?" he asked, tilting his head to the side. He watched me, seeing the hatred I knew made my eyes burn.

"You took everything from me," I said, the words coming out as brittle as they felt. He might not have been responsible for the events that had led to my downfall, but it all went back to him. To his existence, and to the stupid bond that stretched between us, ignoring my desire to tear it to shreds as if it had some right to my soul despite my objections.

He raised a hand to touch my neck, the whorls of his Fae Mark winding on his skin. The black circle on the back of his hand seemed deeper somehow, the shadowed tendrils of pure darkness rolling off it as if he couldn't quite contain the magic that stained him. The ink of his mark extended farther than before, gliding up onto each of his fingers. "Because your life was so incredible?" he asked, his voice raw with fury. "Abused by the Lord of your village. Bled daily and scarring yourself to feed people you'd likely never meet." He lifted my hand from my side, holding it in his grasp and running his thumb over the faint white scars left by the thorns of the Twilight Berry bushes. The circle that had once seemed dull compared to the rest of my Fae Mark swirled to life beneath his touch. My hand burned as the mark sent a shock wave of searing heat through my fingers, the ink twining around the knuckles to match his.

"What did you do?" I asked, the shock of pain making me try to tear my hand away from his. He held fast, refusing to release me while my skin burned, sizzling as the heat of the mark finally started to fade and the ink settled into my flesh.

"When the Mist Guard tried to kill you, your fear awakened the winter part of your *Viniculum.* You've relied on it to protect you since that moment and never tried to access the other part of you, which comes from the Shadow Court. Even so, that option is there, waiting dormant inside of you until you choose to use it for the first time. Everything I can do, you can do on a lesser scale, Little One," he said, gesturing to the dead around him and the way they waited for his wordless command. "If I am the God of the Dead, then the mirror of my power enables you to raise the dead as I do."

I swallowed, staring down at the new ink on my hand and wishing it away. I wanted nothing to do with the necromancy that he'd forced upon me, the insidious magic I hadn't asked for or needed pulsing through my body. It crouched, dark, heavy, and menacing inside of me.

"It was time to awaken that other part of you," Caldris said, tipping his head to the side as he watched me go to war with what was inside mine. I wondered if he could hear it. Did the mate bond gave him access to my internal thoughts—the one thing I'd thought was safe from him?

The only part of me he couldn't touch.

"I don't want it," I protested, shaking my head and aiming a glare up at him.

"It's as much a part of you as I am," Caelum said, and I chastised myself for the name I couldn't help but use for him. The God of the Dead wasn't the man I'd spent weeks with. Caldris didn't fit the man I'd fallen head over heels for despite my better judgment.

I'd known he would only lead me to heartbreak in the end; I just hadn't expected this.

My heart hurt even worse after his admission that he was looking for Mab's daughter; his presence here wasn't even about me in the end, but about the daughter of the Queen of Air and Darkness.

"How can you be a part of me when I didn't even know your real name? Why *Caelum*?" I asked, ignoring the cold dread in my veins that I wouldn't like the answer. Would it hurt me more or less if the name turned out to be a throwaway? If the name I'd come to love with every fiber of my being turned out to be a lie.

But the Fae couldn't lie.

"It's my birth name. The one my mother gave me when I was born—before Mab stole me from my crib and brought me to the Shadow Court to punish her," Caelum admitted, answering the question of how he'd been able to give me a false name. In all likelihood, it was more his true name than the one the world had come to know him by.

Caldris was the lie, the name Mab had forced upon him to steal his identity.

The admission tugged at my heart. The thought of a baby stolen from his home and brought to a place he claimed was ruled by the most monstrous of the Fae was something entirely unimaginable. I couldn't even begin to think of what that must have been like as a boy, growing up with the Queen of Air and Darkness.

My breath left in a sudden huff with the realization that struck me in the chest. She was his *stepmother*. His father's wife. The woman he'd spoken of, who had been so cruel to him that she'd ruined his relationship with his father, was Queen Mab.

I shook it off, trying to shove away the pity I felt for a life like that. His tragic backstory didn't make up for what he'd done to me, and what he clearly intended to continue to do.

I would not be a prisoner in my own life again, even if I had to kill him to gain my freedom.

He stared back at me, searching for a reaction I wouldn't allow him to find even though it lingered inside of me, eating away at me slowly. I willed him to leave me alone, glaring at him to harden myself against the empathy I didn't want to feel.

He pulled back slowly, heaving out a sigh of resignation as he twisted his lips in thought. He stared off into the distance briefly, before turning that blazing stare back to mine. "I have to go summon the Wild Hunt," he said finally, raising his brow as if he waited for a protest from me. When he didn't receive one, he turned on his heel and began to walk away.

The dead closed rank around me, entrapping me within the circle of their protection in his absence.

I couldn't help the question that sprang free from my lips in spite of my determination to keep quiet. "Why did they fight you? Surely they have to know who you are."

He looked at me over his shoulder, the corner of his mouth tipping up into a smirk. "You think a member of the Wild Hunt can see through the glamour of a God?" he asked, turning back in the direction he'd been walking and leaving me with that one bit of information. The arrogance in his voice made me feel foolish, realizing how little I understood about the differences between The Wild Hunt, the ordinary Fae the books called the Sidhe, and the Gods themselves.

The basic premise of their hierarchy was simple enough, the Primordials being the most powerful beings to ever exist and the Gods their children. But just how much power divided the Gods and the Sidhe?

Caldris sauntered over the rubble of the city street, leaving the Fae Marked and me behind, with his trusty army of the dead to guard us. I spun inside the circle my personal guards had formed around me, refusing to watch him walk away and shoving aside the memory of the day I'd watched his ass when he strolled into the hot spring the first time I saw him naked.

It was not the time, and he was not the man to be lusting over. He wasn't even a man at all.

I took in the sight of the other Fae Marked on their knees, corralled into their own circle that I'd abandoned when I ran.

The corpses kept them trapped within, but they moved freely inside the barrier. The glares on their faces felt heavy on my soul, with hatred for myself and what I'd led right into their midst overwhelming me.

"I'm sorry—"

"Save it, Fae Fucker," one of them said, spitting on the ground as if I deserved nothing less than what fate had in store for me. Maybe they were right. I turned my eyes to the ground at my feet, letting them drift closed as I fought back the trembling in my limbs.

The first chance I got, I would set them free, but how was I supposed to do that when I couldn't even help myself?

Something wet and sloppy collided with the side of my brow, obscuring my vision as it splattered across my face. The Marked laughed as I raised a hand to wipe the mud away, flinging it to the ground as a second handful launched through the air.

I twisted to the side to avoid it, wincing as the wet, half-frozen substance struck me in the side of the neck. It dropped into my tunic, warming as it slid over my skin. I looked over at the male who had spit on the ground when I tried to apologize. He glared at me, his mouth twisted into a snarl that dared me to reduce myself to their level.

To gather mud into my own hands and join in their brutality.

Another clump of mud came from the other side of their circle, catching me on the cheekbone. I held back the cry that burned my throat as the ground-up rubble from the destruction of the city bit into my skin. Another followed, and then another, the mud covering me and my clothing as they aimed through the gaps in the upright corpses surrounding me.

I turned my back to them, looking back the way Caldris had gone. He was nowhere in sight, and I suspected oblivious to the humiliation and raw agony the other Marked rained onto me.

I wouldn't even have done this to a Fae. I wouldn't have degraded and demeaned any living being in such a way, but they did it to me—one of their own. To someone who could have been a friend under different circumstances.

Pain burst through my shoulder. White heat that brought me to my knees. My hands clapped against the stone beneath me, my right arm collapsing beneath my weight. The side of my face struck the surface of the stone, pain radiating through my skull and making my vision swim.

Fighting back the nausea swirling in my gut, I raised my left arm over my head and twisted it behind my back. Reaching for the heat burning through me, my fingers brushed over the hilt of a dagger. It protruded from my shoulder, making my arm hang lifelessly at my side.

I couldn't wrap my fingers around the hilt, couldn't quite grab it to pull the blade free from my flesh. Dropping my left hand to the ground and pushing myself up to my hand and knees, I fought to get my feet underneath me. I slipped in the mud, not bothering to protect myself from the clods they continued to sling at me. We all knew I deserved it for falling for his lies, and maybe, if I was lucky enough, they'd find another throwing dagger and kill me before Caldris could bring me back to Alfheimr. My promise to my brother still resonated in my memory, the knowledge that I needed to die before I ever set foot on Faerie soil even more important now. I couldn't allow Caldris to win. I couldn't let him get that happy ending he imagined with me at his mercy.

"You brought him here," one of the Marked accused, her voice cracking through the air like a whip as I struggled to my feet finally. I swayed, my head throbbing and arm useless at my side as I slowly turned to face them. "If it weren't for you, we'd still be free."

"We came here to rescue you. We wanted to bring you to a safe place where the Fae wouldn't be able to find you," I said, hanging my head as I looked back over my shoulder. "At least, that was what I believed. I didn't know he was Fae."

"A likely excuse," she said, crouching down to gather more mud from where what had once been a garden touched the edge of the stone road. These people didn't know me. They didn't know anything about Caelum and I and the complex history we shared. But they were right that I'd been party to the decisions that had led him here, even if they didn't understand just how unwilling my part had been.

Another mud clump thudded against my chest, splattering onto my throat and chin. "Enough," a deadly quiet voice said. The air around me went still, seeming to freeze in time with his fury as it washed over me. I knew from personal experience, the fathomless anger that manifested in the quiet was far more dangerous than the shallow rage of a man screaming in my face.

Cold, calculated fury was far more terrifying.

I spun to look at Caldris in all his glory as he stalked toward me. The dead parted for him, allowing him to pass through without a word. He raised his hands to my face, grasping my head in his palms and brushing the mud from my skin with his thumbs. He glared at the scrapes on my cheek from rubble in the mud, his gaze drifting to the swelling on my other cheek where I'd hit the road as I fell.

He didn't touch the knife in my shoulder, but I knew he had to have seen it. He would have noticed the gleaming hilt as he approached. His nostrils flared as he lowered a hand to my neck, hovering over my skin as if he couldn't quite bring himself to touch me. When he finally did, his hand cupped my shoulder, his fingers touching the skin that throbbed around the knife. He pulled his hand away, staring down at the blood on his thumb for a moment before he drew it into his mouth and sucked the red fluid from his skin.

"Which one?" he asked, gesturing toward the group of the Fae Marked with a nod of his head.

I swallowed, shaking my head as I refused to answer the question. Even if I'd known which one had thrown the dagger, I wouldn't have condemned them to the fate waiting for them. I could feel the fury pouring off of Caldris in waves, and I knew that whatever he'd do to the people he thought had hurt me, it wouldn't be good.

"Will you kill the mates of your own kind?" I asked, tilting my head to the side.

A growl rumbled in his chest, the sound completely inhuman as he snapped his black eyes back to them. Indecision warred with fury on his face, fighting for dominance before he finally grasped the hilt of the dagger where it protruded from my shoulder.

He pulled it from of my flesh as I cried out in pain. My knees collapsed beneath me as he caught me, holding me steady while he used the same knife to drag the blade across his wrist.

The scent of his blood mixing with mine in the air drew a gasp from me, an unwanted shock of familiarity as he raised it toward my face. Blood dripped from the wound he'd made, splashing against the ground at his feet.

I swallowed, shoving down the odd twisting in my gut. An urge I couldn't begin to understand swelled within me. It wasn't hunger, wasn't anything so familiar to me, but it felt like a recognition of completion waited within his blood. "I would rather feel the pain of a thousand blades than bear the knowledge that any part of you is inside of me."

His head tilted to the side as his blood continued to drip to the ground. "Should I remind you that my blood is already inside of you? That you've taken my cock? That my very fucking soul exists within you?" he asked, his dark eyes holding mine captive.

He dragged his thumb through the blood on his wrist, pressing it against my lips, so the desire to open for him became almost unbearable. He pushed harder, forcing my lips to part so that he could touch his blood to my tongue. The flavor of it washed over me, drawing a whimper from my soul as he pulled back. The skin of his wrist knitted back together as I watched, feeling my own wounds heal with a tingling warmth that left the area feeling tight. "I will not have you suffer needlessly, my star. Especially when, no matter what you do, you will never be able to carve me out of your very bones. I own your soul. Nothing matters beyond that."

3

ESTRELLA

*C*aelum's army moved through the broken streets of Calfalls—the city that had once been his and where, as Caldris, he'd been worshiped by the humans who lived there.

The city he'd destroyed when they'd turned on him, torturing him and cutting him into pieces.

There was nothing quite as disconcerting as watching the finger bones of a skeleton tear fabric from the hem of a woman's dress to wrap around the gash cutting into her bicep. The dead tended to the living, caring for their wounds as the surviving Fae Marked huddled in the circle of their protection and flinched back from the oddly gentle touches.

The remaining part of the army that he no longer needed dropped to the ground without ceremony, and the animation he'd instilled left them with the crumpling of their flesh to the ground. The thumps against the earth resounded through my soul, a reminder of the deaths I'd caused with my own ignorance.

Caelum moved to one of the fallen Marked that he hadn't been able to save before the Mist Guard cut him down, touching his fingers to the man's eyelids gently and closing them. He glanced over at one of the skeletons, watching as it walked to the dusty earth beside the stone-paved street and dug the bones of its fingers into it. It pulled the dirt onto the stone, clearing a hole as another skeleton moved away from the group to help.

"What are they doing?" I asked, watching with something between confusion and horror as they continued to dig. They didn't stop, despite the fact that any living person would have felt the pain of all that dirt shoved under their nails.

Nails that they didn't have, I reminded myself.

"Everyone deserves a burial," he said, giving me a look that clearly communicated his disapproval.

"Burial?" I asked.

"It is an insult to the Primordials not to return all bodies to the earth so they can rejoin the cycle of life," he explained, watching as the skeletons kept digging. He turned to me suddenly, stepping up behind me and leaving a breath of space between us. My hands twitched with the need to move and my feet with the need to increase my distance. But I wouldn't let him know how much his proximity bothered me, refusing to give him that satisfaction. He would twist it into something different, on the wrong side of the line that barely existed between love and hate.

That morning, I'd loved him more than anything. Now, I hated him more than anyone I'd ever known.

"We burn our dead," I said flatly, looking at the dead man lying on the ground.

Caelum jolted in a flinch, grabbing me by the shoulders and spinning me so he could stare down at me. "You don't. Not anymore," he said, grasping my chin between his finger and thumb. "I am required to give all Fae and Fae Marked their proper rites in death. Anything else would be barbaric on my part."

"So, because it isn't what you believe, it's automatically wrong?" I asked, crossing my arms over my chest and pursing my lips.

"No. It is wrong because all beings deserve to know they will be a part of this world after they've passed. To take what they once were and burn it is a crime against them," he said.

"Because that's what you believe."

"Because I am the grandson of the Primordials themselves. Because I understand the dead and death more than perhaps anyone else in the two realms. Because for centuries I have guided souls to the Void to await the judgment of The Father and The Mother."

"What do you care what becomes of us after we're gone? You didn't know him. You likely never will," I said, and I realized the vehemence had faded from my voice. I wanted to understand, wanted to grasp why this male, who seemed to value so little, cared so much for what came after our souls left our bodies. And yet, he was willing to desecrate these bodies and pull them from the ground for his purpose, depriving them of their so-called burial rites.

The skeletons finished digging the shallow grave for the Fae Marked male, and Caelum crouched down beside the man to lift him into his arms. He lowered the body into the hole carefully, reaching into the pocket of his trousers and pulling out two shining silver coins. He placed one on top of each of the man's eyelids, turning his attention back to me as I studied him intently. "I care because I would want someone to do the same for you if the time ever came. I care because the witches cursed us to maintain the balance of nature after the Fae became too powerful. The cycle of life is all a part of that balance, and to disrespect it is to threaten nature itself."

"Why the coins?" I asked, closing my eyes as the skeletons began to push the soil they'd pulled from the ground back into the hole.

"The ferryman doesn't work for free. Without the coins, the souls may not be permitted to cross the River Styx and enter the Void for decades. I've paid his fee countless times over my centuries of life, but I am not in Tar Mesa to do so now. All who die in the meantime are vulnerable," he explained, stepping away from the hole in the ground and making his way toward the center of the street where the other Marked waited.

He raised his hands from where they hung at his side, tendrils of inky darkness spreading from his palms and forearms to fall to the ground all around us. The corpses of the Mist Guard rose once again, moving to the dirt expanse outside the city center. They knelt on the soil, digging their hands into it in the same way the others had dug a hole for the man.

"There is something cathartic about watching your enemies dig their own graves," he said, turning back to me. His eyes glowed blue, the power pulsing off his body turning the air suffocating. The breath was wrenched from my lungs, leaving them seizing in my chest when that powerful gaze narrowed on me.

Even knowing what he was now, even seeing him in all his glory, there were still traces of the man I'd fallen in love with. There were still notes of the human within the God, and I wondered if it would ever not hurt to look at him.

"Don't look at me like that," he said, brows drawing together as he seemed to understand the emotion consuming me. But something else matched the heartache within me: malice rending my insides as the thing inside me fought to get free. My heart convulsed in my chest, phantom claws digging into my beating flesh, as if the creature they belonged to might devour me to gain its freedom. His enemies digging their own graves only made me want the same for mine. His soul only drew from the darkest parts of mine, making me long for that sweeping vengeance I shouldn't want for myself.

"Caelum," I said, my voice a plea even though I didn't want to offer any weakness. What existed inside me now had never been there before, the shadowed tendrils on my hand begging to reach out and touch the power he used to control the dead. They called to me, tugging me toward them as if I belonged more with the dead than I did with the living.

"Do you know how much it hurt? To know that every time you looked at me, you didn't really *see* me?" he asked, stepping toward me. Each slow step brought his power closer, wrapping me in that suffocating embrace as the scent of musky decay, like the rotting of leaves in autumn, washed over me. There was something fresh and crisp behind it, the smell of Caelum permeating through the haze that came with his power. "To know that if I showed you my true form, you would run from me?"

"Do you know how much it hurts to know that everything was a half-truth?" I asked, bending over and pressing a hand to my heart as I fought for control. He would tear whatever he'd put inside me free, by force, if he touched me, yanking the power I didn't want out of me.

"We have all the time in the world, min asteren," he said, pausing a step away. As if he could sense that I wouldn't be able to tolerate his touch, wouldn't survive being dragged one more step away from my humanity. "You'll see soon enough that everything I have done has been for you, to ease the inevitable transition in your life and protect you from what's coming."

"What's coming? Do you mean something other than

being forced to be your mate?" I asked, and if it hadn't been for the pain riding my body, I might have scoffed. He acted as if he were the victim, and he had no control over what happened to me because of the bond I hadn't asked for.

"I cannot force you to accept the mate bond," he said through gritted teeth. "No matter what you think of me right now, the Fae do not cross some boundaries that humans have no qualms about crossing. We do not rape. We do not force a bond that will last for an eternity the way you would have been forced into a marriage you didn't desire."

"You'll just force me to come to Alfheimr and live by your side, either way," I said, my legs threatening to give out beneath me. The God of the Dead narrowed his eyes on the hand that I pressed into my chest, as if I could shove that power back inside of me and keep it from escaping. He tipped his head to the side, raising his hand with the circle on the back of it to linger over my chest.

"No," he said, shaking his head sadly. He dropped his hand slowly, his shocking bright blue eyes clouding to black as he glanced over his shoulder at the place where the Mist Guard dug their own graves. All but one of them dropped into the holes they'd made, pulling dirt back onto themselves as the remaining members assisted in the burials. "If you choose it, I will leave you to live out your life in the Winter Court. My mother will care for you like one of her own, and I will stay away."

I studied him, my brow furrowing as I fought to understand why he would make that concession. Why would he allow such a thing when he'd gone to so much trouble to make me fall in love with him? This entire conversation felt like a trap. "I don't understand."

"You are mine, and I am yours. But I will not force you to be with me if you do not love me the way I love you, my star.

You'll be safe in the Winter Court, and you will die your true death when your natural time comes," he said, his eyes dropping to the ground beside me.

"And where will you be?" I asked, pondering all that I knew of Caldris. All I had were questions about the truth behind the hints he'd given me in his tales of his life.

"Until the day comes that you're willing to accept me as your mate, my place must be in the Shadow Court. And should you die your final death as a human, I will join you in the Void to await judgment," he answered, watching as the final Mist Guard lowered himself into the last remaining hole. One of the skeletons broke off from the Fae Marked, taking up the task of burying him properly.

When the skeleton had finished burying the last of them, cutting their uniforms from sight entirely and leaving us with nothing but the long-since dead, Caelum held out a hand for me. His power lessened to a less-suffocating force with the number of dead he needed to control cut in half, and the air returned to my lungs in a rush. "Why would you allow that?" I asked, ignoring his offered hand.

"Because until you accept the mate bond, I am the same as I have always been. You aren't the only one who knows what it is to be a prisoner in your own life, min asteren. I would see you as free as possible rather than have you imprisoned at my side."

"Then leave me in Nothrek," I said, wincing when his fingers wrapped gently around mine. He cradled my trembling hand, running his thumb over the shadow mark on the back.

"I won't leave you here to suffer and die before your time comes. You'll be comfortable in Catancia and able to live a full life, if it comes to that," he said, dropping his forehead to mine. Pain lingered in his dark eyes, which were tinted by a burst of blue behind the obsidian, leaving no doubt in my mind that he still hoped I would change my mind.

I couldn't. Not with the betrayal he'd forced me to endure. If I couldn't trust him, then how could I even begin to trust that he would have my best interest at heart, if I accepted the mate bond thrumming between us?

I felt it tugging at me every time he came near, pulling tight in the moments when his eyes landed on mine. His glamour had done far more than just disguise his appearance; it had masked the bond that connected us, lessened it in a measurable way.

"And what I want for my life doesn't matter to you at all? I was ready to choose death once. I'm not sure what makes you think I wouldn't choose that again, if it meant my freedom," I said, staring into that stunning deep gaze. He raised a hand to my forearm, the contrast of his golden skin against the deep bronze of mine drawing a gasp from my mouth. He'd always been fairer than I had, but now his skin gleamed like the shimmering reflection of sun on snow-covered fields.

"You were ready to die?" he asked, his voice dropping low. We hadn't spoken of it in depth, had never really delved into the fact that I'd been only moments away from death when the Veil collapsed. His eyes narrowed, his nostrils flaring as he stared down at me. "I felt your resignation before I broke through the Veil. Would you care to explain?"

"Not particularly," I said, evading the question in its entirety. Caelum knew about Lord Byron and his disgusting interest in me, but he didn't need to know the details of just how horrible that fate had seemed to me.

Caelum had my secrets. Caldris didn't get to have more.

A strained laugh rumbled up his throat, both uncomfortable and amused. "I did ask you not to lie to me," he said, raising a brow as he remembered all the times I'd done just that in far less serious situations.

"Like I care what you want," I scoffed, twisting away from his presence. He took my hand in his, twining his fingers between mine as he guided me away from the place where his dead guarded the remaining Marked. They whispered amongst themselves as he led me back the way we'd come, leaving them as I looked at them over my shoulder. "Where are we going?"

"We have one more dead to tend to," he said, his voice dropping low as we maneuvered through the city streets. We passed by the stone I'd vaulted off of when the iron chains had caught me around the throat, then walked down the winding road to return to the main street where Beck had disappeared and Melian had been stabbed.

I broke free from his grip when her crumpled body came into view, hurrying across the ruined street to drop to my knees by her side. I hadn't been able to go to her in the moments after the attack, when my focus on survival had to take precedence over an injury that I knew even a Fae Marked couldn't heal.

My hand trembled as it hovered over the wound in her torso and the blood and gore seeping out of it. Her body shuddered, a ragged breath escaping her as she forced her eyes open. Her Fae Mark glowed with a hint of red, the power in her *Viniculum* working to save her from something that it couldn't prevent.

"She's alive!" I shouted, turning to find Caldris waiting at my back. He stared down at her with anguished eyes, and it struck me that Melian didn't even have the strength to glare at him. Seeing her eyes soften when their gazes connected was potentially the worst of all realizations, a concluding factor in just how far gone she was. "You have to heal her."

Caldris's lips pursed as he turned his gaze to me. "I would if I could, min asteren."

"You just healed me for something that barely mattered! Just give her your blood—"

"Blood magic only works within the Mate Bond. A Fae cannot heal a human who is not the other half of our soul," he explained, making me hang my head in despair. I needed her to live, to tell me what to do. He stepped away, giving me a moment to grip Melian's hand in mine and lift it to my cheek. Blood covered hers, as if she'd tried to reach down and hold her entrails within her body to prevent the death she knew was coming.

"It's alright," she whispered, her breathing ragged. "Would rather die than go to Alfheimr, anyway."

"It's not alright. You have to get back to the tunnels and warn them about Caelum. I should have listened to you. I shouldn't have been so blind to what he was," I whispered, the words hovering between us.

Her lips twitched into a sad smile, knowing as well as I did that it was true. All this time, and he'd turned me into a fool. "You have to get away from him," she said, pausing to swallow painfully for a moment before she continued on. "You've seen how powerful he is already. Just imagine what would happen if he completed the mate bond and accessed his full potential. No matter what it takes, Estrella, you cannot allow him to take you to Alfheimr."

Her words cut off as her eyes bored into mine, her fingers squeezing my hand weakly. "I won't. I promise," I said, knowing that no matter what happened, I needed to honor my promises to her and my brother.

I couldn't allow Caldris to take me to the Faerie Realm.

Her eyes drifted halfway closed, her body sagging even as she continued to breathe. "Put me out of my misery," she groaned, dropping her hand from mine to touch her wound once more.

Caldris seemed to hear her plea even though he was far enough away that no human would have heard it. He unsheathed his sword as he stepped closer to us, ignoring my wide-eyed stare. "Close your eyes, Melian," he said, dropping a hand to her eyes. He pressed them shut the rest of the way. "May you find peace in the Void until your next life calls you back to us, or may you find peace with The Father in Valhalla."

"Thought women were The Mother's dominion?" she asked, her voice barely a whisper.

Caldris smiled at her even though she couldn't see it. The first genuine smile I'd seen him give to the woman he seemed unable to tolerate. "Humans would think that, but The Father and The Mother are not the sexist constructs that you believe. The Father will welcome a warrior like you with open arms." Touching his sword to her neck, he smoothly cut a path across it, ending her life quickly without endangering her heart or forcing her to the true death before what might have been her natural time. Her arm fell from her torso, sliding down to rest on the rubble covered ground as Caldris returned his sword to its cross sheath on his back.

I stared down at the woman who had been the leader of the Resistance and had seemed larger than life in a world where women were considered lesser. The sound of bone dragging against stone pulled me from my contemplation, and I watched as the skeleton Caldris had summoned picked up a rock and used it to dig into the earth beside the road.

"Let me perform her human burial rites," I said, wanting to honor the passing Melian would have wished for if she could have chosen.

Caelum's eyes were blue as he stared at me, shining like

the first winter frost on the lake. "I am bound to give her a proper burial," he said, and though he looked apologetic for what he had to do, there was little doubt in my mind that he should have conceded to what a person would have chosen for herself.

I knelt in silence as the skeleton dug her grave, watching when Caelum gently lifted her into his arms and lowered her into the hole in the ground. He placed two silver coins on her eyes, the gleaming metal dragging a strangled sob from my throat before he scooped the first handful of dirt back onto her body. He and the skeleton worked in tandem to bury her, until Melian was gone from sight and only the earth remained.

4

ESTRELLA

aldris turned to me once Melian was gone from sight, his gaze softening as he took in the moisture on my cheeks. "I'm sorry, Little One," he said, reaching down to grasp my chin between two of his fingers. The coolness of his skin against mine penetrated through the numbness claiming my body, filling me with a cloying sadness that threatened to overwhelm me.

For a few moments, there hadn't been the fear for my survival or of what would come, if I didn't get away from the male who wanted to claim me as his mate. There'd only been the strange, lingering desire to once again feel that contentedness I'd felt at the edge of the Veil. With the Void waiting for me and calling my name, I'd known that for even just a little while, there wouldn't be any more pain.

This world was ugly. It was raw and bitter and filled with far too much death to be worth continuing on. The ghosts of my past and the people I'd loved would haunt me for an eternity if Caldris had it his way, and I didn't think I was strong enough to survive that.

"I want a funeral pyre, when my time comes," I said, the

words sounding empty as the hollowness of my voice penetrated the small distance between us. I focused my attention on his face and the pain that twisted his features at my harsh declaration. He recognized it for what it was: a rejection of everything that defined him. "No coins on my eyes. I want my soul to wander and wait for passage. I want more time before I come back to you in the next life."

His eyes drifted closed, his lips twisting to the side as he sank his teeth into the bottom one aggressively. The melancholy that shone in his dark eyes when he opened them once more nearly stole the breath from my lungs. "You want to hurt me, my star? Is that your goal? As if I did not already have to endure centuries without you?"

I stood from the place where I'd knelt in the dirt and watched the skeletons bury Melian, rising to full height as Caldris's hand fell away. "I only want nothing to do with you," I said, lifting my chin high as I looked him in the eye. "If that means I must wander aimlessly without a place to call home, then so be it."

He smiled sadly, lifting his hand and resting it against the Fae Mark on the side of my neck. "You would only be punishing yourself. There will be no next life for you. No more reincarnation to bring you back to me. This is your final life, min asteren. We have already lost so many years," he said, grabbing my hand from my side. He placed it on his *Viniculum*, mirroring his positioning as a pulse of warmth flooded my body. Like a closed circle, his energy thrummed through me and back to him, connecting us in a way that felt far more intimate than the nights he'd been inside of me with his glamour between us. "Please, do not waste our last chance at happiness."

"It is bold of you to assume I could ever be happy with the man who lied to me," I said, my voice breathy as he touched his forehead to mine. The darkness in his eyes peered into my soul, threatening to steal the thoughts from my very mind. I had no doubt he would use them against me if he could find them.

"I am not a man, min asteren. You'll have to stop holding me to the standards you would place upon a human," he said, his thumb caressing the length of my jaw. "The Fae have different urges. If a human were to lose his wife, he would find another eventually. The Fae have only one mate. There is only one being in all of creation who can make us feel complete. Only one who can bring us the joy of children. What do you think a human man would do if he were placed under those circumstances?"

I kept silent, the empty air between us all the answer I needed to give. Human men took what they wanted without thought. They forced us to be subservient to their needs, all while acting as if we were revolving doors.

Replaceable.

"The fact that they would behave badly doesn't excuse your behavior. It just means that you're all evil, and I'd clung to the hope that maybe there was one good man in this Gods-forsaken world. Thank you for showing me how wrong I was to hope," I said, tearing my eyes away from his. The severance of the connection between us made it feel impossible to breathe in the moments that followed immediately after.

"Perhaps then I should have taken you from the companionship of your brother that night in the barn? Cut him down for daring to stand between me and my mate and taken you to my home then and there? I gave you what most never have: a chance to know me, a chance to love me, before I stripped away everything you thought you knew about yourself." The hand at the mark on my neck shifted downward, his palm pressing into the edges where it paused just above my heart.

"You can pretend to hate me all you want, min asteren, because I know the truth."

"What truth is that?" I asked, my voice trembling as he dug his fingers into where the neckline of my dress revealed my chest. My breath caught with his bare skin against mine, only the slick coating of mud separating us.

He guided my hand down from his neck, shoving it inside the loose laces on his tunic to touch the bare, golden skin beneath. Resting it over his heart in a direct mirror of his on me, he smirked as he struck his palm against me.

My heart stopped beating.

One second passed. Then another. I waited for the steady thrum to fill me all over again, waited for my body to feel like it could function once more as I glanced down in horror at his hand where it touched me. The silence around us seemed too loud without the echoing of my heart pumping blood through my veins.

I strained against the strangled breath I fought to release, my eyes flying wide in panic. Even through the haze of terror, my palm against his chest remained still. There was no beating of his heart in his chest, either; nothing to show that he was even alive as his face twisted with the grimace that must match my own.

He pushed his hand against my breast once again, the beat of my heart resuming as if it had never stopped. My chest expanded, the breath I hadn't realized he'd robbed me of filling my lungs. His heart throbbed in a rhythmic chorus with mine, matching the exact cadence of mine's song. "We are two halves of one soul. The heart that beats inside your chest is mine and mine alone."

"Don't ever do that again." My lungs heaved as I tore myself back from his embrace, putting much-needed distance between us. I nearly fell to my ass with the force of removing myself from the connection that strengthened with every moment I spent with him in his true form. He raised his gaze to mine, letting his hand drop to his side as he peered at me through his lashes with his eyes glimmering dangerously.

"Do what?" he asked, his head tilting to the side as something feral stole over his features. He reminded me of a predator watching its prey in the moments before it strikes. "Remind you that we are irrevocably bound, no matter what feeble lies you tell yourself? The Fates have chosen us for one another. Even with our bond incomplete, it is stronger than most."

He raised his hand, his palm facing mine. My hand rose as if commanded, pressing against an invisible barrier between us that reminded me so much of the day I'd touched the Veil and felt a presence on the other side for a fleeting moment. A single golden thread of fate appeared, glittering in the fading light as I watched my fingers move back and forth. The strand wrapped around my middle finger and extended across the gap between us to wrap around his.

"Even you cannot escape your fate, my star," he said, pressing his hand forward until the thread wound its way around our joined hands. "If you die, I will follow."

"I have died twelve times, and yet you're still here to torture me," I said, pulling back as he entwined our fingers.

"We had not met then. Our bond hadn't strengthened. You weren't in your final life, min asteren. All of those things contribute to whether a Fae will follow his mate into the afterlife. Bond completed or not, we're connected now," he answered, watching as the thread disappeared from view. I tore my hand away, finally, freeing myself as I stumbled backward. I turned to face the rubble covered road that would take me back to the other Fae Marked.

"How can the bond strengthen when I can't even stand to

look at you?" I asked, glancing briefly at him over my shoulder. The remnants of the man I'd thought I loved nearly cleaved my heart in two, but the male staring back at me was so much more than he'd ever been. Taller, broader, more menacing and dangerous, and somehow breathtakingly beautiful, in spite of the harsh set of his ethereal features.

"The first rule of existing in the world of the Fae: you should never turn your back on a predator," he said, stepping up behind me. He didn't touch me for just a moment, his presence lingering at my spine. I kept still, refusing to turn to look at him and give him the weight of my gaze. Not with the way my eyes burned with tears, or the way my grief clung to my every limb.

I hadn't known Melian for long, and I hadn't always liked her, with her abrasive personality, but she'd become someone I cared for and respected in that time. Knowing that she'd joined the numbers of the dead—she was past my reach alongside my brother—the grief I hadn't allowed myself to feel when my life had been in danger threatened to swallow me whole.

His arm pressed into the backs of my knees, sweeping me off my feet and making me weightless for a brief moment as Caldris lifted me into his embrace. He cradled me into his chest, tossing me into the air ever-so-slightly so that I shifted my body in his grip and wrap my arms around his neck in a panic.

"Put me down!" I protested, clinging to him in fear that he might do so in a less-than-caring manner. We both knew that if the roles had been reversed, I'd have been the first to drop him upon the ground and hope he hit his head on a rock.

"I find I am very uninterested in that option," he mused, striding forward with long steps over the uneven terrain and the cracks in the stones as if they was inconsequential to him, even when I knew I'd be more likely to fall upon my face.

"Where are you taking me?" I asked, turning a panicked gaze over his shoulder. The Fae Marked were in the opposite direction, and I couldn't imagine he wanted to put too much distance between us and them.

What if they escaped?

"To the falls to clean you up as best we can," he answered, stepping up onto a particularly jagged rock. The edges of my fingers brushed against the hilt of his sword, longing to draw it and press it to his throat. To take my freedom in violence and blood, the same way he would own me. "That would be unwise, min asteren. We both know you won't kill me."

I couldn't be sure if the word choice was intentional or purely coincidental. *Won't, not can't.* One day, I was determined to prove him wrong.

"Perhaps it isn't your life I mean to take," I said as he rolled his neck. My fingers dislodged from their grip around the back, drifting down to grasp the fabric of his tunic tightly.

His frame went solid, the muscles of his chest tightening beneath my fingers, as he flinched away from the words I spoke. I didn't meet his eyes, staring at the side of his neck and unwilling to allow him to see the fear my words caused me. I'd been content to go to the Void once, content to end my life even while suspecting that it may be my final life after the ritual in the woods on Samhain.

But knowing for certain I'd face the judgment of The Father and The Mother, with them knowing my last act was one of cowardice, was an entirely different death to die. Before, I'd tried to choose death over a life as a prisoner. Now, I felt as if I'd use death to escape my fear of the unknown and the twisted, gnarled thing Caldris had planted inside of me, the bond between us that threatened everything I thought I'd known about myself.

If *this* was what The Fates had chosen for me, would The Father and The Mother be angry with me for rejecting it? Would they cast me into Tartarus and sentence me to eternal damnation?

Was Tartarus even real, or just another construct to keep us obedient to the Gods we worshiped in Temple?

The roaring of the falls grew louder as we approached in silence. The tension of his body never eased, never returned to the calm I'd come to expect from him even in the face of my anger. The tears burning my eyes finally fell as the trap of this cursed bond closed around me.

It was only when he'd stopped beside the pool at the base of the falls that he set me down, lowering me gently to the rock. I clung to his shirt, rubbing my cheeks against it as I tried to hide the evidence of my crying. He had to feel the wet stain upon his clothing, but he said not a word and allowed me to try to find some semblance of my dignity.

When I sniffled, wiping the last of the moisture off my face, Caldris grasped the hair at the back of my head in his fist and guided my head away from him with gentle pressure as I released his tunic and stared up into the brightness of his blue eyes. They were so unlike the obsidian stare I'd grown used to, so unlike the warmth I'd found in that dark stare.

They were so...*other.*

"You will not harm yourself. Is that understood?" he asked, his voice gruff as his probing stare searched my face.

"I do not take orders from you. Maybe you should consider the kind of desperation I must feel to even think of it. How much I must want to be rid of your stain upon my life that I would be willing to slit my own throat just so that you could never touch me again," I snarled.

He glowered as he rolled his head to the side, the patience fading from his expression. "It would be pointless in the end. I will heal any injury you suffer, min asteren," he said, releasing his grip on my hair. My neck tilted forward with the loss of pressure, dropping toward his and bringing our faces closer than I wanted.

"Why won't you let me go? I don't want you. I don't want to be your mate. Surely you would rather spend your time with someone who does," I protested, closing my eyes tightly as I turned my head away from his.

He swept my hair over one shoulder, baring my neck as his lips dropped to brush against the *Viniculum.* A surge of awareness flooded through me, the heat of his body sinking into my front as he knelt in the dirt in front of me as if there were no clothes between us. "You are too young to understand what we share. Just because you would take it for granted now does not mean that you will not come to appreciate me in time, as your fear and prejudice against my kind dissipates. You have a lifetime of untruths to overcome, but I can be patient for you. I have already waited centuries to feel the love we share. I would wait one hundred more."

He murmured the words against my skin, the silken caress of his breath washing over my Fae Mark and sending an unwilling shiver through my body. The image of him between my legs flashed through my head, a rapid succession of images from my memory. They were twisted, distorted and shown from his perspective, so that even though I remembered the memories themselves, they were new—different altogether. My thighs clenched as Caldris trailed his nose over my neck, inhaling deeply.

I shuddered. "Do you ever think of anything besides sex?"

"Oh, Little One, what I feel when I'm inside of you isn't about anything as mundane as sex. It's about being united with you as one. Our bodies moving in tandem and our souls melded as closely as they can be. It isn't about fucking you, but about being inside you in every way. The moments when you orgasm are the only ones when you open yourself to me, when you share your feelings so that I may feel them too," he said, nipping at the top of my neck sharply. "Besides, you quite liked that for someone who hates me," he teased, as he continued to breathe me in, trailing his teeth over my skin.

He drew away slightly to tear fabric from the bottom of his cloak, dipping it into the frigid water of the pool beside us. I flinched away as he touched the icy fabric to my skin, wiping away some of the mud on the side of my face with gentle fingers. His gaze drifted over me, the tenderness in his gaze stealing the breath from my lungs.

"I hate you more than you could possibly imagine," I murmured, fighting back the urge to slap his hand away. It warred within me, fighting against the parts of me that needed his gentleness and soothing. The cruelty of my own kind made me feel as if I'd been dragged against the stones of the riverbed, my skin flayed to expose the raw parts of me I didn't want anyone to see.

"What can I do to lessen that?" he asked, rinsing the cloth in the pool and touching it to the side of my neck that was caked with mud. His fingers gently worked to clean me, ringing the cloth out so that the water didn't make me any colder than necessary.

"Let them go," I said, fully aware that imploring him to free me would be pointless. He had already made it clear that he would never be willing to accommodate that desire, but perhaps I could negotiate for the others.

"After what they've done to you, you would still seek their freedom?" he asked, raising an eyebrow as he dipped the cloth beneath the neckline of my dress.

I swallowed, shaking off the involuntary response to his touch. "They're scared. They see me as an enemy, and I can't blame them. I would likely do the same if I were them—"

"You wouldn't," Caldris said, cutting me off. "No matter what rage is in your heart, you are not capable of doing something like that. You very well may kill to survive. You may harm and maim, but you would never demean someone in such a pointless way. The sole purpose of that was to hurt your heart, not to protect themselves."

I scoffed. "I don't think you know me half as well as you seem to think you do," I said, turning my head away from his.

He reached up, grasping me by the chin with gentle fingers and turning me back to him. "I don't think you know yourself at all."

He held my stare, the challenge in his gaze blazing as he dared me to deny those words. I couldn't, I couldn't find a way to refuse the truth in what he was saying. My life was a stranger to me, but even worse, I didn't feel like I knew the person hiding within my skin anymore.

"I hate you," I whispered, fresh tears burning my eyes and nose.

His face softened further, pain lancing across his brow as he pursed his lips and hung his head forward. "I know," he murmured.

The gentle expression only served to make me angrier as the sting of tears sharper, gathering moisture in my eyes. I shoved him back, pushing against his chest as I fought them back down. *"I hate you!"* I screamed, my face twisting with agony.

"I know, Little One," he said softly.

"Would you say something else?! Stop acting as if you are the victim in this. Stop acting as if I am wrong because I will not forgive you."

"What would you like me to say? Would you like me to tell you that I think you are behaving as a spoiled, prejudiced brat?" he asked, dropping the cloth to the rocks as he glared down at me. "That in a few years, you will come to regret the words you've spoken to me in anger? Those years may feel like an eternity to you, but they are *nothing* to me. You will come to your senses and learn to appreciate what I offer you. All I need to do is wait."

My chest heaved, my breath coming in sharp gasps as I fought through my rage. I hated his words, because I knew there was truth in them. He had the kind of time, the kind of lifespan, I couldn't even dream of.

He just had to wait.

I shoved his chest again, wincing when he caught my wrists. He held me still, staring down at me as his eyes bled to that familiar darkness I'd stared into so many times before. "You cannot hate me without hating yourself, Little One. Think of that the next time you want to blame me for this bond. I didn't choose you anymore than you chose me." His words lashed against me, harsh and hurtful and all the things I knew myself to be when I was angry. "I am just not spiteful enough to throw you away on principle."

I bitterly mocked him. "So fucking romantic, and you wonder why humans believe the Fae to be brutes.".

"Is it romance you want right now?" he asked, trailing gentle fingers over my wrist. They teased me slowly as he released it, raising his hand toward my throat and touching it gently. "Or do you want me to be the monster you've already made me out to be?" His palm clasped around the front of my throat, fingers wrapping around it as he leaned forward and touched his forehead to mine.

All traces of gentleness were gone, only the bright-eyed stare of the monstrous Fae I knew him to be.

"I think we both know the answer to that question," he said, trailing his nose against the side of mine.

"Shut up already," I snapped, and my gaze strayed from his intense stare, dropping to his mouth and toward the sinful curve of his lips set into a harsh line.

"Gladly," he growled. He closed the distance between us finally, crashing his mouth down upon mine. It was the opposite of a smooth seduction, the antithesis of the careful way he normally touched me. This was the monster of Faerie, the beast under his skin unleashed as his teeth bit my bottom lip and he tore a gasp from my lungs.

He surged inside the moment I opened for him, his tongue sweeping against mine as he angled his head and took from me. I pushed back against him, shoving at his chest in an attempt to pry his mouth from mine as the taste of him claimed me, spreading across my senses in a primal way that made me want to mark him with a claim of my own.

He pulled back, his lungs heaving and cheeks flushed as he stared at me. His knees rested upon the ground as he stumbled back awkwardly on them, giving me the distance I'd demanded as I fought to regain my breath.

I stared at him across the yawning chasm between us that seemed to widen with every moment we looked at one another. His lips tipped up into a smirk that said everything I didn't want to hear, a condescending reminder that I would willingly give in to the monster I wanted nothing to do with. But the ember of a flame burned inside of me in the darkness, watching for the moment it could burn his world to ash. Waiting for my moment to rise, to remind the world why it should never underestimate a woman wronged.

My eyes dropped to his mouth, to his lips swollen from the brutality of his kiss. "If you want me to keep my hands off of you, then I highly suggest you stop looking at me like that, my star."

"I'm not looking at you like anything," I said, swallowing around the lump forming in my throat.

"There's a fine line between love and hate, Little One, and you are looking at me like you can't quite decide if you should kiss me or kill me." His lips spread into an alarmingly arrogant smile.

"You're the bane of my existence," I said, shaking my head with a bitter smile as I tore my eyes off his lips and tried to shake off the desire I had to feel his mouth on mine and have his arms around me, surrounding me with warmth once more.

"And you are everything I have always wanted and more," he said, and the words might have been sweet if it weren't for the bitterness of them. His expression filled with malice, as if he couldn't help but blame me for not wanting him the same way he wanted me. "Keep lying to yourself, min asteren. I promise you I am not foolish enough to believe the lies that twist your tongue or the way they contradict the pounding of your heart in time with mine. I know all your secrets."

I grimaced, my gaze connecting with his for a moment that hung suspended between us. My lungs heaved with exertion as if I'd just run through the ruined city, my body taut with the restraint that kept me sitting on the stone. All the while, he just pinned me with that agonizing glare that sank deep inside of me, feeling wrong on an instinctive level.

Fuck.

I moved before my brain processed it, lunging forward off my rock and moving toward him. He caught me in his grasp, his hands going to the backs of my thighs as he guided my legs around his waist. My mouth crashed down on his again; I plunged my fingers into his hair as I devoured his mouth with mine. He shifted as I grasped the crown on his head, tearing it from the top of his silver locks and tossing it to the side. It bounced off the stone beside us, shimmering in the light of the setting sun as we separated for a brief moment to watch it.

Caldris smirked and raised his eyebrow, his gaze coming back to mine in a playful challenge. "Should I put it back on? Perhaps my mate would like to fuck a King?"

"You're no King," I said, dropping furious fingers to the laces of his tunic. I tore them open, lowering my grip to the place where the part of him I needed was tucked into his pants and yanking it out.

"*Yet*," he said, the words hanging between us. I didn't want to think of the implications of that statement as I pulled his tunic off over his head, dropping it to the rocks beside us. I leaned forward, capturing his mouth with mine once more. I wanted nothing more than to forget who he was for a time, to allow myself to feel something that wasn't the agonizing grief that threatened to consume me.

Grief for Melian. Grief for the man I'd loved who had never existed at all.

His chest rumbled as he drove his tongue inside my mouth, a growl coming from the depths of his soul as he lowered me to my back upon the ground. The earth pressed into my spine as he followed, laying the weight of his lower body atop mine and tearing at the laces of my tunic. He yanked them free, sliding a hand inside to cup my breast beneath the fabric.

I lowered my hands to his trousers, frantically unknotting them with panicked fingers that couldn't seem to function with the way his tongue plunged into my mouth over and over, or the feeling of him pinching my nipple and adding pain to the sensations washing over me.

As soon as his laces were untied, I reached inside and wrapped my hand around his length, pumping him from root to tip and taking immense satisfaction in the groan that came in response. He shoved his trousers down below his ass and reached between us to untie mine.

He deprived me of his mouth as he kissed his way down my body, his face trailing over the fabric over my stomach as he peeled the pants down my thighs. Pulling off my boots and the pants along with them, he tossed both to the side before he covered me with his weight once again.

The ground was cold beneath my ass, the dirt pressing into my skin like ice in contrast to the warmth of his body as he settled between my open thighs. Laying his body over mine, he claimed my mouth with his as I reached around to grab him by the ass. Without fabric separating us, the heat of his shaft was like a brand searing into me.

He groaned, pulling back from my mouth to stare down into my face as I looked down the narrow space between our bodies. Everything about him seemed more intimidating in this form; his body, larger and more defined, swallowing mine whole beneath him. Despite his nickname for me, he'd only made me feel little a few times in the weeks I'd known him.

I understood the nickname far more now that I had seen his true form. Any human would be small compared to him.

"Say the word and it all stops," he said, even as his face twisted. There was no doubt that stopping would come at a cost for him, and the petty part of me wanted to make him pay it. Instead, I reached between our bodies and guided him to my entrance, pinching my lips together.

"I don't want you to pretend to be sweet right now," I said, the breath hissing out of me when he stared down at the space where his cock pressed against my pussy. One drive forward and he'd be inside of me, spearing me alive with the very thing I should hate more than anything. "You're a God. So fuck me like one."

He growled, shoving his hips forward until the tip pushed into me. My body fought to stretch around him, granting him entrance when it still seemed so impossible no matter how many times I'd done it. "A God is worshiped, min asteren," he said, rolling to his back and holding me on top of him. He placed a hand on either side of my hips, pushing me to sit back on his length and take him a little deeper while a strangled gasp caught in my throat. "A God sits back and lets those beneath him pleasure *him*. Not the other way around. Is that what you want? To serve me until I come?"

A growl built in my throat, my lips twisting with something feral that didn't belong to me at all. Caldris smirked up at me, his point made. No matter how much I tried to convince myself this didn't mean anything, I would never want to be like the women who'd come before me.

Because he was mine.

"You are the mate of a God," he said, using his hands on my hips to lift me and then drop me further down on his cock. Over and over again, working me open bit by bit until I settled atop his thighs and he pressed against the end of me, filling me completely. "I am the one who worships you."

He reached up, wrapping a hand around the back of my neck and pulling me toward him until his mouth captured mine again. He raised his hips in time with the movements he guided from me, filling me with every stroke, dominating me from the bottom. "Gods," I groaned, wrapping my arms around him when he flipped me to my back once more and moved within me. The slow, methodical dance of his hips brought his length rubbing over the spot inside me that made me soar. I wrapped my legs around him, hooking my ankles together at the small of his back as he drove deep.

"That's right, my star. I'm your fucking God," he growled,

the words a reminder of a moment of honesty I hadn't understood. "And you, my mate, are Gods-damned perfect."

He plunged into me, dropping a hand to the apex of my thighs and circling my clit. The words he didn't say danced in my head, the phantom of a memory flashing through me as he stared down at me in another time, another place. "*Now come for your God.*"

My vision filled with myself, as he'd seen me that day, my face twisted in overwhelming pleasure. Now, my pussy spasmed around him, grasping onto his cock as I came and an animalistic groan filled my ears when he followed me over that edge and filled me with warmth.

My head dropped back to the ground beneath me, my breathing ragged as I struggled to remember my own damn name. I had a feeling I didn't want to remember, because I'd come to regret everything I'd just very willingly participated in.

My life had been punctuated by many lows, but fucking my enemy was a new extreme.

5

ESTRELLA

*C*aldris never separated from me, his weight continuing to press down as moments passed between us. Suspended in time, lingering and waiting for reality to come crashing back, I fought to regain my senses.

His breath washed over the ink of my Mark, the vines seeming to writhe in response to his proximity. "Min asteren," he sighed. The instinct rose within me to chase away his fears of how I would react, but I couldn't.

I jolted when his mouth touched the mark, his lips moving over it in a smooth caress as if he knew it by heart and worshiped every line on my skin. "Get off of me," I said, placing both hands between our bodies. The feel of my fingers brushing against his mark sent a tingle of awareness through me, a warning that came from somewhere deep inside of my soul.

That part of me wanted him close, wanted to draw his very essence into my lungs and hold him there, and yet I couldn't stop the panic consuming me.

What had I done?

"Don't," he said quietly, pulling back to stare down at me.

He cupped my neck with his hand, his gaze soft as those unfamiliar eyes studied me from within a face that I didn't wholly recognize. "It is natural to seek comfort in the arms of your mate. Don't carve this into something ugly."

"This could never be anything *but* ugly," I said, my throat clenching around the sob that tried to escape. "I let you..."

"You are grieving, my star. The loss of someone you were growing to admire, the loss of the man you thought I was and the human life we could share. You will do whatever it takes to chase away that well of numbness that exists inside of you, even if that drives you into my arms," he said, the words striking me in the chest. They were too knowing, too similar to what I referred to as the hollow inside of me that threatened to swallow me whole.

With every day, with every revelation, it grew into a widening chasm I would never escape if I fell into it. There was only the gleaming of stars in the sky to look up at from a well surrounded by shadows.

"Don't talk to me as if you know anything about me," I said, shaking my head to rid myself of the comfort that came from someone understanding what existed inside of me. Something alive had been there before the fall of the Veil, watching and waiting, as if it were alive and tangible, knowing it's time would come soon enough.

"We are the same. I spent centuries chasing away that void within me before you were born to your first life, taking small comforts wherever I could find them. I do not know what it is within us that leads us to that empty well, only that nothing good can come of falling in," he said, touching his forehead to mine. The show of gentle affection made the rebellion within me wither and die, the tears that burned my throat finally reaching my eyes as I pinched them closed.

"I need you to get off of me, Caelum," I said, pulling my

hands from his chest, awkwardly gesturing to our hips where we remained joined. Where the God of the Dead was still inside of me.

"Please," I whispered, the quiet word sounding more like an admission than I wanted. He could have my rage and my anger, my betrayal. But he couldn't have my pain.

He was silent as he withdrew from me, finally slipping free as my body seemed to mourn the loss of him. It was so at odds with the relief in my mind, the panic worrying at the edges fading when he rose to stand between my feet. His footsteps scuffled over the rubble-laden street as he moved away from me, leaving me to slowly open my eyes and push up to a sitting position. Wrapping my arms across my chest and fighting back the sudden chill in my body, I curled my knees up and tried to slow my panicked breaths.

Fae Fucker.

The words rang in my ears, knowing that while I might have been able to claim ignorance all the other times I'd allowed him to touch me, *this* time I'd known exactly what I was doing.

I rested my cheek against my knees for a moment, staring in the opposite direction of where Caelum stood. I was all too aware of his presence by my side, my body feeling his closeness even if I hadn't heard his quiet footsteps as he moved. Fabric rending finally forced me to turn my attention toward him, resting my other, wet cheek against my knees.

He held a scrap of cloth in his hand, torn from the hem of his shirt. He dropped it back to the ground next to him in a pile of the clothing he'd gathered. Holding out his other hand to help me up, he raised a brow as if it was as innocent a gesture as any, but nothing he did was harmless, everything served a purpose.

I wanted nothing to do with any of it.

I set my hands on the ground beside me, pushing myself to stand on shaking legs. They wanted to buckle beneath me—to give into the bone-deep weariness that radiated from within. I swayed slightly as I forced myself to stand before the God of the Dead with my chin high. Shaking off the vulnerable girl who'd tried to huddle in on herself with shame for what she'd done, I stared into the dark eyes of a monster and refused to cower.

"There's my star," he said, folding the scrap of cloth in his hands. He flattened it against his open palm, reaching forward as he held my stare in a silent challenge. Sliding it between my thighs, he used it to clean the evidence of his pleasure from my skin. Never glancing down at what he did or where he touched me, he quirked a brow when I refused to flinch from the sensitivity between my legs. "See how brightly you burn when you lean into all that hatred in your heart? Think of what you could do if you didn't waste it on the one person in this world who loves you more than anything."

He tossed the scrap of fabric to the ground, straightening his pants and retying the laces. I stood pantless before him while he began to dress himself, glancing down at my missing clothing for a moment before I returned my attention to him. "I will never forget the man I thought you were, or how much I loved him. But I will spend the rest of my life trying to forget you ever existed."

He winced as I crouched down to grab my pants, turning them right side out and shoving my legs into the holes. Yanking them up my legs until they settled around my hips, I did my best to ignore the flash of pain that I felt from him. It was dampened, as if it was my own emotion circled back at me, weaker but recognizable all the same.

"Don't make me your villain," he said, staring at me. With his shirt still lying on the ground beside him, his golden skin gleamed where the sun drifted over the horizon. The moon appeared in the twilight of the evening sky, dancing with the sun in a brief serenade before she would vanish for the night.

"You did that all on your own, *Caldris,*" I said, his name on my tongue feeling wrong in every way. He grimaced as if he agreed, even though it was his name in truth.

He heaved a sigh, bending down to angrily snatch his shirt from the ground as I sat in front of him and pulled on my socks and boots. He shoved it over his head, forcing his arms through the sleeves as his hair danced in the light breeze. "One day, you will realize that you know nothing of this world, Little One. A lesser male, a lesser *mate*, would leave you to rot in the misery you would create from your own ignorance."

"But let me guess? You will never let me go," I said, rising to my feet and standing before him. "That doesn't sound like they're lesser to me. It sounds like you're just more selfish."

His features twisted as he studied me, his top lip twitching as if an animalistic need to snarl threatened to break through his composure. "Is it selfish to protect you against your reck-lessness? Against how quick you are to judge me for some-thing you do not even begin to understand? I told you once; I would burn the world for you if you so much as asked it of me. What do you think I would do if I lost you? What exactly do you think the purpose of a mate bond is? The witches created them to right the balance of the world—between the Fae and the humans—so that nothing was out of order. A mate is chosen to be our balance. *You* are my balance. Everything good that exists inside of me comes from you. If I lost you, you might as well burn the world to ash," he said, stepping closer until he leaned over me. Forced to tip my head back to meet his gaze, I almost wished I hadn't bothered. "So tell me again, Little One, am I the selfish one?"

He stared at me, his eyes glimmering as my own anger

raised to match his frustration that rolled off of him in waves, coating the air with the sickly scent of death. I glanced over at Melian's grave, the reminder of it causing something completely foreign to sweep over me, striking into my chest and threatening to knock me off my feet.

"You can't put that on me," I said, staring at him in horror. He couldn't possibly mean to put the fate of the world on my shoulders. As if in rejecting him, I rejected the world and condemned it to a fate worse than death. He raised his arms, gesturing out to the city around us and the rubble of the streets and skeletal remains of buildings that had probably gleamed in magnificence during their prime.

"I ruined this city for vengeance over what they'd done to me. For the way they betrayed me. Is this what you want the world to look like? Is this your hope for your home and the people you claim to love and want to protect?" he asked, scoffing because he already knew the answer. He knew I would do what was necessary for the greater good, because where he didn't care, I did.

"Of course not," I said, shaking my head from side to side. Calfalls was devoid of life. It was death and decay and destruction. There wasn't a single trace of humanity left, aside from the Fae Marked hiding in the rubble, so desperate for protection from the Fae that they would hide in a place where there was no food or water that wasn't tainted by the ash of the city's remains.

There was just nothing.

"You can't use the world and this twisted sense of the greater good to force me to be with you. To make me love you. That's not how it works, Caelum," I said, my voice coming out strangled. He stepped closer, touching his hand to my cheek and cupping it gently. So at odds with the tension pulsing through his body, as if he was a moment away from exploding into a violent rage.

As if he was just a second from madness.

"That's not what I'm trying to do," he said, heaving out a sigh. He stroked his thumb over my cheekbone, his expression softening as he considered his words more carefully. "I have lived for centuries. I have seen what this world does to good things—to beautiful things. I have lived without kindness and been betrayed by people I should've been able to trust. This world is ugly and it is filled with brutality." He paused to smile sadly down at me. "And then came you."

Something in his expression made my heart flutter in my chest, threatening to cleave me in two with the bittersweet pain there. "Your essence flows down the bond between us— light and good, tainted by my darkness. But at your core, there is this well of beauty that flows from you. You don't love easy, but you do love hard. And I have spent centuries feeling you fall in love with men who didn't deserve you. Feeling your heart flutter for men who would never have been able to give you what your soul craved in the end, and knowing that, I was trapped on the other side of the Veil waiting for you. Just waiting for centuries to be able to hold you."

"Caelum," I protested, shaking my head to try to dislodge his grip.

He held me steady, staring down at me as if he needed me to hear the words I didn't want to hear. "And then it broke, and I met you and you were everything I'd ever dreamed you would be and more. I felt you fall in love all over again, but with me this time. I see in your eyes that you wish you could take it back more than anything, but you can't. Because you and I both know what you felt; we both know you loved me with everything you were. More than you ever loved your husbands in all your past lives. You still do, and you can't wish that away, because you were born to love me, whether I deserve it or not."

I studied him for a few moments, trying not to think about how it would feel if our roles were reversed. I couldn't begin to fathom the idea of him entertaining another woman. The thought of it alone made a rage so unlike anything I had ever known burn through me. To feel that, and know it was love, over and over again for centuries, I didn't know if I would survive. But I didn't want sympathy for him or empathy for the situation he'd been forced into by some wicked play of fate at the hands of the witches.

I just wanted to be free, to be myself, and I just wanted to not love him.

But he was right. Something in me couldn't let go of Caelum. It couldn't separate the man from the male; I knew they were the same person. A manipulation on the surface, but I'd seen glimpses of Caldris in Caelum. In the way he protected me against everything. In the way he wanted to possess me, body and soul. And in the fact that he'd left Jensen to die simply because he'd wronged me in that library.

I didn't have an answer for him, not wanting to agree with what he said and give him the satisfaction of knowing that I loved him. He didn't deserve that. He'd lost the right to those words from me, and whether or not I could control what I felt, I could control what I spoke.

He groaned, hanging his head forward. The severance of our eye contact...hurt, and I hated myself for it. Hated feeling like I'd betrayed him by not offering him the assurance he needed, after I'd given in to the temptation to feel his skin on mine when it was the last thing I should have wanted.

I hated myself and what I'd become.

"I won't lose you again," he said, lifting his head until his eyes met mine once more. "I will follow you, because what remains after you're gone will be a broken shell that that will do more harm than good. All I want is to be with you. Tell me how to make that happen, Estrella."

I narrowed my eyes, trying to come up with a solution. There was nowhere we could go where we wouldn't be a danger to the people around us. There was no way we could go to Faerie without risking whatever Brann had warned me about, and no way we could stay in the human realm now that people knew who he was. We couldn't go back to the tunnels, not with Melian and the others dead and no answer for how we alone managed to escape the Mist Guard. Too many coincidences; too little time.

"I don't know how," I said, in lieu of an answer.

He nodded, as if the answer were exactly what he'd been expecting as he studied my face. Placing a chaste kiss against my forehead, he finally stepped back and took my hand in his. "You need to rest. I can feel how tired you are."

He guided me back toward where the other Fae Marked waited, all but forgotten until now, making guilt rise inside of me. I shouldn't have cared. They wouldn't have cared about me. "We're staying here?" I asked, looking at the darkening sky.

"For the night. The Wild Hunt will be here by morning." We rounded the corner of the street, the others coming into view. They huddled together in a circle, facing out toward the skeletal remains that guarded them. With their backs pressed together, it would be a long while before any of them went to sleep for the night.

Caldris picked up my discarded cloak and guided me to a dirt clearing on the other side of the street from them. He sat down, tugging me into the space between his knees until I leaned back against him. I immediately felt a target on me from the glares of the other Marked who undoubtedly saw the embrace for what it was.

I squirmed against him as he draped my cloak over my front, cocooning me in warmth. "I don't want to sleep here tonight," I said, something about the haunted city bringing a chill to my skin in spite of his body heat.

"Neither do I, Little One," he said, his chest rumbling against my back. "I hope you never have to experience the kind of pain that I suffered here. We'll leave at first light, but for tonight, don't go wandering off with any spirits who try to tempt you away."

"Spirits?" I asked, glancing around the darkening street. There was nothing unusual, no sign of anything but us and the Fae Marked.

"They can be quite vengeful, and they have a good reason to hate me," he said, wrapping his arms around my chest. He pulled me tighter into his body, and in spite of the independence that made me want to push him away, I snuggled tighter.

How could I fight a vengeful spirit that I couldn't even see?

6

ESTRELLA

I snuggled deeper into the warmth on the side of my face, the soft tingling of fingers running through my hair drawing me from the depths of my sleep. Hovering in that space between sleeping and waking, I tried to shrink away from the touch. I didn't want to wake up and face the reality that haunted me, worrying at the edges of my awareness and threatening to dissolve all the peace I'd found in the realm of dreams.

"It is time for the stars in the sky to rest for the day, Little One, and that means the star I hold in my arms must rise," Caelum murmured, his voice resonating in the depths of my soul. I'd have recognized it anywhere, even with that somehow *other* baritone that tainted it from the man I'd known.

"I don't want to wake up," I grumbled, pressing farther into the fabric beneath my face. It was coarser than I remembered his shirt being, and a quick peek from a barely cracked-open eye confirmed he'd shifted us while I slept. My head rested in his lap, my body curled up on my side.

"What pleasant dreams they must be to keep you from waking. Perhaps you should make them your reality. You hold that power within your grasp," he said, his voice taunting as I closed my eye once more before he could notice. He stretched forward, jostling me only slightly as he grabbed my hand in his. He traced the circle on the back, drawing a shudder from me as the contact awoke that shadowed thing that existed inside of me. "With the God of the Dead wrapped around your finger, you can mold the world into whatever you want it to be." He seemed to grasp the thread of fate, tugging against it to remind me of the very real tether between us.

Finally opening my eyes to see the flash of gold shimmering in the rising sun, I ignored the weight of his stare on the side of my face where he peered down at me. "I don't want to mold the world. No one person should have that kind of power."

"Those who do not want it are the only ones who should wield it in the first place," he said, his tone turning melancholic. I tilted my head, turning so that I could stare up into the sadness that had claimed him so suddenly. "Unfortunately that isn't often the case, in my experience at least. Even if those who rule weren't always evil, power like that has a way of corrupting even the kindest mind."

"Do I have a reason to fear Mab? Is she why you'll leave me with your mother in the Winter Court instead of taking me to the Shadow Court with you?" I asked, swallowing against the bile rising in my throat at the thought. Someone, *something*, had repeatedly injured this Fae so severely that he bore the scars of those lashings to this day. I'd barely endured being beaten with the Priestess's cane.

"You have every reason to fear Mab," he said, nodding his head in agreement. "She knows better than anyone what power a completed mate bond would give me. She would do anything to prevent that from happening, even if it defies the Accord that protects human mates from being harmed in the games of their Fae. She couldn't kill you, not without sending me spiraling into the final stages of madness, and she much prefers me when I'm reasonable and cooperative. So she would keep you alive, locked in her dungeon probably. She knows that I would do anything to protect you," he said.

I forced myself to sit up, moving away from the heat of his body. I wished I could stay there forever, that I could let him hold me and chase away the reality of what we'd done. Of what we'd become, and everything that waited for us if we ever reached the shores of Alfheimr.

He sat on the ground in the same place I'd left him, his clothing unruffled as if he'd never laid down and let himself sleep. If he'd been human, I suspected I would have found circles beneath his eyes or some sign of his exhaustion from his sleepless night keeping watch. I didn't know how the skeletons or corpses worked. Did they continue to follow his orders when he slept, or did they stop doing his bidding the moment he closed his eyes and drifted into the other realm?

"And you think your mother can keep me safe?" I asked. I didn't want to say the thought that danced in my head. I didn't want to sound bitter, but she hadn't even protected her own child. She'd allowed him to be stolen from his crib when he was nothing but a baby. If what he'd told me as Caelum was still true, he'd continued to live with his father and stepmother, never really knowing his birth mother. So how would the Queen of Winter protect me? Why would she protect me? I was nothing to her, especially if her own son mattered so little.

"She won't make the same mistake she made in the past, and she understands better than anyone how valuable a mate is. Mab refused to allow her to be with hers, violating the Accord by keeping him bound to her through the ties of a political marriage. When they defied that and came together for one night to create me, she imprisoned my father in the caves of Tar Mesa until she killed him," he explained, settling an open palm against my lower back. I couldn't bear to look at him, to think of the life he must have lived under the care of the woman who'd killed his father. "She'd long since found possessing the heir of her rivals to be a much more convincing motivator, so she didn't need him anymore because she had me. My mother won't allow me to suffer her fate , knowing my mate is in Mab's clutches."

I nodded as if I could even begin to understand the kind of torture it would be to know that my enemy had someone I cared for. Mab wasn't my enemy yet, but it sounded like she would be if she knew I existed.

I glanced over to the other Fae Marked where they began to awaken, watching as their wide eyes looked toward the edges of the city. On the other side of the street, one of the side roads plunged into a cavern. All life seemed to disappear into the hole that opened into the earth, as if something massive had emerged from the depths of despair. "That was where Calfalls buried the dead, back when the city was thriving," Caldris explained, brushing my hair over my shoulder. His worked through the knotted ends, pulling tangles free with a gentleness that made a chill sweep over me.

"That's where they were buried when you raised the dead and brought Calfalls to its knees," I said, making a mental note to wander closer if I ever got the chance to move at will. I was filled with the sudden need to understand how deep the pit went, how far into the earth the dead had been buried and just what kind of force it must have taken for so many to *rise.*

The faint image of a woman emerged from that same street, her form nothing but a wisp in the wind as her dress billowed in shades of white and gray. The trees were visible through her form, far more transparent than the riders of the

Wild Hunt had been. I turned toward Caelum, grasping his forearm with my ragged nails. "Is that a spirit?" I asked, swallowing as I tried to resist the urge to press further back into his body and the comfort I knew I would find there.

"The Wild Hunt is coming," he said, nodding his head as if that explained anything. "Unruly spirits are drawn to the Leader of the Hunt, following him across the land until they find their own version of peace." He tilted his head back toward the crater in the ground, where more spectral forms of men and women, *children*, rose from the pit. They floated, their feet never touching the ground beneath them, though they moved in the same way they would have alive. The woman approached us first, standing at the intersection of the streets and pausing there. Her eyes landed on ours for a brief moment, shocks of black against her ghostly pallor. There was a hole in her chest, a dark chasm that had to have been a fatal wound.

Unlike her, some of the other spectral forms were whole, their ghostly bodies intact from less traumatic deaths, but the ones who had died violently bore the signs of that on their spirits.

"I thought death was supposed to wipe the slate? Give us a fresh start?" I asked, thinking of the promises the High Priest had made. I wanted the oblivion that came with it, the ceasing of all the suffering I'd endured in this life.

"It does, once we find our way to the Void. Until then, we wander with the memories of who we once were. It is why a quick passage across the River Styx is a kindness, Little One. Nothing good can come from having time to stew in our own regret," Caldris answered.

The female spirit finally turned her stare away from us, looking back over her shoulder toward the chasm as the first rider of the Wild Hunt appeared over the crest of the cliff. The same male who had nearly seen me that night in the woods, and the same one who had fought against Caelum on the cliff after my brother had been stabbed by another one of the riders.

He held his head high as his skeletal horse rounded onto the street, hooves clattering against the stones. A group of others followed, their numbers fanning out behind him and the spirits that paved the way. The leader's eyes landed on Caldris as he lifted me to my feet, standing tall as the other Fae Marked huddled together. In spite of the fear on their faces, there wasn't even a flicker of power flashing through them. The *Viniculum* on their necks never came to life. It had no need to protect them against what any normal human would think of as danger. The Wild Hunt would never be a hazard to the Marked—not when their entire purpose was to find them and bring them to Alfheimr.

Caldris stepped up beside me, exchanging a long look with the leader of the Wild Hunt. When the rest of the spectral forms crested the hill from the empty graves, there were nearly twenty of them, all standing in a similar pattern to what I would have seen from a flock of geese flying away for the winter.

The leader's horse took the first step. His bony hoof rang against the stone, the clap echoing up the road. I would never forget the eerie sight from my memory, how the blue markings on his face stood out, even at a distance. They all had them, those same icy blue lines.

As the horses' steps brought the riders closer, some animals dragging carts behind them, the hounds of the Wild Hunt jumped from the steep bank one by one to follow the riders. There were a dozen of them, all ghastly appearing with venomous shadows dripping from their jowls. Fangs as thick as my wrist gleamed in the light of the rising sun, protruding from the places where their skin had rotted off their faces.

I swallowed as I imagined what it must have been like to be their prey and to be able to see those fangs tear through skin and flesh until the moment of death finally came.

A group of three white wolves followed behind them, their ears tipped in crimson. Caldris's lips tipped up into a smile at the corners, reminding me painfully of the playful man I'd known. The three beasts broke free from the group, racing past the riders of the Wild Hunt. With the sight of their bared teeth and snarling faces to terrify me, I dug my nails into Caldris's sleeve.

"Caelum," I muttered, realizing the beasts didn't intend to stop. They seemed to grow with every leap that brought them closer, until they stood taller than my waist.

The smile slid from Caldris's face, a look of irritation crossing over it briefly before his jaw clenched. "Fuck," he grunted, tearing his arm free from my hand. The first of the wolves leaped and struck him in the chest the next moment, knocking him back a step as he caught the massive creature. Its hind legs dropped to the ground, the front paws bracing against Caldris's shoulders as he stared at the wolf that was nearly as tall as him. "Don't you fucking do it—" The wolf yipped happily, licking a long line up the side of Caldris's face and making a shocked gasp break free from me.

The second of the wolves collided with the back of the first, knocking both the wolf and Caldris to the ground. It scrambled to its feet, prancing happily as the two of them nudged Caldris with their noses and nipped at his hands when he tried to swat them away.

I was so busy watching their interaction that I never saw the third wolf coming for me, the force of its body striking into my chest knocking me off my feet entirely. I landed hard, my back thudding against the dirt behind me and stealing the breath from my lungs. "Fenrir!" Caldris shouted, but I was trapped by the enormous creature crawling over me. He prowled forward until his snout lingered over my face, one enormous paw on either side of my head. The wolf's head tilted in an animalistic way that was so like the God of the Dead it was almost painful, his eyes considering me.

I swallowed back my nerves, meeting his stare. He seemed to find me lacking, and to see all the weaknesses that I knew lingered just beneath my surface. I dug my fingers into the soil beneath me as I pushed myself up to get closer to the wolf's nose and the teeth that he bared at me when I moved. "I don't relish the idea of hurting you," I said, staring into his garnet eyes. "But that doesn't mean I won't if you don't get off of me this instant."

He huffed a breath, that red stare twinkling for a moment before his nose twitched, then the wolf smelled me, tipping his face toward my neck as I grabbed a fistful of the dirt beneath me and readied myself for a fight that I stood no chance of surviving. His wet nose touched the side of my neck, drawing a shudder from me as it connected with the swirling lines of my Fae Mark.

Just when I thought I was a breath away from having his mouth wrapped around my throat, the wolf licked a long trail up the side of my neck and cheek. His expression wasn't as enthusiastic as his companions' had been when they'd greeted Caldris, but there was a grudging acceptance to his stare when he finally stepped back.

Caldris had risen to his feet, glaring down at the wolf who'd knocked me over. The others sat by his side, their ears pointed up as they watched me clamber to my feet. "You do not *assault* my mate. You protect her," he said as Fenrir approached him. He was the biggest of the three, his head level with Caldris's stomach.

The other two stood, making their way to me and sniffing at the hands that I kept perfectly still at my sides. My fingers twitched despite my best intentions when one of them pressed his wet nose against my skin, using his head to guide my hand up on top of it. I scratched the fur there, watching as he rolled his neck in satisfaction like any of the stray dogs I'd seen in Mistfell.

"They have been completely insufferable," the leader of the Wild Hunt said, steering his skeletal horse closer. He stopped just in front of me, but his eyes remained pinned on Caldris at my side. "The next time you think to leave them with me—don't," he warned, dismounting with a grace that defied logic.

Where all the other spirits floated awkwardly, appearing lost, this man was a person in all ways.

Except he wasn't.

His ears were lightly pointed at the tips where his darkly shadowed hair was pulled back from his face, falling into the fur-lined hood of his cloak. Those white eyes were eerie as he shifted his attention from Caldris, pinning me with a look that felt so similar to that day in the woods.

So many questions danced in my head, so many thoughts about that night or the one that followed when he and Caldris had fought on the cliff.

His fur-lined cloak was open at the front, straps of leather criss-crossing over his breast to connect the two sides. His skin beneath it was bare in spite of the cold weather, a swirling tattoo of pale blue ink dipping over his chest and coming to a low point at the start of the definition of his abdomen.

Caelum growled behind me, the low rumble of sound

making me jolt in place as I spun to meet him with wide eyes. "Look at him a little longer, my star. I dare you."

The urge to defend my curiosity rose within me, my cheeks heating with embarrassment. The leader of the Wild Hunt chuckled, his full lips tipping up on one side in a completely arrogant expression. "I won't complain, Beasty," he said, the reminder of the name filling my veins with ice. "Anything that gets this one all riled up is a bonus in my book."

I glanced over his shoulder, my eyes skimming past the feathers woven into the strands of his black hair. The shadowy, slightly transparent riders of the Wild Hunt sat astride their horses, faces completely disinterested. I looked among them, carefully searching until my gaze landed on the one I wouldn't ever be able to erase from my nightmares. His face was committed to my memory, angular with incredibly high cheekbones.

His lips were thin, his nose slightly arched through the bridge until it came to a point at the end. His dark hair was long, hanging loosely around his shoulders except for the pieces he'd pulled back from his face and pinned to the back of his head with two bones. His gray stare met mine, a glare I didn't deserve in his eyes as his nostrils flared. The look of annoyance was fleeting, his attention turning away from me as quickly as it had settled, deeming me unimportant, dismissing me as if I wasn't worth his time.

He'd killed my brother, taken the last of my family from me for no reason other than his own vicious crusade against the humans.

I darted forward, stepping through the gap between the wolves who were determined to sniff every part of my body. Wrapping shaking fingers around the dagger on the leader of the Wild Hunt's belt as I passed, I pulled the blade free from the sheath and raced toward the male who deserved death more than any of the others.

They'd all meet their fate if I had my way, but I owed one a debt that could only be repaid in blood.

"Estrella, no!" Caldris yelled, something in his voice sinking inside of me. It reminded me of the times when I'd fled the danger threatening us, when I'd sworn to stand by his side only to do the opposite in the end. I brushed it off, shaking my head as I reached the skeletal horse of the rider I would kill. His steed reared back as I grabbed him by the cloak hanging at his side, putting all my weight into the pull as I tore him down to the ground. He stumbled off the side, falling to the ground in a disgruntled heap before he vaulted to his feet.

"You're going to be a pain in my ass. I can feel it," he said, brushing the dust off of his clothes. "Of all the blades, you just had to steal *Dainsleif?* Ignorant girl."

I swung for his middle, dismayed when he jerked back suddenly in surprise. I didn't know why it would shock him that I'd try to disembowel him. The last time we'd met I'd stabbed him with his own dagger. "I don't know what that means, and I don't fucking care," I said, spinning the dagger in my grip.

"Then perhaps you shouldn't play with toys you don't understand," the leader of the Wild Hunt said behind me. "*Dainsleif* was forged by the dwarves and cursed to demand the payment of a life anytime it is wielded in battle. When drawn, it requires a life debt from you."

I shrugged. "That's perfectly fine with me. I've no intention of letting the male who murdered my brother walk away."

The leader quirked a brow, turning his curious stare toward where Caldris watched from beside him. "This mate of yours suits you. She's vicious."

"Isn't she?" Caldris agreed, running his hands over what

would have been the muzzle of the horse's bony face. I didn't dare to think about the implications of the God of the Dead finding that appealing, or of the fact that I apparently suited him in such a way.

I turned my full attention back to the rider who needed to die, watching as he rolled his eyes. "You are no help," he said, glaring at the leader. "How am I supposed to fight her when Caldris will skin me alive if I hurt her?"

"You're not," the leader said, lifting a hand to examine his nails as if he didn't have a care in the world. "But I think I'll enjoy watching her play with you anyway."

"I don't plan to play with him," I argued, lunging for his middle. He narrowly avoided the thrust that would have caught him in the belly, twisting to avoid it with the kind of skill that took centuries to hone. "Just kill him."

"You stabbed me three times, you fucking little menace! I'd say we're even," he protested, dodging back when I swung for him again. The blade warmed my hand, the magic within it throbbing through my arm. It wanted blood.

It wanted a debt to be paid.

"For fuck's sake, Aramis. Just let the woman stab you already. *Dainsleif* will demand a life, regardless of who pays it. It might as well be yours," the leader of the Wild Hunt said, crossing his arms over his chest. He slowly leaned his weight back into his skeletal horse, crossing his feet at the ankles as the steed curled its neck to nudge his shoulder affectionately.

"But dying is so inconvenient," the rider, *Aramis*, said. I didn't stop to consider those words before I took the opening he'd given me, thrusting the blade into his chest. He faltered back for a moment, staring down at the dark blade the same way Brann had when the rider had killed him. He dropped slowly to his knees as I pulled it free, watching as black blood spilled free and coated the ground at his feet. It poured in a smooth flow, without any of the rhythmic pumping I'd expected. He glared at me one last time before he fell to his face in the dirt, that inky black stain spreading beneath his body.

The leader of the Wild Hunt stepped beside me, taking the blade from my hand and sheathing it. "Now we wait for him to rise again."

"For him to rise? I just killed him," I said, glancing toward Caldris. He might have the ability to raise the dead, but from what I'd seen they weren't themselves anymore, only the bodies of who had once lived.

The leader made his way back to his horse, pulling a pack down from the back before he turned to me once more. "You cannot kill that which is already dead."

*O*ne of the other members of the Hunt rolled Aramis to his back, but otherwise they left their comrade lying in the dirt. Caldris's words about wanting to ensure all the dead received the proper funeral rites hung over me, a confirmation of everything the leader had said.

He wasn't dead, and my blood debt seemed impossible to ever really pay.

"Holt, this is my mate, Estrella," Caldris said, pushing off his place next to the horse and moving toward me. He tucked a lock of my hair behind my ear, the amusement on his face making me clench my jaw in frustration. "Estrella, Holt is the closest thing I have to a friend."

Not a friend, but the closest thing. If that didn't tell me the kind of man my cursed mate was, then I wasn't sure what would. "Then why did he fight you on the cliff?" I asked, crossing my arms over my chest.

Caldris grinned, turning back toward his *friend*. "He didn't know who I was at first. Even the Wild Hunt can't see through the glamour of a God, and by the time he put it together, we had to keep up the pretense for your sake. Until you flung your stubborn ass off the fucking cliff anyway."

"Such a shame I didn't die doing it," I snapped. I leaned away from him as much as I dared, risking tipping over to put distance between us without actually showing how much his closeness bothered me.

"Only you would wish for death rather than allow yourself to be loved, my star," Caldris said, his lips tipping with a hint of mockery that didn't reach his eyes, making light of something that shouldn't have been funny at all.

Holt chuckled, giving Caldris a look that communicated something silently between the two of them. I didn't doubt they knew each other well, but Holt's glance also didn't need translating.

Good luck with this one.

"Is that all of them?" Holt asked, nodding over his shoulder to where the Fae Marked waited within Caldris's circle of the dead.

"For now. There are more in the tunnels I told you about," Caldris said, the shock of his confession tearing a ragged gasp from me. I turned a wide-eyed stare his way, wondering how he'd been able to communicate with the Wild Hunt when he rarely left my side.

The memory of finding him missing that night in the woods struck me, the brutal twist to his features when I'd stumbled upon him in the trees.

"You didn't," I whispered, voice thready with horror. Holt gave Caldris space, moving away from us as the other riders dismounted their horses. "Please tell me you didn't."

"They belong with their mates, my star. They'll be safer once they're united with the Fae who will do anything to protect them," he said, lifting his chin as he stared down his nose at me.

"They trusted you," I hissed, shaking my head in disbelief as my throat burned. "They gave us shelter when we needed it."

He scoffed, his lips twisting with cruel malice and derision. "No. They trusted *you*. They gave *you* shelter. I was just another body to use as a soldier, and if you had allowed it, Melian would have run me through herself. I will always appreciate that they gave us a place where you could rest safely for a while, but I do not owe them loyalty they would not show me."

"I should have let her kill you the moment she warned me," I snarled, twisting away. I gave him my back, unable to look him in the eye. To betray the Resistance when he could have simply left them in peace was an act I wouldn't forgive. "There are entire families living there. Children who need their parents. What if one of the Marked is a mother? A father? What happens then?" I asked, feeling the moment he stepped up behind me. His presence was soothing, even when he'd been the one to cause me distress in the first place.

I hated to draw comfort from the very monster who needed to be slain.

"We will not separate families if we can help it. The Marked need to come to Alfheimr, but children and spouses will be allowed to come with them. We've taken a great number of the Fae Marked across the boundary since the fall of the Veil," Holt called out. He lifted a pair of shackles from his horse. "But we've not yet run into that situation, as all those we've encountered thus far have been on the run and already had to leave their children behind, if they had any. Many of the women found that their own husbands wished to kill them, and many Marked men found their wives took the children and ran."

"That won't be the case with the Resistance. Many of them

have lived in the tunnels their entire lives. They won't be on the run or have been turned away by their spouses," I explained, trying not to think of children being left behind—of families torn apart. No matter what Holt said about the way they would handle those instances, I had dozens of reasons not to trust him.

"We'll deal with it when we get there, *min asteren*," Caldris said, gripping my forearm lightly and using it to turn me back to face him. I kept my gaze pinned on the thick leather covering his chest, finding the intricate curve where the metal of his armor crossed over his heart fascinating in my effort not to meet his eye. He gently snagged my chin, pulling my gaze up to his with smooth but efficient force. "You shouldn't worry about them. I promise, they will not bother to care about what happens to you."

"I can't exactly blame them for that. I wouldn't care what happens to me either," I said, twisting my chin out of his grasp. I looked over his shoulder, watching his frame slump when my mouth parted in shock. Each of the Wild Hunt carried shackles in their hands, moving toward the Marked. Caldris's army of the dead stepped away, creating an opening for the riders to slip into the protective circle.

The humans struggled, pressing at the barrier the Hunt formed in an attempt to fight their way to freedom. A woman slapped both her hands down on Holt's chest to shove him back, but he held steady. He was gentle as he captured her wrist and pulled it to him, settling the weight of the cuffs on her arm. She sagged beneath them, the reaction far greater than I would have expected from simple chains. Her knees buckled, threatening to force her to the ground.

"What have you done?" I asked, staring at Caldris in horror. They weren't just shackling them in chains. They were putting them in *irons*.

Caldris hung his head forward, his expression filled with his distaste for what was happening—for what he was allowing. "They cannot be permitted to hurt themselves," he said. I stared at the Fae Marks, at the *Viniculum* that was supposed to protect us but had never once moved against him or the Wild Hunt. It didn't protect us against the very creatures who put it there.

"They can't use their magic against you. They can't fight you. What are you preventing them from doing?" I asked, pushing on his chest until he took a step to the side. I moved beside him, my view of what was happening around me now unhindered. I didn't dare go any closer to the Fae Marked. The memory of the mud and the knife they'd thrown at me was far too fresh in my mind. I didn't want to hate them, but I'd be a fool to trust them.

"They may not be able to use the *Viniculum* against us, but they can use it against each other if they think one of them is a threat," he said. The words hung between us, the unspoken meaning clear as he heaved a sigh.

"You mean they can use it against me?" I asked, straightening my shoulders.

"Yes," he agreed. There wasn't even a cursory nod to accompany his statement, nothing to indicate that he'd just shaken my world upside down again, turning it over until everything spilled upon the very ground at my feet.

"That implies we have some control over the *Viniculum*. That would imply we can learn to wield it as a weapon," I said.

"Because you can," he returned, nodding his head. "The *Viniculum* is an instinctive power that is there for your protection whether you seek to use it or not, but that doesn't mean you can't practice and learn it like any other kind of magic. You can call upon it when you wish. All you need to do is try." The statement recalled the revelation that I could raise the dead, an echo of his power existing within my body.

"I don't want to be like you," I said, thinking of the darkness that lurked inside of me. I didn't want to touch it; didn't want it to come out more or to once again feel all of that rage come bubbling to the surface.

"Oh, min asteren," he said, pausing as he tilted his head and studied me. Sympathy filled his gaze, remarkably similar to pity, and for the first time when he looked at me I felt naive and childlike. "You already are." There was a barely present taunt in his voice, a note that someone who didn't know him as well as I did might not have even noticed.

But I did. I saw it for what it was—a reminder of everything I didn't want to be.

"I'm not," I argued, clenching my jaw as I stared back at him, willing him to see everything I hated in him. "I could never do what you have done."

The Wild Hunt continued to shackle the Fae Marked, the cries of their misery and pain striking me in the chest each time as I stared at my mate who would condemn them to such a fate. I didn't think it would have been necessary to shackle them at all, if it hadn't been for me and the way they'd tried to hurt me.

He was willing to agonize a dozen men and women, plunging them into the depths of exhaustion, all to keep me safe from harm. Under any other circumstances it might have been almost sweet, but in this it was only wrong. "You think I don't feel the need for revenge that courses through you? I know how much you long to make Lord Byron bleed for what he did to you," he said, snagging my gaze with his.

"That doesn't mean I should embrace that part of me. Nobody is in control of my actions but me. If I sink to his level, I'm no better than he was," I returned, shaking my head sadly. There were many things in the world I didn't think I wanted to be, but being like him was the worst I could imagine.

"You have never harmed an innocent. You've never violated a girl who should have been under your protection. You will never be Lord Byron of Mistfell, Estrella. But what you can be is an avenging fury on the battlefield." He leaned into my space, finishing in a growl, "And I cannot wait to see you burn it all to the ground." His lips tipped up into the slightest hint of a smirk, as if he could just imagine the portrait he'd painted in his mind.

"The only thing I intend to burn is you," I hissed, ignoring the whimper of one of the wolves as he stepped up to my side. Without thinking, I rested a hand on his head, unable to stop myself from glancing down at the red-eared beast.

Caldris's eyes dropped to the affectionate touch I gave to the animal, his lips tipping higher in satisfaction. The insufferable ass acted as if it was him I petted and not the wolf. All of his satisfaction quickly faded from his face as Holt stepped up to his side, holding out a pair of shackles. "In you get, Beasty," he said to me, his voice sympathetic.

"Over my dead fucking body," I said, the memory of iron searing into my skin fresh in my mind. The others didn't seem so affected, their bodies weakened but not outright harmed.

"It's not necessary. She won't hurt the others," Caldris said, hand on Holt's arm as he pushed the shackles down and away from me. I felt the weight of the probing stares of the Fae Marked watching our interaction, waiting to see if I would be forced to endure the same fate as them.

Holt turned to him in surprise as he lowered his voice. "If you show her preferential treatment, you'll only make them hate her," he said.

"How fortunate for me that they already do," I retorted,

crossing my arms over my chest and glaring at the leader of the Wild Hunt.

"Then do not give them another reason to act on that hate. You are one of them. The only difference is that you're lucky enough to have your mate here with you. He's not stuck waiting back in Alfheimr for you to be delivered to Mab. Only a select few Fae have been allowed to cross into Nothrek to search for their mates—those who are most loyal to her. You are already privileged enough. I have to insist, Cal." Even past the clear friendship between the two of them, Holt still looked to Caldris for approval. I turned his statement over in my head, wondering how many of the Fae had been ordered to remain in Alfheimr and had to rely on the Wild Hunt to find their mates.

I shook off my curiosity, turning to glare at Caldris as he slowly accepted the shackles from Holt. "We are people, who have done absolutely nothing wrong. We are people who you claim to value. If this is how you treat your valued equals, I should hate to be your enemy. You cannot treat us like prisoners."

"You know nothing of imprisonment," the God of the Dead snarled, the sudden vehemence in his voice knocking me back a step. His face twisted with the words, with the absolute scorn on his features. "You think I am your captor? That I'm the equivalent of a jailor?"

I took a step back as he moved even closer, his breath kissing my cheek as he arched a brow in cruel mockery. "Stop it," I said.

"I will always treat you well, min asteren. Even when you are too foolish to see the truth right in front of you. You were determined as mine before your soul was ever born. This bond is not a prison. It is a haven from the ugliness of this world, a person predetermined to love you. To belong to you."

He cupped my cheek in his palm, his touch gentle despite the scathing reprimand on his face.

I reached forward, grabbing the dagger from his side and touching the tip of the blade to his throat. A warning. A silent demand that he keep his distance and not press his fortune when I wasn't feeling too receptive to his advances. What I'd done before had been a mistake—any doubt I'd had of that had vanished the moment he put the other Fae Marked in chains.

"Your haven feels like a dungeon," I said, twisting the knife in my hand when he leaned closer. His eyes gleamed, something like amusement shifting across the tension of his face.

"You really must stop pointing sharp things at my throat, my star. One of these days, you might slip. Then just imagine how guilty you would feel," he said. He suddenly lifted his arm, grasping my wrist and pulling my arm away from his throat quicker than I could even follow the movements.

He freed the dagger from my grip, shoving it back into its sheath and lowering my hands to the front of my body until they were pinned between us, with his grip tight on my arms but not painful.

"I will fight this war with you until the day I die," he said, dropping his forehead to mine. He clasped the first shackle around my wrist, watching as my legs caved beneath me from the shock of energy fleeing my body. The iron didn't burn me, some sort of barrier protected me as he winced. He clasped the second around my other wrist, his eyes filled with remorse as he treated me like the prisoner his very words claimed I was not. Warmth pulsed off the shackles, as if the iron knew there was only a thin barrier between it and my skin, and if it could just burn through it, it would burn through me.

"I'm sorry, min asteren. This isn't how I wanted it to be." My skin itched beneath the shackles, the flesh reddening from the heat coming off of the iron. Caldris's gaze dropped to them, to the growing redness that seemed to spread like a rash. Holt followed his stare, his brow furrowing when he found what Caldris was fixated on. "That's not supposed to happen," Caldris said, turning to look at the other Fae Marked, who seemed unharmed.

"It must have something to do with your magic being more potent as the grandson of a primordial. None of the others have been affected in this way," Holt said, clenching his jaw as he stared down at the shackles.

"Give me the keys," Caldris said, holding out his hand.

"No," I protested, pinning my so-called mate with a glare. "If this is good enough for them, then it's good enough for me. I will not roam free while they suffer, so if you want to unshackle me, then you'll need to unshackle them all."

"Unfortunately for you, Beasty, your mate has no jurisdiction over the rest of them. The Wild Hunt is responsible for returning them to their mates, not the God of the Dead," Holt said. He dropped the key into Caldris's hands, and I flinched back as he worked to unlock the irons.

"If you treat me differently, I will never forgive you for it," I warned, glancing toward the people suffering the weakening effects of the irons as the remaining members of the Wild Hunt brought them to the carts and loaded them onto them.

The rider of the Wild Hunt I'd killed stirred on the ground, coughing roughly before he tossed me a quick glare and stood as if he hadn't been dead only a few moments prior. Another approached cautiously with a living horse trailing behind him as the key turned in the lock on my shackles, the hinges parting to allow fresh air to touch my fevered skin.

"Add it to your list," Caldris grumbled, tossing the irons and key back to Holt. He turned to greet the mount, not the rider, touching his face against the muzzle of the onyx horse.

Taking the reins, he put his foot in the stirrup and mounted the steed.

I glared up at him for only a moment before I turned to follow the Fae Marked as the Wild Hunt loaded them onto carts, looking for one that had space for me to squeeze in. Holt caught me around the waist, hoisting me up in front of Caldris, who reached out to grab me, scooted back slightly, and settled me in the saddle in front of him.

He reached around me, trapping me in place as he shifted the reins in his grip. His breath touched my cheek and the side of my neck as he leaned into my space. "You ride with me, min asteren. Always."

8
ESTRELLA

*T*he sun shone down on us, defying the winter that tried to take hold as we navigated around the falls and climbed steadily up the embankment. Moving around the cliff face that I'd navigated with Caelum and Melian only days before, I couldn't help but glance back at the wreckage of the city below.

Walking into it had been a surreal experience, a legend coming to life around us, painted in the shadows and crafted from the nightmares of what shouldn't have been possible. Leaving this legendary place with the very God who'd caused such destruction wrapped around me seemed unfathomable, like the most intricately designed tragedy.

The narrow pathway wouldn't have been wide enough for the horses, let alone the carts they pulled behind them, filled with the Fae Marked. The three white wolves surrounded the horse I shared with Caldris, enormous sentries that would have blended in with the snow on the ground had it not been for those contrasting, red-tipped ears.

The God of the Dead touched his chin to the top of my head as his horse strode forward, leaning his weight into me slightly as we slowly climbed straight up the embankment. I tried not to grasp the horse's mane too tightly, not wanting to harm the sole creature that seemed familiar to me. The skeletal remains of what might have been Caldris's victims all those centuries ago clambered up the dirt, boney fingers digging into the soil as they climbed.

It was not only the God of the Dead who surrounded me, but an army crafted from corpses and spectral forms. Of beasts and hounds that the legends could never have painted an accurate portrait of.

Holt rode at our side, his white-eyed stare focused on the ground in front of him as he searched the top of the hill. "You won't hurt him," Caldris murmured, making me jolt in his arms.

"Who?" I asked, relaxing my hands slightly as I realized he must have meant his horse.

"Azra," Caldris answered, reaching forward to pat the horse on the side of the neck. "You won't bother him if you grab his mane."

"You have far too much hair to be so casual about hair pulling. Has no one pulled your hair?" I asked, turning back to look at the shoulder-length mane that surrounded his face. It shouldn't have been possible for it to be somehow masculine and only serve to add to the roughness of his beauty.

"No one has dared," he said with a chuckle, the rumble sliding up my back and sinking inside of me. His voice was deep as he tipped his head down, angling his mouth toward my ear. "Though you're welcome to try."

As we finally crested the top of the hill, Caldris steered Azra back in the direction of the tunnels. "We need to detour first," Holt said, his gaze straying in the opposite direction.

"No. We need to get across the boundary as quickly as possible," Caldris argued, tightening his hands on the reins.

"As much as I would like to join you on that endeavor, my sentry reported a group of Fae Marked hiding out in the village of Black Water. A regiment of the Mist Guard was too close for him to try to get them out on his own," Holt said, turning his skeletal steed away from the tunnels.

Another horse moved up to the other side of us, halting as I turned to glare at the male on its back, who'd run my brother through. Caldris sighed. "What do you want, Aramis?"

"The little menace has proven she needs to be shackled more than the others," he growled, glancing over his shoulder as he and Caldris kicked their horses into a quick walk to follow Holt. "You may be inclined to give her preferential treatment, and Holt may allow it because of who you are to him, but that doesn't mean she won't make the rest of us nervous. Even now, sitting in the carts and surrounded by the Wild Hunt, the other Fae Marked speak of their hatred for her. Of how she sold out her own people just to be comfortable. She should be shackled and riding in the carts with the rest of them."

Caldris growled, and when I turned to look at his face, his lips turned down with a snarl. His arms tightened around me, squeezing into my sides to the point of discomfort. "Go ahead and try it."

"Fucking mated pairs. I swear to the Gods, you lot are the stuff of nightmares. It's not like I'm suggesting she take one of us for a ride—"

"This would be the part where you should shut up!" Holt called back without even glancing toward his companion.

"You should listen to him," Caldris said, his voice lower than usual. Something *other* tinted it, as if the power of death itself could bleed into his voice. His eyes flashed with blue, a silent warning amplifying his words.

It faded as quickly as it had come, as if there wasn't the

power necessary to back up whatever rage loomed inside of him.

"Sometimes I think it's fortunate for us all that the Fates kept you from her for so long," Aramis said, shaking his head. "Anything that could rival Mab's power with that cursed crown atop her head shouldn't be possible."

"Are you determined to be stabbed again? I'm sure Estrella would be so eager to oblige that I wouldn't even need to bother myself," Caldris said as I twisted forward. I tried not to chuckle, shoving deep inside that part of me that found humor in his dry wit. "Or was there a point to you pissing me off?"

"She needs to be shackled, Caldris," Aramis said. He reached into the pack slung over the horse's rump, pulling out a pair of shackles. Everything inside of me withered at the mere sight of them, recalling the way it had felt like my soul had been sucked out of me through the connection.

"My magic is too potent. They damn near took her down," Caldris said, shaking his head.

"These aren't iron, just regular bronze," Aramis said, holding out the shackles. Caldris sighed, reaching out to accept them from the other male. I felt him nod at my back as Aramis kicked his horse into a trot to follow where Holt walked ahead of him.

"Tell me again how I am anything but your prisoner," I said, wincing as the cool metal touched my wrists. True to Aramis's word, there was no burning sensation or heat that radiated from within the bronze. Caldris leaned forward as he draped the reins across Azra's neck, nuzzling into the curtain of my hair. His mouth trailed over the delicate skin of my neck, drawing goosebumps to the surface. "The only time I want you chains is when it's to my bed, with you writhing and willing," he murmured, pressing the weight of the first shackle over my left wrist. He snapped it shut, my arm sagging slightly beneath the weight.

He trailed his fingertips over the back of my hand, pressing it down and into Azra's mane just in front of my lap. His fingers laced through mine then into the horse's hair and making me feel pinned and surrounded.

He didn't give a single care for the Wild Hunt and Fae Marked who followed us, our audience not bothering him in the slightest as he made my imprisonment into something intimate. "Do you have any idea how many times I'll make you come for me?" he murmured, slipping his free hand down my arm to touch the wrist that was still free. His touch brought all my desire for him to light, forcing something that belonged in the shadows to emerge for all to see. He raised my free hand, placing it beside the other as he wrapped the other shackle around and snapped it closed. Twisting the lock on each wrist, he made sure to settle my hands with their heavy weights in my lap as he pulled me to sit back against him.

I hadn't realized how far I'd leaned forward, trying to evade his too-familiar warmth at my spine.

The shackles clanked together as I shifted to look out over the open land in front of us. Mountains loomed in the distance to the Southeast, but spread out before us was a vast and empty plain, beyond the trees draped over the pathway from the once busy and prosperous city.

Azra's hooves clomped against something solid beneath the thin sheen of snow covering the ground. The steps of Holt's and Aramis's horses up ahead revealed what looked like the remains of cobblestones, jagged and uneven from centuries of neglect.

Despite the curiosity that threatened to consume me, I refrained from asking what this place had been in its prime. I wanted nothing more than to hold the answers to the past, to pick the brain of my ancient mate so I could know everything that had come before me.

The things that he must have seen—experienced—were beyond my imagination.

Azra halted suddenly, freezing in place as the rest of the Wild Hunt walked past us. "What is it?" Caldris asked, leaning forward to pat the horse on the neck. His body went taut at my spine, every muscle tightening as he responded to the horse's sudden nervousness.

Fenrir growled at my side, the sound a low rumble. He nudged my foot with his nose, meeting my eyes with his red stare that seemed to say a thousand words. "Something is wrong," I mumbled, glancing toward where the Wild Hunt continued on with the Fae Marked loaded into carts. They glared back at us, their eyes full of condemnation as I tried to listen beyond the sound of the wheels over the cobblestones and the squeaking of the bolts with every bump. Caldris canted his head to the side, doing the same thing as he watched ahead of us.

Holt spun suddenly to pin us with a look that communicated everything between the steps of his skeletal horse. "Fuck," Caldris grunted, leaning into me slightly. He swung his leg over Azra's rear, dismounting to stand beside him as he patted the top of Fenrir's head. "*Cwn Annwn*, hunt," he said, and the three white wolves disappeared into the woods at our sides. We waited in silence as time seemed to slow, the howling of the wolves echoing through the forest as Holt turned back in the direction he'd been traveling.

The first arrow came from the right, thudding into the side of Holt's steed. The horse turned its head to look down at the arrow protruding from its ribs, shaking its head and stomping a hoof in fury. Aramis took the lead, pushing his mount onward as Holt dropped back to join with the rest of the Wild Hunt to surround the carts.

Aramis shouted as his horse whinnied, and I watched as a person emerged from the branches in the top of one of the pine trees. "Look out!" I yelled, drawing the eye of the lurking figure. His blade shone in the sun, casting a glare as he sawed through a rope disguised along one of the branches.

On the other side of the path, the reflection of the sun gleaming off a dagger mirrored the same image. "Get them out of there!" Caldris ordered the rider of the Wild Hunt just ahead of us. The male nodded, moving his mount forward to catch up with the one pulling the cart.

He was just in the center of the copse of trees when pine needles rained from above, a cloth barrier parting until red dust gleamed in the sunshine as it fell on top of them. I would never in my life forget the screams as the powder burned into their flesh, or forget the way they huddled beneath their cloaks to protect their bodies.

I watched in horror as the cloth fell down bit by bit, men sawing through the ropes until it came close to us. In a ripple, the sky above seemed to open as they peeled back the fabric they'd painted to mimic the trees.

Caldris's stunned gaze found mine for a moment and then he moved in a blur. Snatching me off the horse, he pulled me down so abruptly that Azra reared and knocked me back. Fury swept over me alongside my fear, driving my senses higher as I prepared for the impact. Staring up at the sky, falling backward with my hands shackled in front of me, I watched the iron dust rain from overhead.

Blackness fluttered at the edges of my vision as I landed on top of Caldris, his body breaking the fall from the horse. He rolled me beneath him and yanked the cloak off his shoulders, covering my body with the fabric and himself as I fought to catch my breath, his pained grunts resounding between us.

My ears rang as the darkness of the cloak surrounded me, keeping me pinned to the ground as I waited for any sign that the iron dust had dissipated. I felt it surrounding me, draining the power from my *Viniculum* and leaving me without that strange buzzing in my blood that usually came alongside threat of danger. The power that wanted to defend me was gone, stolen from me as the breath in my lungs.

"Fenrir!" Caldris called, finally shoving his body off of mine. He swept the cloak off of my shoulders, helping me to sit up. Glancing around myself, I took in the iron dust covering everything and glanced down to where Caldris's hands were burned. His flesh had turned an angry, mottled red, blisters appearing on his skin where the dust had seared through his flesh.

"Caelum," I whispered, staring at him in shock.

I longed to touch the injuries, to feel for myself the sacrifice he'd paid in burning flesh. I needed him to be the monster, the villain who would take and take from me, but there was no denying his willingness to give pieces of himself for my protection.

Leaving the cloak he'd sacrificed on the ground between us, he stood from where he'd knelt in front of me, his eyes roaming over my face and body to search for injury. "Are you hurt?" he asked, taking the key to my shackles from his trouser pocket. He unlocked them, carefully avoiding touching my skin with his ruined, charred hands.

"You know I'm not," I said, swallowing down the tightness in my throat and the surge of emotion within me. I couldn't feel these things—not when we were still enemies.

He nodded, expelling a sigh of relief before he turned back to the looming battle just outside of our bubble. "Guard her, *cwn annwn*," he said as the wolves approached. The term must have been a name he used for the group of them, and curiosity burned through me.

Now was not the time for questions.

He glanced toward the wolves as they surrounded me, their fangs and jowls red and dripping with blood. In front of us, the hounds of the Wild Hunt did the same with the carts full of Fae Marked. As my guardians snarled and snapped at the air around them, I sat in the circle they formed. Caldris stepped forward with fluid, animalistic grace. His army of the dead lay upon the ground, their corpses unanimated once more as the tang of iron filled my lungs.

Caldris pulled his swords from the sheaths strapped across his back, the base of his neck gleaming and dripping blood from where the iron had touched his skin. He strode forward into the edge of the trees, disappearing from view as a scream tore through the air.

A body fell from the trees, already dead by the time it landed. The Mist Guard stared up at the sky with blank, unseeing eyes in a slashed face.

"I think they pissed him off," I whispered, reaching down to pet one of the wolves. I rolled my wrists, flexing them in this moment of freedom. I knew he intended for me to be able to defend myself should the fight reach me, but the least he could have done was given me a blade.

Asshole.

The female of the wolves turned her ruby eyes up to me, her mouth, ears, and eyes all tainted with the color of death. The low growl she gave beneath her breath settled through me, feeling like an extension of the bond I shared with Caldris.

Shouts rang out from the woods as he finally appeared, his clothing and armor bathed in blood. The Wild Hunt fought with the Guard members emerging from the other side, and still the corpses remained on the ground. The skeletons didn't move, and I knew it had to be the iron surrounding us and buried in his skin that rendered Caldris's controlling magic useless.

Even the bond between us felt distant, as if I couldn't just reach down and pull on the strand of Fate that tied us together.

Glancing toward the tree line opposite of where Caldris fought, I watched Holt cut through man after man, taking them down with the sort of lethal grace I'd always imagined the Fae would have. He fought as if he'd been trained alongside Caldris, the two of them moving in sync even though they weren't anywhere near one another.

A member of the Mist Guard stabbed one of the riders, breaking through the barrier they'd formed. Others followed, their sheer numbers proving to be a challenge to the Wild Hunt as they were weakened by the iron.

Fenrir bared his teeth at the Guard who came closest to me, the fiercest growl I'd ever heard coming from his chest as Caldris snapped his head toward us. Our eyes connected for a breath, his attention unwavering as he dropped his sword and pulled his axe from the sheath. He swung it in an arc, embedding it in the face of the Guard who'd dared to challenge him. The man froze in place, the center of his face disappearing entirely as Caldris's axe collided with it and bit deep. Raising a foot and pushing on the other man's chest, Caldris tore the axe free with a splash of blood as the body fell to the ground in front of him.

"Do me a favor, Beasty," Holt called, demanding my attention while riding toward me. He pulled the knife *Dainsleif* from its sheath and tossed it to me. I caught it by the handle with both hands, the familiar pulsing warmth spreading through me as the cursed blade demanded the price for drawing it. "Stop eye-fucking your boyfriend and kill something already."

"My mate is not your rider!" Caldris yelled as Holt rode past him, cutting down a member of the Guard in his path. Holt merely chuckled in response, his smile lighting up his face as he fought and slayed his enemies. I felt like anyone who smiled during a battle was not someone I felt particularly motivated to attack, even before understanding that he couldn't die.

Fenrir nudged my free hand, his eyes gleaming with the need for blood. I felt it hum through me, as if an extension of the distant bond I shared with Caldris. The blade in my hand seemed to warm all over again, spreading the heat of its curse through me and smoldering in my blood like red-hot coals in the fire.

Black hovered at the edges of my vision, bathing the world in an unnatural darkness as I spun the dagger in my grip. The whimper of one of the hounds of the Wild Hunt made Fenrir snap his head to the side, his focus going entirely to where the animal fell to the ground. A Mist Guard stood over the enormous half-rotten hound, scowling as he raised his sword.

I took a step forward before I'd even realized what I was doing, the other foot never landing as Fenrir slid his head between my feet and knocked me off balance. Another one of them urgently nudged me as I stared at them both in surprise. Swallowing back my nervousness, I held Fenrir's gaze and straddled his large, furry body.

I'd barely settled onto his back when he bolted forward. I grasped him by the fur, hanging on for dear life as he raced into the fray. Men shouted around me as the other wolves tore through flesh, spraying blood all over me as we passed.

The man who'd been about to stab the hound spun to face

the enormous, snarling wolf barreling toward him, raising his sword as fear lit his eyes. But Fenrir stopped, slowing to a walk and tipping to the side to help me get down.

He curled his neck around my body, offering support as I stepped toward the man and gripped my dagger tighter. The moment felt ceremonial, like a sacrifice, like tearing a bit of my soul from me to fight alongside the very creatures I was supposed to hate. But the low whimper from the forest floor made me stride forward toward the man, keeping the dagger at my side as he glanced at the wolf waiting behind me.

"How nice of you to separate from the rest of them," the Guard said, shifting the sword at his side as he stepped forward. The magic of *Dainsleif* writhed in my hand, whispering through my mind with its cry for blood. It sank into the hollow inside of me, reaching in with taloned fingers and pulling my hunger to the surface as I tilted my head to the side in the same way I'd seen Caldris do on so many occasions. From the corner of my eye, I watched Fenrir mirror the movement as if he felt compelled by the unique bond we shared through his master.

The *Viniculum* was silent, still against my skin as the iron coating the ground suppressed the magic of the Fae, but the cursed blade still pushed, demanding a life in reparation. The Mist Guard struck, his thrust slow and lazy as I twisted to the side to avoid it and sliced the dagger across the man's wrist.

He gasped, yanking his hand back as blood dripped to the ground beneath him. Pressing his free hand into the wound, he tried to stem the bleeding that would become inevitable. The blade in my hand hummed, the blood expelling from the man's wound faster and faster as we watched.

He struck again, desperation driving him to attack with more speed. I twisted too slowly, wincing as the blade cut into my skin, slicing through the flesh of my bicep and burning it beneath the press of iron. Fenrir growled at the same moment Caldris roared, the sounds of the two of them filling the air around us. Only the hand I laid atop Fenrir's head stilled him and stopped him from taking the life that was mine to demand.

I wanted the blood I was owed.

It poured free from that wound at his wrist, but the brutality within me demanded more, driving me to kill until nothing remained. I twisted *Dainsleif* in my hand, letting the blade lay parallel to my forearm as I swept it in an arc across the man's throat. Blood splattered across my face as the flesh parted beneath the blade. Staring into the split in his skin, where layers of muscle briefly showed, I watched as he dropped his sword and pressed both hands into the wound.

He fell to his knees, that pulsing warmth in the dagger dispersing as death came over the man. "I don't like men who hurt animals. Even if they are halfway to the grave," I said, feeling that hollow inside of me burn. His eyes turned unseeing, blood pumping from the wound at his throat in horrifying waves as I glared down at him.

Fenrir pressed his nose against my hand, turning my glare away from the body in front of me and severing the connection I felt between us. The Void called to him, the pull on his soul lingering at the edges of my awareness.

I stared into the red eyes of the wolf, his knowing expression making me swallow and glance toward Caldris. The God of the Dead continued to fight, cutting down members of the Mist Guard left and right to get to me. He seemed unaware of the pull of the afterlife on the souls, of the way it tempted my very soul to leave my body.

I stepped toward the injured hound, crouching down in front of him and extending a hand slowly. I swallowed as he bared his teeth, a growl rumbling through his chest. Pulling my hand back, I waited and watched as he finally lifted his head and extended his neck. What remained of flesh on his nose wrinkled, working to scent me. I avoided the venomous shadows dripping from his jowls, touching only the top of his head as I glanced down to the wound in his side.

Already the skin worked to knit itself back together, covering the mangled mess of flesh and bones it had revealed. "Will you be alright?" I asked, scratching the fur on top of his head as the hound leaned into my touch.

The Wild Hunt were all too busy to answer my question, but I would have sworn I saw the hound give the faintest of nods, if it hadn't been impossible. My life appeared to be filled with impossibilities as of late, but that one was something I wasn't quite ready to consider.

Fenrir wagged his tail, lying down beside me to make his body lower. I stood and swung a leg over, climbing atop him once again as he slowly rose and prowled through the carnage. He didn't pause to allow me to get down again, with the debt of the dagger paid. He used his teeth to snap through flesh and bone, tearing through the Mist Guard that remained as he made his way to Caldris.

My mate stood staring at me where I sat atop one of his wolves, darkness gleaming in his eyes as he looked over my body and found me mostly unharmed, despite the blood covering me. "Good boy," he said when Fenrir finally closed the distance between us, stepping up and rubbing his nose against Caldris's chest.

When his attention came back to me, something dangerous lurked behind the onyx of his eyes. "You should get off the wolf now, min asteren."

"Why would I do that?" I asked, the words feeling different. Like my voice had changed, like some of the magic I so often heard in Caldris's voice had tainted mine. It echoed between us, and Caldris tilted his head to the side as if he heard it too.

"I need to tend to your wound," he said simply, but something darker laced his words, desire crackling through the air between us as we stared at one another.

Fenrir broke the moment, spinning suddenly to face away from Caldris as he moved. I saw the arrow coming for my chest too late, raising the dagger in my hand too slowly to deflect it. Squeezing my eyes shut so I wouldn't see the iron-tipped arrow embed itself in my flesh, I waited for the pain.

The pain that never came.

Warmth spread across my back. I opened my eyes slightly to find Caldris pressed into the back of my right side, his fingers wrapped around the wooden shaft of the arrow. It rested only a breath from my heart, so close to finding the target that would end everything.

I glanced up at him as he tossed the arrow to the ground, watching as the two other white wolves advanced on their prey. They surrounded the last remaining member of the Mist Guard while the entire group watched, toying with him.

"Finish it," I said, not wanting to watch the wolves make a game out of death. Out of the fear of a man who thought he was doing the right thing. And maybe he was, for all I knew. I couldn't exactly say the Fae had been overly kind to us or done anything to disprove the claims that we would be like pets to them.

Caldris murmured against me, his words twisted and his voice filled with cruelty. "He is fortunate that you survived." He brushed the hair away from my neck. "Otherwise I'd have kept him alive to play with him over the course of years. Let the *cwn annwn* have their fun. They are far more merciful than me."

I closed my eyes to the sound of tearing flesh as they

finally ended the life of the last Mist Guard, the squelching sound of blood too much for me. It pulled at the part of me that reveled in it, the twisted piece of me that was drawn to the souls that lingered, waiting to move on.

Fenrir lowered himself to the ground so that Caldris could pull me off his back, looking to the wolf with an amused expression. "Why is it you never offer me a ride?"

Fenrir chuffed, turning his back on Caldris and going to rejoin the other two wolves.

"You're all bloody," Caldris said, reaching up to touch my chin. He paused, staring down at the mottled, still healing flesh as his skin knitted itself back together and slowly pushed the iron from his body.

"Sorry, I don't see a bath anywhere. Do you?" I asked, scoffing as I looked at him. The male was covered in gore from head to toe, but Gods forbid I be, too.

"Did I say I wanted you to wash it off?" he asked, tilting his head to the side as he studied me. "Because that was not my intent, I assure you. I want to fuck you while you're covered in the blood and death of our enemies who thought they could take you from me."

I swallowed, the intensity of his dark stare making my throat ache with sudden dryness. "That's not—"

"Normal? You are my mate. I could spend an eternity buried inside of you and still want more, Little One. There will *never* come a day when I do not enjoy watching you bring men to their knees and cut their throats when they underestimate you. You would do well to remember that," he said, raising his hands so that I could see the silver shining within his skin. "The only reason I haven't taken you is because I cannot touch you without hurting you."

I swallowed, staring at the injuries he'd sustained for me

and uncomfortable with the feelings of gratitude that knowledge left me with. "You shouldn't have—"

"You are my mate. I will *always* protect you, min asteren. No matter what the cost," he murmured, his deep eyes gleaming as he stared down at me. I sank my teeth into my bottom lip, unsure of what to say in the face of the weight of his confession.

Things would be easier if he were just a monster.

*C*aelum's skin was slow to return to normal, his body pushing the iron free over the course of the next few hours as we traveled. We left the corpses behind us, the bodies too damaged by the iron covering them for his power to raise them from the dead.

Only one grave had been dug, for the only Fae Marked male who'd taken an iron-tipped arrow to the heart during the chaos of the battle. The others had been protected after the first assaults rained arrows down on us.

Caelum was careful not to touch my skin as we rode through the snow-covered plains. There was no shelter to be found, nothing to conceal us as we traveled. After the assault we hadn't been prepared for, the Wild Hunt surrounded the humans, with the hounds sticking close to them. It gave me some measure of comfort to know that if nothing else, they would protect the lives of those they'd rendered incapable of protecting themselves.

Even if the iron powder would have done that anyway.

"You didn't know about the iron dust," I said, staring down at the blistered skin of his hands where he held the reins. The sight of them resting so close to my once-again shackled wrists felt so wrong, the two most extreme instances of how my mate could treat me held in one glance. The deepest part of me wondered if the Fae Mark would return to his skin where it had melted away, to paint the new flesh with the symbol of our bond. The absence of the circle on the back of his hand and shadowed tendrils covering his fingers made something inside of me long to touch him. I needed to caress his skin until the ink returned to what I had grown so fond of exploring with tentative fingers by candlelight in the tunnels.

"I didn't," he agreed. I felt him shake his head behind me as, carefully avoiding his skin that was still tainted by iron dust, I clutched onto his forearm to steady myself when Azra stepped over uneven ground. My shackles clinked together as I moved, the chains connecting them dangling below my wrists to brush against Azra's mane. "We knew humans had been given centuries to devise new weapons to use against us, but I never could have imagined something like that. An ambush like that could actually threaten the Fae, if the Mist Guard were to have enough numbers to overpower a group. Not all Fae are as skilled in combat as we are. The Sidhe have had little reason to fight since the last war with the humans."

"But most of the Fae aren't here, are they? Aside from that one that we saw in Tradesholde, I've not seen any except for you and the Wild Hunt," I said, pursing my lips. Perhaps that was because of my limited interactions where the Fae hunted for their mates, but it felt far more significant.

"Mab will have been very selective about who she allows to wander into Nothrek. There is great power to be found in controlling the fate of one's mate. Even the most vocal of her opponents would be inclined to cooperate with her if she were to hold the other half of their soul in her grasp," Caldris explained, leaning forward until his chin rested against the top of my head.

"She would do that? But I thought you said the Fae considered their mates to be sacred? A bond worth protecting at all costs? Why would the Queen of Air and Darkness go against something like that?" I asked, releasing his forearm as Azra steadied on more even terrain. It took everything within me not to push up the sleeve of his tunic so I could touch the mark under there and reassure the frazzled part of my soul that he was still mine.

That part of me was nothing but a traitorous bitch, and I wanted nothing to do with her.

Caldris pulled on Azra's reins ever so slightly, slowing the horse's gait until we dropped to the back of the group. Holt's gaze lingered upon us as his steed strode past, and he gave a nod of understanding.

"Mab does as Mab pleases. She holds no respect for what the Fae protect at all costs. She will stop at nothing to gain more power, doing whatever it takes to maintain it and keep the other Courts loyal to her," Caldris said, resting his hand against the pants covering my thighs.

The blisters had just begun to fade, the pink and white of new flesh forming where they'd been only moments before.

"How did you come to be raised by your father and stepmother?" I asked as I thought back to all the pieces of the puzzle he'd given me. I knew Mab had hated him all his life and his father had done very little to protect him from the consequences of her ire.

He sighed, his weight heavy at my spine. "She had her daemons steal me from my crib in Catancia when I was a few days old. They killed the guards and women who were caring for me while my mother and step-father were distracted by an urgent meeting with Mab. She made no secret of her fury that my mother would dare to touch her husband, so my mother thought to smooth over the ruffled feathers."

"Your mother was married to another man as well? And he tolerated her affair with your father?" I asked, completely unable to understand a world where a woman could do such a thing. At Mistfell, to be with anyone other than the man chosen to be our husband was likely to have us retrained by the priestesses or hung, while the men were free to do as they pleased.

"Marriages come after mate bonds. My mother and father were fated mates, but my father was already in a political marriage with Mab by the time my mother came of age. Usually when that happens, the political marriage dissolves amicably, but Mab wasn't willing to respect tradition and return to her brother in the Summer Court. She only came to be Queen of the Shadow Court through marriage, and to give that up would mean no longer being Queen."

The snow gleamed in the growing darkness as the sun began to set, the Wild Hunt pausing in the middle of the clearing. Caldris pulled Azra to a halt, keeping his distance from the group as the riders dismounted their horses and pulled materials from the carts to set up a few tents to sleep in.

"But children cannot exist outside the mate bond, and my parents didn't have a chance of producing an heir with either of their spouses. They came together one Winter Solstice, planning to hide the affair and the resulting child from Mab by claiming the child was a consequence of my stepfather's affair with his own fated mate. Unfortunately, Mab is quite gifted at gleaning the truth through riddles and play with words. She always knows what questions to ask and how to phrase them, and she accompanies those with more painful interrogation methods. My father wasn't able to keep their secret. So, she took me to punish my mother, and quickly realized just how loyal a woman will be when you hold her only child in your power. I was the first of the children she stole, but I was far from the last."

"She's taken others?" I asked, my horror mounting. It was no wonder Caldris felt no sympathy over Mab's missing daughter, but if children couldn't exist outside the mate bond...

Who was Mab's mate?

"Most of the Court royals don't have children to steal," he admitted, shaking his head. "But she's taken at least one child from every Court, the highest ranking offspring she could get her hands on. Maylea is the sole heir to the Spring Court, Rieka is the daughter of the Summer King's best friend, and Lycus is the Autumn Queen's nephew. There are others—the children of advisors who thought to challenge her—all uniting to create an elite force of unwilling Fae who cannot defy her because of the way she bound us to her magic when we were too young to fight back. Sometimes I wonder if the lack of access to our mates and potential offspring has had the benefit of slowing her reach of power. You cannot steal what a Fae does not already have."

He kicked Azra forward as I fell into silence, the darkness reigning as it descended upon the plains in truth. The absence of trees to shelter us from prying eyes made me nervous. Even if I didn't want to travel with the Wild Hunt, I didn't want to experience the feeling of iron dust sinking into my skin if the Mist Guard happened upon us, either.

"The two of you take the tent all the way at the end," Holt said as the riders of the Wild Hunt ushered the Fae Marked into the three remaining tents.

"We don't need an entire tent to ourselves," I said, thinking of the dozen Fae Marked being crammed into three tents. "I assure you privacy is not necessary."

"I need Caldris rested come morning. He won't sleep if he has to worry about the others stabbing you in your sleep. I'd rather you didn't ride him until the sun comes up, so he can get some sleep, but privacy is necessary in this instance I'm afraid," he returned, winking at me with an infuriating grin. He turned away to help get the Fae Marked safely tucked inside their tents for the night.

I ignored the flush staining my cheeks. I would not be riding anything until the sun came up. Caldris dismounted Azra from behind me, reaching up with mostly-healed hands to grasp me around the waist and pull me down. The tent he guided me toward was small, a simple tan linen draped over a wooden post in the center. The canvas was secured to the ground in four corners, the front flaps of the fabric tied open to reveal the entrance.

"Come, min asteren," Caldris said, placing his hand at the small of my back. He guided me toward the tent, closing the distance between us and the place where we would be well and truly alone. I didn't trust myself to be with him, not with the emotions over what he'd given to protect me from the harm of the iron colliding with the fact that I remained shackled in chains like a prisoner.

The actions were so oppositional. They couldn't come from the same man.

Like warfare, my mind conflicting with my heart, I wanted nothing more than to reconcile the man I'd known with the cruel Fae male who thought the ends justified the means. "You said Mab will want to have control over the Marked. Does that mean they're in danger? That they aren't being brought to their mates?" I asked, letting him guide me into the tent.

He smirked slightly, shaking his head as he turned and drew the fabric closed. Knotting it tightly with the ties sewn into the canvas, he turned to me with a cocked eyebrow.

"Their mates will negotiate for their release. Mab will just get what she wants from them in the process," he said, taking a step forward.

"But wouldn't it be better to find some other place to bring the Marked? Somewhere that nobody can find them?" I asked, stepping backward before I realized what I'd done.

The way he looked at me, his eyes blazing with desire and amusement, felt like an assault. Like he'd managed to weaponize all the things I loved about him, turning me against my own best interest.

"Do you intend to continue to avoid lying down beside me, Little One?" he asked, cocking his head to the side as a laugh bubbled up his throat. There was nothing amusing about the fact that we discussed the fate of living beings, as if they were pawns in a game they couldn't understand.

"That's not what I'm doing," I said, shaking my head, even as his words sank inside me and I knew the truth in them, I took another step backward until the fabric of the tent brushed against my head.

"That is *exactly* what you're doing," he said with a smirk, unlacing the neck of his tunic. He pulled it from the waist of his trousers, lifting the fabric off over his head so he stood shirtless in front of me.

"What are you doing?" I asked, pulling my cloak tighter around myself. It was far too cold to sleep naked, the cool wind outside stealing through the fabric of the tent itself.

I would *not* be keeping him warm.

I swallowed as I tried not to look down at the sculpted muscle covering his stomach, and at the strength in his chest and broad shoulders. He'd been unbelievably attractive as a human man, his body appearing as if it was crafted through hard work. But as a Fae male, there was something about him that no human could hope to achieve. An effortless beauty that reminded me too much of the carving of him in the stone cliff, with the two women kneeling at his feet and ready to worship him.

My throat burned, the acrid taste of bile swirling in my gut as I considered all the women he must have been with before me. All the centuries of history he must have had before finding his pathetic, barely-experienced human mate.

He tilted his head to the side as if he could sense the emotion surging within me, the rage I felt over knowing that countless women before me had known his body in the way I did now. He turned, draping his shirt over the knotted ties in the cloth so that it hung there.

"What exactly is my star feeling jealous of now?" he asked as he turned back to face me. His eyes darkened as he prowled forward, closing the distance between us. He stood before me, towering over me and truly emphasizing how small I was in comparison to him. His Fae size was larger somehow, taller than any man I'd ever known, as if his soul and the power it held was too big for the confines of a mortal size.

"I hate you," I said, unable to deny the jealousy coursing through me. As much as I wanted to deny it, the words wouldn't come past the swirling sickness I felt in my gut.

"Do you often get jealous over toys that you hate?" he asked, bending down to grasp a handful of the undisturbed snow at the edge of the tent. He lifted it to my face, touching the cold fluff to my skin and using the moisture to wipe away the blood splatter that felt hard and crusted on my skin. "Or am I just special?"

"You're a male, not a toy," I said, trying not to look down at the way the melted snow turned pink with the blood he washed from my face.

He grinned slowly, dropping to his knees in the snow in front of me. The position put his head level with my chest, those gleaming and mischievous dark eyes staring up at me through unfairly long lashes. He raised his wet fingers to my neck, his soft and smooth new skin brushing over the mark and drawing a warm tingle of recognition to the surface of my flesh.

He slowly washed the blood from me, showing delicate care as he pinned me with that alluring gaze. "I'll be your toy any time you want to play with me, min asteren," he said, his grin deepening as my cheeks flushed in response to the words. He pressed his face into my stomach, the fabric of my tunic separating us as his hands skated down my sides, skimming over my frame until they settled atop my boots, where he slowly untied the laces. "You still smell like me."

I swallowed, trying not to think of the implications of his statement. "I'd have washed it from my skin if I could," I said, the words coming out with all the venom I wanted to convey. I didn't want to smell like him, didn't want anything to do with him, even if my body did warm beneath his touch.

"I'd just have to cover you in my scent all over again," he admitted, pulling the first boot free from my foot. He moved to the other, depositing them to the side as he stared up at me. He furrowed his brow, shifting his gaze to where my wrists were bound together in front of me, staring at them as if he hated them as much as I did. He reached up, touching the shackle on my left wrist, then he waved his hand over the lock, watching as the bronze pieces separated with a clank. The other followed, then he tossed them to the side and raised my wrist to his mouth. Kissing the chafed skin there, he let his lips glide over the injury.

He stood, lifting me off my feet and into his arms as he carried me over to the bedrolls and set me down on one of them. I curled my legs up to my chest as he ran a hand through his hair. "I'll go get you something to eat," he said, stepping toward the opening in the tent. He made no move to put his shirt on as he unknotted the tie, peeling open the curtain of fabric.

That jealousy pulsed through me again, thinking of the Fae Marked women or female members of the Wild Hunt who might see him.

He smirked as if he knew it would torment me. "Estrella?" he asked as he stepped outside the tent and spun to face me fully. "If you run, I will hunt you down. I think you know now what will happen when I catch you."

He pulled the tent flap closed, leaving the fabric to sway in the cool winter breeze as I stared after him. The desire to flee pulsed through me, my limbs tingling with the need for freedom. With the need to move, to wander in the darkness as I had always done.

To roam beneath the stars.

I stared at my boots where he'd set them to the side, trapping me on the bedroll if I wanted to avoid the snow soaking through my socks. Putting them on would cost me valuable time, but I sprang to my feet regardless.

Stepping over the snow and wincing as the cold bit my toes, I shoved my feet into my boots and tied the laces as quickly as humanly possible. Dashing for the entrance to the tent, I slowed just inside the flap and peeled it back slowly.

"Going somewhere, Beasty?" Holt asked, framed by the parted fabric of the tent opening. Arms crossed over his chest, he curled up a brow in challenge as I sputtered and searched for the words that might defy what we both knew to be true.

"I was just—"

"Spare me your lies. Do yourself a favor and turn your skittish ass around and sit back on that bedroll before Caldris gets back and has to be disappointed in you all over again," he said, nodding his head back toward the inside of the tent behind me.

"Disappointed in *me*?" I asked, my outrage growing. Only by the grace of not wanting to needlessly alert Caldris to my escape attempt did I keep from raising my voice. "He pretended to be human so I would fall in love with him."

"Yes, disappointed in *you*. You've got your head stuck so far up your own ass, you can't see that he would do anything for you. He pretended to be human to give you time to get to know him before you had to deal with the pressures of being his fated mate. Stop acting like an unappreciative brat and see what is right in front of you." He shook his head as he glared down at me, then he stepped to the side, holding out an arm. As if I would bolt past him and take the opportunity to run when he would be able to point Caldris in the right direction. "He is the same male he was a week ago. The only thing that has changed is you."

"You expect me to believe you're just going to let me go?" I asked, narrowing my eyes on him.

"I expect you to believe whether or not you try does not matter to me in the slightest. He will find you and he will drag you back, even if you're kicking and screaming while he does. It all seems like a pointless waste of energy, if you ask me, but that's your prerogative." He shrugged, his lips tipping up with a slow and calculating grin. "Unless you're hoping for the reward that will come when you're caught. If you want your mate to fuck you, all you need to do is say the word and I'm sure he will be happy to oblige."

"We are not having this conversation," I said, rolling my eyes and stepping back into the tent. Holt and I both knew he'd effectively made it impossible for me to run, implying I would want the resulting outcome when Caldris was finished hunting me through the woods.

The unfortunate reality was that I didn't doubt it. Even when my brain knew better than to desire the man who was my mate, my body and my heart couldn't quite understand why he was bad news in a way that was totally and completely impossible to take.

"You're in the world of the Fae now, Estrella Barlowe of Mistfell," Holt said, bowing in what felt like a mockery of respect. "Your human sensibilities do not matter, because there will quickly come a day when your mate wants to fuck you for everyone to see. When he wants to take you beside the fire while the Wild Hunt watches and listens to you scream his name. *That* is what the Fae do. We take what is ours and we claim it for all to see," he said, making my cheeks flush with the memory of the Resistance watching us.

Of the way they'd witnessed his mouth between my legs, his cock spreading me wide and impaling me in the aftermath of his battle with the cave beast. I struggled to find the words to brush off his statement, and to pretend I didn't have first-hand knowledge of everything he spoke of.

Holt tilted his head to the side, a wide smile spreading his lips. They gleamed white in the shadowed, translucence of his flesh. The feathers tied into his hair shook as a sharp laugh bubbled up his throat and he tossed his head back in mirth.

"Oh, Beasty. He already has, hasn't he?"

I turned away, stomping over to the place where Caldris had left my boots. I tore open the laces in my rage, keeping my heated face turned away from Holt's probing stare as I stomped back to my bedroll, feeling defeated. "There's a special place in the afterlife for creatures like you," I snarled when I finally leveled at him the strongest glare I could summon through my embarrassment.

"I certainly hope not. I would hate to miss out on the show," Holt said, turning away from the tent as I pulled the blanket over my lap and snuggled into the chilled, knitted fabric. I willed the heat in my body to warm it, trying to shove away the horrifying arousal that built with the thought of being with Caldris in that way.

That wasn't me. It may be normal to the Fae, but I was a human. I'd been born a human, and for the love of Gods I would die as one as well.

Holt stayed in place, not speaking another word while we waited for Caldris to return with the food he'd promised. My stomach growled as if to emphasize the need for it, the rumble resounding through the tent.

"Would have been hard to find something to fill your belly in the dead of winter," he said pointedly, driving the point home that I didn't stand much chance of survival on my own. As if I didn't already know that. As if the bitter, short time Brann and I had survived on our own had been anything but an obvious symptom of my own inadequacy.

Holt's head tilted to the side suddenly, his attention snapping to the sky as he glanced overhead. "Stay inside. If you want any chance at survival, stay inside the fucking tent, Estrella," he said, snapping the fabric of the tent closed and shutting me in darkness.

Long moments passed in silence as I waited, listening for the sound of *any* form of movement outside the tent. There was nothing, as if the world itself froze.

I jolted when the fabric of the tent finally peeled back, Caldris's frame stepping into the tent in a hurry. His shoulders slouched in relief when he found me sitting atop the bedroll, the hand holding a plate full of food dropping lower as he took the first step toward me. "Did she leave at all?" he asked, spinning to pin Holt with a look that was so full of fear my heartbeat ramped up in response.

What the fuck was going on?

Holt looked at me, his meaningful but expressionless stare penetrating through me. "No," he said, surprising me. Though, I supposed, I hadn't set foot outside the tent, but that was only due to his interference. "She never left the tent." The words were not a lie but a carefully crafted statement to avoid the truth.

Caldris kicked off his boots, lowering himself onto the bedroll beside me and leaning forward to touch his lips aggressively to my forehead. "Thank the fucking Gods," he murmured, and even with his mouth pressed to my skin I could feel his attention shifted to the other man.

"What's going on?" I asked, pulling back and staring up at him in confusion. There was something so out of the ordinary about his concern, something that didn't make any sense with the lack of commotion and nothing but quiet to fill the air.

"Have you seen them like that before?" Caldris asked, ignoring my question. His probing stare was still intent on Holt, the man who was a mix of white and shadows, of wisps of air that made a somehow corporeal form. He looked paler than usual when he shifted his attention to me briefly.

"No. She's growing impatient," he said, touching a hand to his chest. Caldris mimicked the motion, rubbing his hand over his heart in a way that made my own ache.

"Who?" I asked, hating that I was entirely and completely lost in the conversation that seemed to concern me.

"Mab," Caldris said, his dark stare meeting mine. His eyes danced over my face, worry filling them as he sighed. "A murder of blight just flew overhead. They're looking for something."

"Mab's daughter?" I asked, my attention shifting between the two of them.

"Possibly. More likely she's looking to see what's taking me so long. Trusting her children isn't her strength," he admitted, hanging his head forward briefly before he turned and nodded to Holt. The other man tied the knots on the tent door, disappearing from the crack between them and leaving us alone once again.

"She calls you her children?" I asked, my brow furrowing as I considered how horrifying that was, when she'd stolen them from their real families.

"Not out of any sort of love," he said, shifting his position to get more comfortable. He lifted a piece of bread to my lips, letting me take a hesitant bite out of it. It was far from fresh, stale and crunchy around the outside, but it still tasted like one of the best things I'd ever eaten. My stomach rumbled in response as I chewed, watching as Caldris took another bite from the same piece. "It's a reminder to our families that she owns us now. That's all."

He lifted a piece of dried meat to my mouth, letting me take a bite of it with a grimace. He smiled as he tore off his own bite. After laboring to chew and swallow my piece, I asked, "How does she get away with it? Why is it that no one has tried to leave?"

He lifted a hand to touch his chest all over again, rubbing the spot where he and Holt had touched previously. "That's a story for another time, Little One, and not one that should be told over such delicacies as these."

His playful grin nearly stole a laugh from me as he lifted the stale bread to my lips once more. "Where did the food come from?" I asked, thinking about what food must be like in Alfheimr. If the gardens at the edge of the boundary had the most verdant land in Nothrek, it seemed unlikely that anything else would be true of the land of Faerie itself, but such things didn't necessarily travel well.

"Oh, you know, they got a little hungry so they carved the

horses down to the bone," he said, waving the meat stick back and forth with a raised brow.

I scoffed at his foolishness, taking the bread from his hand and stealing another bite while he bit into the meat. "Did they steal it?" I asked as I chewed.

"Stealing is a strong word," he said, trailing off as he looked away from me. His gaze dropped to where I held the remaining bread resting against my thigh. With his newly-healed hand, he grasped mine and lifted it to just in front of his mouth. His eyes held mine intently as he guided me forward so that he could take a bite from it.

He chewed thoughtfully, feeding me the last bite of the meat as I opened my mouth. He placed it on my tongue, leaving me with the scorching intimacy and feeling how he made such a simple moment feel sexually charged.

"One day soon, we'll lie in a bed in the palace at Catancia with a fire roaring in the corner of the room. I'll feed you twilight berries by hand," he said, holding out his hand to demonstrate the size of the decadent berries.

"No." My voice came out snappier than intended, my body leaning away from his as I realized I'd swayed toward him, drawn to him like a moth to the flame when I should have wanted nothing more than to stay as far away from him as I could.

The twilight berries were just one more reminder of the games of men; of why they were dangerous and never to be trusted.

"No?" Caldris asked, his brow furrowing in confusion. "No one in their right mind can say no to a twilight berry." He laughed, the rich sound of it grating over my skin in all the wrong ways. My body felt too hot, even feverish as I thought back to all the things I'd lived at the hands of the man who held authority figure over my life.

All he'd wanted was to raise me, and to groom me to be his wife one day. I'd been young enough to be his daughter, and that age difference was staggering.

Caldris was old enough to be my earliest ancestor, for Gods' sake.

"I can," I said, shoving the blanket away from me. "I hate them."

"What am I missing?" he asked, setting the plate to the side and leaning into my space. He snagged my chin with his thumb and forefinger, turning my attention back to him and meeting my gaze with his probing stare.

"Nothing," I said, feeling my eye twitch with the lie.

"Nothing? Like your scars?" he asked, his voice dropping lower as he glanced down to where I wrung my hands together. "Tell me, Little One. I want to know just how long I need to make him suffer before I grant him the gift of death. Are we talking about decades of torture, or am I sending his soul to the pits of Tartarus to be pecked to death by the blight for an eternity?"

I swallowed, trying to think of a response that would spare me this conversation. I didn't want to have it—didn't want to give Caldris any more of my secrets. He shouldn't get to own this part of me, but the bitter girl who wanted revenge would revel in the knowledge that Caldris would wreak vengeance on my tormenter, long after he'd lost me.

I wanted to be better than this. I wanted to be the strong survivor I'd spoken of with Melian, turning my back on those who'd wronged me, not wasting energy on things like revenge.

"Somewhere in the middle, I would wager," I said, my lips twisting into a dry smile when I raised my eyes to his. His glare seemed to enfold me in darkness as his nostrils flared. "But these aren't the sorts of conversations we should be having over delicacies like this," I said, shoving the last bite of bread into my mouth and chewing to delay the conversation.

"How convenient that you just ate the last of it then, min asteren," he said, releasing my chin and gathering my hands into his. He stared me down, trying to compel me to speak my truth.

"Am I your equal?" I asked instead, glancing down at my hands clutched in his. "Or am I just a pet like the humans have been taught?"

"You are my mate," he said, reaching out to touch his palm to my face. He caressed my cheekbone with his thumb, the intensity of his stare making me want to believe the words more than anything.

"Then give me your truth," I said, leaning my face into his touch instead of pulling away from it for once. If he could turn his love into a weapon, if he could use it to make me need him when I didn't want it, then maybe I could use his love for me against him.

Use it to learn the truth of everything that was coming.

"You know my truth," he said, his mouth turning down as he considered my words.

"Why did you touch your chest when Holt said Mab was getting impatient? What power does she have over you that makes you cooperate with her wishes, even when you think they're wrong? Why can't you defy her to save me from a life that I do not want?" I asked, reaching out to shove the plate to the side.

"Those aren't secrets I keep for my own benefit. I'm protecting you from the pain the truth will cause, my star."

"If I am truly your equal, then I do not need your protection. You cannot have it both ways, where you demand my secrets and I get nothing from you. If you want me to believe a word you say, then you have to start by being honest with me.

Until that happens," I said, shifting up onto my knees in front of him. I lifted my tunic from where it bunched around my knees as I unclasped my cloak with the other hand, letting it fall to the bedroll behind me. I shifted forward, straddling his outstretched legs until I settled in his lap. Leaning down to touch his face with a gentle hand, I stared into the familiar dark eyes that took my breath away with every glance. "You will not get to own any more of my secrets."

His hands settled on my hips, the heat of his palms feeling like a brand upon my soul. "This is a most cruel punishment," he said, tipping his head back as I leaned over him. My hair fell around us in a dark curtain, offering a feeling of intimacy in the darkness around us.

"Tell me," I murmured, trying not to respond when his fingertips brushed against my ass and squeezed.

"If I tell you, will you make love to me tonight?" he asked, leaning up until his mouth was only a breath from mine. He rubbed the curve of his lips against mine, teasing me and seeking to twist my daring game into something he could use to his advantage.

"You can only have one reward. You can have my body wrapped around yours, or you can have the reason I will never be able to stand the taste of twilight berries," I said, drawing his attention back to the issue at hand. He alone could choose which he wanted more: my body or my mind. My pussy or my secrets.

He pulled back as he considered his choices with a serious look on his face, then he nodded, lying back on the bedroll beneath him. His hands stayed at my hips, holding perfectly still even though I felt the tension in his grasp. He wanted to guide me to roll my hips over him, to mimic the movements I would make if I rode him.

"Mab has my heart," he said, and everything inside of me

froze at the words. Of all the things he could have possibly said, that was the last thing I'd wanted to hear. To think that I could be in love with a male who loved someone so evil; I felt like my heart might splinter in my chest.

He lifted a hand from my hip, grasping mine as he pulled me forward. Pressing it against his chest where his heart lay, he mirrored it with his hand on my breast as he had once before.

"Don't," I protested, my eyes snapping wide just before he clapped his palm against me.

My heart ceased to beat all over again, the ringing in my ears drowning out all sound as I swayed forward. Still, Caldris pressed my hand tighter to his chest, his lips moving despite the grimace on his face. "*Feel*," he mouthed, and I dug my fingertips into his skin.

His heart didn't beat, his chest lying still but for the slither of something moving slowly within his breast. I watched the skin move in a slow wave as something inside of him caused a rippling in his flesh.

My mouth dropped open in shock, with no air for me to draw past the overwhelming feeling of death hovering on the edge of my awareness. It threatened to pull me under, to take me to the calling Void waiting for me.

Caldris clapped his hand against my chest once more, starting my heart all over again and pulling me back from the foggy edge of existence. From the place between life and death, waiting to cross the river.

I drew my hand back with a sharp gasp as something inside his chest rattled. "What is it?" I asked, my voice conveying every bit of horror I felt.

"One of Mab's serpents," he answered, dropping his head back to rest against the bedroll as if his own exhaustion was too much to bear. "Wrapped around my heart."

"You meant she had your heart, *literally?*" I smacked my palm down against his chest as I scrambled to disentangle from his lap. The fucking asshole had to know how I would have perceived that. How much it would have broken me.

He raised a hand to his chest and the reddened skin where I'd slapped him as he reached up with the other to me back down until I sprawled across him. Rolling me beneath himself, he shoved my thighs wide and inserted his hips between them.

Rolling himself against me, he left me with little doubt as to what he would choose if forced to make the choice between my body and my secrets. "You thought I meant I loved Mab?" he asked, his voice shocked as a chuckle resounded from him. "Why would I love a monster when I have a perfectly beautiful, sweet mate lying beneath me?"

"There was *someone* you loved. You said it was complicated even though you didn't miss her anymore. If it wasn't Mab, who was it?" I asked, staring up at him as he filled my gaze.

He smiled down at me sweetly, lifting a hand to cup my cheek as he looked at me with so much affection and longing that I lost the ability to breathe. "You, Estrella. It was complicated because I couldn't reach you, but I spent every day missing you, anyway. Waiting for the day when I would get to know you," he said. My heart stalled all over again, no supernatural reason for it aside from the way he made it flutter and skip a beat with his admission.

While I'd been talking about the man who took my virginity, he'd been waxing poetic about... me?

I swallowed, biting the inside of my cheek as he grinned down at me. "I told you it was a good thing he was already dead. Your *Viniculum* eased his suffering. If I could hunt down every man who touched you in your previous lives and end them permanently, I would."

"Unless you plan to allow me to reciprocate with the women you were with while I was trapped in this endless cycle of reincarnation, that hardly seems fair," I said, turning my head away to try to comprehend the reality of what he'd said.

Of the way it made me feel.

But he wasn't done shaking my world and turning it over, it would seem. He grinned, leaning forward to tease my lips with his. "Your list would be mercifully short, my star. There has been no one since the moment you came of age in your first life and the bond snapped into place."

I paused, trying to think past the ringing in my ears. "What?" I asked stupidly, blinking up at him as I turned my face back to him in shock.

"So that you cannot try to say I twisted my words, I'll be clear. I have not kissed a woman. I have not touched or fucked or allowed any to touch me in that way since the moment I knew you existed. I would never disrespect my *equal* in that way," he said, running his nose along the side of mine. "I was no innocent in the centuries before your creation, but I would have waited a dozen more for you."

"So that night in the spring beneath the stars, you hadn't had sex in..."

"Over three hundred years," he admitted, sitting up beneath me. His stomach flexed with the motion, and then his face was directly in front of mine. His features were open, nothing shuttered in his expression as he willed me to see the truth of the words.

"Have all the Fae repressed their..." I paused thinking over the words to properly convey what I needed to say. "Urges if their mate was on the other side of the Veil?"

"Not all of them, but some, I'm sure. It is a difficult thing to convince yourself to be loyal to your mate when you know that, somewhere out there, she is taking other men to her bed. There were times when I wanted to punish you for doing so," he admitted, reaching out to cup my cheek. "But I couldn't, because I knew it wouldn't be fair to you. You didn't know about me, but I knew you better than I knew myself."

"I don't know what to say to that," I admitted, sighing as I stared into his eyes. I'd never considered that he might have been celibate for so long. He'd remained loyal to me when I couldn't have been to him: the man I didn't even know was out there waiting for me.

The image of him with two human women kneeling at his feet flashed through my mind, a reminder of all that he could've had if he'd so chosen. It made his celibacy hit harder, knowing there wasn't a single man I'd met in all my life who would have done such a thing for me.

"There's nothing you need to say. I did it because I never would have been able to stomach the touch of another woman on my skin," he said, leaning forward to nip at the tip of my nose. "Now, tell me about the twilight berries."

I blanked, staring back at him in shock. I'd thought he would choose the physical intimacy that he craved from me. "What?"

"You said if I told you what power Mab holds over me, you would tell me why you cannot stand the taste of twilight berries," he explained, reaching forward to tuck a lock of hair behind my ear. He huffed a little laugh as realization set in, the sound bittersweet as it reached my ears. "I will always choose you, min asteren," he said, his brow creasing as he stared at me in something akin to confusion. "Your body is just the packaging that gives the other half of my soul a home. I have failed as your mate if you do not already know that."

"I think I should have known that," I said, the breathy whisper escaping even though I didn't want to speak the words aloud. Caldris grinned at me, his smile shining in the darkness surrounding us. In the enclosed tent, there were no moon and stars above to offer any light in the night. I wasn't sure I was supposed to be able to see as well as I could.

At least not when I'd been human.

"Lord Byron liked to make me sit on his lap so he could feed them to me while he tended to the wounds on my hands that I earned picking them during the harvest," I said simply, watching as Caldris's gaze dropped to the thin white scars on the backs of my hand.

"And how old were you when Lord Byron started doing this?" he asked, his voice dropping into that timbre where it no longer sounded even remotely human, the depth where the God-like quality of his power crept through his throat and coated the air.

"Seven," I said with a sigh, watching as he reared his head back in shock. "When I got older, he would make me feed them to him while he—" I paused, unable to find the words for the horrors that had started as soon as I'd come of age.

"While he what?" he asked, his eyes narrowing on my face. His voice wrapped around me, raising goosebumps on my arms as I sensed the danger that would come from my admission.

"While he fucked the Ladies of the Night who came to pleasure him. He would have me sit on the edge of the table in front of him while he sat in the chair and a woman either rode him or sucked him off."

Caldris shifted me off his lap, depositing me gently onto the bedroll beside him as he stood. There was no care for the cold as he paced around the small enclosure of the tent. "Did he touch you?" he asked, his body tense as he rolled his shoulders. His hands clenched at his sides, but he didn't give me his eyes for a moment as I hesitated to answer.

The rage rolling off of him made me wish he'd chosen the physical intimacy instead. "Come back to bed," I said softly, forcing a smile to my face that he couldn't see with his back turned to me. The thought that he might not want someone who had been so damaged, so violated, rolled through me, a finger of doubt I never wanted to feel.

"Did. He. Touch. You?" he asked, spinning to pin me with his bright blue stare. The wind outside made the fabric of the tent flap viciously as a burst of winter weather tore through the camp. People shouted outside, drawing my attention toward the ties in the canvas.

I swallowed nervously, pulling a blanket up to my shoulders, wanting the cover it could provide. "Not those nights," I said, evading the truth of what had happened on the ones when we were alone in that Gods-forsaken library.

"Not those nights," Caldris said, his head tilting to the side as he scoffed bitterly. "But others?"

"He didn't fuck me if that's what you're worried about," I snapped, scowling up at him.

"Did he violate you? Touch you sexually in ways you didn't want?" he asked, the question leaving no room for me to evade it. I didn't want to lie to him; I wanted to give him the same respect I could expect from him, and something in me felt compelled to do just that.

My bottom lip trembled as I prepared for the word that I thought might change everything between us. For the answer that could drive him away once and for all. It should have been what I wanted, the answer that I would state proudly in an effort to gain my freedom. "Yes," I whispered, the sound cracking between us like a whip echoing through the tent.

His breath came in deep, shuddering gasps that shook his entire body as he rolled his neck from one side to the other again. His jaw clenched as he glared down at me, his blue eyes bleeding to black before he reached down and snatched the plate off the bedroll.

He exploded, throwing it at the side of the tent with a roar that echoed within me. My very *being* seemed to go still in response to the sound, my soul aching down to my core.

He stormed to the doorway of the tent, ripping the ties loose. The flaps flew open in the wind from the storm surging outside, thick layers of snow falling from the night sky as he disappeared into the storm itself. "Caldris!" I called out, scurrying to follow after him.

The cold bit into my feet as I trudged through the snow outside the tent, emerging into the storm and looking around for any sign of the God of the Dead. "What did you fucking do?!" a male voice shouted at me as Holt appeared from the haze of snow. He stepped up beside me, touching a transparent hand to my shoulder.

"He asked about the man who hurt me," I said, turning a fear-filled gaze up to the leader of the Wild Hunt.

"Fucking Gods," he said, reaching down to take my hand in his. Revulsion filled me, the startling wrongness of any touch other than Caldris's filling me with a surge of nausea. "He's going to bring the blight back here. They will feel this kind of power, and when they catch sight of it, she'll send someone to investigate what made him this angry. She has been trying for centuries to get any kind of reaction out of him; do you understand me? She *cannot* know that you exist. Fix it, Estrella," he said, pulling me through the camp as members of the Wild Hunt tried to hold down the tents that threatened to blow away in the storm Caldris had brought down on us.

He stood in the center of the plain, ice and wind swirling around him in a vortex. Above him, clouds roiled in the sky as he slowly raised his hands from his sides. "Caldris!" I called, raising a hand to cover my face as snow made my skin sting with the cold.

There was no response, leaving me to believe he was lost to the storm entirely.

I hurried forward, daring to enter the eye as the violent gusts of wind threatened to toss me to the side. I finally stepped up next to him, resting a firm hand on top of his forearm and trying to force it back down to his side. His stare was like tumbling into the darkest of nights when it finally fell on mine. "Stop this," I said, wincing when he pinned me with a glare.

"He needs to die," he said, his voice guttural.

"This isn't the way. Think of all the people you'll hurt doing it like this," I said, trying not to even consider the number of people who stood between Caldris and Byron. He would take out them all with a storm like this.

"What should I care about any of *them*?" he asked, his lips lifting into a snarl. "Did they protect you from the monster who wanted to hurt you? Did they offer you shelter when you were forced to run from the only home you'd ever known? They do not deserve to live."

"Caelum," I said sadly, reaching up to cup his cheek. I fought against the violence inside of me, and the desire for revenge I wanted to pretend I was above. "I don't want this. I want to slit his throat myself. I want to be there to watch the life fade from his eyes the way my father's did when Byron made me watch. I want him to know it was me who killed him. Don't take that from me."

The darkness of his eyes softened as a brutal smile twisted his mouth. His hand raised to cup my cheek, a mirror of the way I touched him as the winds around us slowly eased.

"I wouldn't dare to deprive the world of your vengeance," he said, dropping his forehead to mine. "And when he makes his way to Tartarus for his crimes, I'll have an eternity to make him suffer."

"You can do whatever you want with him after I've killed him," I said, the lack of interest in my tone showing my exhaustion. Caelum sensed the faltering of my energy, or he realized that I was standing in the snow in only my socks. Lifting me off my feet and leaving me with no choice but to wrap my legs around his hips, he carried me back to our tent and the refuge waiting for us there.

I pressed my face into his shoulder, trying to escape the prying, curious eyes of those watching us.

I was asleep by the time we reached the tent.

*M*y back was warm from the heat sinking into my skin through the fabric of my tunic. My face felt too hot against the bare skin pressed into it. I pulled away slowly, shifting lower and sinking into the fabric of the bedroll beneath me as I slowly peeled my eyes open. The canvas walls of the tent surrounded me, billowing gently in the wind that was almost nonexistent compared to the howling I recalled from the night before.

I turned to glance at Caldris over my shoulder, his eyes closed as he slept peacefully. The chains of my shackles clinked as I moved, drawing a wince from me as I waited for him to wake from his slumber. In his sleep, his face always smoothed into a relaxed expression that I so rarely saw on him. With the absence of emotion, he looked all the more like the carvings and portraits I'd seen of my Fae mate.

Void of all humanity, a specimen of unrivaled beauty who was missing that spark of life inside of him, as if he spent far too much time with the dead he held power over.

I turned forward, trying to ignore the throbbing of my heart and the way my blood heated as I studied him. My visceral reaction to him erased any doubt I might've had about the truth to his confession that he was my mate. After rolling slowly so I wouldn't alert him as I moved, I screamed as a play of shadows materialized in the tent.

A wisp of dark tendrils in the air, he was even less tangible than the ghosts that had accompanied the Wild Hunt the day before. Here was nothing but a tangle of darkness and gleaming golden eyes.

Caldris moved from behind me, jerking into a sitting position as the sound of his sword being pulled from its scabbard rippled through the early morning air. I stared up in horror at the shade of a man lingering at the entrance to our tent.

"Pardon me, ma'am, but would you happen to know how I got here?" the shadow asked, leaning forward with a curious expression on his face. His feet were rooted into the snow-covered grass, the tendrils of shadow sinking into the earth itself as if it was what connected him to the plane of the living.

Caldris dropped the tip of his sword to the ground in front of me as his body shook our bed with laughter. "What the fuck is so funny?!" I asked, swinging my hand out as I spun to look at him over my shoulder. He'd gotten to his knees behind me, his trousers pressed into the bedroll beneath him as his golden skin gleamed in the dawn light.

"You screamed like you were about to die," Caldris laughed, his chest shaking as he released the hilt of his sword entirely and let it drop to the ground in front of me. I resisted the urge to grab it up and use it to run him through.

Barely.

"Of course I screamed, you ass! There's a *thing* staring at me," I said, fumbling over the word for such a creature. He wasn't a ghost, and he wasn't a member of the Wild Hunt. He was somehow a being crafted from nothing but the air itself, with only the light from his eyes to distinguish his features.

"I have seen you attack a member of the Wild Hunt with all the bravery of a warrior and none of the fear that you should have felt," he said, dropping to his side on the bedroll and snuggling into my back all over again. He curved his body around me until we fit like the perfect, seamless pair that he seemed determined to convince me we would be. "But the shadowed face of a shade is what drives fear into your heart."

"What is it?" I asked, crossing my arms over my chest and forcing myself to sit up. I wanted nothing to do with the rumbling amusement bubbling in his chest behind me, or with the way his laughter warmed my soul against the cold surroundings.

"The shades are people who are drawn to the Wild Hunt, while they sleep. The soul leaves their body for a brief time as we pass near them, giving them the opportunity to join the Wild Hunt while it rides. They are just the unrealized potential of the soul before it has fully vacated the body," he explained, wrapping strong arms around my waist and tugging me down to lie on the bedroll.

He shifted, leaning his upper body over mine as one arm came down on the opposite side of my head and he filled my vision. Then he spared a single glance for the shade lurking in the corner, whose expression plagued me with an odd sense of curiosity.

He looked so...*lost*.

"Go haunt someone else," Caldris said, his voice deep with command. As if compelled, the shade retreated from our tent, dissipating through the canvas and disappearing into the early morning light.

"If he isn't dead, does he still need to listen to your command?" I asked, thinking about the potential reach of the powers of the God of the Dead. How close did one need to be to heed his orders? Could he control the living in the same way?

"He is neither dead or alive at the moment. His heart continues to beat in his body, and he'll return to it with the sunrise believing he's had an adventurous dream. He listened because only a fool would remain when a male tells him to get out when he has the warmth of his mate beneath him," he said, leaning forward to run his nose along the side of mine.

The odd intimacy was something he so often did, which I'd grown to appreciate and even love in our brief time together.

"Oh," I said, shifting my gaze to where the shade had drifted through the fabric. It was so different from the corporeal forms of the Wild Hunt, leaving me to struggle to wrap my head around all the creatures that existed and I had somehow never experienced. "Why can I see them now when I never did before?"

"The magic of Alfheimr has opened humans up to all sorts of senses they didn't possess when it was confined to the other realm. The spirits and shades have always been there, even when you couldn't see them, but you are not likely to see that which you do not open yourself to," he explained. Seeing my discontent at that explanation, he leaned over to touch a kiss to my wrist.

"How are you feeling?" he asked, drawing my attention away from the erotic image of his mouth against my skin. It should have been a sweet moment when he simply tended to a minor injury.

Even if he was the reason it was necessary.

"Tired," I admitted, sighing when he raised my hand to rest beside my head. He threaded his fingers through mine, mirroring the motion with his other hand as well. With the shade gone, I glanced around the tent, trying to remember how we'd come to be lying upon the bedroll when the specter had appeared. "What happened?"

"You fell asleep as I was carrying you in from the storm," Caldris murmured, leaning his body over mine as he stared down at me. "Until you accept the bond and the power that comes with it, the *Viniculum* will pull the energy it gives you when I use too much of my own too quickly. You've had a very long, tiring few days, and I suspect the *Viniculum* was all that sustained you for so long. The power will return slowly, and I'll do my best not to overdraw again."

"So the exhaustion I felt was purely because I was human again for a few moments?" I asked, swallowing around the confusion that left me with. I didn't want to consider being human a weakness, wanted to think of it as a strength that made me care about those around me. But there was no denying the fact that I wanted to roll onto my side and go back to sleep for the rest of the day.

"Yes," Caldris said with a smile. "What's wrong, my star? Did you not enjoy the reminder of what it was to be human? That feels dangerously close to admitting you enjoy some aspects of being my mate."

"Fuck you," I said, but my lips curved up into a smile that I couldn't seem to prevent with the way his eyes gleamed happily.

"I would be happy to, but I'm afraid your scream has awakened the entire camp," he said with a chuckle. Even as he said the words, he gripped my hands tighter in his, the touch defying what he spoke. "It is most fortunate that you and I both know you do not have any aversion to having an audience."

He shifted my hands higher, grasping both wrists in a one-handed grip as his other trailed down my arm, tickling against my skin through the fabric of my tunic. His fingers toyed with the laces at my chest, drawing them apart slowly to reveal a line of cleavage.

I stared up at him, fear pulsing through my veins. I knew what it was to be with him; I knew how it was to have him moving inside of me. To have allowed it while I was consumed with my grief had been one thing, but in the aftermath of the intimacy we'd shared the night before and the weight of our confessions, this felt like an entirely different beast.

"Wait," I whispered. The word cracked through the silence and Caldris froze immediately.

He stared down at me with his brow furrowed, his features conveying so much hurt and so much confusion, I immediately regretted the fact that I wasn't able to be with him in this moment. "What's wrong, Little One?" he asked, his voice gentle in spite of the surge of emotion I could feel coming from him.

The rejection wandered down the bond, striking me in the chest to confirm that he knew exactly what was wrong. "I can't," I whispered, letting my eyes drift closed as I spoke. I didn't want to hurt him; not under his gentle stare, feeling as if I held his heart in my hands. "You lied to me. Call it what you want, but you knowingly deceived me. I loved Caelum, but you are not him."

He released my hands, rising to his knees beside me and staring down . The sudden vulnerability from him staring down at me, his face taut with the pain of rejection, forced me to sit up and cross my arms over my chest. "I thought we were coming together last night," he murmured, the ache of his melancholy surging into me. "But I'm not getting anywhere with you, am I?"

"I'm just not ready for that," I said, fully knowing that I was giving him mixed signals. I'd allowed him to take me after we'd buried Melian, and I couldn't find the words to explain that this felt heavier *because* of the way he'd worked inside my heart since that moment, not in spite of it. "It doesn't mean that I'm not..." I floundered, rubbing my hands over my face as I tried to find the words.

"You could let me in, you know," he said, reaching forward to pull my hands away from my face. He touched the side of my temple, his fingers coasting over my skin gently. "Our bond would allow us to speak without words—to feel without having to articulate it—but you keep your mind closed to me."

"I feel like you already know everything. Like you can sense what I'm feeling," I explained, leaning away from his fingers. I didn't know how to open myself to him so he could feel the torment lashing through me, but I also knew that I wouldn't do it, even if I could.

I wouldn't give him that part of me, not when even I couldn't understand the mess inside my head.

"I've learned to read you very quickly, but it isn't the same. I want to be one with you, min asteren. I want to feel your emotions as if they are my own. Let me in," he urged. His eyes were sad as if he already knew what my answer would be, and he turned his head away when I didn't reply.

"I need time," I said finally. "You're right. We... There was progress last night, but I'm not ready for you to make love to me with all of that hanging between us. It's too much. It's more than just sex—"

"Of course it's more than just sex. I am your mate, Estrella. We are incapable of anything less than the complete melding of our souls. If you've convinced yourself that all the times that came before this were anything less, then you are further lost to me than I thought," he snapped, rising to his feet.

"That's not true! In Calfalls, it was closer to anger than love," I said, clinging to the fact that I'd given him a different part of me in that instance.

"Trust me, Little One; if it's a hate fuck you're after, I would be happy to oblige you right now." He shoved his feet into his boots, grimacing as he stormed toward the entrance.

"Where are you going?" I asked, rising to my knees as the blanket fell around me. He paused there, the canvas fisted in his grip as he glared at me over his shoulder.

"You want time? Have it," he said, tearing the flap open and stepping into the early morning sunrise. He turned to glare at me from the other side, the hatred in his gaze burning through me so hotly that I raised a hand to touch my heart. He ignored it, yanking the canvas closed and knotting it together to seal me inside.

Alone.

I stared after him for a few moments, convincing myself that he would come back. That there would be opportunities for me to put words to the torrent of emotion that plagued me, and to the confliction of hating him and loving him all at the same time.

It felt like he was unmaking me, unraveling everything I'd been raised to believe and forming something new its place. My soul, my heart, couldn't stand the constant battle of confusion.

The mixture of want with the horror that followed it.

He didn't return, leaving me staring at the canvas ties as my eyes burned with the threat of tears. I lay down on the bedroll, hating that it smelled of his unique spearmint scent, and stared at the canvas surrounding me, wishing I could undo that conversation.

Whenever I tried to articulate the feelings within me, I somehow made it all worse. I couldn't fix it when he was just *gone*, but letting him inside my head wasn't something I could accept just yet. There was no telling how he might use it to manipulate me into doing what he wanted.

My tears stained the bedroll beneath me, letting out all the anguish I hadn't been able to release since I'd learned the truth. There'd always been prying eyes, always been my mate looking to see if I was okay.

The sound of canvas opening at my spine made me turn to see if it was Caldris who had returned, but I only found Holt standing there with his arms crossed over his chest. The blue markings across his chest gleamed in the gap where his fur coat didn't cover him; how he could tolerate the cold winter air against his bare skin was beyond me.

"Get up," he said, stepping forward and grabbing my boots off the ground. He set them beside the bedroll for me to step into, gathering my cloak from the ground and holding it out for me. "Time to pack up camp, and it looks like you're with me today, Beasty."

"Where's Caldris?" I asked, standing slowly and shoving my feet into my boots. I tied the laces quickly, wincing when I thought of how often Caldris insisted on doing it for me. He'd been gone for a matter of moments, and the empty space he'd left already mocked me.

"Gone for a ride. He'll catch up eventually," he said, swinging my cloak around my back as I stood in front of him. Other riders of the Wild Hunt stepped into the tent, working to pack up the bedroll and the blankets as Holt guided me outside.

My steps faltered as I glanced around the campsite the Wild Hunt worked to dismantle. "He left?" I asked, searching for any sign of Caldris or Azra.

Holt only nodded, his lips pursed judgmentally as if to say just how badly I'd fucked up. "He left," he agreed finally, guiding me toward his skeletal horse. "So now you get to ride with me."

Tears bubbled free at the thought of Caldris being so done

with me he would willingly allow me to ride with another male. To be held within his arms. "Did he approve that?" I asked, turning a teary stare up at him.

Holt rolled his eyes, drawing me into his chest as his arms settled around my back awkwardly. He patted me in an attempt to soothe me, making a harsh laugh burst from my lips. "Not directly, but he knows damn well I can't exactly put you in the carts. They'll tear you apart," he said, glancing over to where a few members of the Wild Hunt guided the Fae Marked into their carts.

Indignation struck me in the chest, knowing that was where I belonged, in all fairness. Riding with Caldris had been one thing because he was my mate, but now?

"I'm Marked and I do not see my mate here to accompany me on the journey," I said, pulling back from Holt. I held out my wrists, waiting for my shackles. He glanced down at my free wrists with a disgruntled sigh, waving a hand so that a new pair appeared from thin air. He secured them to my wrists, eyeing me like he didn't particularly agree with where the conversation was going. "It only seems fitting that I ride with the rest of them."

He sighed, hanging his head backward as if I was insufferable. "You do realize they dislike you greatly, correct?" he asked, chin dropping as he pinched the bridge of his nose.

"I've gotten that impression, yes," I agreed, stepping toward the carts. Holt accompanied me, groaning as we approached the only cart with a space for one more to join. I climbed into it without his assistance, taking the seat on the end and resting my shackled wrists in my lap.

With my cloak settled around my shoulders, I tried to snuggle into the warmth it provided. I'd grown so used to having Caldris's heat at my back to warm me, I didn't know how I would fare without it.

The other Marked were silent as Holt shook his head at the vagaries of human women. He lifted the gate to the back of the cart, giving me something to lean into so that I could feel a little more secure. Judging by the glares I received from the others, I would need it.

"May the Gods be with you," Holt said, striding toward his skeletal horse. He mounted smoothly, raising two fingers to the sky in a silent command, and the Wild Hunt moved forward as one with his.

"The Gods left us the moment we were marked by evil," one of the men said with a snarl, his lips twisting with malice as he glared at Holt.

"Might have wanted to say it *after* he was out of earshot," a woman said, rolling her eyes to the sky as she leaned back. The cart rolled forward, jostling me to the side as the wheels navigated the uneven terrain.

"Why bother? The little spy will tell him everything, I'm sure," he snapped back, the lot of them bickering like children. I stood very little chance of them ever growing to tolerate me when they didn't even seem to like one another.

"I'm not a spy," I said simply, propping my elbow on my knee and resting my head in my hand. I still felt too tired, body drained of the energy that had bolstered me through the journey thus far.

"Like your mate won't use his cock to pry anything out of your stupid little head," another one of the women said, her glare scathing as she settled it onto me.

I turned my head away, ignoring the ire she leveled at me and wishing there were something more interesting to stare at. "I don't think you understand how the human body works," I remarked, turning back to her with a saccharine smile. "It isn't my mind he's penetrating when he fucks me."

A few of the others in the cart gasped, strangled laughter

bursting free as they looked at me as if I'd left my mind on the ground behind us.

"You admit you've been intimate with him?" the woman asked, crossing her arms over her chest as if she could protect herself from the depravity that wafted off of me.

"I hardly think there would be any point to denying it. We all know you heard us when we were in Calfalls." I shrugged, feigning confidence. The reproach in her gaze sank inside of me, illuminating all the dark hollows of doubt that I struggled to reconcile with the male who treated me well. "You might try it when you find your mate. Your overt lack of understanding of sex could be part of why your face is pinched up so tight it looks like someone sewed it that way."

She scoffed, turning her attention away. She was older than me by far, and I'd have been shocked if she didn't have a human husband of her own waiting for her to return. As much as I might wish we could all get along, I didn't think there was a chance of that happening.

At least not yet.

I'd take the begrudging acceptance that I was not one to be pushed around and the tolerance that came with that. We could coexist without liking one another.

"Yes, we all heard you scream for him," she said, snapping her attention back to me with a cruel smile. "Just because you're willing to debase yourself in such a way, doesn't mean the rest of us lack the self-respect to do so, Faerie *whore.*"

I tilted my head as I studied her, remembering a time when that insult had made me cringe. Now, there wasn't a single reaction in me; not a cringe or a flare of anger at the accusation.

"I didn't just fuck a Faerie," I said, shrugging my shoulders as I leveled a glare at her. "I fucked a *God.* Remember that, the next time you think to trick yourself into believing that it was any kind of life, lying in bed with your legs spread for the flaccid flesh of the husband they chose for you."

"The Fae are no Gods," one of the women said—the one who'd criticized the male for speaking too late.

"Odd, he definitely feels like one when he raises the dead or calls up a storm great enough to tear Nothrek in two," I argued, twisting my head to her.

I wasn't sure why I defended my relationship with him, not when I'd been so determined to get out of it, but the bastard was in my head, swimming along with my thoughts even after he'd left me alone. I hated him. I wanted him. There was no middle ground in the passion between us, no neutral space for indifference.

"The power of the Gods does not have limitations," she said back, raising her shackled wrists. "They are not weakened by iron or by something so insignificant as love."

"Or maybe the Gods you believe in are just grandiose tales told by men who want to keep you subdued within the confines of the world they created. All I know is that I will never stand a chance at wielding the kind of power Caldris has. I'll never have a fraction of his ability to bring the winter, or of his dominion over the dead. That makes him a God to me. If The Father and The Mother would like to argue otherwise, I'll be waiting for that riveting discussion. As they do not waste time with paltry peasants like me, though—" I shrugged, grinning at her with a smile that felt torn straight from the depths of the underworld "—I'll stick to the God who can be bothered."

"Interestingly enough, he seems to have lost interest in you already though, hasn't he?" the man asked, smirking arrogantly. "Or is there some other reason that you've been abandoned?"

"Trouble in paradise already?" a woman asked, their scathing laughter echoing through the air.

"Am I a whore for entertaining him? Or am I pathetic for losing his interest so quickly? I do apologize, but I can't seem to decide which logic is more convenient for you at this moment," I said, earning a chuckle from the rider on the skeletal steed that pulled our cart. The woman beside me grasped my forearm at my eyeroll, digging her nails into it, her features harsh.

"His lack of interest in you after you've whored yourself out is what makes you pathetic. You couldn't have been half as good a lay as you seem to think you are for him to abandon you so readily," the man said.

"Would you care to find out for yourself?" I asked, smiling sweetly. "We can even place wagers on how long it takes for Caldris to kill you when he finds out you touched me." The crack of the older woman's hand across my cheek snapped my head to the side, my skin burning as I processed my shock.

"Okay," Holt interjected. He pulled his steed to a halt, dropping back to pace beside the cart until the rider stopped as well. "Let's go, Beasty," he said, sighing in frustration as he reached underneath my armpits and lifted me from the cart.

Depositing me on the front of his saddle, he did the best he could to refrain from touching me more than necessary. His arms closed around me, that pervasive sense of wrongness filling me as his cool body touched mine.

"I don't like it any more than you do, I promise you that," he grunted, kicking his horse into a steady walk once more. "Try not to move too much. I do like my head attached to my shoulders. Growing a new one is painfully slow and inconvenient, and we have a lot of ground to cover. No time for Caldris to sever it for me when he returns for you."

"What the fuck is wrong with them?" I asked, my frustration leaking into my voice as I turned to glare back at the humans who seemed much more comfortable with me gone.

"They're human," Holt scoffed. "All of you lot have that same attitude. Whatever they've told you in the centuries since the Fae have been gone from these lands, the teachings lodged deep. It will take time to undo all that hatred."

"And yet you are not so patient with me and would condemn me for the fact that I am not fully committed to my mate yet," I said, trailing a finger over one of the bones making up his horse's neck. It felt exactly how I imagined a bone would, the surface smooth and somehow porous-feeling all at once. I sighed, looking out at the expansive plains around us.

Would it be so much to ask for some change in scenery?

"You're different from the rest of them," Holt said, his voice dropping low as if he knew it was an unfair assessment. "You knew him before you knew what he was. You loved him exactly as he is, now he is just more. They did not have that benefit. They will go to their mates knowing what they are, and their own prejudice will stand in the way of their happiness. It is unfortunate for them because they will likely waste countless years to their own bitterness. You have the chance to finding happiness before you arrive in Alfheimr. The chance to stand united with your mate before you face all that will try to tear you apart once you arrive in Faerie. You would be a fool to waste such an opportunity."

"Or perhaps I would be wise to be cautious," I said, snorting at the black and white way he saw Caldris's and my relationship. There was no room for the betrayal of his deception or the fact that I was still recovering from it.

"Sometimes, we fight with the most fervor against those things that we need most," he said, his voice dropping lower until it was barely more than a murmur. "Would you like to hear a story, Beasty? Caldris says you quite enjoy them." I flushed, not wanting to even consider what else he'd told Holt about me.

"What kind of a story?" I asked, my words a mirror of what I'd said to Caldris the first time he'd tried to tell me a story to settle me down for the night.

"The story of how I came to be the leader of the Wild Hunt," Holt said, shifting me forward in the saddle to gain some more room for himself. "I was a hunter—called to the hunt when I was alive as well. My band of men and I traveled around Alfheimr, taking trophies of the most brutal of Faerie creatures. Until we encountered the Erymanthian Boar, I'd never known defeat. But that boar sliced my arm open with his tusk," he said, holding out his arm and lifting his fur-lined coat to reveal a long, jagged scar carved into the ghost of his flesh.

"It doesn't look fatal," I said, taking his arm in my grip. I twisted it from side to side, staring at the way the flesh glimmered in the sunlight streaming down upon us.

"If it had been a normal boar, it wouldn't have been," he said, pulling his arm back from my grip as one of the other members of the Wild Hunt raised a brow at him in warning. I rolled my eyes to the sky, retracting my own hands from what had been an entirely innocent touch. "But the Erymanthian Boar has poison in its tusks."

"Poison strong enough to kill a Fae?" I asked, blinking back my shock.

"Yes. It sinks into the blood and travels through the body until it reaches the heart, slowly dissolving the beating flesh. There is no cure, so I was killed by that damned boar. When I went to the Void, The Father offered me refuge from the Asphodel Meadows in the Kingdom of Valhalla."

"What are the Asphodel Meadows?" I asked, wrapping my mouth around the unfamiliar term. Holt froze at my question.

"It is where the majority of souls go upon their final death," he said, his voice laced with confusion. "They didn't teach you about that?"

"They told us that all souls are selected to either join The Father in Valhalla or The Mother in Folkvangr. There is no other final resting place."

"That is simply appalling," Holt said, shaking his head. "There is Valhalla, Folkvangr, the Asphodel Meadows, and Tartarus. Where you are destined to go depends on your soul; on the quality of it and the calling that runs through your very being. The Father chose me for Valhalla since the hunt was in my blood, but I offended him greatly when I asked to be given a second chance at life, so I could continue with my purpose of hunting. I chose what I thought I wanted over the peace I needed."

"You rejected The Father himself?" I asked, unable to withhold a snort . If the image painted by the Temple and the High Priest was anything to go by, The Father was not a portrait of forgiveness.

"I did, and he cursed me to the Wild Hunt for all eternity for it. I stalked the realms, searching for criminals who needed to be punished within the depths of Tartarus, so that I might drag their souls to the underworld. Until Mab came into power, anyway."

"That's what the Wild Hunt is meant to do?" I asked, my brow furrowing at the snippets of information he provided.

"Before Mab and before the Veil, that was my life's purpose. It was a good life, even if it was meant to be a curse. It has never felt more like a punishment than it does since I've become Mab's errand boy, collecting the Fae Marked as if they are criminals. I long for the day when someone wrenches her from her throne and feeds her to the creatures of Tartarus," he said, his grip tightening on the reins in front of me. "Caldris can be that someone, if you allow him to be. Think of that the next time you want to reject him so cruelly that he rides off on his horse without a shirt. He could be the savior of everything if you weren't so stubborn."

I swallowed, choosing to remain silent in the face of his venom. There was nothing to be said when he was so angry with me. Saving the world wasn't meant to be my responsibility, and it shouldn't come at the expense of my dignity.

And yet, how could I choose between myself and the freedom of so many imprisoned by the Queen who held all of Faerie in her hands?

11

I sat on a blanket thrown on top of the snow, the fire at the center of our campsite keeping me warm. Holt draped an additional blanket around my shoulders as the rest of the Wild Hunt set to work putting up the tents. "I'll put a man on you tonight, but he'll stay outside the tent. Try not to get into too much trouble without Cal here to physically hold you down. I don't relish what he'll do to my riders if he finds out they had to put their hands on you."

I lifted my shackled hands toward the fire, nodding wordlessly. An entire day and Caldris hadn't returned, leaving me to the unease of being with creatures I didn't know. I didn't want to contemplate how I would feel waking up to another shade in my tent without him here to protect me. Fenrir lay beside me, earning a glare from Holt as he settled his upper body atop the blanket and lay his head on my lap like a pampered beast.

"Caelum wasn't always this way," I said, huffing out a breath. It might be ridiculous, but I needed him to know that the man I'd slowly fallen for hadn't behaved as if I were his property. He'd been protective, but as much as his teasing had made me want to stab him, he'd been charming, in a sense. "He was sweet in the beginning. Not so concerned with the fact that other men might look at me wrong."

Holt paused, turning back to face me with a sigh. "Have the two of you discussed the mate bond at all? Aside from just skating over the fact that you have one?"

I shook my head, knowing there had been time for Caldris to explain the ins and outs of how it would work. We'd had the entire day before, sharing a horse, when he could have taken the time to explain it all.

Holt groaned, dropping to a sitting position on the blanket beside me. He kicked his legs out in front of him, keeping his slushy boots off the fabric and lying back to stare at the night sky above us. "If you were to accept the bond, the instinct that drives him to be so possessive would ease," he explained, turning to pin me with a sharp look. "It would not disappear entirely, but it wouldn't feel as if—"

"He's going to suffocate me with it?"

"Yes, that," he agreed with a chuckle. "If you accepted the bond, he would know your mind. He would know exactly what is in your heart, and other men wouldn't matter because he'd know without a doubt they didn't have a chance of stealing you away from him. It is practically unheard of for a person to have an affair outside a mate bond once they've been formally bound to another."

"He has always claimed that it isn't me he doesn't trust, but the people around me. If that's the case, what good would it do for him to know how I feel about him?" I asked, dropping back to lie beside him. I kept my distance from him physically, but allowed myself to enjoy the sight of the moon and stars glowing in the sky above.

My biggest complaint about sleeping within the tent was the lack of night sky above me.

"It isn't only your feelings that are revealed. Your minds are open to one another. That means there will be no secrets between the two of you, no moments when a male tries to make a pass at you that he is not aware of. He can tailor his actions around what has already happened rather than trying to guess at what he might not know," Holt explained, rising to his feet. He moved to the skeletal horse waiting nearby, opening the pack slung over the horse's rump to pull an old book from it.

He held it out for me as he returned, allowing me to stare at the leather binding as I reached out with tentative hands. I ran my fingers over the surface, unknotting the tied laces keeping it closed. Opening to the first page, I ran my fingers over the words staring back at me.

Kateadh yn Psychid.

"Fracture of the Soul," I said, earning a quirked brow from Holt.

He studied me intently, waiting for me to flip through the pages. "I wasn't certain I believed Cal when he said you were able to read the Old Tongue fairly well. That book details everything that occurs during the splitting of the soul for the mate bond. Every consequence and every benefit to accepting it. It's all in there."

"Why would you give me this, if it will tell me the negative effects of agreeing to a bond with Caldris?" I asked, turning a shocked stare up to him.

"Because it will also show you the positives greatly outweigh the negatives. I have been Mab's errand boy for centuries; even before the Veil was formed she often sent me here to collect the Fae Marked. It wasn't often that I encountered a human who was willing to listen, to learn what might exist beyond his or her own prejudice. I keep that for the ones who will see."

He started to walk away, but I quickly turned and asked one more question. It burned inside of me and urgently needed an answer, because I didn't have it in me to read the book out of order, needing to absorb the information in proper form.

"When you say the benefits of the bond, do you mean to Caldris or to me? Is there something more than increasing his power to act as an incentive for him to complete the bond?" I asked, needing to know if there was a nefarious purpose that I didn't yet know.

I wanted the truth. I just had to hope that the Faerie rules of lying applied to the dead Fae of the Wild Hunt.

"Increasing his power?" Holt asked, furrowing his brow as he hung his head in his hands. "I guess that's one way to refer to it." He returned to the blanket, kicking off his boots and bending his legs to sit on it beside me. I pushed to sit up as well, the book cradled in my arm, as he extended a single finger. Fenrir grumbled beneath his breath, rolling to his back and giving me his belly for rubs.

A gleaming black claw protruded from Holt's finger, shimmering in a way that made my throat tighten nervously. But he only extended it to the snow in front of us, drawing a stick figure male in front of me and a stick figure female beside him.

He drew a curved line connecting the two figures, hanging below them, but left two patches of snow to disrupt the path. "Say this is you and Caldris, and the line is your bond. The bond is incomplete, and the connection between you is severed in places. His power has to flow to you to offer you protection, but you were also gifted a part of his power when your souls were cleaved in two. He has half and you possess the other half, but with only this one pathway for that power to travel between you, broken as it is, all that happens is a collision in the bond. You cannot share power in the way you are meant to, and it weakens you both."

He dragged his sharp nail through the snow, curving it over the line he'd already drawn. "When Caldris accepts you formally, the line between the two of you solidifies. Because you will have accepted him, too, and we both know that day will come soon enough—" He drew another line curving above the two figures, solid and uninterrupted as the one beneath them. "You will have unhindered access to him as well. It forms a circle, a fluid path for exchange of power. He can give to you and take from you all at once, as the power does not belong to one person alone. It is shared between you."

"But that would mean that the human mates of the Fae become..."

"Fae? At the root of it, yes. They become immortal and they share in their mate's status and power. They become equal," he answered. "It is why it is so insulting when a human believes they will be nothing more than a pet to their mate. We give as much as we take, as it should be."

"Is this why Caldris said it was unusual for a Fae to take another Fae as a mate? How would that work with a mate bond?"

"The same way," Holt answered. "It is rare because the cleaving of souls was intended to create balance. We believe that a fracture only results in two Fae souls when those souls are destined to bring about change, something that aligns with the designs of the witches. As you can imagine, if the two Fae complete the bond and share their power with one another without restriction, it could change a Fae from a regular Sidhe to almost God-like in his abilities."

"What happens when one of the Gods mates with another Fae? Would the Sidhe become a God? Would they become

Primordials?" I asked, running my fingers over the book in front of me as my curiosity threatened to devour me.

If there was anything that drove me to desire more, to seek out answers, it was the wonder that hid within all magic. I desired to unravel it and understand how it worked at its core. "That's never happened," Holt said with a shrug. "Many of the Gods have not yet found their mate, despite centuries of searching, and have somehow clung to their sanity by the grace of the witches and whatever they have planned. But of the Gods who have found their mate, only one pair mated with another Fae and accepted the bond in full. They did not become Primordials, despite both of them being Gods in their own right."

"Primordials are born, not made," I said, mulling over the thought.

Holt stood once again, staring down at me intently. "Get some sleep. The book will be there tomorrow, and I hope it helps you to understand the instincts driving your mate to behave more brutishly than you would prefer. The Fae are half-feral as it is, Estrella. Deny a male his mate, and you risk awakening all the instincts that Caldris would sooner protect you from. That's why he left you. Not for his benefit, or because of his rage, but because if he didn't, he may find he did something he regretted and couldn't take back." He stepped away, leaving me to my thoughts as I stared down at the book.

All around me, the camp settled in for the night. The Wild Hunt didn't need sleep and kept an eye on me as I sat beside the fire. I knew that I needed to rest, and that my body was still recovering from the draining pull of Caldris consuming too much magic.

But the book called to me.

I rubbed Fenrir's belly and turned the page.

꠱ ꠱ ● ꠱ ꠱

*M*y body jostled as something shifted me closer to the fire, settling behind me. I groaned, rolling forward until my ribs slid over the top of the book. Gentle hands pulled it out from underneath me, setting it to the side as heat covered my back and slid beneath the blanket with me.

"You left me," I said, stating the obvious as my sleepy state fell away.

Caldris nuzzled into the back of my neck, pulling me tighter into his chest. "I didn't think you would care. What's wrong, min asteren? Did you miss me?" he asked, his voice teasing as if he could brush away the neglect I'd felt with him gone.

The absolute bone-chilling depression I'd felt the moment he'd walked out on me, wondering if he would never return. If I'd gone too far, even when I didn't intend to, and lost the one male who would love me beyond everything.

I shifted forward out of his grasp, sitting up and trying to ignore the prying eyes of the Wild Hunt as they watched. The rest of the Fae Marked slept peacefully in their tents, the moon and stars lighting the night sky above as I turned away from the fire and skewered my mate with a glare.

"You are not about to come back from Gods-know-where and act like nothing ever happened," I said, flinching back when he sat up and reached for me.

"Little One," he said, the smile dropping off his face.

"You could have been killed. You could have been caught by the Mist Guard and tortured for all I knew, and I'd just be *stuck* here surrounded by fucking dead people!" I yelled, stepping off the blanket. Shades lingered in the distance, observing the Wild Hunt with interest and probably waiting for them to do something far more entertaining than sit around a fire or socialize amongst themselves at camp. The book sprawled open on the blanket in front of where I'd lain, and Caldris's eyes fell to it before he raised his stare back to me.

"It would appear you've been making good use of your time while you're *stuck* here," he said, picking up the book as his eyes skimmed over the page I'd been reading when I fell asleep. "It seems Holt has been inserting himself where he does not belong as usual."

"Just because you're determined to keep me in the dark doesn't mean everyone shares that sentiment. Did you stop to consider that maybe if you told me the truth of what was coming and what might be expected of me, I could make a better choice for my future?" I asked, reaching forward and snatching the book from his grasp. I'd only made a small dent in my reading before my exhaustion claimed me and my eyes drifted closed, only to be awakened by the return of my mate, who thought he could leave me without him for an entire day.

"Am I supposed to believe that you would relish knowing I'm inside your head? That there is no part of you or your history that would be safe from me? You can only tolerate my touch when you convince yourself you hate me," he said with a scoff, his anger from that morning showing on his face.

"Cal, perhaps..." Holt said, stepping up beside us.

"I'll deal with you later, Huntsman," Caldris said, turning to glare at his only friend with eyes so black I swore I would never see the sun shine again when he turned his dark stare back to me. "I think you've done enough."

"He protected me when you abandoned me," I snapped, ignoring the way Holt hung his head in his hands.

"Don't stand up for me. You'll only make it worse. He isn't

capable of being rational right now, Beasty," Holt argued, raising his hands and backing away.

Caldris growled, the irrational rumble in his chest grating on my nerves as I dropped my hands to my sides. "I didn't want you to touch me this morning, because you *terrify* me," I said, my voice coming out soft.

He turned his gaze to me, his attention so fixated that Holt managed to slink back into the darkness and evade his notice. My throat burned with the threat of tears, brought with the knowledge that all around us, the Wild Hunt heard me confess my greatest weakness.

They heard the emotion in my voice, the way I was barely capable of withholding the tears gathering in my eyes as I said, "I didn't want you to touch me because I know it is more than just sex. Because I can feel you working your way inside of me all over again."

"My star...." he said, reaching for me as I gathered up the book off the blanket and stood. I turned my gaze away from him, looking over to the tent and the privacy it offered. Feeling on the verge of breaking, I ignored the way he vaulted to his feet to follow me.

"You're so quick to judge me, Caldris. To condemn me for the fact that I barely know you. I've had a matter of days since I found out the truth of who you are, and you cannot even be patient and give me that time to grasp what it means for me and my future? I will not be with a male who feels entitled to my body just because he has my heart," I said, dropping my eyes to the ground at his boots.

"That wasn't what happened," he said, stepping into my path as I made my way toward the tent. "I chose you over your body last night, if you want to look past your own anger. I will *always* choose you. It's about you withholding part of yourself from me. It feels like a punishment, and I won't be led around by my dick just because you think you can offer your body when it serves your purpose and withhold it when it doesn't."

I groaned, my hands clenching into fists as I glared up at him. "You are such an asshole!" I yelled, making to move past him.

He grabbed me by the forearm as I went to storm by, halting me as he tugged me into his body. "And you are so stubborn that you won't even let yourself see what you're doing. The way you keep me at arm's length. If I get too close to your heart and you risk admitting that you're as obsessed with me as I am with you, then you withdraw your body from the equation. But I bet if I slid my hand into your leggings, you'd be wet for me now. Your anger lets your body hum for me without your guilt."

"You're disgusting," I said, glancing around at those who had stayed to watch. Swallowing past the sudden anxiety trying to crawl up my throat, I ignored the pulse of awareness that came from staring into the watching faces of the few female members of the Wild Hunt.

Caldris's chest gleamed in the moonlight, the bare skin he'd displayed since leaving our tent that morning drawing the attention of all who wanted him and couldn't have him. Or maybe they already had, for all I knew. Holt appeared to have been around for longer than I had existed, if his time in the Wild Hunt predated the Veil. I'd have already been taken to the other side if I'd been born before the barrier was created between realms.

Caldris followed my gaze, that arrogant smirk twisting his lips as he brushed my hair back from my face. "You think they're watching us because they want to see us squabble?" he asked, leaning into my space. "They're watching us because they're hoping I'll bend you over and fuck the attitude right out of you, Little One."

I blanched, turning to look at him in shock. The words were a direct confirmation of what Holt had told me the night before when I'd thought to run while Caldris was getting food. An implication that they fully expected him to fuck me while they watched. "That isn't going to happen."

"Maybe not tonight," Caldris agreed, pursing his lips in thought. "But we all know it's only a matter of time before you embrace your true nature and all that goes with it. You want to lay your public claim over me just as desperately as I want to push you to your knees and shove my cock down your throat, so they can watch you choke on it. I want all the males to wish they were me, to know that your pretty, sharp tongue is mine to paint with cum."

I stilled, the image he painted causing heat to flush through my cheeks.

He touched his lips to my jaw as he murmured the darkest secret torn from my soul. "And you want them to know that you're the only one who will ever have my cock and my cum again."

I shook my head, backing away from him suddenly. My skin flamed, a denial coming to my tongue and falling away just as quickly. I turned for the tent, shame coursing through me as Caldris let me go.

We both knew he'd won that battle.

12

ESTRELLA

$\mathscr{W}$e crossed over the first of the Twin Rivers at
their shallowest point, the black water rising
up to lap against the sides of the carts. The Fae Marked
squirmed back from the cold water, huddling into the middle
as if they could avoid the plunge into icy depths.

I stared down over the side of Azra, trying not to think of
what might lurk in the waters below. Even at their shallowest
point, I'd long since heard tales of the horrors that hid within
the dark water clouded by the tiny creatures that swam in
schools under the surface.

"You won't find the kraken in these waters, Little One,"
Caldris said with a chuckle. We'd ridden in mostly silence
through the day, only punctuating it when we absolutely
needed to speak to one another. I wasn't certain that I could
push past the embarrassment I felt over our conversation the
night before, after he'd awakened me beside the fire.

Every lingering gaze of the males and females of the Wild
Hunt made me question if they were waiting for the very thing
Caldris had said they were.

I remained quiet, ignoring his appeasing factoid that the

kraken wouldn't harm me, as Azra's hooves clashed against the rocks covering the bottom of the river. The bridge that connected the Isle of Ruin and the Dark Isle wasn't far enough away to give me any sense of comfort. I knew without a doubt that the kingdom's bridges would be patrolled by the Mist Guard searching for Fae on the run. The bridges had been secure even before the fall of the Veil; now stepping foot on one would only result in a slaughter. Given that I traveled with the Wild Hunt, I didn't think it would be the humans who'd pay the price of that battle.

"You can't ignore me forever, you know," Caldris said, his voice tinged with the amusement of a male who liked to challenge me. All he would accomplish with such absolute statements would be daring me to do just that.

"I'm not ignoring you," I mumbled in spite of myself. I resisted the urge to turn and smile at him over my shoulder, feeling as if the grin would be too obviously laced with the venom that consumed me. "I am merely choosing not to interact with you. There is a significant difference."

"The significant difference being that you understand how our verbal spats are as much foreplay as when I have you beneath me?" he murmured, the deep timbre of his voice brushing against my skin. It sank inside me, trying to raise the bond between us as if I needed the confirmation that his words were true.

Azra touched the soil of the Dark Isle, rising up out of the water and onto the rocky shore as I jostled from side to side. Only Caldris's arms wrapped around me held me firmly in place, my body still not accustomed to the balance required to ride, particularly without stirrups to slide my feet into.

"The difference being that I understand nothing I can say will ever change your mind about a damn thing. You think you've been accommodating in allowing me time to get to know you. I think you deceived me to serve your own purposes. We'll need to agree to disagree on that front," I said, looking out over the treacherous, rocky land of the Dark Isle as it sprawled out before us.

"I don't think either of us is wrong. I didn't have a choice if I wanted to protect you and infiltrate the Resistance, but that doesn't mean I wasn't more accommodating than most of the others will find their mates. They'll be thrust into Fae life without time to adjust to the bond, and you should know better than anyone how, even incomplete, it can take some getting used to. You're unlearning everything you've been raised to believe. I understand that," he said, guiding Azra to lead the way. Night had fallen over the Dark Isle, plunging us into darkness with only the stars glittering in the sky above. At the edges of the land, where the stones met the sea, sharp rocks curved up toward the sky as if they themselves could spear the moon.

Azra walked past them slowly, clinging to the stone walkway that led through the island. The carts rolled behind us, guided by their macabre skeletal horses and the ghostly riders of the Wild Hunt. Given the gruesome surroundings, I thought our procession likely fit in far more appropriately in this setting than we had on the gleaming frozen plains of the Isle of Ruin.

"If you understand that, why did you storm off when I didn't welcome you inside my body? That was not the way an understanding mate should behave. That was how an entitled, arrogant ass reacts to being denied what he wants," I accused.

Caldris chuckled lightly, pressing into me further as if my tongue was just another symptom of my lack of fear of him. I supposed it was. He might be taking me back to Alfheimr against my will, but I didn't fear that he would hurt me physically.

Reasonably or not, I'd never once feared he would force himself on me, but I refused to allow that to be enough. It wasn't consent unless it could be given freely, without fear of consequences. Incurring his wrath, even if it wasn't violent toward me, for saying "no" negated all of that.

"You may find this difficult to believe, my star, but I did not react so negatively because you wouldn't allow me to fuck you," he said, giving me time for that to sink in. "I can say it one hundred times over and never convince you it's the truth, but I would live centuries without knowing the pleasure of your body if you so much as asked that of me. What angered me was the way you shut me out of your heart, and the way you pushed me away when I got too close to you once again. I can be content without your body so long as I have *you*. Do not deprive me of the mate I have waited centuries to know; not now that I've finally been able to truly know you."

That silenced me as I considered his declaration. He was so virile, and had been so desperate to be inside of me several times a night in those moments we'd shared in the privacy of our bedroom at the Resistance base. Imagining him as anything else was impossible.

Caldris tugged Azra to a stop with the shadowed figures of enormous rocks and half-dead trees the size of Mistfell Manor looming in the distance.

Black Water.

I could barely see it from where we stood, only the vague outlines of things too imposing to be real. From the books in Lord Byron's library, I knew the village existed on stilts, of homes that rose out of the black river itself and were connected only by bridges.

"I'll send a small team to investigate," Holt said, walking his steed up beside us. I stared down at the village, watching as the flames of what I'd assumed to be torches glinted, burning brighter and brighter as they seemed to grow continually.

"It's on fire," I whispered, shock keeping my voice low as I drew the connection. I felt the moment Caldris and Holt's attention turned to the village below with more acute vision, and felt the glance they shared with one another.

"Fuck," Caldris groaned, undoubtedly torn between the need to keep me safe and the drive to help any of the Marked who might still be hiding out in the village itself.

"Go!" I yelled, waiting for Azra to obey my command. He didn't move, waiting for the order from his master as Holt shouted his own commands to the riders behind us. A group of them remained to guard the carts of the humans, but he and a small number charged forward, disappearing down the hillside. "Would you go already?!"

Fenrir charged forward, the figures of the other wolves following at his heels.

"Son of a witch," Caldris groaned as he tensed his thighs, and Azra darted forward with the shift in his seat. "If you get yourself fucking hurt, I will smack your ass until it's red. Do you understand me?" The words should have elicited objectionable images, but instead all I could imagine was the way he would stroke his hands over my burning flesh when he was finished with my punishment.

The way he would build heat inside another part of me.

Not the fucking time.

He groaned as if he could sense the path my thoughts had taken, pressing his groin farther into my rear as we rode down the embankment. With the steep angle, I had no choice but to lean back into the comfort of his embrace or risk falling forward over Azra's neck.

The lights of the fires came into view the closer we came to the wooden bridge that ran through the center of the village.

The gnarled trees twisted toward the sky, ancient beings that had once been striking and powerful but had died after the Fae were locked out of our world.

The village of Black Water was burning.

The first riders of the Wild Hunt reached the bridge, their horses galloping over it as they went toward the flames. Riders jumped from their horses, submerging any container they could grasp to gather water to douse the flames.

At my spine, Caldris summoned the cold of a winter storm, filling the air with snow as we rode into the fray. I jumped down from Azra as we crossed, ignoring Caldris's sharp curse as I slipped through his grasp and landed upon the wooden bridge. I rolled forward, absorbing the shock as I looked around.

The red stain of blood covered the bridge, turning the sun-bleached wood a deep wine. I barely restrained my nausea as I glanced over the edge of the bridge to the jagged stone teeth that curved to the sky. There were bodies impaled there and left to bleed into the black river below, hanging limply with eyes facing up, toward the indifferent stars.

Holt made his way to the hut at the center of the flames, the one where almost nothing remained, as I looked among the bodies to see if I could find any survivors. Caldris called my name, compelling me to turn to face him suddenly as he rode back toward me with a thunderous expression. The punishment he'd threatened waited for me, but I walked toward the edge of the bridge.

Away from the flames, away from the worst of the carnage, somehow, the figure in front of me drowned everything else out. I walked slowly toward him, moving as if in a dream as those around me dashed back and forth and tried to douse the flames that threatened to bring about the end of Black Water.

Kneeling on the bridge, I grabbed his small form and carefully maneuvered him to his back. The blank, unseeing eyes of a boy half my age stared up into the night sky, his vision as white as the moon itself.

Vaguely, as if underwater, I heard Caldris calling my name. His voice distorted with the rushing in my ears, with the pure ice flooding my veins. My fury rose; the neck of the child in front of me didn't bear the mark of the Fae.

There was no reason for the death, no reason that a boy who'd had never been given the chance to become a man lay butchered in the street, the slash of a sword laying open his chest. The mark on my neck seemed to freeze altogether, silent, as if it could not bear the torrent of emotions inside of me.

It came alive just as suddenly, darkness bleeding out from my body. The stars twinkled once before the heavens darkened as if clouds covered the moon and stars and plunged us into a void where there was absolutely nothing.

Where darkness was our only friend—the only ally to bring about the end of all suffering. The end of pain.

Cool wind touched my skin, kissing against me as my rage surrounded me. As wrath filled me and threatened to consume me, to mold me into something I had never been before.

"Estrella, calm yourself," Caldris whispered, stepping in front of me. His gaze snagged on the boy's body before lifting to my face, the contact of his shocking blue eyes pulling me back slightly from the void.

The fires glimmered around me, burning out and plunging us into total darkness, blanketing the world with the nothingness that claimed me.

He stared down at me intently, something searching in his gaze as he raised a hand to my cheek. The stars glimmered once more, casting their light down on Black Water as smoke rose to the sky from the houses where the fires had blazed.

The flames were gone, extinguished as if they'd winked into thin air.

Caldris's confused stare held mine, the first sign that he was just as baffled as I was by me and what I'd become for a few moments. "What are you, Little One?"

*E*strella leaned back in the bathtub, her head hanging over the edge of the metal basin as steam rose from the hot water. The survivors of Black Water had been all too willing to give her the hot water for a bath after she'd extinguished the flames threatening to consume their homes. They'd given a hut for us to share, as well, while the other Fae Marked took another.

Only a few homes had been destroyed by the flames, the rest remaining untouched where they curved along the bridge-forged path of the village. The stilt-based homes surrounded the ancient, gnarled trees that had been grown by the Fae centuries prior, before their trunks grew twisted in the absence of the magic that helped them thrive.

Her eyes were closed, her lashes fluttering against her cheeks as she settled into the warmth of the water. In the moments when I'd touched her immediately following the wave of darkness she pulled from the sky, she'd been cold to the touch, like plunging my hands into the frozen falls.

The heat of the water finally returned some of the color to

her bronze skin, bringing her lips back to the pinkish hue that was so much more natural than the blue that had tinged them.

A knock came on the door of the hut we shared, drawing me to step outside and leave Estrella in peace. In the wake of whatever had happened to her, she didn't care in the slightest about her nudity in front of me, as if all sense of concern for such things was suddenly irrelevant.

Holt peered into the room, heaving a relieved sigh when he saw Estrella's head hanging over the tub. He couldn't see her body from this angle, but I still swung the door closed with a jarring thud nonetheless.

"What the fuck was *that*?" he asked, crossing his arms over his chest. He seemed unsettled, as if whatever he'd experienced from the distance across Black Water had been enough to shake him to his core.

"I don't know," I admitted, glancing back toward the hut.

"Her anger took the flames out of the air. It extinguished the stars in the sky without so much as a conscious thought. She cannot be human," he said, glaring back at me as if I was in denial.

But he hadn't seen the stars glimmering in her eyes, the galaxy shimmering in the depths of her dark stare. With pinpricks of purple and golden light, an eternity stretching out before me and threatening to suck me in.

There was nothing human in that gaze.

"She has to be human. How else did she end up on this side of the Veil?" I asked, not daring to allow my thoughts to stray to the one explanation.

To the one Fae I knew of who had come across the boundary just before the Veil was formed.

"Maybe you need to consider that your mate and the female you're looking for are one and the same," Holt said, staring at the door to the hut as I forced myself to meet his gaze. "It would explain her extreme reaction to iron. She reacts as a Fae would, Cal."

"She isn't Fae," I said, feeling my glare harden on him. "You will speak to no one of this. Do you understand me?"

"Of course I won't," Holt said with a huff, but the nervousness in his gaze did nothing to reassure me. "But all of the riders here felt it. All of the humans who witnessed it know that something happened, even if they aren't aware of how significant it was."

"I'll deal with the humans. Make sure your riders know that I will cut out the tongues of any who even think to speak of what happened here. Did any of the Fae Marked of Black Water survive?"

Holt shook his head, a silent answer for the horrifying reality. I'd lost count of the bodies that had been run through, impaled on the claws surrounding their island, or drowned in the black water they called home. "You can't just will this away. If she is what we suspect she is...that kind of power, Caldris." He sighed, shaking his head in disbelief. "Think of what the two of you could do once she accepts the bond."

"*If* she accepts the bond," I said, clenching my jaw. Estrella still wasn't any closer to accepting me as her mate than she'd been when we were on the run, and she'd feared the Fae chasing her more than anything. If she didn't accept it, and she turned out to be...

Gods.

"She *has* to accept it. Now more than ever. Power like that could rival Mab herself! Mab won't let her exist as a neutral party. If you cannot get her interests aligned with yours, then Mab will do whatever it takes to worm her way beneath Estrella's skin and convince her that her path is right," Holt said, hanging his head forward. "I know you care greatly for her. I know you love her, but she is not just a person if this is true. She is a weapon. You must make sure you are the one to wield her."

"She's my mate," I said, my brow furrowing as I glared back at the man who'd been my best friend for as long as I could remember.

"I've been around longer than you can even imagine," he said, pulling his shoulders back as if he needed to remind me that, while I might be a God, I was a rare second-generation God. Countless Sidhe had existed before I'd been born—including Holt. "I don't think your mate bond has as much importance as you think it does. Not when we're speaking of matters that could change the very fabric of the world."

He shook his head, taking a step back and disappearing into the night without another word. Even hours after Estrella's show of power, after riders of the Wild Hunt had taken the bodies to land for a proper burial, the night still seemed darker than it had before.

As if she couldn't quite release her grasp on the eternal darkness clutched in her fingertips.

I stared up at the night sky, at the swirls of stars and at the mists between the eternal, burning galaxies, and at the way they shimmered together, as if everything was connected.

Swallowing and glancing back to the hut behind me, I pushed on the handle and swung the door open. *My* star hadn't moved, her head tipped back in relaxation and her fingers clenching the edge of the metal basin. From her middle knuckles down to the tips, her fingers were tinted black, as if she'd dipped them into paint.

But no paint shimmered with the glimmer of the stars above.

"Are you going to continue to stare at me? Or are you going to get into the fucking bath already?" she asked, lifting her head. Her neck cracked as she turned her face to me without opening her eyes. As if she sensed exactly where I stood, sinking into the mate bond farther than she'd ever allowed.

She opened her eyes, her long black lashes fluttering open to reveal eyes that still reflected the midnight sky set within her bronze face. I couldn't say that I didn't miss the green of her gaze when she tilted her head to the side and raised an eyebrow at me impassively, but I also couldn't say that her starry-eyed gaze didn't feel right.

It felt like her, yet an eternity stared back at me in spite of the fact that Estrella was fairly young as far as souls went.

"I wasn't certain you would want my company," I said, stepping closer to the basin.

She didn't move to hide her nudity, letting her breasts stay exposed above the waterline in the bath. She bent her knees until they broke through the surface, spreading her legs wide enough to accommodate a place for me to fit my body between them. "Is that invitation enough for you, my suddenly-chivalrous mate?" she asked, a playful smirk lighting her face.

"You're playing with fire, my star. Am I supposed to take an invitation when you're under the influence of some strange magic? You'll condemn me for giving in to the temptation in the morning," I predicted.

I brought my hands to the black leather and metal that covered my chest, unbuckling the straps and peeling the armor off my shoulders. Draping it over the chair beside the fire, I moved my hands to my tunic and slowly unknotted the laces at the chest . Her dark gaze dropped to the motion, and the monster lurking inside of her practically purred in delight.

The self-satisfied look on her face nearly broke my resolve; I wanted nothing more than to bend her over the tub and fuck her until she couldn't function. "Perhaps," she admitted, shrugging her shoulders as if it was inconsequential. "But when has anything like my regret or self-hatred ever stopped you from taking what you wanted?"

"I won't fuck you in this state, Little One," I said, pulling the tunic over my head. As inappropriate as it might seem in the morning, however, I did fully intend to get in the bath with her.

By the time she got out of the water, it would be cold. It was pragmatic to share a bath.

She sank her teeth into her bottom lip as she raked her eyes over my chest and down the muscles of my abdomen, lifting her chin and draping her head backward over the lip of the tub again. She lifted a hand still tipped with the night, waving it passively as if it mattered little to her. "Whatever you say, *Caldris*," she said, the timbre of her voice seeming to echo through the enclosed space of the hut.

I shucked my trousers down my legs, ignoring the way she cracked one eye open to peer at my nude body. Kicking my pants off along with my boots and socks, I ignored the hungry look in that eye as I moved to the side of the tub, beside her feet, and slowly stepped inside.

"Your cock doesn't seem to be in agreement with your vow of abstinence, my love," she said. My cock twitched at the endearment she'd never used, and the admission it contained, but my heart clenched in my chest. I longed to hear her say it when she wasn't high on the effects of using her own magic for the first time, or riding the aftershocks of a show of power that many Sidhe could never hope to achieve in their lifetime.

She spread her legs wider as I lowered myself into the tub on the other side, sliding my own legs to cradle her body between them. The tub was large, thank the Gods, allowing me to nearly stretch my legs in the space, but Estrella lifted her legs once again until she draped her calves over the edge, giving me an unimpeded view of her body.

"Estrella," I warned.

"Ooo using my name," she said, raising her head to meet my eye. Her full lips curved up, spreading into a shameless grin that exposed her brilliant white teeth. "You must be annoyed."

She tossed her hair back, lowering her upper body into the bath water and wetting it until it clung to her shoulders when she emerged.

"You aren't aware of what you're doing," I said.

She tipped her head to the side, something animalistic filling her features for a moment. "I know exactly what I'm doing," she said, grasping the edge of the tub and pulling herself up to lean toward me. She stared at me, those deep-set, dark eyes full of mischief as she lowered one hand from the edge of the tub to rest against my upper thigh. She trailed dark-stained fingers over my skin, and it took everything in me to force my body not to react to the sensual touch.

"Come out and play with me, my mate," she murmured, the words an echo of what I'd said to her once when I wanted her to show everyone what she was capable of. Somewhere in there, my Estrella waited to emerge and would be horrified by her actions. She moved that intrusive hand toward my cock, the tips of her fingers brushing against my shaft as I forced a swallow and reached down to stop her. She pushed her bottom lip into a pout, dropping back against the tub with an aggravated sigh. "When did you become such a bore?"

I smirked, wondering how the magic beneath Estrella's skin would change her. Once she accepted her place in my life, once she was ready to be mine completely and accepted the magical bond that existed between us and everything that went with it, would she be this needy for me?

Fuck, but I had to hope so.

"I became such a bore the moment my mate grew so

angry she summoned the darkness of the night sky to do her bidding," I said, taking her hand in mine. I ran my fingers over the dark tips of hers, drawing her attention to them. Her brow furrowed in confusion for a moment, a second of vulnerability entering her expression before she shook it off.

"I'm not angry now," she said, arching her back into the basin as she yanked her hand from my grip. She rested it against her chest, trailing those traitorous fingers over the swell of one breast until she cupped it in her hand, kneading the flesh and putting on a show. "I just want to feel something good."

"Banish the stars in your eyes back to the sky where they belong," I ordered, wanting to see if Estrella could find a way to control the power consuming her. Magic like this; it would devour an untrained woman. Turn her inside out and erase all that had existed of her before it manifested, if she remained too long in its clutches.

"I don't want to," she pouted, sliding her hand down over the slight contour of her stomach. She was still too thin from the life of poverty she'd lived in Mistfell, and our time on the run without access to comfortable feasts three times a day didn't help matters.

I couldn't wait to see her thrive in Alfheimr, to watch her face as she ate the delicacies I would serve her.

Her hand traveled lower, sliding between her thighs to stroke her pussy gently.

"Fuck," I cursed, snagging her hand in mine and pulling it away and out of the water. Her scent hung in the air, tantalizing me to remind her that part of her was mine alone. "You need to let go of the magic, Little One."

"It's so *cold*," she said, and even with the warmth of the water surrounding us, her hand felt cool to the touch, as if the coldness radiated from within her. "Nothing hurts in the cold."

"You're numb," I said, tilting my head to the side as I considered her words.

She nodded, turning her wrist until her palm faced the roof of the hut. She ran her thumb along the underside of those black fingertips, meeting my stare. "I don't want to hurt again," she said, the first trace of vulnerability leaking back into her voice. "Don't make me give it up."

"Little One," I said, my voice softening as I leaned forward. I snagged her around the back of her neck, letting the skin of my hand and the Fae Mark there brush against hers. She jolted, as if the contact of our swirling inks threatened to ground her—to pull her back from the edge of an abyss. "The only time pain truly ends is when we enter the Void after death. To live is to feel pain."

"Then maybe I don't want to live anymore," she protested, yanking her head back from mine. I touched my forehead to hers, holding her steady as I touched my other hand to her cheek.

The crash back to reality would hurt. It would leave her feeling like a half-empty shell of herself without the power filling her.

"You want to live," I said, pressing my skin more tightly to her mark. She flinched back again. "The dead cannot feel pleasure. Come back to me, and I'll fill that emptiness in you with me for the night, min asteren." I promised her the one thing I suspected could bring her back from the lure of the magic in her veins.

It wasn't only me that the mate bond affected, despite Estrella's unwillingness to acknowledge that she was just as insatiable for me as I was for her.

She twisted her head to the side as if she might dislodge

my grip, but I held her tight, staring into her dark eyes as the stars slowly faded from them. It wasn't a fast process, and our bath water cooled as her eyes filled with tears and the black faded to her normal green.

Her fingertips stayed painted in the night sky, that change refusing to leave her. It would make it far more difficult to hide what she was from any who passed us by. Should we encounter another Fae, they would know that my mate was no mere human.

They would likely come to suspect the very same thing I already did.

"Caelum," Estrella's soft voice whispered finally, the first of her tears falling and skimming over the skin of her cheek. It sparkled with the displaced power removing itself from her body, and she sucked back a rough gasp as air filled her lungs.

She winced in pain, the crash back into a human form taking everything from her. I released her finally, standing and stepping out of the tub. She grasped the sides, but whereas before it had seemed natural, as if she couldn't contain that aggression in her body, now it was pained. Her nails dragged over the metal surface of the basin as she clung to it, her head lolling to the side with the sudden effort of holding it up.

I quickly dried myself with the linen beside the bath, reaching into the tub and pulling her free from the water. She shivered the moment the cool air kissed her skin, shoving her face into my neck as if she could suck the warmth from my body.

"It hurts," she gasped, her skin raising with the tiny pinpricks of goosebumps.

"I know, min asteren," I said. I dried her quickly and efficiently with the linen, discarding it to the side and maneuvering her to the bed we'd borrowed for the night.

I could only claim ignorance for so long if she continued

to show signs like this. I could only claim a reasonable doubt to a point, before my orders from Mab would interfere with my ability to protect my mate.

I crawled into the bed after her, tugging the blanket up to cover us both as I pressed my body against the side of hers. She shivered, leaning into the touch as if she needed it.

"I can take some of it from you," I said, keeping my voice low.

Estrella's confused stare met mine, and she nodded. "Please."

"You'll have to let me in. I can siphon it through the bond, but there may be side effects. It would not be unexpected for you to seek out more of a physical connection with me, unless a time comes when you choose to sever the mental link," I explained, watching as Estrella's eyes rounded. She pressed further into my body, leaving me with no doubt that it wasn't the physical aspect that made her hesitate.

It was the knowledge that I would be inside her mind; I would see all the vulnerabilities she tucked away and tried to hide from my prying eyes. I'd infiltrated her heart. She'd given me her body. Her mind was her last stronghold—the one with the potential to change everything for us—and she damn well knew it.

14

ESTRELLA

*H*e waited, lying quietly beside me, remaining patient as he studied my face for any answer I might give. My body throbbed, the pain extending through every bone and muscle that lurked beneath my skin. I couldn't seem to grasp where I began and where I ended, the power that had extended out from me feeling as if it had changed my very nature—my very being—down to the core.

He could help me. He could take some of the pain through the bond, but I'd have to allow him to access my mind for a little while to do it. I didn't have time to understand what he might see, or if he'd be able to root around inside my memories or search through each and every one of my conscious thoughts.

The one nagging thought that persisted through all of these possibilities, the one motivation, was that I would gain equal access to him. I'd be able to see inside him, to feel how *he* felt. There would be no questioning his motives after something like this. I'd know if the love he claimed to feel for me was real or if it was another fabrication—another exaggerated truth to suit his purpose.

I nodded, meeting his vivid blue gaze with mine. His eyes flashed with frost, like the first snow falling behind his lashes. "I need the words, Little One," he said, his forehead dropping against mine.

He held my stare, watching me work through the consequences of what I would permit. I could handle the pain, even as it threatened to tear me limb from limb. What I could not do was pass up the opportunity to understand him, to have a firmer grasp on what our bond meant to him.

"Yes," I agreed, giving him the verbal assent he required. My consent, in something of this magnitude especially, mattered to him. He would not take my mind by force.

Caldris nodded, raising his head slightly to stare down at me. He raised a hand, cupping my cheek and touching the edge of his palm to my Fae Mark. "Close your eyes," he murmured softly, and I did as he commanded. Letting them drift closed, I focused on the comforting feeling of his thumb coaxing my skin. On the way it beckoned me to a place where part of me slumbered, waiting to awaken. "I want you to visualize the bond between us. What do you see?" he asked, his voice soft and low.

I hesitated, twisting my mouth and feeling exposed as I imagined the golden thread of fate between us. "It's a thread, like spun gold shimmering in the candlelight," I said, lifting a hand as if I could touch it. I plucked it with a single finger, the vibration in the thread itself making my heart quicken, putting the rhythm of its beat out of time.

Caldris gasped, making my eyes fly wide open. He stared down at me in shock, touching a hand to his chest for a moment before he shook off whatever had come over him. "Keep your eyes closed, min asteren," he said, smiling softly as I let them drift closed once more.

One day, I'd ask about the shock on his face when I'd

touched the thread of our bond. One day, I'd gather that thread into my hands and play with its very creation.

"Follow that thread back to yourself. There's something blocking our bond, something in the way, not allowing me to reach you. What is it?" he asked, that soft bass lulling me nearly to sleep. I forced the tiredness away, running my fingers along the thread. My soul hummed inside my body, the vibration of my touch along the thread pulsing through me entirely until I reached the blockade.

"It's my window," I said, abandoning the thread to reach trembling fingers out to touch the cracked glass of the window in my shack in Mistfell.

"Your window?" Caldris asked, his voice laced with confusion as I tapped a single finger against the crack.

"From home. It even has the fabric stuffed into the cracks in the wood beneath the window pane," I said, the first hint of laughter coming into my voice. I hadn't realized just how much I'd missed my freezing, half-decrepit bedroom. How much I wished to go back to those nights lying beside the fire to keep warm, the roof over my head doing nothing to protect me from the creatures that called to me in the night. "I used to sneak out through it at night and go wandering in the woods."

Caldris chuckled, leaning downward to touch his forehead to mine. "Of course you did, min asteren," he said. He ran his nose along the side of mine, the wintergreen of his breath tickling my cheek. "Open the window, Estrella. This time, I want you to let something in. I need you to open it and let me in."

In the seam between the two window panes, the gold thread shimmered—pinched between the wood frame of each pane just below the latch. Opening it should have been a simple thing, but I couldn't tear my fingers away from the crack that my father had complained about when he'd installed it in the house.

The very crack that was the reason we could afford the window at all; a castaway from one of the wealthier villagers who paid him for his labor with their discarded material.

Opening it to Caldris, letting him enter my private space where I laid my head at night without fear of judgment from the people around me, felt like opening myself to a new life.

To a new chapter.

"Open the window, Estrella," Caldris said, his voice soft and coaxing. I shifted my fingers toward the latch at the center, and toward the golden thread that seemed to sway in the breeze outside the window, extending out into the dark of the night.

Calling to me. Summoning me to the darkest parts of myself.

The latch squeaked as I flicked it open, hanging on its hinges as it flipped to the other side. For a moment, nothing happened, and I stared at the still-closed window in surprise. Until the sudden gust of winter wind tore through, blowing the panes open in a sudden blast of frosted.

It struck me in the chest, sinking inside of me as visions of winter filled my head, of snow falling through the night sky. There was nothing but the bitter cold, nothing but the shock of damp wind upon my skin.

Something *else* filled me in the next breath, a shadowed figure making his way toward me in the vision. His silver hair gleamed in the moonlight, blue eyes glowing from within his shadowed face.

"Open your eyes, min asteren," Caldris said, drawing me back from the imagery inside my head. I let my eyes open slowly, afraid of what I might find. When they settled on his stormy blue gaze, the breath tore from my lungs.

My back arched up from the bed as my consciousness filled with him so suddenly that I didn't know what was me and what was him. He grasped my hands in his, pinning them gently to the bed beside my head as he lowered his mouth to my neck and ran his tongue over the mark of his possession.

My soul was full, his consciousness pressing against mine as he drew the pain from my body and absorbed it into his own. That hollow within me was nowhere to be found, so profoundly full that I had to wonder how I would ever return to the emptiness when the moment was over.

If I would ever want to.

For just a few moments, I was whole.

"Caelum," I murmured, my voice coming out strangled as I fought my way through the waves of emotion pouring off of him: affection, pride and satisfaction.

Love.

Gods, the love felt endless, as if it would continue through an eternity and never bend, never break. He pulled his face out of my neck, brushing a strand of hair back from my cheek. His brow was furrowed with the pain he siphoned from me, taking and bearing as if it was his own, only to save me from suffering.

There was so much warmth in his gaze despite that pain, I would never be able to question whether or not he loved me. Never again. This was the kind of love stories were made of, the kind that poets wrote sonnets about. The kind little girls dreamed of finding when they lay in their beds at night and tried to imagine the man who would one day become their husband.

"There you are, my star," he murmured, gently touching his lips to mine. I longed for more, longed to see inside his head, but I couldn't do more than feel the emotions washing over me. There were no tangible thoughts or actions, only the emotions that drove him forward.

The motivation for his every action, every twisted truth, spilling out across the world for me to see.

I sank into his kiss, rising into his embrace and deepening it. He possessed my mouth just as he possessed my soul, angling me the exact way he wanted as he slanted his lips over mine and drank from my soul.

"I love you, Little One," he murmured, pulling back just enough that the words were murmured against my mouth. The words crashed over me, the meaning behind them burrowing deeper into my soul and plucking the thread of our bond as if it were his to play with.

I couldn't speak the words in return, couldn't seem to voice what he could already feel coming from me, thanks to the access I'd given him to my mind. He smiled, his eyes knowing, even if I didn't give him the words back.

He knew. Without a doubt, he knew exactly how I felt for him in the moments when I rolled my hips against his, seeking the heat I knew he would give me. "Tell me what you want, my mate. I'll give you anything." Grinding his hips against me, he notched himself against my entrance, gliding through my tender flesh until the head of his cock brushed against my clit and sent a shudder rolling through me.

"I want you," I murmured, lost to the sensation as I dragged rough nails down the skin to either side of his spine. "Please," I begged, reduced to only my need to feel connected to him. Opening my mind had only made me crave the rest of him and the connection that could deepen—both inside our minds and outside of them. I needed to explore one final entanglement of our bond while our minds and emotions danced. To take him inside me and see if he felt even more right than the moments when he'd joined his mind with mine.

"You'll have to be more specific, otherwise I am likely to wander," he whispered, a chuckle lightening his voice as he moved farther down the bed. The movement drew his length away from where I wanted it, and he only laughed when I whimpered in protest.

His mouth covered my nipple in the next moment, nipping at the flesh lightly as his free hand worked my other breast. He kneaded it in the way I had only minutes before in the bath. The first stroke of his tongue against my nipple sent a wave of heat flowing through me, then he curved it around tightened peak and sucked until my back arched.

I ground myself against him, seeking the friction he seemed determined to deprive me of as he kissed his way down my stomach. He paused as he spread my legs wide, placing his shoulders between them and staring down at me. "You need your rest," he murmured, leaning forward to lick a clean line from my entrance to my clit. He wrapped his tongue around the bundle of nerves at the top of me, maintaining eye contact the entire time as he tormented me. "But I'm afraid there won't be any sleep for you tonight, min asteren."

He hooked his arms around my legs, pressing a firm hand into my lower belly and using that hold to pin me still. He worked my clit with soft, torturous strokes of his tongue as his eyes held mine. Just when I thought he might give me enough to bring me to that edge of an orgasm, he drifted lower and slid his tongue inside of me with gentle pressure. I groaned, plunging a hand into his hair and trying to guide him back to where I wanted him.

His laughter rippled through my body, sending pulses of pleasure that made my legs twitch. "Greedy little thing," he said, trailing gentle kisses over my flesh. He left no part of my pussy unexplored, reacquainting himself with it as if he'd been separated from it for years instead of a matter of days.

The torment seemed to last forever, building the heat inside of me to a crescendo and then easing off just when I thought I would spiral into the heavenly abyss. "Caelum!" I begged, using my grip on his hair to tear his head back. "Either make me come or get out of the way so I can do it myself," I ordered, the darkness I'd danced with earlier in the night bleeding back into my voice.

Caldris's gaze turned black, his lips twisting with a cruel smile as he watched me balance between the two versions of myself. With the access I'd given him to me and my mind, he knew we were not separated as far as he'd initially believed.

I didn't know her; didn't understand where she'd come from. What I did know was that the monster who danced beneath my skin was me without inhibitions. She was me without fear, knowing she was terrifying enough to destroy any who thought to make her face the consequences of her reckless behavior.

"If you're going to play with yourself, perhaps I should fuck your pretty little mouth while you do it," Caldris mused, leaning forward to lick another path through my flesh.

"Make me come, and you can fuck whatever you want," I said, pushing his face closer to my pussy. He grinned into me, licking and sucking and tormenting me to the brink of madness.

"There's something I want to hear before I let you play with my cock, Little One," he said, dropping his thumb to my clit while he fucked me with his tongue.

"What?"

"Tell me you love me," he said, rising from between my legs. He rubbed his face against my belly, spreading my own arousal over my skin as he leaned over me. His cock hung between us, so close that I could reach out and take it in my hand. I did just that, rubbing my thumb over the tip where his own arousal had gathered and smearing it onto his skin.

Using it to lubricate him as I worked my hand up and down his shaft.

"That's not very nice. I thought you were trying to prove to me that you aren't a monster," I said, lifting my hand from his cock to my mouth. I licked my thumb clean, watching the way his eyes narrowed on the movement.

Just a day before, I'd have been horrified by my actions. I'd have been appalled to be so demanding and carnal, much preferring to let Caelum take charge when it came to our sexual encounters.

But something new had awakened within me, and I was wanton in a way I had never been before.

"Fuck," he groaned, gliding his hips forward until he brushed against me. He shook his head as if snapping himself out of a trance, guiding his fingers to the space between my thighs as he stroked me. "I'm not a good male." His fingers filled the void his mouth had created, plunging inside of me and pumping slowly as his thumb continued the assault his mouth had begun. "But I'm *your* monster, my star. Now tell me what I want to hear. I want to hear you say the thought that is rattling around inside your beautiful, twisted little mind." He hooked his fingers forward, stroking over a place on the inside that made me see the stars as my eyes drifted closed. "Give me your truth," he ordered.

"I love you," I gasped, the words coming out strangled. I hated the truth in them, hated knowing that he was aware they were far from a lie.

He plundered my mouth with his, the taste of me washing across my senses as he pressed more firmly with the thumb on my clit. His fingers left the tunnel of my body, leaving me suddenly empty until he replaced them with the head of his cock.

He thrust forward, uniting us suddenly as he pushed

through the quivering flesh waiting for him. His groan matched mine, vibrating between us as I looked down between our bodies to stare at the place where we'd joined. Watching as he disappeared inside of me, pressing forward until he filled me completely.

He raised my hand to where his thumb stroked me, replacing it with my own dark-tinted fingers as he grabbed my hips and raised them up, lifting my ass off the bed. "You want to watch me fuck you? Is that it?" he asked, his hips rolling as he worked himself in and out of me. He thrust forward sharply, filling me quickly as I watched his flesh disappear inside me, and then retreated slowly. "Come on my cock, min asteren."

I stroked my clit, working myself closer to the peak of my orgasm as he took me. My body obeyed the command, primed from his seemingly endless torment and the way he stroked over that spot inside of me carefully, with precise control.

I came, my fingers falling away from my body as he continued to move within me through my orgasm. His strokes became rougher, his body taking what it needed with my pleasure obtained and my confession of love given.

Caldris lowered me to the bed, letting my ass rest against the surface as he covered me with his body. His mouth claimed mine, devouring and uniting us in yet another place as I wrapped my legs around his waist and lifted my hips to meet him stroke for stroke.

"Fuck," he groaned when I dragged my nails over his back, reaching down to take his ass in my hands and pull him in harder, deeper. He took the encouragement for what it was, seeking his own pleasure as he fucked me into oblivion.

When he came, he filled me with him and his ragged groan echoed through my body, striking me through the bond as his pleasure consumed me and sent me tumbling into a second orgasm. I lay beneath him, trying to catch my breath before I opened my eyes.

The moment his gaze clashed with mine, I knew he'd meant every word about not allowing me to sleep that night. He pulled back and thrust forward, gliding through my tender flesh until I whimpered.

He rolled us over, keeping us united as he softened inside me. After he stood and picked me up, the bathwater was cold as he stepped into the tub and lowered us into it, settling me on his lap so that I sat on his cock.

The urge to move claimed me, forcing me to make tentative, testing rolls with my hips. He groaned but smiled up at me, dropping his hands to sides and guiding my uncertain motions. "I want to feast on your pussy and fuck you until the stars in the sky fade and the sun rises on a new day."

He ran his thumb over my mouth, a teasing lilt filling his voice as he continued. "And I believe you owe me the haven of your mouth, min asteren."

Fuck.

15

ESTRELLA

I pulled open the door when the knock came, revealing the fresh face of one of the village women. She held a massive bowl of crystal-clear water in her hands as she gave me an indulgent smile. "I thought you might like some clean water to freshen up this morning, my Lady," she said, glancing over my shoulder. The sheets on the bed were a rumpled mess from where I'd only just untangled myself, barely having the time to slip Caldris's tunic over my head.

"I'm no Lady," I said, giving her the most awkward smile I thought she'd probably ever seen. I stepped aside, shuddering to think of what a mess my hair probably looked like as she placed the bowl on the table in the space.

"I'm so sorry," she said suddenly, clasping a hand over her mouth. "How foolish of me. I don't know what to call the mate of the God of the Dead? Does that make you a Goddess?"

The horror on her face brought a startled laugh from my throat. "I'm just a woman. A harvester in fact," I admitted, ignoring the strange prickle of discomfort that made me flush. Would I...have a title?

Oh, fuck *that*.

Caldris appeared in the doorway from the back, where the wooden walkway extended around each home. His shirt was missing, his trousers slung low on his hips. I was fairly certain that my hair was a matted mess given our activities of the last countless hours, but his lay in perfect waves to his shoulders. The crown was missing from the top of his head, tossed to the side at some point after we'd ended up in the hut.

The events of the early part of the evening were slightly hazy, as if I'd experienced them from behind a fogged window and only been a witness to them instead of an active participant.

The woman gaped at him, watching as he closed the distance between us and leaned down to touch his lips to mine. It soothed the part of me that was tempted to rise up, which was so possessive of him that I wanted to smack him for daring to expose any part of himself to wandering eyes.

When he pulled back, he smirked down at me as if he knew the exact thoughts in my head. I realized with a shock that he might not know the choice words swirling in my head, but he knew the feeling. He knew the jealousy and possessiveness that consumed me, because he could feel it.

He grinned, wrapping himself around my back and resting his chin on top of my head. "As the Crown Princess of the Winter Court, her formal address would be 'Your Highness'," he said, brushing the mess of my hair to the side and leaning down to lay a quick kiss upon my neck. I shivered, both from the touch and the callous reminder that I wasn't my own person any longer.

"We aren't married," I said, swallowing my nerves as Caldris walked around the village girl. She flushed at him, spinning and pressing a hand to the wall behind her as he lowered his hands into the water and leaned over the bowl. Raising handfuls of water, he splashed it onto his skin. His face was beaded with water when he turned his heated stare my way, taking the small, folded linen off the table and using it to dab himself dry.

"Aren't we?" he asked, the teasing lilt in his voice making me shake with laughter. From what he'd said, there would be a ceremony if I were to accept the mate bond. Something that would mark the acceptance of one another as our fated match, *that* was when I would consider us wed.

I laughed, the sound sharp and full of disbelief as I gaped at him. "Not even close, you arrogant prick," I said, crossing my arms over my chest. The girl rounded her eyes, staring at me as if I was either very foolish or very brave.

"Hmmm," my mate hummed, stepping around the table to close the distance between us once again. He snagged my chin, staring down at me intently with gleaming blue eyes. "We'll have to remedy that then." Everything in him seemed *more*, both pleased and empowered by the step we'd taken toward the completion of our match.

My nerves made me want to slam the metaphorical window in his face, to close myself off once more, but...I couldn't quite bring myself to do it. I *liked* having him in my head, experiencing everything he felt. I thrived off of knowing what emotions surged through him and feeling the way he saw me. If loving him was wrong, if feeling whole with the connection blazing between us was a sin, I never wanted to be virtuous again.

"This is the part where I think it would be wise to give us some privacy," Caldris said, turning to quirk a brow at the girl watching his display with wide eyes. She scurried from the hut, grabbing the door by the handle and pulling it closed behind her. It slammed in her hurry to leave, making me gasp and smack my palm against his chest.

"That was terribly rude. She was kind enough to bring me fresh water for the morning. I'll need it to make my hair resemble something other than a bird's nest, thanks to you. And Void knows I cannot climb back into the tub again," I said, glancing toward the metal basin. I'd lost track of the number of times Caldris had submerged us in the water, cleaning my body of the evidence of his love making just to cover me in it all over again.

I didn't even want to think about all of that being in my hair.

Maybe I should go submerge myself in the Black River. It was probably cleaner.

"They would bring you fresh bathwater if you asked," he said, grinning at the disgust on my face at the thought of it. I'd only been half-aware of what was happening the night before, when they gifted us with the hut for the night, warming water in metal buckets by the fire and filling the tub until the steam filled the home.

"Just because you're comfortable being waited on, does not mean I am," I argued, pulling my chin out of his grasp. The people of Black Water had already done far more for me than they needed, mistakenly believing they owed me a debt for extinguishing the flames.

Guilt lanced through me, knowing that hadn't even been my intention. I was just...angry.

I was tired of the useless, senseless death, and seeing the boy lying dead on the bridge for absolutely no reason or fault of his own had been enough to set me over the edge. I longed to hunt down the Mist Guard who had cut him down, to return the favor so slowly he had no choice but to watch himself be skewered by my sword.

"Hey," Caldris said, drawing me back from the moment of rage. "Until we understand what's going on with the dark-eyed little monster you harbor, I think it's best that we keep your more...volatile emotions under control."

"Did you just call me a monster?" I asked, narrowing my eyes at his face. "I'm fairly certain you admitted that you were a monster, just last night."

He shrugged, dropping his hand, then moved to the bed, sitting on the edge and leaning forward. With his legs spread wide and elbows on his knees, he steepled his hands in front of him and stared at me with a playful smirk on his face. "Who says we can't both be?"

"It isn't funny! I need to know how to control the *Viniculum* so it doesn't happen again. I don't—" I paused, considering the admission. Even though he had to know how I felt about it, the broad strokes didn't necessarily communicate my horror. "I wasn't in control."

"Come here, Little One," he said, beckoning me to him when I hesitated. I shoved aside the self-doubt, walking toward him finally. When I stood before him, he reached forward, snagging me by the hips and guiding me until I strad-dled him and sat on his thighs. The fabric of his trousers rubbed against the most intimate part of me, eliciting a shock to the oversensitive flesh from our night of passion.

The interlude had been exactly what I'd needed. The perfect solution in the moment to the pain coursing through me and the fact that I felt like I would come out of my skin at any time. Like my body could no longer contain what crouched inside of me, waiting for a moment to break free.

"What happened last night wasn't because of the *Viniculum*," he said gently, his hands gliding down to touch the bare skin of my thighs. He slid his fingers beneath the hem of his tunic I wore, the gentle caress dancing over my bare skin and drawing a sigh from me. With the bond linked between us, one more step taken to unite our souls, everything felt amplified. I couldn't be certain if it was because I could feel his desire for me mirroring my own, but something in it was incredibly empowering.

It made me feel free, rather than tethered. As if I could conquer the world with him at my side.

"What are you talking about? Of course it was," I said, laughing as I stared down into blue eyes that held mine.

"The *Viniculum* gives you access to my abilities through the bond. I do not have the kind of power you displayed last night. I've never controlled the darkness itself, *min asteren*. That had to come from something inside of you that has been lying dormant all these years because of the Veil," he answered, distracting me from his words with the slow, methodical circles he drew on my thighs.

"But I'm human," I protested, shaking my head. I had a human father and mother, a human brother.

"As far as I can tell, yes. You feel very human, but that doesn't mean there isn't something in your bloodline. Maybe the Fae Mark awakened it, or maybe the surge of power from the collapse of the Veil caused it. We'll never really know how the Veil might have influenced magical beings who were born in the human realm and never knew access to their power," he said.

"If I'm not human, what am I?" I asked, not wanting to consider the possibility of being Fae.

"I'm not sure, and unless you take the time to reawaken that part of you further when we're in a safe place, we may never learn the truth of your lineage. You could be descended from witches, Fae, Daemons...the list is never-ending, *min asteren*." He shifted his hand closer to my ass, brushing his fingers over the skin there and grinding me down on his lap.

The distraction served its purpose, sending a pulse of pleasure through my body, but I didn't miss the diversion for what it was. "You're keeping something from me again," I said, gasping as one of his hands left my rear and slid between our bodies to touch my core. He stroked his fingers through the wetness there for him, always ready at the slightest encouragement for the mate I hadn't wanted.

For the male I couldn't seem to get enough of, no matter what that said about me.

He stroked my clit with his thumb, slipping two fingers inside of me. My body stretched to accommodate him, a twinge of soreness making me clench down on him as he worked me open slowly. "I have a suspicion, but I'm not certain about it. If there comes a time when I believe it to be true, I'll tell you. Until then, I won't have you worrying over something that could be nothing. Is that fair?" he asked, curling his fingers to make me throb with need.

"Nothing is fair when you're doing that with your fingers. I can't think straight," I admitted.

He chuckled, leaning forward to nip at my bottom lip as he pressed harder on the spot inside me. "That is entirely the point, Little One. I want you *mindless* with need for me."

"It's working, you twisted bastard," I said, but I smiled in spite of myself. As much as I wanted the answers to what he suspected about me, there were far more pressing matters at that moment. Especially when I could feel the emotions motivating his silence and avoidance.

Whatever it was, he genuinely wanted to protect me from it, and if Caldris thought I needed to be protected from something, I was inclined to agree with him.

Some secrets were better left in the dark.

He dropped his other hand to the laces on his trousers, unknotting them quickly and lifting me so that he could shove them down his thighs. His cock sprang free between us, pressing against my core as he removed his fingers from me. "Now come sit on my cock, my star."

Now *that* was not something I would argue with.

16

ESTRELLA

I ran a hand over my perfectly braided hair, my mind flashing back to the tender way Caldris had brushed it, dipping the brush into the fresh water to help tame the frizz as he worked through the snarls. The action had been so at odds with our position, me facing him, staring into his eyes with his cock softening inside of me, after I'd ridden him to my orgasm and then he'd fucked up into me to achieve his own.

Now, my shackles clanked as I lowered my hands again to the horse's mane in front of me, the return of the metal chafing against my wrists. "How do you know how to braid so well?" I had asked, leaning into his touch as he managed a perfect fishtail braid and draped it over my shoulder.

"I have lived for countless centuries and experimented with all manner of hairstyles, *min asteren*," he'd answered, the honesty in the confession soothing the rising jealousy inside of me. I wanted to ask if there had ever been anyone who'd mattered to him on an emotional level before me, or if I was the first he'd ever showed such care to. "What has my star feeling jealous now?" he asked, leaning forward to murmur the words into my neck. Beneath us, Azra's gait was slow but steady, navigating the white plains back toward Mistfell and the boundary that would take us to Faerie.

"Have you ever loved someone before me?" I asked, wishing I could take the words back the moment they were free and hanging in the air between us.

"No," he said, touching his lips to my mark before he pulled back slightly. "Even before you were born, I knew I was just passing the time while I waited for you. That probably sounds horrible, but the Fae know the score. They know that for most of us the mate bond is the goal to achieve. That is when love comes for us."

"Does anyone ever reject the bond?" I asked, turning to look at him over his shoulder.

"Sometimes," he said, his voice sad. "Not everyone can love the person The Fates choose for them, unfortunately." We rode in silence for a little longer, Caldris understanding that I needed the time to consider the information he'd given me over the course of the morning. I wasn't human, and the Fae believed that love was the most important thing; it was important and worth protecting, no matter what form it chose to appear in.

While humans forced their women into loveless marriages with men who would never appreciate them, the Fae protected love at all costs.

I sighed, my body twinging with discomfort when Caldris went solid at my spine. The procession halted, pausing in the road as he pulled Azra to a stop. Above the path up ahead, something swayed, hanging from the canopy of the trees.

The strength of the winter winds was enough to force the object to move despite its size, the tree limb creaking with the strain. Rope wrapped around the branch, digging into the bark and dangling down to wrap around the neck of a woman.

As her body spun in a circle, I caught sight of the tipped ears that marked her as Fae. Her chest was torn open, ribs bent outward, broken and dangling from her torso with torn, red flesh clinging to them.

Her heart was missing from her breast, no doubt burned in the small pit in the ground beneath her where the snow had melted and the grass was burned from the soil.

Caldris leaned into me, swinging his leg over Azra's rump. He didn't glance back at me as he walked toward where the Fae female hung from the tree, but something in the rigid posture of his body felt dangerous. There was nothing coming down the bond, no overwhelming sense of fury or even the slightest tinge of anger. "Caldris?" I asked, flinching when he swung his sword to the side. He cut the rope where they'd entwined it with the tree to wrap around the trunk and pull it taut.

The woman's body fell to the ground in a heap—lifeless in a way that even a human couldn't have reincarnated from. Even if she became animated by the God of the Dead, she wouldn't be alive. She'd be a walking corpse.

Caldris turned to us, his eyes gleaming with black when he met my wide stare. There was no trace of blue in that night-filled gaze, no trace of anything but malice as his rage crashed into me so suddenly that I flinched back.

"Fuck," Holt cursed, dismounting his skeletal horse. He turned to me, taking my reins in his grip and handing them to Aramis. He reached up and waved his hand over my wrists, releasing the shackles there. "Get her the fuck out of here."

Aramis nodded, angling his horse to line up parallel with Azra. He kicked his horse into a canter, making Azra pick up the gait to follow as I shifted my weight forward and struggled to keep my seat. He raced back the way we'd come, Azra following at his side with me atop him, leaving the others behind. Azra whinnied his protest, tossing his head as if he didn't want to leave Caldris.

"What are you doing?" I demanded, fighting him for control of Azra's reins.

"We need to get you as far away from Caldris as possible right now," Aramis said, meeting my stare for a brief moment. The path was almost treeless as we made our way back in the direction of Black Water.

We should have just stayed in the hut for an eternity, like I'd wanted, hiding out there and living full lives in secret. The only thing that had kept me from asking to do just that was knowing we would bring more danger to the people who lived there. The next time the Mist Guard found them harboring the Fae Marked and Fae alike, they would burn the village to the ground along with everyone in it.

Aramis stopped suddenly, pulling Azra to a halt as he looked around the clearing. There was nothing to be seen, not a sign of danger as I spun to look at him with ragged breath. "What's wrong with him?" I asked, wheezing and trying to adjust my position in the moment of stillness.

"He spent fucking centuries without his mate; that's what's wrong with him. It would be enough to make a Fae go feral under good circumstances, but when you factor in what he's lived through, the possibility for the loss of control grows," Aramis answered, continuing to look around the clearing. He guided the horses into a trot, his journey much more cautious as his body was consumed with tension.

The rage blazing down the bond was like nothing I'd ever known, rivaled only by my wrath the night before. It was all-consuming, terrifying in its intensity. It threatened to burn the world to the ground and claim the ashes as his war prize. "He's never been like this before. I don't understand what brought it on."

"Mab killed his father and strung him up. Left his body to hang there, rotting in her throne room for *weeks* when Caldris was only a century old," Aramis answered, turning to look at me. He swallowed, his gaze straying over my shoulder. I spun, finding a lone figure standing in the snow a few feet away.

My mate tilted his head to the side, his posture inhuman as he stalked forward toward us with slow steps. "Get off the horse," Aramis said, tossing the reins back over Azra's neck.

"But you said—"

"Get off the fucking horse before he kills it to get to you," Aramis ordered, jumping down from his own steed. He slapped it on the rear, sending it back toward the group we'd left. I had to hope they were still alive—at least those of them who were alive in the first place.

Blood dripped from Caldris's hands, his nails curved into pointed, black talons. His sword was gone from his hand, not a weapon in sight as he approached Aramis.

I dismounted Azra, sending him to follow Aramis's horse with a nervous swallow. Aramis put distance between us, stepping away slightly as Caldris headed straight toward us.

"You coward," I hissed back at Aramis, my lips twisting with a snarl as I stared into the gleaming eyes of death. Even feral, even lost to the rage and madness consuming him, I had to believe Caldris wouldn't hurt me.

Right?

"He will gut me and feed me my entrails while I watch," Aramis said, quirking an eyebrow up at me as he glanced down my body. "He just wants to fuck you, and given the noises I heard coming from your hut last night, you aren't entirely against the idea."

I turned away from him, facing the male prowling toward me. His hands were still at his sides, those black nails gleaming in stark comparison to the snow that fell behind him. "Caldris," I said softly, ignoring the way the sound still seemed to crack through the silence.

The fact that Holt and the others didn't try to intercede didn't bode well for us at all, and the menace on his face made me swallow nervously. His eyes turned toward Aramis, his lips peeling back into something resembling a snarl as he studied the other man, who seemed desperate to put more distance between us.

"Fuck!" Aramis yelled, dropping to his knees in the snow, making himself submissive.

"You can't even fucking die!" I yelled, watching as he bowed his head and lowered himself to the ground.

"That doesn't mean it won't hurt like a fucking bitch, you menace. Would you just give him what he wants already?" he asked, staring at the way Caldris's boots carved through the snow. It fell steadily, landing on my cloak in heavy layers and covering my hair in white flakes, then scattering as I flinched away from the male prowling toward Aramis. There was no doubt he would tear the other man limb from limb while I watched. I stared at him, considering the vengeance I couldn't achieve on my own through his death.

Would his pain ease the part of me that called for blood?

"Estrella, please just give him what he wants," Aramis said, his voice nearly quivering as he stared at Caldris's boots. "I am sorry about your brother, but you're *alive* because of what I did."

"Who said I wanted to be?" I asked, tilting my head to the side. That darkest part of me rose from within, enjoying the way he huddled in on himself in fear. For a single moment, I didn't want to stop the bloodshed—I wanted to join in.

Caldris stopped with his boots directly in front of Aramis's head, leering down at the other male with that brutality etched into the lines of his face. Gone was the male I knew, the one who would regret what he'd done when he came back from this madness that possessed him.

It wasn't protectiveness for Aramis that forced my hand, but the knowledge that I would always want Caldris to stop me from becoming the monster I feared. I would want him to intervene, to keep me from committing sins I couldn't take back when I emerged from the dark well inside of me.

"Fuck," I hissed, the realization jolting me as I turned and ran in the opposite direction of Aramis. I raced due East, hauling my body over the snow-covered plains as quickly as I could manage. Trees loomed in the distance, and I didn't know why, but I focused on them as my plan for escape.

I knew as well as anyone that there would be no escaping the Fae chasing me.

I glanced over my shoulder, expecting to find him following close behind, enjoying the chase, thriving on the thrill of hunting down the mate who dared to run from him. I halted in place, spinning back to look at Aramis kneeling in the distance.

Caldris was gone.

All I felt coursing down the bond were his rage and the way it mingled with his excitement. I turned my head to the side, studying the snow between Aramis and I for footprints that I couldn't find. There was only one set, only my sloppy trail through the snow as I raced as if my life depended on it.

I spun around, only to crash into the black leather and metal armor of my mate. He stood before me, the remnants of shadows floating off his skin as he stared down his nose at me while I touched my palms to his chest to catch my balance.

Caldris's eyes were fathomless, void of all light as he stared down at me. He raised a single hand to capture one of mine, his thumb trailing over the black circle on the back of my hand. His voice was barely a whisper when he finally spoke.

"Why do you continue to run from me, my star?" I pulled on my hand, trying to get him to release me as those dark eyes gleamed.

"You're scaring me," I said, taking a step back. He released my hand, following the movement as I took another step.

"There's no need to be afraid," he murmured, his voice soft in spite of the tension gripping his body as he followed me, mirroring my movements as a predator toys with his prey.

"What happened to you?" I asked, stopping my steps altogether.

He lifted his hand from his side, touching a talon to my cheek. After trailing it over the skin there, sliding it over my lips and chin, he pressed the tip into the front of my throat. The threat hung between us, unspoken as he stared at the point of contact in confusion. "I hate that you don't want me."

"That's not what happened. We were in a good place this morning, and then you saw the body," I said, a shocked gasp leaving my throat as his hand wrapped around the front of my neck. He used that hand to guide me back, sweeping my legs out from under me and maneuvering me carefully to the ground.

I was weightless for a few moments, falling to my back in the snow as he leaned over me, pressing his weight into the hand he held at my throat. "Caldris," I groaned, reaching up to grab his wrist. Aramis had been so certain my God wouldn't hurt me, so certain I'd be safe.

"The body," he said, voice dropping low as he leaned further over me. His face filled my vision, drowning out every-thing beyond him as I fought back the urge to struggle. His hand on my throat hadn't restricted my breathing yet and I wanted to keep it that way. "If they can do that to a Fae female, what do you think they can do to you?" His chest rumbled with a growl, sounding like one of the wolves, making his entire body tremble with the force of it. "You who are so frag-ile, my vicious little mate."

He flicked his nail against my skin, slicing through the surface to prove his point. The wound burned as cold air kissed it, my shocked gasp hovering between us as he lowered his head and licked the bead of blood from my skin. His tongue lingered against me, the slow drag of it over my flesh making me shiver despite my terror.

He lifted his free hand so I could watch as he pressed his nail into his own skin, puncturing his finger until a single dot of blood welled to the surface. He squeezed my throat, forcing me to open my mouth as I gasped for breath. Pressing that finger onto my tongue, he forced his blood into me and watched as the tiny scratch on my throat healed in response.

"What do you want from me?" I said, my voice harsh as he relaxed his hold.

He released my throat finally, pulling at the laces of my tunic where my cloak hung open beneath me on the snow. "You. Bound to me in every way," he said, trailing a nail over my chest as he yanked the fabric down to reveal my breasts. I didn't stop him, letting him take what he wanted.

It wasn't so much out of fear that I allowed it, out of knowing it was what he needed. He needed me to not fight, to not shun his nature and the bond between us. I lifted a hand to touch his face, cupping it gently as he cut my skin with his nail. A tiny rivulet of red slid from my collarbone to my nipple, lighting my skin on fire as he lowered his mouth to it and trailed the tip of his tongue down to follow in its wake.

It healed immediately, the blood he'd given me serving its purpose of undoing any damage he inflicted. His mouth wrapped around my nipple as I slid a hand into his hair, using it to pull him tighter against me.

Encouraging him, I show him that I accepted him and his

nature. I couldn't promise him forever yet, but I could give him this moment and bring him back from the brink in the way he'd done for me the night before.

He groaned, pulling himself away as he fought with the instinct consuming him, refusing to be the monster who took me when I didn't want him. He wouldn't be the man from my nightmares, even if there wasn't a trace of humanity inside of him at present.

I cupped his face in my hands, moving forward to touch my lips to his. He sank into the kiss, his teeth crashing against mine with the ferocity with which he returned it. His tongue plunged into my mouth, dominating me in the way I knew he would with his cock within a few moments. "You'll take my blood every day," he demanded, slashing his nail across his palm.

He held it over my mouth, letting the blood drip down onto my lips as he waited for my response. It was just one more concession, another part of me that I would give to him, but he'd already received what mattered the most. My mind was his, my heart belonged to him, and my body was liquid in his arms. "Okay," I agreed, watching his gaze lightened a fraction when I gave him that.

Caldris pressed his palm to my lips, letting his blood flow onto my tongue. The sweet taste of him seemed even stronger with the connection flaring brightly between us, cool and crisp in spite of the warmth of the viscous fluid as it spread over my tongue and slid down my throat. He stared down at me, his eyes glinting with satisfaction as a little bit of the haze faded away from them.

As his lust for blood settled, his hand remained at my mouth so that I continued to drink from him. I dropped my hands to the laces of his trousers, pulling them open slowly as he studied me. It felt like toying with a cornered animal, waiting for it to strike. I was placating him, giving him what he wanted in the hopes of avoiding the worst of his wrath, but it would be a lie to say I didn't want this part of him too. That I didn't want the swollen shaft I pulled free from his trousers as his feral gaze watched me.

"There you are, *min asteren*," he said, using his other hand to cup my cheek in his massive palm. I wrapped trembling fingers around him, unable to banish the lingering fear that wouldn't seem to leave me.

The wound on his hand healed far too quickly, the taste of him addictive as I licked his skin and sought out more. He chuckled, dropping his hands to my pants and tearing them open with frenzied fingers as I stroked him. He yanked them down my thighs, leaving them bunched at my knees as he flipped me to my stomach and pulled my hips up.

Driving inside with a single thrust, he shoved my body down into the snow beneath me. My face stung from the ice pressing back against me, and from the frozen blades of grass beneath the snow as they dragged over my cheek.

"Gods!" I yelled, pushing up to my hands. He didn't relent, pulling back and thrusting into me all over again with hard, fast drives. This would be no smooth seduction, but the quick, manic fuck of a Fae male driven by his instinct.

To claim. To take.

"What have I told you, my star? I am your *God*." The words caused a shock to roll through me as he leaned over my back and wrapped an arm around the front of my body, pulling me up until I knelt in the snow. His chest pressed into my back as he drove up and into me relentlessly, he wrapped his palm against the front of my throat. The reminder of who he really was, especially when he was buried inside me, shouldn't have made my body clench around him. I'd been drawn to him from the first moment until this one, my soul recognizing what my mind couldn't comprehend.

He was mine. He'd always been mine. Since the dawn of creation, since I'd been born into this world for the first time.

Portraits flashed through my mind, a collage of all the moments we'd already shared, and all those that had yet to come. "Now do you see, Little One?" he asked, his grip tightening as his cock drove through me. His mind tunneled into mine, reaching into the depths of my soul.

The connection we'd shared the night before, taking my breath away in that moment, was a pale imitation of this. Now he showed me how much he'd held back with every portrait he painted in my mind. With the promise of a future I hadn't even known I wanted. In my mind's eye, the skin above his heart gleamed with strange black markings, an extension of the Mark we shared as it curled over his bare chest.

Caldris squeezed my throat, drawing me back from the haven he'd created inside my mind. The reality of my knees freezing in the snow was so much more painful than the utopia that he showed me waited for us on the other side of these hardships to get there. "I asked you a question," he said, his voice dropping deeper as he lowered his mouth to the skin just above my ear and sank his teeth into it. He bruised the skin, worrying it between them.

"Yes, I see it," I admitted, fighting back the sting of tears. I understood now why he was so angry when I fought our bond, why he wanted me to give in and be his mate. Accept him for all he was, above all else, because he saw what waited on the other side.

He saw the beauty in the madness.

But I saw the coming struggle to get there. I felt my lingering heartbreak like a phantom pain, tearing at my insides and trying to claw its way out. Something lived inside of me, and I couldn't shake the notion that it would be freed more and more with every step I took toward my mate.

"Accept me," he ordered, lowering a hand to the apex of my thighs. He stroked the flesh between my legs, bringing me closer to an orgasm as he used my body to find his own pleasure.

"I can't," I said, protesting on a sob. Not in the way that he wanted; not in a way that would commit me to him permanently. There were too many unknowns, too many secrets still hanging between us. I barely knew the male who existed beyond the Veil or the life that he lived there. There were too many questions about who or what I might be, as well.

Caldris growled, the sound feral as he shoved me forward into the snow. I landed on my hands as he placed a hand against my spine, pushing me further down until my stomach touched the snow and only my ass remained in the air. The position was animalistic; it was brutal.

I felt him in the deepest part of me as he drove inside, showing me how gentle he'd always been when he'd fucked me. "*Estrella*," he warned, malice tinting his voice.

"This has to be enough for now," I forced out, turning to look up at him from over my shoulder. "You have my body. You have my mind. I'll take your blood, but I can't accept you fully until I know everything."

He growled but didn't argue. Even in his half-feral state, he knew I'd already given him everything I could for now. Giving him that last part of me felt like signing away my soul, like making a deal with a daemon from the underworld, knowing I would never get that piece back.

He slid a finger inside of me alongside his cock, pressing into the spot that made me see stars. "Oh my fucking Gods," I whimpered, squeezing my eyes closed, the unbelievably tight fit sending me crashing over the edge. I hadn't even known that could be possible.

I screamed my orgasm into the clearing surrounding us, my legs twitching with the force of it as I came down from the high of my ecstasy. While I recovered, Caldris removed his finger from my drenched core, slipping it free from beneath my body. I jumped when he touched it to the *other* place that no one had ever touched.

The one he'd threatened to take one day.

"What are you doing?" I asked, diving forward. His cock dislodged from me as I tried to escape, wincing when he followed after and slid back inside. That finger pressed against my rear entrance all over again, the pressure steadily increasing as he moved his hips, slowly gliding in and out of my pussy with smooth, passionate lovemaking.

The note of something *other* that had filled his voice was gone when he answered me. "If you will not give me all of you in this way, then I'll take it in another," he said, pressing more firmly. He never breached my flesh, keeping the pressure there as if he simply wanted to get me used to the feel of it. To the forbidden touch as he slid his cock through my wet, swollen tissue.

"You are not sticking your fucking cock in there," I protested, shaking my head.

First of all, *ew*. Second of all, *just no*.

"Not today," he said with a chuckle. I glanced up at him, finding amused blue eyes gleaming down at me, the darkness from before faded from his brow. "We'll need a bath and special oils when that day comes."

He moved through me more slowly, covering my weight with his as he reached forward and wrapped my braid around his hand, using it to pull my head back so that he could nip at my shoulder. "Would you fucking come already?" I asked, hating the second orgasm that was building within me. He would be the death of me.

He chuckled, pulling free from me entirely. My body mourned the loss of his skin against mine as he knelt in front of me. "Then give me your mouth, *min asteren*. I want to paint it with my cum."

I flushed as I sat up, crawling to my knees in front of him as he rose to his feet. His cock dangled in front of my face, angry-looking and throbbing with purple veins as I wrapped my fingers around him and stroked him from root to tip. I shifted my gaze up to his face as he let out a ragged groan.

I'd experimented with taking him in my mouth the night before, running my tongue over and exploring his cock the way he did my pussy. He'd lost control long before he'd finished, tossing me down on the bed and fucking me until I felt as if I couldn't breathe.

I leaned forward, dragging my tongue along the underside of his shaft. He groaned, grasping me by the braid and guiding my head the way he wanted. There was no time to explore the way I had the night before, only time to let him thrust into the heat of my mouth. His harsh breaths seemed to echo over the plain and he struck against the back of my throat.

"Swallow around me," he instructed, pulling back and pressing deep once more. I tried and failed, gagging as I tried to understand how I was meant to function.

How I was meant to breathe.

He thrust forward, keeping the pressure at the back of my throat as I swallowed and *finally* managed to take him into the haven of my throat. I couldn't breathe around him, feeling him slide as deep as the angle of his cock would allow. He stared down at me as if I'd hung the moon in the sky, touching a taloned finger to my cheek and wiping away the tear that fell as he made slow, small movements within me.

He pulled free, giving me a moment to suck back deep lungfuls of air before he made shallow thrusts, gliding the head over my tongue. "Again," he instructed, pushing forward. I swallowed, relaxing around him as he slid within me all over again.

As uncomfortable as it was, I watched his face. I watched the way he came undone with his cock in my throat, and knowing I was able to give him that brought me comfort. His hand pressed against the front of my neck as he thrust once more, feeling his cock move against it, consuming him.

He pulled back as he roared, holding me by the throat while his cock twitched in my mouth. Thick, warm fluid coated my tongue, covering it in his orgasm. His hand tightened as his eyes drifted closed, his body relaxing. I wanted to swallow him down, to get the evidence of his pleasure out of my mouth. The flavor wasn't something I would ever particularly enjoy.

"Show me," he ordered when he opened his eyes once more.

I opened my mouth, sticking out my tongue so that he could see it covered in his seed. "That's my good girl," he said, releasing my throat finally. I closed my mouth, swallowing as his dark eyes gleamed with approval.

The words of encouragement shouldn't have meant so much to me, and yet my body hummed with warmth. I was so far gone for the Fae male who claimed ownership of my soul; it was a sin.

He cupped my jaw in his palm, running his thumb over the skin with a gentleness that took my breath away. "Thank you," he murmured, his eyes soft.

"For what?" I asked, my voice coming out breathy.

"For accepting the darkest parts of me—the ugly ones— even if you can't give me those words yet," he said, and the way his brow furrowed nearly broke my heart. I knew what it was to be out of control. To feel like a monster waited to take control of my body.

I'd do whatever it took to bring him back from that brink. "Always."

17

ESTRELLA

$\mathcal{I}$ couldn't quite find my way to sleep that night. The memory of Holt's body sprawled on the ground, bleeding out on the snow and waiting to come back to life by the time Caldris and I returned from our tryst in the snow-covered plains, haunted me.

Not because I cared about Holt; as much as I appreciated the book he'd given me, I still struggled with the knowledge that he was my enemy. He'd been part of the threat that had terrified me as I'd run through the woods with my brother at my side. There was no escaping the life I'd lived and the things I'd been raised to believe. I couldn't change them overnight, but I could feel the shift coming on slowly.

If I could find a way to forgive Caldris for what he'd done, did I really have any place to not forgive the males who owed me nothing? The ones who'd never lied or hidden what they were.

But no, what kept me awake in the night was the memory of the carnage Caldris had caused in his blind rage. He'd torn through several members of the Wild Hunt, spraying their blood across the land in a way that terrified the Fae Marked.

He'd left them alone in favor of pursuing me, but the stark reminder of what he was and the damage he could inflict made me swallow a ball of nerves in my throat. *That* was what had found me in the woods. That was who I'd allowed to sink inside of me and claim me as his to bring him back from the brink of bloodlust.

Aramis's confession of what Mab had done to Caldris's father also hung over me, leaving me with more questions than answers. He slept peacefully behind me, cradling me in his arms in our tent for warmth. I wished I could just ask him the questions I had about his past, but if the memory of his father's death was so traumatic that it resulted in a rage like this, I wasn't certain it would be wise to ask.

I pulled slowly away from his arms, shoving my feet into my boots and moving to the opening of our tent. I worked slowly to untie the strings, moving as quietly as I could so I wouldn't disturb Caldris. Given the exhausting events of the day, I had a feeling even the God needed his rest.

But my restlessness drove me to the book Holt had given me, safely tucked in the saddlebags near Azra. I'd go read by the fire until I became tired enough to return to bed.

"You know, it is fairly rude to sneak out of your lover's bed while they sleep," Caldris said, making me heave a sigh as I spun to face him. One single eye opened, studying me with a quirked brow.

"We don't have a bed," I said, smiling at him playfully. He studied me, waiting for me to elaborate on what would drive me out in the middle of the night without a word. "I couldn't sleep," I admitted, shrugging my shoulders and making sure I kept my posture casual. Given our history, if I gave him any reason to believe I wasn't being truthful, he might think I was trying to escape while he slept.

I didn't want that. Not after the little progress we'd made. I wanted to cling to it and own it as the hard won victory it was. "Is something wrong?" he asked, shifting to sit up. He pulled on his boots, standing to follow after me.

"I'm just restless," I admitted. "I can't seem to turn off my mind. I was just going to go read by the fire."

"I have a better idea," he said, standing beside me and unknotting the ties on the tent. He pulled the flaps open, stepping out into the night and waiting for me to follow.

"You don't have to be awake just because I am. You should get some sleep," I said, nodding my head back toward the tent. I was entirely capable of reading in the middle of a well-protected camp full of dead things that didn't need sleep.

"You're my mate. If you need something, I'll provide it," he said, starting to walk through the snow. I curled my cloak tighter around my shoulders, missing the warmth of his embrace already. I should have stayed by the tent, only the lure of the warmth of the fire was enough to tempt me away. But Caldris carved a path through the outer edges of the camp, taking me around to the side as far from the other Fae Marked as he could. Members of the Wild Hunt watched us curiously, looking just as lost as I was.

He turned to face me when I stopped a few paces away from him, trying to ignore the sinking feeling in my gut. A stern glare from him sent the riders of the Wild Hunt back to their previous tasks, leaving us with the delusion of privacy for a few moments.

He closed the gap between us, raising a hand to hold out in front of him. With his palm facing the sky, he held my gaze as a rush of wind rise from his hand. Snowflakes danced above his skin, hovering in the air in a mini-snow storm, all contained in the boundary of his palm.

He raised my hand with his free one, mimicking his positioning as he turned his hand upside down. Waving that snow storm above my hand, he let the pulse of cold touch my bare skin. It rested above my palm, levitating and following my movements as I moved my hand from side to side. Caldris pulled his hand away, leaving me with the tiny snowfall.

"I know you've been taught to believe that magic is something to be afraid of, and it can be," he said, reaching beneath my hand to cup it in his grasp as I stared at the snow drifting up toward the sky. The magic felt the same as it had when I'd killed Loris, that same threat of something all-consuming as the white lines of my Fae Mark lit up in recognition of my mate's magic. "But it can also be beautiful."

"This is yours," I said, feeling that the magic that sustained the little storm wasn't coming from me. My mark recognized it, but didn't own it.

"Yes," he agreed, and the knowledge hung between us that, even if I managed to pull power from my *Viniculum*, this magic would always be his. "We're going to focus on the Winter Court abilities for now. You seem to favor them, and they're farther from whatever magic is hiding inside of *you*."

I nodded, watching as the magic of the storm faded away. "How do I do this intentionally?"

He gripped my wrists in his hands, touching the Fae Mark and giving me that added connection. "Find the bond. Imagine you're tugging on that golden string and pulling it toward you." I closed my eyes, envisioning the shimmering gold of our mate bond and tugging on it. "Good. Now think of the cold. Think of the snow and the winds of winter. Of the smell of fresh snow and of ice filling your lungs. Push that feeling into your hands, like a spark to bring the winter."

I did as he said, picturing the snow he'd created in his hands and the way it had felt in mine. The touch of cold against my skin with the cool air surrounding me. My hands buzzed with warmth, making me open my eyes.

There waited only my empty hands to greet my gaze, with not a single snowflake floating in the air above me. I sighed, scowling as I tried to think wintery thoughts.

"Not everything can come easy, Little One," Caldris said with a chuckle, dragging his thumb over the sensitive skin at my wrist. "Mastering magic takes a lifetime, and most human mates do not learn until after the bond is completed."

"Is it even possible to learn before that? Who is to say you haven't set me up for failure?" I asked, but I kept my eyes trained on my hands regardless, picturing snow-covered trees beside me.

"Anything that exists is possible, and the magic is already within you." His thumb stroked the *Viniculum* as it curved around my wrist. "You just have to learn to communicate with one another."

"You act like it's alive," I said, huffing a laugh.

He tilted his head to the side. "Of course it's alive. You're tapping into the magic of the world, using the nature around you to do your bidding. If nature isn't life, then I don't know what is."

My understanding shifted, and I closed my eyes as I considered the beauty of the snow for the first time. All my life, it had been a detriment. It had represented the hardship that came with being unable to work the gardens for a season, and with having less food to eat.

Something rose up in me. I wouldn't have said it was magic exactly, but it felt like a drain on my energy, quieting the turmoil of my brain until a yawn burst free.

"I think we've accomplished the goal for the night," Caldris said, releasing my wrists from his grasp. I nodded sleepily, swaying slightly as he turned me and guided me back toward our tent and to the bedroll we shared, so he could wrap me in his warm embrace.

I was too tired to feel defeated and incompetent for not being able to channel the magic that was supposed to be mine now.

That would come in the morning.

)) ● ((

I very much, sincerely regretted my sleeplessness the next morning. Even if it weren't for the way my body slumped back into Caldris's form, the feeling of failure that rode alongside us all day was enough to act as a deterrent spilling from our bedroll in the future.

I'd had plenty of sleepless nights in my life, wandered in the woods at all hours, but none of those had ever left me feeling as exhausted as Caldris's lesson. Still, I flexed my hand in front of me, trying to call the winter air to my palm as if it would come to me as we rode along.

"You should take a break," he said, his presence at my spine both a comfort and a deterrent. He grounded me, giving me a piece of winter that I could hold for my own, but at the same time he felt like a safety blanket in a lot of ways.

If I could surround myself in his presence and allow him to offer me the strength I so desperately needed, then what did I need to be able to summon magic on my own for? When I was in danger, there was no issue calling upon the *Viniculum* that acted instinctively.

He would always protect me against physical threats to my wellbeing, and so would the mark that claimed me as his. "I don't want to take a break," I protested, glaring at my palm. I was never the best at anything, but I just wanted to not be incompetent.

I wanted to be able to summon my power to defend myself against other Fae, even if the *Viniculum* wouldn't instinctively respond in such a way. I wanted to be able to challenge anyone who threatened me in the future.

The last thing I wanted was to be reliant on a male. I'd fled that life with nothing but the dress on my body and my brother at my side. While I'd lost sight of that goal of independence for a little while, allowing Caelum to provide me with a feeling of safety and a place to rest my head at night with the Resistance, I couldn't let go of my goal just because I'd begun to accept that he had a place in my life.

He would be mine, and I think a part of me knew it, even if I wasn't quite willing to accept it fully yet.

"You're exhausted, *min asteren*," he said, releasing the reins with one of his hands and grasping mine. He lowered them both, pressing them into mane in front of me. "A star can only burn for so long before it dies."

"Are you trying to imply that I'll kill myself?" I asked, narrowing my eyes as his chest shook with a slight laugh behind me.

"I'm not implying anything. Pulling too much from the source of your magic can cause death in extreme scenarios. You aren't quite risking that by attempting the trick I taught you, but your body is not used to it. You have to take it slow," he explained.

I sighed, sinking further into his chest and letting him wrap me up in his embrace fully. "I just don't want to feel helpless," I said, turning my head to press my cheek into him. The scent of him washed over me, lulling me closer to sleep on Azra's relaxing gait.

"You are far from helpless, Little One. Not many can claim they've stabbed a member of the Wild Hunt," he said, his voice dropping low. As if he could sense how near to sleep I was from the way my body sank into his.

"I wouldn't be able to claim such a thing either, if he hadn't wanted to take me alive. Let's not deceive ourselves; the only reason I have been able to defend myself against you or them is because you want me unharmed. The world is not the same as it was when Loris taught me to fight in the woods," I said, ignoring the way his breath hitched. I realized in a moment of clarity it was likely the first time I'd spoken the man's name. Given the tension suddenly filling Caldris's body, I suspected it was likely fortunate for Loris that he was already dead. "Being able to stab something isn't enough anymore. What do I do when we arrive in Alfheimr? What of the beasts that roam beneath the stars in Faerie? Will those never be a threat? What of Mab?"

I didn't expect an answer to any of those questions that served the purpose of confirming how useless my limited skills would be in a fight against such creatures.

"First of all," he said, the relaxation gone from his voice. "If or when you encounter Mab, you do not fight her. You run like your life depends on it, because there are some fates that are far worse than death. The things Mab does to her toys cause unimaginable suffering. You run and you never look back."

"But you said you're bonded to her. How am I supposed to run if you cannot?" I asked.

"You'll leave me. I have taken Mab's torment for centuries, and I will continue to do so until I am free. But you, she cannot have," he said, the ominous warning in his voice making everything inside of me tremble. He genuinely feared the Queen of Air and Darkness and what she would do. Not to him.

But to me.

"What reason would she have to hurt me? I'm not a threat to her," I said, furrowing my brow.

"She doesn't need a reason to enjoy the way you scream, Little One. She thrives on suffering, on the sounds that fill her throne room. Her father is the Primordial of Chaos, of everything that came before, and humans once believed that meant she should thrive on silence. On the moments when there was nothing to exist."

"But creation had to start somewhere," I said, my voice trailing off as I considered it.

"Exactly. He created something from that nothing, an entire world spawning from that moment of inception. Some say he hoped to fill the void within him with the noise of creation around him," he explained.

"The opposite of how he feels on the inside," I agreed, again pondering the disappearance of the Primordials. The eternal beings could never stop existing or the world would collapse beneath us, yet from what Caldris had said nobody had seen them for centuries.

Azra halted as the group traveling ahead of us slowed to a stop. We'd ridden at the back for most of the day, seeking the privacy and distance from the Fae Marked so that they wouldn't see my attempt to summon the magic of winter.

They already hated me enough.

"What is it?" I asked, stretching up to try to get a better view through the riders blocking the path. I looked down when I felt shackles settle on my wrists.

"A group of humans," Caldris said, ignoring my huff, his voice uneasy as he guided Azra around the female member of the Wild Hunt who was directly in front of us.

She nodded to him in respect as he navigated through the crowd to approach where the group of people had gathered. "We don't offer sanctuary to people we don't know," Holt said. "I'm sure you can understand the importance of our duty to deliver the Marked humans to Alfheimr, if you are being honest about your intentions and the persecution you have faced."

Caldris pulled Azra up alongside Holt, keeping his distance from the group of people. A woman with dark hair gathered into a braid that draped over her shoulder looked past Holt to meet my stunned gaze. She looked from me to Caldris, a knowing smile spreading across her face. "It would seem death has found you after all, Estrella," she said, the knowing in her gaze turning to friendly acceptance as I leaned forward and dismounted from Azra's back before Caldris realized what I was doing.

I walked up to the other woman, taking her hands in mine and squeezing. "Adelphia," I said, the laughter that bubbled up from my throat of genuine pleasure to see her. Even if her ritual on Samhain had been the starting point of my life turning upside down entirely, I couldn't shake my happy reaction to seeing her.

She'd been kind and accepting in a world determined to force me into a mold of whatever suited each person's needs.

Caldris dismounted Azra behind me, moving up to place a protective hand on my shoulder. Adelphia's smile drifted off her face as she took in the shackles on my wrists and the matching Fae Mark on his neck. "How do you know my mate?" he asked. I looked over my shoulder, finding his eyes narrowed on Adelphia's face.

"You could ask your mate," I inserted, shrugging off his hand. If he wanted to be territorial, he would need to do so in a way that didn't dismiss me.

One of the men stepped forward from Adelphia's group, and I recognized him from when we'd sat around the fire eating cake. He moved toward me as if he meant to touch me, but Adelphia held out a hand to stop him, catching him in the chest. "I do not suggest that," she said, swallowing as her gaze fell to Caldris once again. "We met Estrella on Samhain. She stumbled upon our ritual in the woods before the Veil dropped, and she joined us in our worship."

Caldris tilted his head to the side, stepping away from my body slightly so he could look down at my face. "You participated in a ceremony worshiping the Old Gods?" he asked, his lips twitching in amusement.

"Shut up," I said, rolling my eyes at the satisfied way he puffed up his chest in response to the new knowledge. I didn't have the heart to tell him that I'd merely been curious; it wasn't out of some grand act of faith the way it was for the others.

"It would seem your hatred for my kind does not go as deep as you would have me believe, my star. If you would like to worship me, I can tell you exactly how to—"

He coughed when I slapped his chest with the back of my hand, the chains of my shackles rattling with the motion. "Do not even *think* of finishing that thought."

"Too late," he said, reaching forward to grasp my chin. He tilted my face up, dropping a soft kiss to my parted lips and risking my fury. The moment his lips touched mine, my irritation faded away.

"It's up to you, Estrella. Are they trustworthy?" Holt asked, interrupting the moment so that Caldris pulled back with a glare. I flushed when I realized that Adelphia monitored the interaction carefully.

"Yes, I think so," I said, looking through the group. There were several people I didn't recognize, but I believed Adelphia's intent was pure. She wouldn't do anything to knowingly harm the Fae Marked and what they represented.

"Thank you, Crown Princess of Winter and Shadows," Adelphia said, lowering her head to me respectfully. She turned to Caldris, dropping into a curtsy that looked incredibly uncomfortable in the snow. "We would be happy to pledge our loyalty to the Gods of Old if it suits you, Caldris, God of the Dead, Crown Prince of Winter and Shadows."

I snorted, in spite of my best instincts, brushing off my curiosity of just how Adelphia had come to know enough about the Old Gods to recognize Caldris. "Please don't. His ego is quite large enough, thank you," I said, ignoring the glare Caldris leveled at me.

"I've no need for anyone to pledge their fealty to me," Caldris said, his voice tentative as he slowly turned his gaze away from mine. "I merely wish to co-exist peacefully."

"Unfortunately that is not possible in Nothrek; not for some time now. We're seeking sanctuary and safe passage to Alfheimr. Once the Veil fell, we were all cast out from our villages and hunted down like dogs. Many of our brothers and sisters lost their lives in the escape. Might we be able to travel at your side? We won't make too much fuss."

"Just more mouths to feed," Aramis said, the first words I'd heard him speak near me since his cowardice the day before.

"Attitudes like that are exactly what contribute to the Fae's reputation," I argued. My voice was hard and unforgiving. "If you hope for any humans to believe that you Fae are interested in peace, then you have to start by showing them. Turning away those who are friendly will not accomplish anything but to alienate those who could have been allies."

"Aramis is far too young to remember just how powerful belief can be," Holt said, quirking a brow at the younger member of the Wild Hunt. "The Old Gods were once more powerful than they are now. They were forces to be reckoned with, because the humans believed them to be the Gods of legend." Aramis quieted, pursing his lips together with a scowl.

I was most definitely not his favorite person.

I wondered if it was because I'd stabbed him multiple

times, or if it was just an issue he took with my personality. It hardly mattered either way.

The man was a dick.

"You may travel with us," Caldris said solemnly. He pulled the dagger from his sheath, holding out a hand and cutting along his palm. The knife dragged over his flesh, parting it to reveal a steady stream of blood as he allowed it to drip onto the snow at our feet. "But you will swear a blood oath not to harm any of the Fae Marked."

Adelphia took the dagger from his hand, cutting along her palm without hesitation. It hardly seemed fair, knowing that Caldris's wound would heal within a few moments while hers would take days. She made her cut more shallow, allowing a single drop of blood to drip on top of his. One by one, the rest of her group followed suit.

When that was done, Caldris raised his hand to my mouth. I rolled my eyes, turning down my nose at the healing wound on his palm. "You haven't washed your hands since this morning. I will not be licking your hand."

He grinned as if I was amusing, shoving his sleeve up and slashing the blade across his wrist.

Blood poured onto the snow to prove his point as he lifted it to my mouth, touching it to my lips as I drank what the heart beating in his chest pumped out.

I supposed that would work.

18

ESTRELLA

*A*delphia strolled at my side, her presence calm and soothing. Caldris had only begrudgingly allowed me to walk alongside her and the others chattering about their lives, which must have been wholly interesting for Adelphia to recognize Caldris on sight.

"How do you know so much about the Gods? About the Old Rituals?" I asked, staring down at the bag strapped across her chest. I suspected the skull of a God rested inside it, something I couldn't see the older woman parting with.

"We come from a village that resisted the New Gods as long as they could. Eventually the King sent his Priests and Priestesses to convert our people by force, but by that time we had already hidden our forbidden texts and artifacts in a safe place. The people of our village have done what we can to preserve that knowledge over the generations that have passed since," she said, nodding her head as we continued along the snowy ground. "It was how I was able to recognize your mate."

I nodded as well, having already suspected as much. With the Veil separating the realms, portraits held within forbidden texts were the only way a human woman with a mortal lifespan could know what any of the Gods looked like. My attention swung to the book Holt had given me, strapped into the saddle bags across Azra's rump.

"The night the candle predicted you were slated to die, I sensed the truth in that premonition," Adelphia said, drawing my attention back to her. "I wouldn't have guessed it was a reference to the God of the Dead. I don't typically believe the magic understands nuances like that, and you are very much alive," she mused, reaching out a hand to grasp mine. She kept the movement casual, her voice low as she eyed Caldris cautiously where he rode beside Holt. "Stay close to your mate. I fear something else may be coming for your life, Estrella."

"I fear there are a great many who would want me dead," I said, scoffing with laughter as I brushed off her statement. When I'd stumbled across the ritual in the woods, I'd been shocked by the candle's declaration that death waited for me before the next Samhain. It was my first brush with mortality —the first moment when I was reminded of just how temporary a human life could be. In the weeks that followed, I'd become far more acquainted with death. I'd danced with it more times than I cared to count, and the life where I didn't need to worry daily seemed farther away.

Like a different life entirely.

"All the more reason to stay close to the male who would do anything to see you alive and well," Adelphia said, finally releasing my hand. She cleared her throat, turning her gaze forward on the path we walked across the open plain and heaving a sigh. "I am certain your village did its best to turn you against the Fae. That much was obvious from what I saw in you that night in the woods, but you were willing to join us in our chanting. A part of you has always known the way of the New Gods is not the natural order. Do not let that part of you die when you need her the most."

"I am a firm believer that it's worthwhile fighting for something like freedom," I said, lifting my chin as I glanced at Caldris from the corner of my eye. He continued in his conversation with Holt, but I couldn't help the feeling that he listened intently to every word. It should have been impossible to hear us, but my skin prickled with awareness regardless.

"Oh, sweet girl. What do you know of freedom?" Adelphia asked, her voice sad as she regarded me from my side. Her gaze was a heavy weight on my profile, stealing the breath from my lungs.

"I have fought my entire life to maintain even a small measure of it—"

"There can be nothing small when it comes to freedom," she said, glancing down at the shackles on my wrist with a grimace. "You either have it or you don't, and you were a prisoner in this world before you were even born, purely because you lack a cock. No matter how many times you snuck out in the night, you were always a prisoner—just a rebellious one."

"How am I any freer now?" I asked, clinking the metal of my shackles together pointedly.

"You're not, and in truth, you may never be free in the sense you desire. If you should embrace your path and the mate who is destined to stand at your side, you may find yourself caught in a different kind of imprisonment. But I should think it will be preferable to fearing for your life and the risk of punishment should you fail to comply. I suppose only time will tell," she said, shrugging her shoulders.

"What are you talking about?" I asked.

She smiled, her lips pulling back to reveal her teeth in something that felt far too wicked to be comforting. "Regardless of your feelings on the matter, you are the Crown Princess of Winter and Shadows. That is a title that will come with responsibilities to your new people—a burden that I am sure many would feel trapped under."

"How could a title like that matter? Unless The Fates interfere, the Queen of each Court will probably continue to live for centuries. It isn't as if Caldris will ever see the throne," I said, but my voice trailed off with doubt. I knew nothing of the way Faerie politics worked or how the line of succession worked.

I didn't even know if a royal had ever vacated a throne.

"I would wager that even a Faerie Queen can grow tired when she is not consumed by her thirst for power. From what I do know of Mab, I would agree that she'll never step down, but there is always a chance that Caldris's mother tires of ruling. Think of how many centuries she must have lived before Caldris was even born." Adelphia's voice turned wistful as she considered the thought, but all I could conjure was horror. What would an immortal being, who had lived since nearly the dawn of creation, think of someone as young as me?

I had nothing but an insignificant blip in time compared to that kind of lifetime—an eternity that sprawled out before the immortals and held all the promise of an endless future. We could accomplish nothing in our short lives by comparison.

Except I wouldn't have a human lifespan if I accepted Caldris as my mate. I would live as long as he did. I could live for what seemed like forever.

I didn't know if I would even want that.

"Most would see the promise of immortality as a gift," Adelphia said with a chuckle, turning her smiling face away from mine as she fought back her laughter. "You look as though you've just witnessed a murder."

"Immortality is a great deal of time for The Fates to hurt me," I said, thinking of just how miserable I'd been through most of my life. The thought of living centuries like that....

No.

"It is also a great deal of time for The Fates to bless you," she said, raising a brow and snagging my stare with hers finally. "You could watch your children grow, your grandchildren and great grandchildren."

I paled. *Children.*

I turned a startled glance over to my mate, where he chattered with Holt, and his body seemed tense. His head turned toward mine slowly, something knowing in his gaze as I fought the panic closing my throat.

I couldn't breathe around it; couldn't see past my own stupidity. I hadn't taken the tonic to prevent pregnancy since we'd left the Resistance. "Fuck," I whispered, turning my stare away from Caldris. He motioned toward me, tugging gently on his reins as he made to close the distance.

"Estrella?" Adelphia asked, grasping my forearm in her grip. "What did I say?"

Caldris rode up beside me, staring down at me with his face grave with concern. He didn't speak because he didn't need to ask if I was alright.

He already felt that answer pulsing down the bond between us.

"How do the Fae prevent pregnancy?" I asked, staring up into his blue eyes.

He thinned his lips, his jaw clenching. "They don't, *min asteren*. Children are a blessing that most beg The Fates to bestow upon them for centuries before such gifts are granted. There are exceptions, but it is highly unusual. If you are worried you might be with child, then there is little cause for concern."

"Why not? You said it can happen," I said, trying to ignore the way Adelphia stared at me in keen interest.

"As far as we know, you are primarily human. You will most likely not be able to bear my child until that is no longer true. I would not have risked you falling pregnant before you are ready if I thought there was a chance of it," Caldris said, his face soft as he looked down at me.

I heaved a sigh of relief. "For a moment, I wondered—"

"If I would use a pregnancy to trap you? I assure you, *min asteren*, I want you to accept me because you love me and you cannot stand the thought of a life without me—not because I used a pregnancy to leave you with no other choice. You are young and deserve to figure out who you are before you become a mother. I have waited centuries to see my mate swell with my child. I can wait a few more," he said, smirking when I flushed at the words. He made pregnancy seem almost erotic, like another way of claiming and owning me.

"I'm not even sure if I want children," I said, thinking of the world they'd be born into. A war loomed on the horizon, and I'd already seen the catastrophe and horror that could come from Fae and humans deciding the cloak-and-dagger feud they'd been waging needed to escalate.

Bringing a child into this world would be nothing short of irresponsible.

"You have plenty of time to change your mind. Nothing needs to be decided now," Caldris said, and something told me he understood. He'd been there when I was lost to the darkness over the dead child in Black Water. I shuddered to think of what I would do to the world if that was *my* child.

I wouldn't need Caldris to set it on fire for me. I'd do it my fucking self.

One of the hounds howled from a distance in front of the traveling group. His ears were pointed forward, his enormous jowls dripping with shadows as he turned his face back toward Holt and seemed to gesture him on. The leader of the Wild Hunt snapped straight as the other hounds moved to the front of our traveling group.

"What's going on?" I asked, watching as Caldris turned a stare toward Holt. He nodded, and the rider and a few members of the Wild Hunt kicked their horses into a gallop. Taking off to follow after the running hounds, they disappeared into the distance far too quickly.

"The hounds sensed one of the Fae Marked nearby," Caldris answered, pinning Fenrir with a glare when he stepped up beside me. The wolf nudged my hand with his head, bringing my arm to rest against his fur and settling in at my side. "Don't even think about it."

Fenrir whined, tossing his head and shaking it from side to side. I leaned into his weight, snuggling into the warmth of his fur as I tried not to think about the person's fear. The memory of it flooded through me; the terror of being hunted through the woods was a nightmare I wouldn't have wished upon my worst enemy.

My next breath was a deep gasp as a shout rang through the air, making me shake my head as I tried to steady my breathing.

"No! Let go of me!" a man yelled, his protests falling on deaf ears. I pressed each hand to the side of my head, trying to block out the sounds as I fought for composure, struggling to breathe.

There was movement in front of me as Caldris dismounted Azra. His fingers brushed against mine as he cupped my face in his massive hands and spoke to me. I couldn't hear the words or his voice over the pounding of blood in my head, but his touch was soft. His mouth moved slowly, as if he could calm the racing of my heart and the quick, shallow breaths that couldn't seem to fill my lungs with air.

I knew what came at the end of the hunt. I knew the death that waited for anyone who had the misfortune of traveling alongside the Fae Marked. I dropped my hands from my ears, clutching Caldris's forearms tightly. My nails dug into the leather covering his skin, the material creaking as sound tried to filter through the haze of my panic.

I couldn't do this again.

No. No. No. Not again.

My hands shook against Caldris's arms as he spoke in a soft cadence meant to sooth me. "It's alright, *min asteren*. You're okay," he murmured.

I squeezed my eyes shut, closing myself off from the sight of the white, open plain as a whimper escaped my throat. The metal of my shackles clanked, the sound so like a sword being drawn from its scabbard that I flinched back.

"You're with me. In the middle of a snow-covered plain and with a wolf at your side," Caldris said, and Fenrir leaned into me, brushing his fur against me and nuzzling his nose into my side. "You aren't on the edge of that cliff. You haven't just been running through the woods. You're with me."

My stomach swam with nausea as I peeled my eyes open slowly, staring into the worried blue gaze of my mate as he looked down at me. I was with him, I reminded myself.

With the very monster my brother had tried to kill me to save me from. It wasn't the comfort it had been a few moments before.

I focused on my breathing. Slowing it down with methodical, deep breaths.

When the Wild Hunt and the hounds returned, it was with a Fae Marked male tossed over the rump of Holt's horse, head and arms hanging lifelessly. They swung him off carefully, shackling his hands and lowering him into one of the carts with the others.

"Someone is going to have their hands full with that one," Aramis said, a smile lighting his face as he looked at Holt. It was a game, all of it: the human suffering and the fear we felt in being chased—the deaths we mourned.

It was all part of the thrill of the Hunt for them, and I wanted no part of it.

19

ESTRELLA

*C*aldris slept beside me. His face was peaceful in the moments when his brilliant blue eyes were closed, his posture relaxed as I slipped out of his hold. He'd clung to me as he fell asleep, as if he could feel me drifting away.

I wouldn't question his ability to feel my growing distance pulling through the bond—not with how estranged I felt after watching the Wild Hunt bring back the Fae Marked male they'd caught. Only a few weeks prior, that might have been me.

If it hadn't been for Caelum's deception and interference, I might have been slung across Holt's horse, dragged back to the carts, and shackled with the rest of them. My brother would still lie dead in a heap at the bottom of the cliff, leaving my heart in tatters and wishing I'd managed to go with him.

The bond between us was silent as my mate slept. It should have been peaceful, the knowledge that the only emotions plaguing me at the moment were my own. Instead, it left me unsettled as I tried to understand where I'd gone wrong. When I'd allowed the link between our minds as a way to take my pain, I'd given myself to Caldris in a way I'd planned to take back.

I'd intended to wake the next morning and slam that window closed, cutting him off from my head and my heart as best as I could. But I hadn't. I couldn't be alone all over again —not when I'd finally felt like I had somewhere I belonged, for the very first time.

I sat beside him, staring down at the golden skin of his face and the relaxed seam of his mouth. My eyes slid down his shirtless form, dropping to where he'd trusted me enough to rest his weapons beside the bedroll. There was no attempt to put them out of reach or make it harder for me to get to them any longer. My shackles lay on the other side of them, deposited for the night until he would need to put me in them once again to placate the humans who already hated me.

I'd done nothing to free them in spite of my promise. I'd settled into my place at Caldris's side in all the ways I swore I would never do, and it hadn't been until I'd been reminded of the fear *they* caused that I recognized what I'd done.

I had taken the easy road—allowed my heart to dictate what my mind knew to be wrong. Mate or not, the Fae Marked deserved to go free, and I already knew I probably wouldn't survive an attempt to set them loose.

Not when Caldris was gone and I was no longer the mate of anything.

I reached over his body slowly, wrapping my trembling fingers around the hilt of his dagger. I lifted it carefully, easing it out of the sheath and wincing at the light sound of iron against leather. Weakness plagued me when I touched a finger to the blade itself, confirming that the metal would serve my purposes.

I shifted to my knees beside him, careful not to touch his body with mine. Leaning over him and touching a hand to the bedroll beside his head as carefully as I could, I raised the dagger until I held it to the front of his throat. My cheeks were wet as I stared down at him, my hand making the blade shake as it lingered just off his skin.

I pushed forward and then retreated, choking back the sob that stuck in my throat. Caldris's eyes peeled open slowly, the bond remaining quiet as his blue eyes met mine. There was no surprise in his gaze as it landed on me, as his eyes roved over my tear-stained cheeks. "I wondered what you would do."

"What are you talking about?" I asked, sniffling and turning my eyes down to stare at the knife. I pressed the blade into his skin, wondering why he never flinched back or reacted to it at all. Surely, he had to know the blade was iron. That his death would be final when I cut through the sinew of his neck and carved his heart from his chest.

A strangled sob escaped me.

Caldris reached up to grab my wrist, finally forcing the blade away from his neck while I struggled. But instead of guiding it away from his body, he shifted it down his chest and cut a thin line toward his heart. Pressing the tip of the blade to the skin covering his beating breast, he held my hand steady. "It is yours. Whether it beats or not," he murmured, reaching up to cup my cheek with his other hand. "I have felt your desperation coming through the bond all day, Little One. If my death is what brings you peace, then I will pay that price."

I shook my head, my brow furrowing in confusion as I fought back the torrent of tears. I felt his resignation, felt his lack of fear. "You're supposed to fight," I whispered, sniffling and pulling against his hand.

He held me steady and blood welled at the tip of the blade where he guided my hand and pressed it into his skin. "Why would I want to fight with you? All I want is to love you," he murmured, his thumb running over the skin on the back of my hand soothingly.

"You woke with your own dagger pressed to your throat. You're supposed to fight," I repeated, watching as a tear dripped off my cheek and splashed against his chest.

"If you are able to imagine your life, your future, without me in this world, then why would I want to live?" Caldris asked, running his other thumb over my cheekbone. It smeared through the tears wetting my face, moving smoothly over my skin as I searched for any anger coming from him. There was nothing...nothing but the calm resolution of a male who would welcome death. "I love you, Estrella. I have loved you for centuries and waited for you to be mine. If there is no hope, no chance of you accepting me into your heart in truth, then I will gladly allow you to be the one to end my eternity of suffering. If the last thing I see is your face, then I can go to the Void in peace."

I sobbed as he dropped his hands away, letting them settle against the bedroll at his side. "Stop it," I pled.

"Claim your freedom, Estrella, because if you do not, I will never let you go. Do you understand me? I will not stop until you have accepted me—until you're my mate in truth. I will take from you, but I will give you more love than you could have ever imagined. This is your moment to choose, *min asteren*. You can have your freedom or you can have me, but you cannot have both," he said, his voice gentle despite his harsh words. Despite the fact that he admitted I would always be a servant to this compelling bond between us, mangling my truths and demanding my secrets, I couldn't help but see the gift he offered me.

For once, I could choose. Something. *Anything.*

His understanding flowed through me, coursing through our bond as he felt the emotional mess that choice created in me. The first choice I would make on my own, and it was the one that would tear me in two.

It was the choice that would demand me to sacrifice a part of myself, no matter which way I chose: freedom or love. One was all I'd ever wanted in my nights wandering in those woods, not answering to anyone as I made my way through the darkness. The other...the other was exactly what I'd never dared to dream of.

I shifted my other hand, sitting back and tucking my legs beneath me. The tip of the dagger still pressed to his chest, but I stretched forward with my free hand to touch his lips with trembling fingers as he spoke. "I love you. In this life or the afterlife, my star. I will always wait for you."

I leaned forward as I shifted my fingers to the side, running them over the smooth skin of his square jaw. He held my gaze as I touched my lips to his, a soft, barely-there whisper of a kiss that gently caressed him. He didn't move as I kissed him, and I knew without a doubt he felt the goodbye in that touch. He felt the farewell in my kiss as I twisted my grip on the hilt, digging the blade closer to him and swallowing the sharp intake of his breath that followed.

I pulled away, slowly, staring down at him as his eyes drifted closed, waiting for the death he thought was coming. But it wasn't his death The Fates demanded from me as the golden thread between us sparkled brighter, shimmering despite the lack of light within our tent.

A single tear dropped, splashing against his cheek as I watched. I dropped the dagger, letting it fall to the bedroll beside my mate as his eyes flung open.

It was the death of Estrella Barlowe of Mistfell that The Fates claimed. The death of all I had been before the fall of the Veil.

I sank back, kneeling as Caldris sat up slowly. I couldn't

tear my eyes off the dagger that lay discarded at his side. The weapon I'd held in my hand had given me a way to end it. I could have bought my freedom with his death, and yet I couldn't do it.

I couldn't kill the very being who had brought me my first moments of real happiness. I couldn't end the only male I'd ever loved, even if he was a monster.

He snagged my chin between thumb and finger, dragging my gaze off the dagger. My eyes snagged on the tiny wound above his heart where the flesh slowly mended itself, only the small trickle of blood remaining upon his skin. He swiped a fingertip through it, pressing it to my lips. They parted for him in my daze, allowing him to glide his essence on top of my tongue.

I'd betrayed my people, I realized as he slid that part of himself inside of me. I'd disobeyed my brother. I'd abandoned the Fae Marked who wanted to be free, choosing my own happiness over their liberty, but wouldn't they have done the same? Did this make me worse than them somehow?

"Are you alright?" Caldris asked, shifting his hand to hold my cheek. He gazed at me as if I'd already died, and the throbbing ache in my chest felt as if that might be true. I could no longer hate him for the choices he'd made that led us here or for the horrors of the Wild Hunt.

The weight of those decisions from this point forward would be mine to bear.

"Make me forget," I said, biting the corner of my lip. It was too much, threatening to consume me even if it changed nothing. Our lives would continue on as they had, as if he were the one forcing me to be in a place where I did not belong. Only he and I would know the difference, but that was enough.

"And what if I do not want you to forget that you have chosen me?" he asked, tucking a lock of hair behind my ear. "I have waited a very long time for this moment, my star. Would you blame me?"

"No," I said, shaking my head sadly. Thinking he wouldn't give me the blessed numbness that came from the pleasure he provided. Nothing existed beyond the all-consuming nature of his lovemaking in those moments, and I craved that nothing more than anything.

Come morning, I would be alright. Come morning, I would sink into the routine and pretend that I hadn't completely changed the course of my life and our relationship. I'd pretend I hadn't felt The Fates working in the background, knitting their threads and binding us closer together.

"But," Caldris said, leaning forward to touch his mouth gently to mine. He held my gaze as he kissed me, pulling back only slightly so his words murmured against my lips. His fingers slid down over my neck, caressing his mark on my skin as they went to the laces at the top of my tunic. He pulled them loose slowly, agonizingly, as he held my stare. "I do intend to make love to my mate."

He tugged my tunic off over my head, tossing it to the side as he revealed my nude torso. My nipples pebbled in the cold air as Caldris kissed me. Teasing the seam of my lips with his tongue, he closed his eyes as I opened for him. All I could do was take what he gave, something in me knowing he would not allow me to create a feeling of urgency in his claim.

Not in this moment or the next.

His mouth trailed kisses down the side of my neck, stopping above my heart and kissing the spot where it beat intimately in tune with his. His eyes held mine as he dropped even lower, wrapping his lips around the peak of my breast and drawing it into his mouth. He kneaded the flesh of the other as his free hand worked my trouser laces open, and then he released me entirely to yank them down my legs.

Pulling them off and leaving me naked, he tossed them to the side and made quick work of stripping off his own trousers. He spread my legs as he settled his weight between them, touching the flesh of his shaft to that heated, greedy part of me that couldn't get enough of him. His mouth came down on mine and he kissed me tenderly. Soft, slow, and in time with the rolling of his hips as he thrust himself against me. Rubbing over my fevered flesh, coaxing himself through me as my arousal built and built.

I'd never known he could make love to me without sinking inside of me, or that he could make me feel so surrounded and wrapped in his embrace. He shifted his hips, gliding through the wetness he'd created between my legs to finally notch the head of his cock against my entrance.

I angled my hips, accepting my mate as he slid inside of me. My body clenched tight, fighting against the feel of him moving through me. He opened me to him with slow thrusts, carefully dragging himself over my flesh until I couldn't help the pleasured whimper that he pulled from my throat. He brought his mouth back to mine once more, devouring the sound as if it was his to own. As if he didn't want anyone else to hear it.

This was just us, without a single care or thought for anyone else. This was a private moment between lovers in the night, a fusing of souls that I didn't think either of us understood just yet.

He seated himself fully inside of me, pausing with his groin flush against mine to pull back from our kiss. He stared down, brushing a hand over the wispy hair that clung to the side of my face despite the cold surrounding me.

"Mine," he murmured, and then he pulled his hips back and he began to move. Slow thrusts, slow drags over me and inside of me, I found myself raising my hips to meet his drives.

We moved in tandem, a dance between us as he held my gaze and shared my breath.

This was not just sex. This was the physical manifestation of our love, and tears stung my eyes as I denied the urge to twist it into something filled with hatred. I'd let it go. I'd consumed it for myself.

How could I hate the male who would have let me kill him to take my freedom?

"I love you, *min asteren*," he murmured, reaching between our bodies. He stroked my flesh as he moved inside me, bringing me back to him and the moment and driving me closer to an orgasm that would unravel me.

There was no torrent of pleasure, no rough assault of river waters barreling me toward the falls. It was only the languid flow of gentle waves lapping against the shore, driving me closer to that which would overwhelm me.

I knew I would never be the same.

"I love you, my mate," I whispered back, wrapping my arm around his back and pulling him tighter. My other hand went to the back of his neck, holding him pinned as he brought me to the edge of an orgasm and then sent me tumbling over the side.

He held my stare as I came, his ragged groan filling our tent when he followed. When his weight collapsed onto me, I had no desire to separate us, or to wash the evidence of our lovemaking from my skin. Caldris rolled to his back, keeping our bodies joined as he pulled me with him and settled me across his chest.

He was still inside me while I fell asleep, my ear resting above the strong heart that beat for me. I would hate myself in the morning, but for that moment, I let him lull me to sleep.

20

*T*here wasn't room in the carts, but even if there had been, I highly doubted the Fae Marked would have treated the humans who willingly chose to travel with the Wild Hunt with respect. They would have been met with the same hatred I'd faced the day that I chose to ride with them.

Adelphia and her group walked at our side as she chattered happily with one of the men I recognized from the fire that night. I tried to focus on the book in my grasp, studying the mate bond while I sat astride Azra with Caldris. It might have seemed foolish with the very ancient mate riding the horse at my back, and I didn't doubt he would be willing to answer any question I asked.

The problem was that I didn't know what questions to ask. I didn't know enough to form an educated opinion one way or the other, and I certainly didn't know what to do with any of the information I did have.

"We'll reach Tradesholme soon," Caldris said, the name of the city where I'd thought I'd lost him sending a shock through my system. I hadn't thought of the possibility of traveling through the same city as before and wondered if that was wise.

"Is it really smart to travel through the city? After the force we met the last time?" I asked, wondering about the carts and all the spaces we would need to pass through. We would never fit the horses or the carts through the tunnels we'd used the last time, when we escaped.

"We'll send a scout ahead to determine if there are too many Mist Guard for it to be safe. This is where your human friends will come in handy," he said, nodding his head toward Adelphia. She nodded back, as if only the mention of scouting for the Wild Hunt was all she needed to know it would be her duty.

"You don't have to agree to this," I said to her.

"It is my honor, Princess Estrella," she said, smiling slightly.

"That is not my name," I groaned, dropping my head back against Caldris's chest.

"I think you will find that, regardless of where you end up in Alfheimr, regardless of the Court you choose to call home, and whether or not you accept your bond with me as your mate, there is not a place in the five Courts where you will be anything less than royalty," he said, his chuckle vibrating through my body. His emotion sank into me, finding me through the bond and making my own lips tip into a smile that matched his, even though we spoke of things that would lead to my great discomfort.

That happiness froze inside me the moment a *caw* sounded through the air, Caldris's fear spiking like something tangible. He snapped his gaze to Holt, jumping down from Azra's back in a fluid move as he yanked the hood of my cloak up over my head without a word. Holding out a hand to accept the bow and arrow another one of the riders tossed to him, he caught one in each hand and knocked the arrow in place, pulling back the string.

"What's going on?" I asked, grasping my hood so that I could pull it down.

"Leave it," he ordered without taking his eyes off the sky. I froze in place, the lack of attention he paid me and his fixation on the path a random bird might fly making everything in me go taut. He watched the sky, circling around the clearing as other riders of the Wild Hunt did the same with the bows they held. "We cut it down. No matter what," he said, and the others nodded as they moved in symmetry. I watched the sky, narrowing my eyes to fight off the sunshine that seemed to bounce off of all the white surrounding me.

A single streak of black cut across the sky, a lone blight flying quickly as it journeyed back toward the boundary between realms. Several arrows shot forward, none able to reach the creature as it flew through the sky.

Caldris took a deep breath, exhaling slowly as he released his arrow. The winter wind followed its path through the sky, pushing it forward and allowing it to reach higher and farther than the others had gone.

A splash of red burst from the crow as the arrow struck him, a tangled mess of black feathers crashing toward the ground as it fell. It landed on the plain up ahead, and I swore the Wild Hunt held still.

Watching and waiting.

"If she was looking through its eyes, she will not be pleased with what you've done," Holt said, swallowing as his white stare met Caldris's.

My mate looked up at me, his gaze locking with mine for a moment before he looked back to the other male. "I know," he said simply, striding toward the bird on the ground. I stayed back, knowing I needed to keep my distance from the cursed spy for the Fae.

"You cannot keep her from learning of your mate's existence forever," Holt added, walking up beside Caldris as the two of them stared down at the blight on the ground. Caldris reached forward, snatching the arrow and tearing it free from the monstrous bird's flesh. "Too many people know of her."

"We just need to buy time," Caldris said, turning to look back at me. My breath caught, knowing exactly what he meant. Time for me to accept him. Time to complete our bond, making him strong enough to fight back. Time to set off the events that I imagined would lead to a new war amongst the Fae.

I swallowed, contemplating how I felt about the idea that we were just buying time. That my acceptance of the bond was unavoidable, and with the knowledge that his freedom hung in the balance—and after my inability to kill him the night before—could it ever really be any but? Could I handle being responsible for him being indebted to a woman he so clearly hated? That enjoyed torture and would find pleasure in the way I screamed?

I didn't think I could.

I dismounted Azra, stepping closer to where my mate stood over the blight. When the black feathers of the bird came into view, I noticed the slight golden shimmer to them as they glinted in the sunlight. Its eyes gleamed with amber, the light in them fading as life left it. I stayed out of its line of sight, but felt compelled to step forward and get closer. Whereas I'd felt compelled to put distance between myself and the blight on the night I'd seen one spying on me in the woods before the Veil fell, this drew me closer.

"It's alright," Caldris said, holding out a hand for me as I took it. I stepped into his side, staring down at the creature with an odd feeling rushing through me. "You've seen one before." He observed me, the confused tension on my face as I dropped into a crouch.

I couldn't resist the urge to reach out with trembling fingers, to stroke the dead bird on its feathers. The softness of them touched my skin, something in the glittering darkness calling to me. So close to matching the colors of my fingertips, which I couldn't seem to bring back to their normal bronze. The gold in them flashed, as if recognizing the blight as its amber eyes glowed once more.

It decayed before my eyes, its body disintegrating slowly as the feathers disappeared to reveal skin...then bones... then nothing. Only the snow beneath its body. It vanished from view entirely, and it wasn't until the snow shifted that I realized it hadn't disappeared.

It had merely changed. Something slithered through the grass beneath the skiff of snow, a baby snake wrapping itself around my pointer finger as I stretched out a hand.

"Through death comes life," I said, the words feeling torn from my soul as I turned a stunned expression up to Caldris. He flinched back from the sight of the snake wrapped around my finger, swallowing as he studied me.

"Estrella," he said, and the concern in his voice made me lay a tentative hand back to the grass where the blight had been. The snake vanished with a curl of my hand, the yellow and green of its scales disappearing and leaving us behind in a world washed in white.

"What the fuck was that?" Holt asked, staring at Caldris. The two men exchanged a silent secret as my mate took my hand and pulled me to my feet. He ran his hand over mine, searching for any sign of the snake or the blight I'd touched.

"Where's the snake, min asteren?" he asked, studying my

hand. He shoved the sleeves of my tunic up, searching along my arms.

"It wasn't time for it to be born yet," I said, knowing instinctively. The image I'd had, the snake curling around me, had been a flash of its future life. A moment of what would come after the soul rested in the Void.

A reincarnation revealed.

Holt turned his stare to me, crossing his arms over his chest. "Yeah, because *that's* not fucking creepy or anything."

The city walls of Tradesholme loomed, looking far different as we approached the front gates. There was something macabre about the way they appeared out of the trees, but I couldn't quite get a feel for what caused that shudder to roll through me. Adelphia had scoped out the city itself, advising that, while there was a small force of the Mist Guard waiting, it didn't appear to be large enough that the Wild Hunt couldn't handle them.

It was small enough that they'd need to have a death wish to fight at all. Even so, as we crossed over the land in front of the gates, I had to swallow back my nausea.

I was not made for war. I was made for peace and a cuddly blanket in a comfortable chair in a library with a book in my hand. And I was so tired of the fucking cold.

"You stay by my side. No matter what happens," Caldris said, his voice ringing through me with a sharp command. He behaved as if I had any intention of separating from the one person in the world who would do anything to keep me safe.

"I don't have a death wish," I reminded him, wincing when

I felt his amusement through the bond between us. "Okay, I don't have a death wish at the moment."

He laughed, the sound rich and filling my soul with a moment of warmth in the face of the coming tension and a possible battle. The memory of the blight's blood staining the snow hung over me, threatening to consume me. I'd never been drawn to something that wasn't alive before, or had any inclination to move toward it.

To touch it.

But I knew beyond the shadow of a doubt the snake that had appeared to me had been a vision of the blight's future life. Of what was waiting for it after the Void.

Caldris had been mostly silent on the issue as we moved forward and closed the distance between us and Tradesholme, but I felt his confusion and his fear. Fear that I'd put there, and it horrified me to think the legendary God of the Dead was afraid of what I might be or what I might become.

What the fuck was I if I wasn't human?

I glanced over at Adelphia, recalling the words she'd spoken to me on the night we'd met. There was beauty in knowing who I was, and in embracing that in spite of the potential consequences.

But what was I supposed to do when I didn't have the slightest fucking clue?

We neared the gates, the clank of armor sounding as the guards protecting the city stepped forward. Leveling their spears to face our traveling group, I looked past them to the real horrors swinging from the city walls.

No matter what I was, I was not this kind of monster.

Tears pooled in my eyes, taking in the sight of bodies dangling from the perimeter walls. A warning to any who dared to enter. Duncan's face was ashen, his body swollen in death, but at least he'd only suffered a single strike to the heart that had ended him in a permanent way.

What they'd done to Jensen was a different beast entirely, and I felt the way Caldris stiffened at my spine. Almost nothing remained of the other man, his flesh torn from his bones. Nothing human had caused that kind of suffering, not when the Mist Guard was far more interested in cutting out hearts and calling it a day.

"He was already dead, min asteren. I swear that to you," Caldris said. Cool air rushed over the back of my neck, surrounding me with the chill of the male I was mated to. The male I was fairly certain I would accept as mine, even if only to offer him peace from the turmoil of his relationship with his abusive stepmother.

"You did this?" I asked, wringing my hands together in my lap. I avoided touching him, my thoughts roaring in my head. He'd said he hadn't killed Jensen, and I'd believed him. I most definitely believed him now, knowing that he couldn't lie.

"The power I unleashed to kill the Mist Guard who attacked us did this," he confirmed, sighing heavily. "But I waited until after Jensen had already been stabbed through the heart to reveal myself."

"Did he see you? Before his heart stopped?" I asked, a shudder of horror rolling through me.

He'd called my name.

Jensen had been an asshole, but he'd tried to warn me. He'd tried to do the right thing in a situation that was complete shit. Even knowing he wouldn't be around to benefit from me knowing the truth, because his death already loomed. He'd tried to warn me.

My throat clenched, the threat of tears burning and my eyes stinging with the realization. I'd hated Jensen; I had far from mourned his death.

Fuck.

"Are those tears for him, Little One?" Caldris asked, his voice dropping lower. Even if he hadn't killed the man, I knew he would in this moment had he lived. He'd already wanted to in the past, and knowing I would have any kind of emotion for him would only worsen that.

"Not in the way you're thinking," I said, touching his hand to settle his rage. The last thing I wanted as we made our way through a city full of people was for him to go into a bloodlust over something that no longer mattered. "I just...I wouldn't have thought he'd try to warn me. I would have imagined him wanting to leave me to the fate I chose, feeling self-satisfied when he died because he knew something I didn't. When did I get so cynical?"

"You've probably always been cynical," he said, his voice settling slightly as he fought off the hint of bloodlust, realizing that the turmoil he'd felt in me actually had almost nothing to do with the other man and everything to do with myself as a person, and the changes I hadn't wanted to see. "The life you've lived would demand that. Those who have been taught to expect the worst tend to do just that. Jensen gave you no reason to expect otherwise from him. Not with his behavior in the short time you knew him."

"He was a creep," I agreed, trying to reconcile that with the man who had tried to save me from my own choices. I should have known better than to believe he was entirely evil. Real people existed in shades of gray.

Holt approached the gates, sitting astride his unearthly steed and leaving no doubt to the fact that he was anything but human. The Wild Hunt could not conceal what they were, so they would not even be bothered to try.

He pulled his sword from the sheath, letting it hang at his side as he tilted his head in that animalistic way the Fae had.

"I promise you, I cannot die. But you can, and you will, if you choose to engage in this fight."

His words echoed over the plain outside the keep, bouncing off the stone behind the guards' backs as they exchanged frenzied looks with one another. I hated the knowledge that their deaths loomed, and even knowing their cause was not just, nothing could stop me from regretting the fact that they had to choose between life and what they believed in.

That was no choice at all.

The first guard laid down his spear, shaking his head at the others as he moved toward the gates. He spoke to someone on the inside, and I could just imagine the panic in his voice when he asked them to open the gates. To allow us passage, because the Wild Hunt would go through that city even if they had to scale the walls.

Caldris guided Azra forward, and I saw the moment of recognition when another one of the guards laid eyes upon him. He too dropped his sword, smacking his fellow guard in the chest and pointing with horror on his face.

"If you lay down your weapons, we will not kill you. We have no quarrel with those who do not wish us harm," my mate said, his voice ringing with command. Everything inside of me warmed, knowing without a doubt that he would hold true to his word. Loving him for the show of mercy that others would not have given him.

He would never go back on his word like that, and if he tried, I'd gut him myself.

"We wish no one in the city any harm. We are merely passing through on our way to the boundary," Holt called.

"You know we cannot allow you to reach the boundary!" a voice called from the top of the stone walls. The guard in question held a bow and arrow in his grasp, the quiver pulled taut and an arrow notched at the ready.

"Don't throw away your life for someone else's war. Life is about the choices you make, and you always have free will," Holt said, something bitter entering his voice. I thought of all of those here who were cursed to ride for eternity, and of Caldris, who was enslaved to a woman who made him do all manner of things he didn't believe in.

Would she make him hurt me? Force him to be the one to peel the flesh from my bones?

I swallowed back my nausea, wishing with every passing day there was another place we could go. That he was not bound to return to Mab's side with her daughter in tow.

The gates opened and Holt hung his head forward. My body tensed, preparing for a trap as he guided his horse into the open city. We followed behind him, and Caldris wrapped his body around mine more tightly so that he could shield me from any attacks that came from above.

I couldn't breathe, just thinking of what would happen and the innocent people who might be hurt if it came to a fight. Children raced through the courtyard, their mothers chasing after them as they caught sight of the Wild Hunt entering the gates.

A guard stepped forward, walking into our path as he tried desperately to keep his hand off his sword. His fingers twitched at his side, ready for anything, but Holt smiled.

Kindly, if not a little painfully, as if he wasn't entirely used to offering human pleasantries.

"If you'll follow me, we would like to see you through the city before the Lord awakes and realizes what we've done," he said, his gaze darting around nervously.

"I do have one condition for our quick passage," Caldris said, speaking up from behind me. The guard's eyes shifted, tracking over me and the mark on my neck. He grimaced, closing his eyes as if he realized just how disastrous the legendary Caldris increasing his power could be for anyone who made themselves his enemy.

"What would that be?" the guard asked, his voice a low murmur.

"Cut down the dead and bury them in the earth," Caldris commanded. He hesitated, as if he knew I would not like whatever he had to say next. "Except for that one," he added, pointing toward Jensen's desecrated corpse.

The guard hesitated, studying Caldris as he tried to figure out the motivation for such a request. We did not bury our dead. We did not treat them with the respect they were due, only burning their bodies in the way of the religion we'd had shoved down our throats forcefully since the time we were born. "It will be done. I'll see to it personally," the guard said finally, turning and walking the winding path through the city.

The Wild Hunt walked forward, following after him as I sat in shock and tried to come to terms with the declaration my mate had just made. "I thought everyone deserved a burial?" I asked, turning to look at Caldris over my shoulder.

His eyes were dark as he met my gaze, flurries of a winter storm floating through them. "Everyone but him," he growled.

22

ESTRELLA

I'd thought we were the entirety of the Wild Hunt.

  I'd been wrong.

We marched toward the Hollow Mountains, our group forming a single line as we navigated the narrow paths through the trees. The carts jostled from side to side all too often, the underbrush and leaves on the forest floor disguising the tree roots and stones that made for a rough journey.

I knew the moment we stopped at the cave entrance that something was wrong. The stillness of the air around us made it impossible to suspect otherwise. "Come on, Little One," Caldris said, dismounting behind me. He helped me down as I stared at the opening, swallowing down my discomfort of all that was to come.

These people knew me. They would recognize me and with my association with Caldris at my side, they would quickly realize that he and Caelum were one and the same. This was the moment when I faced the reckoning for my own ignorance. The people in the carts hated me even though they didn't know I'd been the one to stand up for the Fae at my side.

These people would despise me, and I deserved it. I'd had the opportunity to kill him, and I hadn't been able to do it.

"I don't want to go in there," I said, shaking my head as Caldris reached out to take my hand. Night was beginning to fall all over again, the air cooling around us. The daylight hours grew shorter and shorter with every day that passed, costing us valuable time on our journey.

"It's a warm place to sleep for the night. A place that can offer us all baths and comfort in the middle of our journey. You know we cannot miss that opportunity when it presents itself," he said, but his eyes were soft with the sadness he knew I felt.

"Don't you want a group to go in and fight first at least?" I asked, watching as they were unloaded from the carts and led into the caves. Their eyes were wide, their expressions tormented as they made their way into the dark caverns. "I can't imagine you want to put the Fae Marked at risk if they decide to fight, and surely you have to be aware that they *will* fight."

"Holt sent a regiment ahead of us. As soon as he received word from me that you knew my secret, he sent a team to infiltrate the tunnels. We couldn't risk the people here realizing they'd been compromised, and I didn't know how long they would go without word from Melian before they grew wary," he admitted, and a shock rolled through me.

He was always planning ahead, maneuvering for every possibility as if his life depended on it. I guessed when it came to the possibility of finding Mab's daughter, it very well might. Holt emerged from the cave, connecting eyes with Caldris and nodding in reassurance. A few of the riders stayed behind to tend to the horses, seeing to their needs and positioning them in the canopy of the trees for the night. The rest of the members of the Wild Hunt strode into the entrance to the caves, Adelphia and her group following behind them. They moved slowly, studying the cave entrance and taking in the exterior.

Perhaps if they didn't make it to Alfheimr, they would return here.

"Everything's clear?" Caldris asked, looking over my shoulder to speak to the other man. I turned in place, maneuvering so that I could watch the interaction fully.

Some part of me hoped the books hadn't been endangered. That they were safe, despite the battle that must have raged. I turned my eyes to the forest floor, noticing the disturbed snow where fresh packed dirt had been laid upon the ground.

"How many?" I asked, turning my blistering stare to Holt.

He held my gaze, lifting his chin in a way that told me he knew exactly what I meant. Still he played the fool, pretending as if he didn't. "How many what?"

I stepped away from Caldris, making my way to the upturned dirt and crouching low. I touched a hand to the burial place, lifting the loose grains into my hand as my shackles clanked. The ground should have been frozen, should have been more difficult to bury people within it.

But that didn't seem to stop the Wild Hunt from hiding the casualties of their cause.

"How many did you bury?" I asked, and a hush swept over the forest.

"Only what was necessary to gain access to the Fae Marked within the tunnels, and to gain enough advantage to be able to rest here for the night, *your highness*," Holt said with a sneer. "We do not kill without purpose. We are to bring the Marked and Mab's daughter back to Alfheimr. That is all."

"And what if Mab's daughter is within one of these graves?" I asked, turning to look at Caldris. "How can you kill in the very community where you are searching for a person you have never seen?"

"They did what was necessary," Holt said, defending the choices his riders had made in his absence.

"They did what was easy," I corrected, standing from my crouch. I moved closer to Holt, stopping directly in front of him and staring up into his ethereal face as he glared down at me. "If you want the humans to stop hating the Fae, this is not the way. This has to stop."

"Unfortunately for you, I only take orders from one female," Holt said, his lips peeling back from his teeth to form a cruel, twisted smile. "And you are not the Queen of the Shadow Court."

I tilted my head to the side, that hollow inside of me filling with ire. It roiled near to the surface, waiting to be called upon as the cold of stone filled my fingertips. They trembled, tingling with the nearness of death. "If Mab is defeated, who inherits the throne?" I asked him, keeping my voice measured. As if I was genuinely curious. In my reading of the tomes the Resistance had gathered, I knew enough to know the Faerie Courts were to be passed down from ruler to first heir if the Kings and Queens who ruled over them were to pass.

"There are technically two heirs to the Shadow Court," Holt said, evading the statement as best he could. He knew the trap he'd walked into.

"Yes, the daughter who could very well lie buried in these graves thanks to your riders' foolishness, and my mate. Tell me, if he is to be King of the Shadow Court, what would that make me, Hunstman?" He stared down at me, animosity in his features.

I didn't know what had happened after the moments in Black Water when I'd summoned the darkness to my fingers, but something in Holt had shifted, turning away from the slightly friendly and amusing male he'd been previously and embracing the fact that we seemed destined to be enemies.

Whatever he suspected I was, I swore he saw it dancing in my eyes as he swallowed and clenched his teeth. "The Queen of the Shadow Court," he said begrudgingly, looking over my shoulder to where Caldris watched the exchange. He didn't move to intervene, allowing me my moment.

I couldn't be certain what had come over me; not when I still resented the idea of being royalty. But sometimes, in the quiet moments when nobody was watching, part of me craved the moment when the world would see what I could be. Something insidious, lurking inside of me and waiting for the right moment to strike.

Holt glared at Caldris, turning on his heel and making his way back to the caves. "Holt?" I asked, making him pause in his steps. He turned to look over his shoulder, his glare cast on the ground rather than meeting my pointed stare. "Do try to remember that only one death separates you from taking orders from me."

He spoke not a word, turning to face forward and walking into the caves. "Easy, min asteren," Caldris said with a chuckle. His touch settled on my shoulder, calming the inferno senselessly raging inside of me.

"Did your glamour protect me from the more unpredictable aspects of what it is to be Fae?" I asked, spinning to pin him with a glare. My emotions were too intense, leaving me with the unsettling feeling that I wasn't in command of them anymore. They would break me and consume me, tearing me apart from the inside and leaving me only a piece of who I'd been before.

"Somewhat, but not to the level that would cause strong surges like you're having. The Fae are volatile, but not in this way. I suspect this has more to do with what our bond has awakened that already lived inside of you," he said, and the bond pinched, as if he was keeping that label from me. I had the distinct impression that I could find it if I really pushed, but given the way I'd been behaving...I didn't think I wanted to know just yet.

That felt strange. Like there was something wrong with me for willingly living in ignorance when it came to my own heritage and the monster that lurked beneath my skin.

"I don't suppose you're ready to tell me your thoughts on that matter?" I asked, my gaze softening as I studied him.

The adoration he showed as he raised a single palm to cup my face, capturing my cheek in its strong embrace, nearly took my breath away. "Are you ready to hear them, Little One?" he asked, his brow hitching up ever-so-slightly. He knew the answer, knew the hesitance that rattled around inside my head as I tried to process my own willful ignorance.

"I can't exactly make that decision without knowing what it is you would tell me," I said, causing a sharp bark of laughter to escape Caldris as he released my cheek and placed his hand on the small of my back. He guided me forward, inching me toward the cave entrance as my breath came in deep, shuddering gasps.

I could *feel* the warding, feel the magic Imelda had used to protect the tunnels from prying Fae eyes. It felt like a snap, a rope splitting in two as we stepped across it finally and moved into the protected bubble it had created inside. The noise of the woods outside faded away, leaving me with the distinct impression that we were in another world entirely.

"Is there any information I could provide that you would find acceptable?" he asked as we stepped inside the cave tunnel. The corridor opened up ahead of us, helping us to navigate our way toward the passage with the hole in the floor.

To the home of the Resistance.

All was quiet as we approached it, like the calm before the storm. But it wasn't terror of the cave beasts that struck fear into my chest this time, or fearing that they might be waiting around the corner to strike.

It was the humans who waited within.

"Probably not," I sighed, stopping to stare down into the hole that would take me to the base. That would take me to the baths where Caelum had fucked me for all those people to see, where he and I had slept in our little shared room, and I'd been entirely oblivious about the predator in my bed.

"The members of the Resistance are already in their rooms for the night so that we can all use the kitchen and bathing chamber in peace before we have to deal with the turmoil that will come tomorrow," Caldris said, nudging me forward. "You don't need to worry about an altercation just yet."

I nodded, dropping my body into the hole. I landed on the balls of my feet, crouching down to place a hand on the stone. Caldris followed behind me, leading me through the winding tunnel until we emerged into the cavern that was usually bustling with life.

Like the shadow of a memory, I saw a flash of Imelda leaning over the table, her white eye gleaming against her dark skin and the glowing white crescent moon on her forehead shining in the dim lighting.

I turned to the side, catching a flash of movement—a head of dark hair and golden skin disappearing into one of the tunnels. I furrowed my brow, turning toward the tunnel and looking down the void.

There was nothing to be found.

But I'd have sworn...

I shook it off as Caldris snagged my chin, looking down at me in concern. My mind lay in tattered strips, as if I couldn't differentiate reality from memory. From the torment of the family I'd left behind, come to haunt me until my dying days. "Did you see that?" I asked, turning a shocked stare up to my mate.

He shook his head softly, his brow tensing with concern. As if he could feel the shadows of madness scratching at the edges of my mind, he guided me toward the kitchen. "Food will help," he said, but even he had to know he wasn't convincing anyone with those words.

Food couldn't help the inability to tell the past from the present, or the threat of the future hovering just out of reach, as if I could grasp if I would just reach out.

I wouldn't.

23

ESTRELLA

*A*s it turned out, food couldn't help the games my sanity seemed to want to play, but it didn't hurt, either. With my belly finally full and hunger sated with fresh stew and bread, I allowed Caldris to lead me up and out of the tunnels, to the hot spring above the surface where he'd first touched me, and where I had no doubt he intended to do it again.

I didn't have the energy to try to convince myself I didn't want that. Something feral within me wanted to bathe in his scent until I had the comfort of knowing if I had to face the hatred of the people I'd wanted to join, I would do it with him all over me. With his presence to support me through the confrontation.

Was I...really hoping to have the smell of sex with him on me?

I swallowed. I didn't know what that urge was and where it had come from, but it was decidedly *not* human. "What was that thought?" Caldris asked as we approached the upper level of the tunnels. He held a torch in his hand, depositing it into the holder near the entrance. Outside, steam drifted off the hot spring, engulfing the area in a warmth that nowhere else had this time of year.

"It was nothing," I said, turning my flushed stare away from him. My cheeks felt overheated with something like shame consuming me. I shouldn't be so embarrassed by the things I wanted and the desires this male created in me, not while knowing there was no reason for such shame. He was the epitome of every sin the people who had raised me to believe was wrong. He was also the reason I would never have to exist in a world where virtue was valued over kindness. I couldn't, not ever again.

"Little liar," he murmured, his voice soft as he stepped up behind me. I stood beside the hot spring, staring into the cloudy waters that were warmed by the heat trapped within the mountain. "I can feel your humiliation now. There's no reason for you to be embarrassed about anything when you're with me."

He unclasped my cloak from around my shoulders, guiding the fabric away and tossing it to the side so that it fell in a heap on the ground. The linen he'd brought to dry us off went along with it, and I resisted the urge to turn to meet his stare. I couldn't look him in the eye when I admitted it to him, even knowing he would probably enjoy the knowledge of my possessiveness.

"I was grateful that I will be able to face the masses tomorrow smelling like you," I answered, for once almost resenting the fact that the hot spring would wash me clean.

"Hmm, is that because you want the women to know I'm yours in a way they never could have expected?" he asked, his voice a hum at my back. It sank into my skin, vibrating through me as I tried to decide exactly what it was that drove my irrational desire.

I was still as jealous as I'd been before, but not in the same way. I wasn't concerned that he would have a tryst with any of them, and was confident in the knowledge that he truly was mine and would continue to be for the rest of our mortal lives. I just didn't want other people to covet what was mine, I realized with a shock. It seemed ridiculous, to be so secure in our relationship and what it meant between us, but unable to let go of that sense of *ownership*.

Whatever I was becoming, I couldn't decide if I loved it or hated it.

He stripped off my tunic, my bare skin pebbling with goosebumps. "I don't know," I admitted, pursing my lips as I tried to decide what it was about all of it that set me so on edge.

"Then we'll just have to make sure you smell like me come morning," he said. The moment his hand touched my bare skin and his lips coasted over my neck, I realized one very clear thing.

It didn't fucking matter.

꙳ ꙳ ● ꙳ ꙳

*S*leep never came. In spite of the way Caldris had made love to me in the hot spring, and the way he'd done it all over again when we came back to the room, I couldn't get my mind to quiet. My restlessness drove me off the bedroll we shared in our private little haven, wishing against all hope and possibility that we could stay in the center of the Resistance for an eternity. When I stayed here, there was none of the conflict that existed outside of these walls, as if it was its own private world, removed from the pressures we would face when we crossed the boundary.

A shelter in a world determined to start another war.

I stepped outside of our bedroom, dragging my hand over

the stone as I made my way through the tunnels. None of the Wild Hunt moved to stop me, not bothering to interfere with my descent farther into the mountain itself.

I grabbed a torch off the wall when I came to the part of the tunnels that wasn't used in the nighttime hours, using it to guide me to the library that had become my refuge. I'd resented it at first, feeling like it was a punishment designed to lock me away and put me in a place where I didn't want to exist.

But it had become a haven, and I was thankful for the respite the books had provided. I only wished more women were taught to read, so that more of them could get lost in the stories that had saved me from real life far too often.

I stepped into the room, finding the books left precisely the way I'd left them. Not a thing had been moved, as if it had become a tomb in the absence of the only person who could read them. My heart wept as I considered leaving them and the knowledge they contained behind, knowing there wasn't a single person who could make sense of the history trapped within these walls. Everywhere I looked, I saw Melian lurking at the edges of my vision. Knowing she was gone, knowing she was dead because of my stupidity and stubbornness, all I could think was how horrified she'd be to see these books go to waste once again.

I stepped behind my table, running my fingers over one of the pages in an open book. It seemed like it had been a lifetime since I'd last been here, reading the words on that page.

It had been a matter of weeks. That was the extent of the time that had passed.

Breath rushed out of my lungs as I was stunned silent with the realization of how much had changed in such a short time —with how much *I'd* changed. I wouldn't have been able to fathom accepting my Fae mate only a week ago. Weeks ago, I wouldn't have been able to comprehend the sort of betrayal that Caelum had committed.

And now I was considering accepting our bond?

He appeared as if I'd summoned him; as if he could hear his name in my thoughts. "You're thinking of me. I suppose I'll have to let that reassure me since you once again snuck out of our bed while I slept," he said, leaning his shoulder against the doorway. The position was so similar to what he'd done in the past that my heart skipped in my chest. I reached up, rubbing the ache it caused.

"How do you know I'm thinking of you?" I asked, averting my gaze to the book on the table. I ran a finger over the page, enjoying the rough feel of the paper against my skin. It was comforting in a way. One thing I recognized when all else had been torn away.

"Your emotions have a very distinctive feeling when you're thinking of me. I've come to recognize what it means when that travels down the bond," he answered.

"What does it feel like?" I asked, unable to help myself. I turned the page, running my fingers over the portrait of a Fae female wrapped in shadows. She stepped forward with a single foot, disappearing into a chasm where no light existed. She emerged on the other side intact, stepping out of that darkness as if it was an easy task.

Caelum shifted, making me turn my attention back to him. It was so unusual for him to waste movement on something that served no purpose. His movement was always intentional, working toward a goal as soon as he chose it. "Bitter," he said with a shrug, his lips twisting to the side as he crossed his arms. "Sweet, guilty, so full of love and hatred in equal measure. It feels as if you know you love me, and you fucking hate every moment of it."

I tore my gaze away, dropping it to the side as I sighed and fought back the sting of tears. "Why couldn't you have been human?" I asked, huffing a bitter laugh.

He pushed off the doorway, closing the distance between us and snagging my chin. Turning my gaze back on me, he smiled softly. "The irony of you wishing for me to be human, when we both know that you yourself are not."

"We don't know that," I said, shaking my head even though he refused to release my chin.

"I don't know what you are," Caelum agreed, heaving a sigh. "But whatever it is, it is not human. Humans do not have the abilities you have shown as of late. It is time to accept that you are not who you thought you were."

"But I had human parents. A human brother. How is that possible if I'm not human?" I asked.

"You thought you were human until a week ago. Is it any stretch to think they might be showing the same symptoms as you?" he asked, posing the question I hadn't considered. If my mother had uncontrollable magic, the Mist Guard and Lord Byron's army would guarantee her death.

Gods.

I shoved the thought away. Dwelling on it wouldn't get me to her side any faster, and I would simply have to work to make sure Caldris offered her protection. Whether she came with us or stayed in Nothrek would be determined as we approached Mistfell.

There were more pressing matters, like the fact that I hadn't killed the male I hated more than anything, because I also loved him more than the thought of my own freedom. I didn't know what to do with that.

"What's wrong, Little One?"

"Is it possible for you to...alter my mind? My thoughts and feelings about certain things?" I asked, holding his stare with a firm one of my own. I wanted the answer, knowing he couldn't lie to me, especially not now when I could feel guilt pulsing down the bond if he tried.

"No. I can force your body to do things if I'm very determined, just as I forced you to run when the cave beast attacked us," he admitted, shrugging his shoulders as he reached out and caught my chin in his grasp. "But that is a short term burst of control. I cannot control your thoughts and your feelings in the long run. That's an entirely different kind of power than I possess."

"Can you influence other people in the same way?" I asked, reaching up to grasp his hand with mine. Even just from the brief glimpses of power I'd experienced, of feeling that surge through me and knowing the way it made me feel and behave in the aftermath, I knew I could never have that kind of power over other people.

I couldn't be trusted.

"No. It's exclusive to the mate bond. It's an instinctive aspect related to protecting our mates. Our human mates are not inclined to leave our side in times of danger, wanting to protect us as that aspect of the bond goes both ways. Unfortunately, human mates are far weaker and more likely to be killed, so sometimes we have to send them to safety in the hopes of saving both our lives," he answered. I couldn't imagine the knowledge he must have had from observing the way other Fae behaved with their mates, while waiting centuries for me to be born, only to not be able to reach me when I finally came to be.

"I don't want to leave all this knowledge here," I said, changing the subject when I didn't have anything to add. It was reassuring to know that he wasn't tampering with my emotions, but it was also terrifying to know that it was *me* who was changing.

Not the sum of the actions done to me, but me as a person. Me as a human...or not.

Ugh.

"I promise you, I will do everything in my power to make sure you have the best library at your disposal. The library at the palace of Catancia is filled with more books than you could read in a lifetime, but I will find anything you desire to add to it," he said, his words encouraging. I stepped away from the desk, my fingers falling from the book in slow motion as if it was a goodbye. "We have much more in-depth records on the history of the Fae and the way our world works than the Resistance could ever hope to have."

"I'm sure you do," I said with a little sigh. "But you can't exactly give me a library if you yourself are a victim of Mab."

"I can promise you my mother will allow you unrestricted access to the library in my absence, Little One. She'll treat you as if you are her own child, because as my mate, you'll be the closest thing she's ever had," he said, his voice dropping low as sadness filled it.

I stepped into his chest, wishing I could give him the words that would chase away the melancholy. "I don't want to be there without you," I said, settling for that confession instead. I didn't want to be *anywhere* without him.

"I don't want to exist without you," he said, returning the sentiment and taking it up to another level. I sighed, breathing in his scent, wondering how long I could really hope to delay the inevitable. He knew how I felt, knew how much his soul tormented mine.

"If you challenge Mab, what happens then?" I asked, feeling the moment his body tensed.

"I cannot do that unless we finalize the bond," he said, wrapping his arms around me. He didn't look down at my face, knowing me well enough to know I couldn't look him in the eye for this conversation.

"I know," I said simply.

"I'll challenge the bonds she placed on me, and if I can manage to break free, I could challenge her for the throne to the Shadow Court."

"Would you?" I asked, tilting my head to the side. I didn't know what I should hope for. If I should long for a peaceful life tucked away in the Winter Court? I wanted that peace, but I didn't know that I could leave others to suffer, either. Not the way the world had abandoned me in my time of need, turning a blind eye to the way Byron had tortured me as a young woman.

"I would do anything for you, min asteren. If you would want me to gain my freedom and go with you to some remote place, I would do it. If you wanted me to take you to explore one of the forbidden realms, I would take you there and we would never have to concern ourselves with Mab again."

"That tells me nothing of what you want," I pointed out, laughter making my chest shake.

"I want to see Alfheimr freed from Mab's clutches, and I don't think anyone will have the ability to do it if I do not aid that cause. None have been able to for countless centuries, and it would be difficult to leave my people to suffer at her hands," he admitted, and I felt the way the words felt torn from him. He didn't want to make me feel trapped by his dedication to help his people.

"I wouldn't be able to live with myself if we walked away," I said, turning my eyes up to his. I swallowed, holding his vibrant blue stare.

"What is it, my star?" he asked, touching a hand to the side of my neck.

I nodded, trying to force the determination and *love* I felt to him through the bond. I needed him to know that the words that came next were partially because of my desire to right the wrongs that had been committed, but the decision wasn't made without love in my heart.

"I'll complete the bond."

The stone tunnels felt more oppressive than normal as we made our way toward the common area in the main cavern. I didn't know if the members of the Resistance would be allowed out in the open, but the commotion coming from the end of the tunnel implied far more voices than just those of the Wild Hunt.

I swallowed back my trepidation for what was to come, shifting my wrists to wring my hands in front of me. The shackles rubbed against my skin, the chain clinking and echoing off the tunnel walls. Caldris turned to look at me, staring down at them with all the hatred I knew he felt for the fact that I needed to be treated as if I was a prisoner.

Some days, I nearly asked him to remove them. The Fae Marked already hated me. They'd made that very clear, and I couldn't imagine them despising me and my companionship with my mate anymore than they already did. His gaze darkened, as if he was only a few moments from tearing the shackles off me. After my agreement to accept the bond, it seemed even worse to be chained.

I wasn't his prisoner any longer, but his partner moving

toward freedom at the end of a fight for his freedom. It was a strange conflict to find myself at the center of, to feel as if I was solely responsible for the deaths that would come, but I could also be a part of the peace on the other side.

If I lived long enough, anyway.

All I knew, all that mattered to me, was that, at the end of the day, Caldris and I would live together. We would fight together. We would die together. There was comfort in that. A constant in the unknown.

We stepped into the main cavern and a hush fell over the space as all eyes fell on us. Holt straightened his shoulders, his hand going to the hilt of his sword as he prepared for whatever may come. Skye, the woman who had fed us on the day we'd arrived the first time caught my eyes, her mouth parting in shock as the breath left her lungs. She hurried over as Caldris tensed at my side, then took my hands in hers with a gentleness that made my heart ache.

"Estrella," she said, her eyes filling with tears as she looked around behind me. "Where are the others? Melian? Duncan?"

Moisture gathered in my eyes as my nose burned, and it was all I could do to shake my head sadly. "The Mist Guard..." I trailed off, not needing to finish that sentence as her eyes drifted closed.

She shook her head slowly, heaving out a sigh. "All is truly lost then," she said, and when her eyes opened she turned her attention to Caldris. She stared into his blue eyes with all the hatred any of them would have felt for the Fae, but as her gaze darted over the features of his face and went to his swords strapped across his back, I watched the ragged gasp leave her lungs. "Caelum?" she asked, stumbling back a step. She shook her head, pressing a hand to her mouth. Her gaze dropped to the matching marks on our skin, and to the way they seemed to move in tandem without Caldris's glamour to hide the similarity. The way they pulsed as one, linking us across any distance between us.

There was no mark on Skye's neck, but she reached up to touch herself as if there was.

"She trusted you," Skye said, those eyes filled with accusation as they turned back to me. The hatred she felt for the Fae was nothing compared to the hatred she held for me, thinking I'd betrayed her people in a way that was unforgivable.

"I didn't know," I said, shaking my head sadly as I gave her my truth. We all had our choices to make and our burdens to bear, and knowing that I'd been the reason for Caldris's deception was mine. But I was not responsible for the half-truths he'd spun, for his grand play to work his way into the Resistance.

I hadn't done this knowingly.

She took another step away, moving into the arms of a man who wrapped her in his embrace. He wasn't marked either, but his glare settled on Caldris exclusively. Why was it that women were always so quick to judge other women? Why was it the woman we vilified, even when presented with the truth that the woman had been a victim of the same deception?

Women needed to be better, to do better, because at the end of the day, *every* one of our actions could see us condemned—while men were free to fuck and murder, to steal and lie, and it was all just brushed off as another day under the sun.

Bitterness rose within me, hatred so blinding I couldn't see past the dark tinting the edges of my vision. At the center of the fog, the man guided Skye forward once again until they stood directly in front of us. He stared up into Caldris's face, his eyes glaring in challenge.

Then he struck, reaching for the dagger strapped to

Caldris's thigh with movements as quick as I'd seen from any human. My mate blocked it easily, grabbing the man by the wrist and holding him. His grip was firm, the man's skin pinching beneath his hold, but given what I knew of Caldris's ability to tear a beating heart from a man's chest with his bare hands, his restraint was admirable.

I stared down at his hold, wishing others could see it for the gentleness it was, for the control it took with strength like his. I saw him through a different lens, turning my stare up to his face as he met my eyes sadly.

Something wet splashed against my cheek, startling me as I turned to look at Skye. She wiped her mouth of spit with the back of her hand. "You didn't know? That doesn't seem to have stopped you from making loving eyes at him now. Spare me your fucking lies, you Fae-fucking whore."

I reached up, wiping the spit off my cheek with trembling fingers. I reached forward, grasping her by the shirt and using it to clean my skin of the traces of her abuse. I said not a word, not bothering to waste my breath as she watched me pointedly, waiting for the response that I would not give.

"Do you have nothing to say for yourself?" she asked, pulling her shirt out of my grasp and crossing her arms over her chest.

"I encountered less judgment from the man who caned me when I failed to please him," I said simply, keeping my expression blank. "But he taught me one valuable lesson. There is nothing I can say to lessen your hatred, because it exists within you. It is not about me at all, but about you as a person and who you will never be."

"Am I supposed to strive to be like you? To stand there and allow myself to be his pet?" she asked, leaning into the side of the man next to her as Caldris finally released him. My mate kept quiet, not offering me a word of defense.

I was glad for it, knowing that, if I was truly to be an equal at his side, then there were some battles I needed to be able to fight for myself. "I would never tell you to be like me. I would advise you to find love in your heart, to find patience and understanding, even if I am incapable of it myself. Because as we've stood here having this worthless conversation that I will not bother to remember in a few days' time, I've already imagined a dozen different ways I could kill you," I said, watching as her eyes rounded with shock. She swallowed, glancing at Caldris out of the corner of her eye. "I do not need the God of the Dead to fight my battles with a human woman; I would do it myself. So no, Skye. Don't be like me. Be better than me."

"The God of the...." she trailed off, her eyes flashing back to Caldris as she stumbled back out of the man's hold. It wasn't surprising that those of the Resistance didn't recognize him. The portraits of him were hidden away in the library of the lower level, where none seemed to go because of their inability to read.

"Do come visit us in Alfheimr, Skye! *Caldris* and I would love to repay the kindness you've shown us during our time here," I called as she disappeared into the watching crowd. It swallowed her whole, taking her as far away from the threat of the God and his violent mate as she could manage.

"I will make sure you regret this one day," the man said to Caldris, turning his attention back to him once Skye was gone from view.

Caldris grunted, pursing his lips thoughtfully as he stared down at the man. There was nothing hostile in his expression, only a resigned truth. "Your lifespan is the blink of an eye. I will rest my head tonight, and by the time I think of you again, you'll already be dead."

The man's mouth snapped closed. It was not easy to be faced with the reality of our own mortality, with the fact that while we could die easily, the Fae had lived for countless centuries. Many of them would continue to live centuries more, and the Primordials—who some of them were the very children of—had been alive before the dawn of creation.

"We intend to leave you in peace when we depart. There is no reason that our relationship needs to extend beyond this day," I said, taking the man's attention off of Caldris.

Caelum. The more I reached out to him with an open heart, the more I longed to separate the man I loved from the legend who controlled the dead. Even if only in my own mind.

"You are taking some of us from our home by force. We will never part as anything but enemies," the man said, his glare unsettling me as he turned his face down to the shackles on my wrists. "How can you wear those? How can you willingly stand beside someone who would treat you as a prisoner?"

"Because even though I may be shackled, he's offered me more freedom than any of the humans in my past have," I said, raising an eyebrow at him. Even if Melian had wanted to promise me a life where I'd be free to make my choices, I would have been trapped within the walls of the Resistance.

Freedom of will came within a cage in Nothrek.

Caelum would do whatever he had to do to make sure that I could roam freely through Alfheimr, and that kind of freedom was something that I would never be able to find in the human realm.

My mate grunted, drawing the man's attention back to him with a startled look. "Where is the witch?" he asked, looking over the other man's head for a sign of the breathtaking woman with the hair that glowed like moonlight.

"I am here, Caldris," she said, stepping out from the group of Fae Marked who surrounded her. She clasped her hands in front of her, hanging her head low as she moved through the crowd that parted for her. Whether it was out of respect or hatred, I couldn't tell, but the emotion that clogged my throat as I realized the truth must have only been a hint of the betrayal they felt.

"You knew who he was all along, didn't you?" I asked when she finally stopped before us, her moonlit-night gaze finding mine and holding it.

"I did," she agreed, nodding thoughtfully. "We've met before, a very long time ago. The Lunar Witches are close with his mother, Twyla, as she is the Goddess of the Moon." She reached out, touching her fingers to mine and raising them so that she could inspect the darkness that tainted my skin. Hers were stained with black, stars glimmering as if she'd dipped them into the night sky itself and managed to trap them within her skin. All too similar to mine, but the stars on mine were far subtler, as if the shadows of the night had been far more prevalent on the evening I touched the sky. "What is this?" she asked, turning my hand over in her grip.

"We aren't sure; there must be something in my lineage—"

"You are a child of the dark. Whatever is in your lineage must have an association with that magic for you to bear this mark. Your mate is aware of that," she said, turning a glare his way as if she could force him to wither on the spot with only a look.

"Yes," he said, drawing out the word as if it was an admission in itself. "But that could be any manner of creature."

"It could, and the markings are not consistent. Two siblings with the same lineage could have entirely different manifestations. This is only one symptom," she said, dropping my hand to my side. "You were looking for me. What is it you require?"

"When we spoke before, you confirmed that Mab's

daughter was brought here after the construction of the Veil. I have to take her back to Alfheimr with me," Caldris said, and Imelda squeezed her eyes closed.

"And if I am unable to provide you with the information you seek?" she asked, her fingers twitching at her sides. I could almost feel the pulse of power as she maneuvered her hands carefully, drawing a subtle pattern on her thigh.

I reached out, stilling the hand that had performed what I could only imagine was the beginning of some kind of spell. Whether it was to defend herself or attack I couldn't be sure, but she glanced down at my hand that held hers and twisted her head to the side, her brow furrowing as she studied me.

"I will burn what remains of the Resistance to the ground to find her. The order came from Mab herself, and you know as well as any that I am bound to complete that order. No matter what it takes, Imelda," Caldris explained, making Imelda heave a sigh.

She nodded once as I released her, turning to look over her shoulder. "Fallon," she called, summoning a woman forward. I recognized her from the common cavern that first night we'd arrived in the tunnels and seen her in passing for a few brief moments in the time we'd spent here afterwards. She was a few years older than I, her dark hair gleaming as it hung down past her shoulders. One side was twisted into two braids that pulled away from her face and clung to her skull, revealing the deep line of a single scar that started at the center of her forehead and slashed through her eyebrow. It reappeared on her cheek, fading into the line of her jaw. Her eyes were wide-set and hazel, dark compared to her pale skin. Imelda put a hand on each of the woman's shoulders, pulling her forward to stand before her.

"This is her?" Caldris asked, tilting his head to the side as he studied her, perhaps searching for any hint of recognition of his tormentor's bloodline within her. I wasn't certain how lineage worked with reincarnation; how someone could still be Mab's daughter after centuries of living and dying and being reborn to new parents. That kind of power had to be etched upon our souls, carrying through our lives in some way.

"I don't know," Imelda admitted, her fingers grasping Fallon more tightly. Fallon's lips turned down into a frown, whatever truth Imelda planned to share something she wasn't entirely aware of.

"What do you mean you don't know?" Caldris asked, his irritation leaking into his voice as he studied the witch.

"There were two children, two girls brought to us for protection the night the Veil was formed. Fallon is one of them and could very well be the daughter you seek," Imelda admitted, hanging her head.

Caldris stilled at my side, his body tensing with the words Imelda spoke. I only knew he'd believed Mab's daughter to be with the Resistance because it was the entire reason for his deception and infiltrating their numbers in the first place. What could possibly interest the witches in the way Mab's daughter could? "Two children?" he asked, tipping his head to the side as he considered the words. His shock was evident in the silence that followed.

I cleared my throat, breaking it. "How do you know? That was lifetimes ago." I studied the woman standing in front of me. She stared back at me, as interested in me as I was in her.

"She bears the witch's mark," Imelda said, reaching down to take Fallon's hand in hers. She raised it, showing me the white crescent moon that appeared to be burned into Fallon's skin—a magical brand.

"It is a mark that each clan of witches has the ability to place upon the souls of the people they are tasked with protecting," Caldris explained, his body remaining tight at my side. "It is not done often, but each clan can only produce the one mark. So the girls would both share the same one, if what Imelda says is true. If the girls were both in the Void at the same time, there would be no telling which was which by the time they were reborn."

"But where is the other girl?" I asked, looking from him to Imelda. Our ability to return to Alfheimr, to stop in Catancia and complete our bond before we could rally against Mab, depended on him finding her daughter to complete his duty to her.

"I do not know," Imelda said with a sigh. She pursed her lips, as if the truth pained her as much as it pained us to hear it. "She was taken from the Resistance by her guardian three lifetimes ago. He must have shielded her from view and disguised her witch's mark. We've tried to find her but have been unsuccessful. She could be anywhere by now."

Caldris groaned, dropping his head forward. "The other girl. What was she that was so significant she needed protecting? Was she the child of one of Mab's enemies?"

"I don't know that either. That information was guarded by the elders. We knew that one of them was the child of Mab and that someone would come for her one day, but only the elders know the truth of the other and what her purpose will be in all of this," Imelda answered, turning her attention to where the Wild Hunt watched from the sides of the cavern.

"Then bring me your elders."

"One is dead at the hands of the other. The other," she said, her gaze connecting with Caldris's, "is the guardian who stole the other child."

"Of course it was," Caldris said, his anger palpable as it filled the cavern surrounding us. "You had better hope she is Mab's daughter and not the mystery being, for all our sakes.

Mab will show you the meaning of pain if she thinks you have some knowledge of her daughter and do not share it. We leave in an hour. Both of you take the time to say your goodbyes and pack your belongings," Caldris said, the order resonating between them. Imelda nodded, the motion followed by Fallon's as she moved to an older couple waiting on the sidelines.

Her family, I realized.

Fallon glared back at Caldris, an odd sort of resignation in her gaze. Whatever she did or didn't know about herself, it was clear that she'd always known the day would come when she would need to leave her human family behind. Our eyes met briefly, nothing but a fleeting moment of connection that seemed to arc between us. It was over as quickly as it began, with Fallon tearing her eyes away from mine and stepping into her father's embrace.

I squeezed my eyes closed, heartache pulsing through me. I knew what it was to leave our family behind, to be forced to go on a journey that we neither chose or wanted.

It was misery, and I was a part of it now.

*T*he Fae Marked had already been shuffled out through the tunnels, led to the surface so they could be loaded into carts and undoubtedly shackled when they reached the surface. I appreciated that Holt and the Wild Hunt spared their friends and family from the sight of them in chains before they left.

I moved through the passage toward the surface, unable to function with the knowledge that had been thrown at me so quickly. Imelda had known the truth, and as she walked alongside me while Holt and Caldris discussed their plans for the coming days, I didn't know if I should be appalled by that. "Why didn't you warn anyone?" I asked her, falling into step with her as she maneuvered away from Fallon.

I had no doubt the other woman would feel the same, that she'd long to know why someone she appeared to be very close with hadn't moved to protect her in the slightest.

"I chose peace over knowledge," Imelda said, her voice soft as it carried between us. The end of the tunnels loomed up ahead, and the first riders of the Wild Hunt stepped out into the winter sunshine to leave the center of the Resistance behind us. There was too much at stake to think of it as a good thing, the missed opportunities for alliances making something inside of me ache.

I wished that we could all be united in our quest to right the wrongs of the world, to find a way to ally us all in our common goals. As someone who had only recently come to terms with all this, it didn't seem likely that it would happen. My heart hadn't been filled with as much hatred, not with the way I'd despised the Lord of my village and the people who'd enabled him to remain in power.

"There was *nothing* I could have done that would have stopped Caldris from taking the Fae Marked to Alfheimr. Even if I'd revealed his identity the moment I laid eyes on him, it would have been pointless. All it would have achieved was death. I chose to hope for peace, and that I could negotiate for the lives of the humans who did not need to die needlessly. I chose to save what lives I could, in the face of a terrible choice resting upon my shoulders," she explained.

I nodded, understanding taking over my features. I didn't want to understand that choice, or that sometimes the greater good meant doing things that we would have once thought were unimaginable. But I related far too much to interrogate her until she was forced to relent that she'd made the wrong decision.

I didn't think she had.

If Imelda had revealed his identity, I would have learned the truth of who he was before he ever touched me. I wouldn't have known the intimacy of having him moving inside me, and I would have been far less likely to give in to that aspect of our relationship. It was easy to accept him inside me when I did hate him, because he'd already been there, and he'd already had that part of me.

The sun shone off Caelum's head as he stepped out into

the light. The gleaming silver of his hair was the color of iced-over snow, of the icicles as they hung from the eves of homes in Mistfell during winter.

I followed behind him, letting him turn around to guide me down to the ground from the tunnel entrance. In spite of knowing I could handle it, I enjoyed the feeling of his helping hands on mine. He set me down a few feet away from the entrance, lowering me down his body smoothly while I smiled up at him. Not so long ago, I would have fought him for the way he seemed determined to take care of me. It was ridiculous to think of doing that now, knowing that his care came from a place of love. That it wasn't a statement of his belief that I was incapable of doing things for myself.

It was just him. Loving me. "I love you, min asteren," he said, confirming the thoughts that he must have seen written on my face.

"And I love you, Caelum," I said, and that part of me who had hated to admit such things because they felt like a weakness finally withered and died. She shriveled up inside of me, abandoning me to the knowing that I could do this. That I could trust someone with my heart and know that it would be safe.

"Imelda? What is it?" a woman asked, and I turned to find Fallon leaning over Imelda where she'd hunched over with her hands on her knees. The black fabric of her dress was bunched in her fists, her mismatched eyes glazed in a way that I wouldn't have thought was possible.

Caldris followed my gaze, taking a step toward her even as we both cursed the interruption to what must have been an incredible moment for him. To have me acknowledge my feelings so openly, I didn't think I'd ever done that.

Imelda looked up from the ground, that eerie stare meeting mine in a shock that sent pain rippling through me.

She stood straight, marching toward me and pushing past Caldris to grab my hand in hers. She lifted it, staring at the side of my palm as I tugged away from her. "What are you doing?" I asked, pulling harder. Her grip remained like a vice, clinging to me as she stared down at my bare skin.

"Imelda, don't—" Caldris said, but she ignored the warning in his tone.

She muttered something beneath her breath, an incantation in the Old Tongue as I tried to translate the words quickly enough to process them. *La solis ne lunat.*

By the light of the moon.

"What are you doing? That hurts!" I repeated, yanking my hand away as a searing pain lit my skin. I turned my eyes to Caldris, finding him staring down at my hand with something akin to horror on his face.

But I couldn't see past the blinding pain, past what was worse than any of the moments when iron had touched my skin. Imelda twisted my hand in her grip, showing me the place where my skin burned and fell to the snow at my feet in ashes. "Revealing your truth," she said, her eyes sad as a crescent moon appeared on my hand.

Fallon stepped up beside us as if she were in a daze, placing her hand next to mine and staring down at the marks on our skin. At the identical moons that marked us as protected by the lunar clan of witches.

I sucked in a breath, snatching my hand away from them both to cradle it to my chest. The smell of burning flesh tickled my nose, easing when Caldris took my hand in his and brushed a cool winter breeze along my skin.

Ending the suffering. Ending the magical branding that was permanently etched on my body.

"How could you not have known this before?" Caldris asked Imelda. "How did you not see it?"

"The mountain cut me off from the moonlight, and the warding I've placed on the tunnels makes it difficult to see through magic that mimics my own, since it covers everything. As soon as we stepped outside, I could see where lunar magic clung to her skin. Where is your guardian, Estrella?" Imelda asked, making me turn a stunned stare up to Caldris.

"I don't have one," I said, shaking my head. "I don't—" My denial cut off, leaving me with nothing but the twisted sense of horror that I would never be able to erase.

All the secrets he'd kept. All the things he'd known and hid from me—all his vague nonsensical statements. The things he swore he would tell me, but had never had the chance.

Brann.

"Where is he?!" Imelda demanded, and I couldn't decide if she wished she could cause his death or if she wanted him for some other purpose.

"He's dead," I croaked, turning my stare up to my mate. "The Wild Hunt killed him when he tried to kill me." I held Caelum's stare. I'd never admitted that part to him outright, but I doubted he didn't know it already from conversations with the riders of the Wild Hunt.

What Brann had tried to do was no secret, but the way Caelum's gaze hardened and a cold wind swept through the woods, I knew he hadn't been aware.

"What does this mean? I can't be the other child. That's... impossible," I said, turning back to Imelda and trying to ignore the raging fury pulsing off of Caelum.

"It means that one of you is the child of Mab, and the other is something else. Who was he to you? Who did you believe him to be?" Imelda asked, and the genuine concern in her eyes made me believe that she had been close to my brother once.

"My brother," I said, heaving out a sigh. "He told me he was my brother, but he wasn't, was he?" Trying to wrap my head around the new truth, I cradled my hand closer to my chest, blinking back the tears that came with not knowing what I was. Had he been keeping me from Alfheimr so desperately because he'd known I was the daughter of Mab? Or because I was some other kind of monster from the depths of Faerie?

"He told me I could never go to Alfheimr," I said, stepping forward into Caelum's embrace. He wrapped his arms around me, pulling me closer to his chest. "He knew something, but I never pushed to know the truth. He said there was nothing waiting for me in Alfheimr but darkness and torment."

Caelum stilled, the meaning of those words crashing over both of us. If I was Mab's daughter, I was the child of the person who had tormented my mate for centuries. I was the offspring of the Queen of Air and Darkness.

Gods.

I tugged away from him, trying to put distance between us. If it were true, I was the daughter of the woman who had imprisoned him for centuries and wrapped snakes around his heart to keep him obedient.

"We don't know anything for sure yet," Caelum said, squeezing me tighter and preventing me from stepping away, but I felt the look he exchanged with Imelda.

I'd summoned darkness when I was angry. I'd seen a vision of a bird reincarnated into a snake when I touched it, and there was a snake wrapped around my mate's heart courtesy of Mab. "If he was my guardian, does that mean he was an elder witch? Can witches even *be* male?" I asked, considering the reality that my brother wasn't human. He wasn't my brother.

But I'd grown up alongside him. I had memories of him being a child at my side.

How was that possible?

"It's less common, but entirely possible. Some of the strongest witches are male because of the way magic manifests. If your brother was your guardian, he was one of the most powerful witches I knew. That was why Twyla named him to the Council as one of the Lunar Elders," she explained, bowing her head out of respect.

"Was his name even Brann?" I asked, sorrow coming in a torrent—a wave crashing over me. I hadn't known Caelum's real name, but to think that I'd gone through my entire life without knowing my brother was an entirely different kind of pain.

"We knew him as Brander," Imelda said, and something inside me eased. It may not have been the same name, but it was similar enough that I felt like I'd still had a piece of him. "He loved you. In all your lives, he stood beside both of you and was your greatest protector until the day he took you away."

"He couldn't have loved me very much if he left me behind," Fallon said, her glare settling on my face. It lacked the heat I would have expected from someone who was interested in making a grudge personal, feeling more like the attention of a woman who felt at odds with herself.

Was she supposed to mourn the loss of someone she didn't even remember?

As our stares held, I felt an odd sort of kinship with her. Something moved between us, like the interwoven strands of fate connected our destinies.

"The two of you lived side by side for ten lives, existing in these tunnels, and you were the best of friends," Imelda said, studying the way we stared at one another.

I turned back to face them, watching with a furrowed brow as Imelda stepped forward and touched her hand to my shoulder. "This was your home," she repeated, confirming the thoughts in my head. "For most of your lives, anyway. I don't know where or who you've been since Brander took you from us, but I knew you then."

"I don't know what to do with all of this," I said, rubbing a hand over the new moon burned into my skin. "Who am I?"

My gaze met Caelum's gaze, his blue eyes softening as he reached down and cupped my cheek. I couldn't imagine he wanted to even look at me ever again—given what I could be.

What we probably both suspected me to be.

"We'll figure it out. Together," he said, and I leaned forward to rest my forehead against his chest, letting him comfort me for just a moment before we moved on to the next phase in our lives. Before we continued on our journey to Alfheimr, all while suspecting that I was the very person he needed to return to Mab.

My step-brother.

I shuddered.

Fucking Gods.

*E*ven sitting beside me, it felt as if there were oceans separating us. Estrella had been quiet since Imelda had revealed that my mate was one of the two children hidden by the lunar witches.

Holt and I had suspected that Estrella might be the daughter of Mab since that night in Black Water when she'd first summoned the darkness and extinguished the flames of hatred. The knowledge that there was just as much of a chance that she was the lost Princess of the Shadow Court as there was that she might be something else...I didn't know how to feel about it.

It would make her the daughter of my greatest enemy, and the stepsister I'd never wanted. What was I supposed to do with that knowledge?

I wished I could reach over to her, pull her into my embrace and not feel the bitter void that lingered between us. If she was Mab's daughter, I would have to return her to the Shadow Court. Our only hope of salvation would come in her acceptance of our bond, in making me strong enough to defy the Queen of Air and Darkness herself.

But would Estrella still accept me? Even suspecting the new chasm that would threaten to keep us apart?

"Do you hate me?" Estrella whispered, her voice too low for the rest of the Wild Hunt to hear. We lingered around the fire, huddled close atop the blanket we'd claimed for ourselves as a few of the others set up the tent for us to sleep in.

"Why would I hate you, *min asteren*?" I asked, turning to look down at her. My voice sounded harsher than I wanted it to, my emotions clogging my throat. I couldn't bear the thought of losing her; not when we'd come so far.

I wouldn't allow Mab to take her from me, too.

"Because I'm her daughter," she said, scoffing as she flopped back against the blanket. She stared at the stars above, moisture gathering in her eyes as her bottom lip trembled briefly. "I spoke to Fallon earlier today. She said she's shown no signs of magic at all."

"That does not mean she doesn't have any," I reminded her. Only a few days prior, Estrella herself had never exhibited any signs of magic outside of the *Viniculum* that marked her as mine.

Estrella turned her head to the side, tearing her eyes off the moonlit sky to finally meet mine. "It doesn't, but am I really supposed to believe it is a mere coincidence I manifested a vision of a snake when Mab herself wrapped serpents around your heart to control you?"

"There could be any number of reasons—"

"Cut the bullshit," Estrella snapped, turning her glare away from me once again. "We both know what I am. It's why even now sitting beside me, you've not moved to touch me. You're keeping your distance because you're disgusted to think your mate is the daughter of that vile woman. You thought you knew me so well, and yet here I am! The spawn of the greatest evil Faerie has ever known."

"Even if you are her child, you are not like her. You were not raised by her in any of your lives, and you've had centuries of history to form you into a woman who cares more about being kind and fair than anyone I've ever known," I said, lying down beside her. My pinky finger brushed against hers, reminding me far too much of that first day I'd laid eyes upon her in the barn when she'd been hiding for the night. "There is a gentleness in you that has not existed inside Mab for countless centuries, if it ever did at all. That is not something that can come from your lineage."

"And what of everything else that is inside of me? What about the thirst for blood and revenge? What of my desire to see all those who underestimated me kneeling before me? Is that the part of me that is *kind*?" Estrella asked, her green eyes meeting mine. The twinkle of stars shone from behind the moss color of her irises, the edges bleeding to the purple of a night sky that bordered on black. "Or is the part of me that suspects the world would be so peaceful if there were no people to taint it and it returned to the nothing from whence it came?"

"Those parts of you do not come from Mab, Little One," I said, my eyes going soft as I studied her. She was so determined to hate herself, and to bear the weight of her need to be liked by everyone around her. "They come from me. They are all the worst parts of me that you provide balance to."

"How do you bear it?" she asked, her voice nothing but a low murmur.

"Bear what?" I asked, knowing she could be speaking of a great many things. Knowing Estrella for her own self-hatred, I suspected she would say something along the lines of a question of how I could stand to look at her.

But that was not what came out of her mouth.

"The thirst for power. The knowledge that you could be so

much more than they believe you to be, if you only let that monster within you loose. How do you control your strength with such finesse, when we both know you could kill a man with a snap of your fingers?" she asked.

Estrella might not have been comfortable with her title in formal settings, but she was born with the need to rise. If Lord Byron had been a halfway decent man, she'd probably have embraced her position as his wife and been the Lady of Mistfell.

But that kind of power would never be enough for my mate. She would be submissive to no man in the end, and would settle for nothing less than an equal at her side.

"First, you must learn to channel your power before you can worry about controlling it. Come," I said, pushing to my feet and holding out a hand for her. The Wild Hunt had long since finished assembling our tent, but I knew Estrella well enough to know she would not fall asleep anytime soon.

She wore her restlessness on her sleeve for all to see, and she confirmed as much when she took my hand and allowed me to pull her to her feet.

Exhaustion waited for her on the other side of training with me. All she had to do was walk willingly into it.

ESTRELLA

The trees taunted me, swaying in the cool breeze. They seemed to whisper in my ear, reminding me that they could dance in the winter breeze far easier than I could channel it into my own damn hands.

"This is a waste of fucking time," I growled, throwing my arms down in frustration. No matter what I did, no matter how I twisted my body and tried to force my will to focus on the cold air I tried to craft within my hands, nothing came from it. I couldn't grasp anything but the darkness pulsing in my fingertips, and couldn't see past it to summon the *Viniculum* to channel Caldris's power.

"You can do it. You just need to be patient," Caldris said, as gentle as he was every sleepless night that he dragged me from our tent to practice.

"Is it because I'm not human?" I asked, staring at him. If I was Mab's daughter, then I was Fae. I didn't have the ears, and had never channeled the magic of nature until the moment he'd marked me when the Veil fell, but there was something decidedly inhuman within me, pacing under my skin.

"We don't know anything yet," he said, his face shutting

down as it had for the remainder of the day when I'd tried to ask any questions about what it would mean for me.

For us.

"How many humans do you know who can turn a dead fucking bird into a living snake?" I asked, tossing a hand onto my hip and glaring at him. He seemed determined to live in denial, never admitting to the glaring similarity to Mab. Nausea swirled in my gut, my body reacting to the knowledge Caldris refused to share.

"Not many," he said, pinching his nose between his fingers. "But you won't be *not* human until you touch the land of Faerie—at least that's what we suspect." The new information shocked me, silencing me as I processed that confession. I'd *change* when I got to Alfheimr?

"And what of the other child? Were there any rumors of another girl who went missing?" I asked, focusing on the things that would matter. If I were to change when we arrived in Alfheimr, I would have little control over that. The instinct to cling to what remained of my humanity crashed over me. I'd lived my entire life, *lives*, believing myself to be a human girl. Simply letting go of that was not so easily achieved.

"It was centuries ago, min asteren. I haven't got a damn clue. I can ask around when we get back to Alfheimr, but by then I suspect we'll have more answers. Your magic is more and more determined to make itself known. There will come a time when it gives us the information we need to decide what you are," he explained, stepping forward and taking my hands in his.

"I understand that you want me to be able to channel your magic to protect myself, but maybe what we need to focus on is the fact that I have magic of my own. Maybe mine is repressed and wants to be let out, but it's blocking everything else from escaping because it's been lying dormant for so long.

Maybe in the past when your *Viniculum* answered, it was because this part of me hadn't awakened."

"I don't think it is wise to encourage your magic to surface," Caldris said, turning to give me his back. "If you aren't trying to control it, there is no telling what it might do."

"Do you believe I'm Mab's daughter?" I asked, noting the hesitance he'd shown with being near me since the discovery. He hadn't tried to get me into the tent to seduce me before we fell asleep, as if he couldn't quite grasp the idea of bedding me anymore.

"I don't know what to believe. Your magic has some similarities to hers, but it also manifests in different ways. I've never known Mab to reincarnate a creature immediately," he said, but the end of the statement hung unspoken between us.

"She seems far more concerned with killing things than bringing them back to life," I said, flinching away from the reality of who she was.

"That is also true," he said, sighing as he relented. "I can't say that you aren't her daughter, but I'm also not confident in saying you are. Either way, we should proceed like we haven't got a clue where your magic comes from or what it is capable of, which means erring on the side of caution." I nodded, letting him raise my hands and encourage me to start all over again.

Even though I knew it wouldn't work, even though I felt it inside of me that I was meant to release some of my own magic before it would let me touch his. Sometimes, love meant humoring someone, even when they were wrong.

I raised my hands in front of me, fixating on that pulsing, twisted darkness that rose up immediately. Taking a deep breath of it into my lungs, I closed my eyes to shut out the blackness surrounding me. Only the light of Caelum's hair and blue eyes stood out in stark contradiction, but somehow the darkness wasn't enough anymore.

It wasn't dark enough to hide the shadows cast by the light of the moon. It wasn't dark enough to hide the very essence of the trees surrounding me, filling the land as if it were overflowing, as if it needed to be taken back to the place where the world was quiet.

My hands thrummed with that dark magic, the urge to bring the shadows to the forefront of my vision overwhelming, but I swallowed against it, holding that part within me and shoving it down into that pit that rested inside my belly, into the hollow that craved oblivion.

Opening my eyes, I looked at the snow-covered branches over Caldris's head, raising my arm and considering what it would feel like if it fell on my head. How the cold would sink into my skin, tickling the back of my neck where my cloak gathered and trapping it there until it sent a shiver through me.

Imagining that cold on the back of my neck, I visualized the golden strand of fate that lingered between us, wrapping cautious fingers around it. Caldris flinched forward, wiping the surprise off his face as he shook his head. Every time I grasped the bond within my hands, each time I turned it into something tangible, he gave me more and more confirmation that it was not the norm to do so.

Just another strike against me—another way that I was strange even to the Fae God who had existed for so long and probably thought he'd seen everything. He was the grandson of a Primordial, and yet my actions mystified him as much as they did me.

I wrapped the thread of the bond around my hand, pulling it taut even as Caldris grimaced like it pained him. The bond could stretch across realms. It could stretch across mountains and the sea and still connect us, but for some reason it pained him when I took too much of it toward me.

I fixated on that cold. On the winter breeze that had blasted over my spine when he saw my scars for the first time. On the way he'd summoned the first snow in his fit of rage.

I would *not* be helpless when the war came. I would *not* rely on him to protect me when battles raged through the land. A funnel of wind appeared in my hand, swirling above my skin like a miniature storm. It caught the snow from the branches hanging over our heads, pulling it down into the orbit of the winds I created.

The snow disappeared into the void formed on my palm at the center of the tempest. Caldris stepped forward, a smile on his face that faded ever so slightly when he stopped in front of me. Grasping my hands in his, holding them from the bottom and supporting them as he studied the swirling, raging storm I held in my palms, he met my eyes with a bright smile.

"It feels like winter," he said, but something lingered unspoken. Winter, tainted by whatever made the snow disappear.

The winds fizzled out under his attention, the storm disappearing as quickly as it had come. Disappointment flashed through me that my moment of success had been so short-lived, while in the wake of the magic, my body sagged with exhaustion.

"Magic always has a cost," Caldris said, dropping one of his hands from mine and reaching up to cup my cheek. "Which is why you take it slow. Build up the resistance to what it takes from you and strengthen it like a muscle. You must be stronger than the magic you call to you, otherwise the cost could be your life. Do you understand?" he asked, and I swallowed back my trepidation.

No wonder he worried so much about me taking too much

from the magic we didn't understand, from the source that I seemed to be able to tap into without even being aware I was doing it.

The consequences could be catastrophic.

"Will that still be the case if I become Fae?" I asked, tilting my head to the side and considering him. I didn't want to change into the very thing I'd hated so much only weeks before, but I'd seen the worst of humanity as well. Evil existed everywhere—in every species and creature. Were humans really any better?

I truly had to wonder about the cost of magic as a Fae. Caldris was stronger than I could imagine, his magic like something that could only exist between the pages of a book. What was the cost of power like that?

"Yes, but your body will be able to withstand more. When your body changes to match whatever your soul already knows, there will be more for the magic to feed from before it becomes too much. As it stands, it is very possible that what you are is already draining from your body just to exist," he said, dropping his hand from my cheek. "Your lives have always been short. Even for a human lifespan. It would make sense if it was because your soul was never meant to be trapped within a human body."

"But we reincarnated. If we aren't human, why would we have done that in the first place?"

"According to our records, the way the witches severed the realms made anyone on this side of the Veil human and tied them to Nothrek. Creatures and Fae alike. Without the magic of Faerie to refill the magic we all draw from, there was nothing to make them anything more than human. The soul became trapped in the cycle of reincarnation because of it," he said, glancing down at my hands.

He stepped back, the momentary reprieve he'd given me

over as his gaze hardened. "Again," he barked, the command lashing through me. Gone was the gentle and caring mate who would guide me slowly through the tremulous waters of embracing what I was meant to be as his equal.

This was the Fae male who commanded armies for an evil Queen, and who expected nothing but the best from the woman who would stand at his side in the coming conflict.

I sighed, my exhaustion washing over me as I raised my hands a little higher and shut my eyes to the harsh expression on his face.

And I tried again.

Fallon grabbed my hand, tugging me away from Caldris's side the next night and toward the blanket she would share with Imelda beside the fire while they waited for their tent to be prepared. She didn't speak a word as she laced her arm through mine, ignoring the male glaring at the back of her head.

She guided me down to the blanket, sandwiching me between Imelda and herself. They closed ranks, surrounding me in the warmth of something that shouldn't have felt familiar. I barely knew the women to either side of me, but there was comfort in feeling the press of them against me.

"What are you up to?" I asked, watching as Fallon got comfortable. She kicked her feet out in front of herself, crossing her legs at the ankles so that the deep brown leather of her pants rubbed with the slightest creak as her boots hung off the blanket.

"What makes you think I'm up to anything?" she asked, leaning back onto her elbows. Her tunic covered her arms, her cloak bunched up behind her back as it draped over her shoulders and hung to the blanket beneath her. She stared up at the night sky, her eyes darting over all the constellations that burned above.

"You're always up to something," Imelda inserted, twisting her lips to the side as she glanced toward Fallon out of the corner of her eye. "Which Huntsman are you hoping to snare for the night? I suppose I'll need to sleep out here."

"You could always join us," Fallon said, and there was no artiface in her voice as she spoke the words. They spoke of one-night stands and the freedom to choose a bed partner for the night as if it came without consequences or judgment. "I'm sure *the* Huntsman would be more than happy to oblige you."

"What Huntsman?" I asked, snapping my head toward Fallon.

"Don't you dare pollute her head with your grand notions of a romance. The Wild Hunt are abominations of nature. I would sooner die than allow him to come anywhere near me," Imelda argued, her nostrils flaring with the slightest irritation.

I'd clearly missed something.

"There doesn't need to be romance involved for you to sit on his face, Imelda. God's sake," Fallon said, and she burst into laughter at the way I leveled an incredulous stare at her. I was no virgin. In fact, Caldris was determined to expose me to all manner of sexual activities, and I was far from against them. I didn't think I'd ever heard a woman speak of such things so openly, without any regard for the members of the Wild Hunt who snapped to attention and turned to look at her. I flushed, wondering what it would be like to do the very thing she spoke of. I'd felt Caldris's mouth, but I'd never been the one in charge.

I felt the moment his attention snapped back to me as he spoke to Holt, pointedly ignoring the heated brand of his stare. We were speaking only just enough to get through the day and would likely go to sleep in silence when our tent was ready.

Sitting on his face was the last thing on my mind when I could barely stand to look at him without feeling guilt over my potential lineage and what that would mean for our bond.

Fallon smiled roguishly at the riders of the Wild Hunt, leaning her weight into the elbow closest to me and giving a playful finger wave.

"A few nights without a male companion would not kill you, you know," Imelda said, but her voice shook with amusement.

"You're silent when you sleep. It is absolutely exhausting," Fallon said.

"Would you like me to snore?" Imelda asked, leaning forward to stare down at her charge with a smile curving her full lips.

"Are you really complaining about something being exhausting when you're meant to be sleeping?" I asked, regarding the hazel-eyed woman at my side with a confused stare.

"I like to fall asleep naturally after I've exhausted myself physically, not lie down and stare at the ceiling. It's dreadfully boring," Fallon said.

"Hence looking for a bed partner for the night..." I said, my voice trailing off.

"There are other ways to tire ourselves out, but I think we would all admit that a skilled bed partner is the most fun," she said with a laugh. She turned her hazel stare to one of the riders, quirking up a brow. He scurried off quickly, leaving Fallon to drop back dramatically. "No one wants to touch me when there's a chance I could be the daughter of that miserable queen."

"You'll live," Imelda said, her laughter making her chest shake. "I'll sing you to sleep."

"Please don't," Fallon protested, her wince showing just what she thought of Imelda's singing. "I'd rather you regale me with tales of what you intend to do to the Huntsman when you stop being so stubborn."

"He's dead, Fallon," Imelda said, rolling her eyes. "I am not being stubborn. I just require the men I fuck to have a pulse."

"A likely excuse," Fallon argued, waving a hand toward the sky. "Where's the fun in limitation?"

"Which Huntsman are you not fucking?" I asked, my gaze bouncing back and forth between the two women.

"All of them," Imelda said.

"She is going to fuck Holt. It's only a matter of time," Fallon said, pushing herself to sit up. She looked over at where the male in question stood with Caldris.

"I'm not going to fuck him. Even if he weren't transparent, the man is insufferable," Imelda protested.

"You should see the way they argue," Fallon said, sinking her teeth into her bottom lip for a moment. "If you don't plan to fuck him, then I suppose you won't mind if I take him for a ride tonight?" Fallon pushed to her feet, turning to face Imelda as she backed toward the fire. Holt waited just on the other side of the flames, his eerie white eyes observing our interaction with far too much interest to be natural.

There was no denying the way they blazed with white hot fury when they settled on Imelda's face, and she clenched her jaw as she turned her attention away from both him and Fallon. "Yeah, that's what I thought," Fallon scoffed with satisfaction.

"Do you ever shut up?" Imelda asked, pushing to her feet.

"Only if you pet me and tell me I'm pretty," Fallon

returned, blowing the witch a kiss as she stood in front of Fallon.

"That's not going to happen."

"Okay, then take me for a walk. I want to see the woods. The trees are so strange," Fallon said, turning her eyes to the edge of the clearing. "I never imagined they'd be so big."

"You've never seen trees?" I asked, standing up as the two women stepped away from the blanket.

"I wasn't allowed to leave the tunnels. For my protection, of course," Fallon said, shaking her head sadly as she stepped toward the woods.

"The first time we stepped out of the tunnels was the first time she felt the sun on her skin since I brought her to the Resistance as an infant," Imelda said sadly. "I tried not to call too much attention to it, but it feels like it should have been an important moment. I worry I did her a disservice."

"I wouldn't have wanted people to watch me at that moment either. I think you did the right thing, for what little it's worth," I said.

"It's worth more than you think. You may not believe you know one another, but you do. The soul remembers, even when the mind does not."

29

ESTRELLA

*W*e rode through the day, and by the time we made our way to the wall of the Gods and the hot spring that awaited on the side of the mountain, my exhaustion was growing to a level I'd never known. I couldn't even begin to believe the way the night before had tired me out so I was falling asleep atop Azra through the day.

Caldris continued to push me, giving me moments of privacy and urging me to try to summon his magic to my command. There wasn't much energy left for me to give, but I did the best I could. Sensing the renewed urgency that came from him, I did as he asked. I pushed, summoning and stretching that muscle that he was determined for me to train.

Neither of us spoke again of what would be waiting for me when I stepped foot in Alfheimr, of what I might become. It hung between us, renewing the distance in our relationship in a way that hadn't been there since the first days after I discovered the truth of his identity.

It seemed fitting, in a horribly karmic way, that I would finally accept Caldris as my mate only for something to tear us apart. In this case, the knowledge that I seemed likely to be the daughter of his abuser. I couldn't imagine what it must have been like, what he must have thought, to know the very woman he hated more than anything was the mother of the mate he'd so desperately waited for. I didn't know everything Mab had subjected him to. I couldn't, when he was always so hesitant to speak of her. I recognized the signs of abuse, the determination to keep his suffering buried, because I felt the same hesitance when talking about Byron.

The wolves whimpered as we dismounted our horses, sitting back on their haunches with sad looks on their wicked face. They were like the scariest dogs I'd ever seen, yet as sweet as the fluffiest of puppies. When they weren't devouring Caldris's enemies, anyway.

"We'll be back soon," I murmured, patting Fenris as I walked past. I leaned down to touch my lips to the top of his head, immediately regretting the way his fur clung to my face. He chortled as if he thought I deserved it for leaving him behind.

Rude.

We passed the wall of the Gods, walking the path carved into the side of the mountain. Holt led the charge and we left most of the Wild Hunt below with the horses. The dead Caldris had summoned to guard us kept the Fae Marked from throwing themselves off the mountain side to escape through death. That would have been my inclination, at least, but it didn't seem as if many of them even considered the possibility.

No matter what they would have done for their freedom, I couldn't judge them for it. Not when it hadn't been so long since I would have done the same. The thought of jumping off a cliff immediately brought Brann to the front of my mind— filling me with a sense of wonder. We were close to the place where I'd lost him, nearing that very cliff where Aramis had thrown him over the edge and left him for dead. I wished I'd demanded answers from him while I'd had him at my side. I knew regret, and what it was to have answers at my fingertips but be so afraid of them, I lost them to time and death itself.

I couldn't afford to make that mistake again.

We rounded the top of the path, the hot spring coming into view. I watched eyes widen as they took in the sight of the statues of the Gods in intimate positions, their reactions so like what I'd probably expressed the first time I'd seen them.

We were retracing our steps, making our way back to the boundary. I wished I could say it was like taking a walk down memory lane—a stroll through the evolution of our relationship. Instead, it felt like it had been another lifetime with the new tension thrumming through us.

I didn't know what to make of it, or what to do about it.

"The dead will supervise as you bathe, to give you some privacy," Holt said, sweeping a hand to point out the army of the corpses who had lined the edges of the landing. They blocked the pathway back to where the horses and the Wild Hunt waited below, forming a line as if they needed that connection to relay information.

"You can wait and we'll bathe when they're done," Caldris said, taking my hand and guiding me back toward the mountain path as Holt settled onto a rock at the edge, facing away from the hot spring itself.

"Not unless you'd like my riders to see her in the nude," Holt called, not bothering to turn around as he delivered the message. "We cannot afford to delay just so the two of you can have a fun romp in the spring. She either bathes with the women or she bathes with the men, there is no other option."

"Have I told you how much I despise you lately?" I asked, narrowing my eyes into a glare that felt like it dripped venom. Even if he couldn't see it, I wanted nothing more than to solidify that glare until phantom talons clawed down his back.

He twitched, rolling his shoulders as he spun to look at me with a shocked expression. I swallowed, keeping my face neutral in an attempt to disguise my guilt.

Had that...?

Nope. We were not going there.

"She has a point," Caldris grunted, bending down to kiss my forehead. He made his way toward the path that curved down to the forest floor below, looking back over at us. "If anything happens to her, you'll find your head on a spike when I'm finished with you."

"Please refrain. Regrowing a head is quite time-consuming," Holt called back, his tone dry. Caldris glared one last time before he disappeared around the corner, and I felt his annoyance course down the bond. He didn't want to leave me; he worried about leaving me. But we all knew it was important we got to Alfheimr as quickly as possible, especially if we were trying to avoid Mab's notice and slip into Catancia first.

"How are we supposed to take our clothes off?" one of the women asked, glaring into Holt's back as she clanked the chains of her iron shackles together to prove her point.

He raised a hand, waving it through the air in a quick flick. The chains connecting the shackles vanished. "You have precisely one minute to get your clothes off. The chains will reappear when that time comes. I suggest you hurry," he said when he didn't hear anyone moving. I bolted into action, shrugging off my cloak as the other Fae Marked did the same. Imelda and Fallon weren't shackled, but they stripped off their clothes quickly all the same, joining in the fray to get into the warmth of the water. Adelphia and the others moved more leisurely, and I got the sense they didn't rush for anyone or anything.

Nobody wanted to be standing bare ass naked in the freezing cold. The moment I stripped off my tunic and the cold air touched my breasts, I wanted to shriek. My nipples would fall off before long. I shoved my pants down and stripped off my boots and socks, stepping down into the water as the others finished stripping.

I'd long since passed the point of caring that my body was on display for people who hated me. After I'd allowed a roomful of men and women to watch Caelum fuck me while we washed away the blood of a cave beast, being nude in front of a handful of women seemed insignificant.

Some of the other women stepped in behind me, their glares settling on my face but easing as the pleasure of the warm water touched their skin and sluiced over them, sinking into them and warming the insides that often felt as if they would never know warmth again.

We'd been fortunate enough that the snow was minimal; it wasn't deep on the ground, and when it did actively snow, it was a light flurry instead of a blizzard. But those too would come, and we were risking the onset extreme weather with every moment we delayed.

The shackles reappeared. I sank as low into the water as I could, turning my back to the other Fae Marked as I reached up onto the stone ledge to grasp one of the cloths the dead had laid out for us to use to wash. I didn't allow myself to think about what my life had come to—corpses setting out my bathing linens. There wasn't any soap, but the warm water would do the trick to some extent.

My fingers wrapped around the cloth, dipping it into the water to get it wet as I raised it to touch my face. I saw Fallon and Imelda moving toward me from the corner of my eye, and I had the briefest moment of gratitude that they would make me feel less alone in a spring full of strangers.

Two hands touched each of my shoulders, pressing down firmly. There was no time to scream. No time to make a sound before I plunged beneath the surface. Water filled my lungs as I tried anyway. The strangled sound was distorted as the water surrounded me. I thrashed, swinging my arms as one of the people who'd touched me swept my legs out from under me.

I plunged deeper, so low their feet came down atop my back to hold me beneath the surface. I flailed, grabbing onto the ankles of one of those close enough. The water tinted pink as I dug my nails into their bare skin, clawing through their flesh in my struggle to survive.

Still they didn't let me up, keeping me pinned to the stone and waiting for my death. With the blood rushing into my head, the water burning in my lungs, and my breath stolen from me, my head spun.

I tried to grasp Caldris's power of winter, tried to find a way to freeze some of the water, but nothing came to me. Nothing responded to my dire need in my panic.

I couldn't focus, couldn't feel the cold when I was on *fire*.

Reaching out with the other part of my bond, I sank into it and wrapped that golden string of fate around my hand. Tugging it toward me, I allowed my panic to flow through me and reach out toward Caldris. I just hoped he was close enough, but I knew I didn't have *time*.

I'd lost too much air already, and clinging to the very last bit in my lungs would only do so much good.

I tugged on our bond again, following it to the army of the dead waiting on the other side. They felt strange, like empty vessels without a soul. Wrong on a level I couldn't explain. I hated touching them, hated feeling their stain upon me.

But I grabbed one, wrapping it in the golden thread of our bond that connected us, visualizing myself yanking it into the water.

Above the surface, someone screamed, the sound muted by the water making my lungs burn. Consciousness slipped away, but I held onto that bond, focusing on it and refusing to release it.

I would bury them all.

My eyes drifted closed, cutting off reality as it all went black.

30

ESTRELLA

There was no twinkle of starlight around me. Only the depths of an inky gloom the likes of which I'd never known. There was no trickle of sunlight, no light of a campfire. I sat up, spinning to look behind me as my hands scraped over the smooth surface beneath me. Even that had no substance, as if crafted from the clouds in the sky, and yet I never fell through to plummet back to the ground below me.

"Caelum?" I called, my lungs feeling as if they might seize, but there was no breath, no movement in my breast. My heart was quiet and still.

I turned forward once more, frantically raising my hand to my chest. My nails clawed at the skin covering the heart that refused to beat, my fear pushing me to my feet. A male figure stepped out of the darkness, shadows twining around his form. His skin was paler than the darkness surrounding him, his eyes set deep into his face and gleaming with the light of stars. Golden threads twined up his arms, wrapping around his hands and forearms until they finally settled against his bare shoulders.

I swallowed, not daring to speak as he took measured,

leisurely steps toward me, as if time was a construct he didn't understand, because he had eons of it.

"Hello, Estrella," he said, his voice striking me in the chest. It was deeper than I'd thought possible, the vibrations of it sinking inside of me. I couldn't tear my eyes away from those golden threads covering his arms, and only his amused chuckle forced me to look up into his star-filled, black stare. "Only you would be in my presence and be more interested in the threads of fate than in me."

"Who are you? Where am I?" I asked, swallowing as he finally halted directly in front of me. Golden threads rose out of the clouds at my feet to wrap around my wrist.

"Answers will come when you're ready for them," he said, reaching forward with a single hand. He stroked a finger over the flesh of my cheek, then air filled my lungs suddenly. I bent over in pain, glaring up at the male as he patted my head soothingly. "But it is not your time yet, child."

I woke from my dream lying on the rough stone beside the hot spring. I sputtered, coughing as water expelled from my lungs. Twisting my body to the side, I vomited the water from my stomach, emptying my lungs of all the fluid trapped in them. One of the skeletons stood between me and the Fae Marked still in the spring, his spine straight as my vision returned.

Holt stood, staring over in shock as I tightened my grip on that golden thread clutched in my grasp. The skeleton crumbled to the ground, giving me a perfect view of the people who had attacked me. Of the four faces I would remember until my dying days, their arms marred with bloodied scratches I assumed they'd gotten from the skeleton who'd pulled me from the water.

Fallon leaned over me, her face flushed and twisted in

concern. I had the vaguest sense of her breathing air into my lungs—of her pressing on my chest in an effort to awaken me.

The cold finally touched my skin, making me realize that I lay upon the stone naked for all to see. I pulled on that golden thread once more, flinching back from Fallon's gentle hands as she touched my face. She mouthed something, her words lost to the roaring of my rage in my head.

At the corner of my eye, the skeleton rose to his feet once more as I lifted the hand wrapped in my mate bond. It rolled its neck around on its shoulders, the bones and vertebrae cracking and drawing Fallon's shocked eyes to the place where it jumped down into the water of the hot spring.

I pushed on the stone, maneuvering to my feet and staring down at the women who had wronged me in such a malicious way. I didn't move my feet, allowing the skeleton to be the one to step forward.

"Estrella stop!" Holt called, the words breaking through the fog in my head. I shook them off, enjoying the way the Fae Marked women scrambled back to avoid the skeleton stalking toward them. The murder they'd tried to commit would haunt them until the moment they died, but it almost made me sad to know it would be short-lived.

Caldris appeared at the pathway that wound up the mountain, his face flushed as if he had run up the hill. I knew he hadn't; I'd watched him appear from thin air. His hand was pressed to his chest, as if he'd been able to feel the way mine had been stopped in the dream that had taken me from the pain of drowning.

I shook off thoughts of the strange male crafted from the shadows themselves.

Caldris took in the sight before him with wide, frenzied eyes—the curl to my hand as my fingers spun the threads and guided the skeleton's steps. His eyes raked over my nudity that was on display as he made his way across the stones. He came to me, swinging the cloak off of his shoulders as he walked and wrapping it around me. I didn't take my eyes off the skeleton, or the vengeance I wanted with a ferocity that took my breath away.

"Estrella," Imelda said, her voice gentler than Holt's had been. I didn't turn to look at her, only hearing her pull herself out of the hot spring. Water slid off her body as she came to stand only a few feet away, but I didn't turn to look at her—not with my vengeance within my reach.

I was so tired of being hurt.

Caldris grasped my hand, his presence at my side like a soothing balm, but I didn't want to let go of the rage. I didn't want to release the fury that kept me warm. Lifting my palm wrapped in the threads of our bond and cradling it in his palm, he turned his stare to the skeleton, his brow furrowing as he focused on it.

It never stopped moving forward slowly, its steps measured as it tugged against the control Caldris tried to exert.

"It's time to let it go, min asteren," he said, his voice tormented as he touched a finger to the golden thread I'd wrapped myself in. The bond shuddered, chasing away some of my rage.

"They've made it clear that it is either them or me," I said, my voice echoing over the spring. "It will not be me."

"They deserve every bit of the punishment you would mete out to them, but think of the mates who are waiting for them. Who have waited centuries and think they're so close to finding them. They deserve better. They deserve the opportunity to fight with them to change their perspectives, the way you have done." He touched the threads again, and a strangled sob clawed its way up my throat, my bottom lip trembling as the rage eased enough for the pain to sink in. I released the threads with a groan, letting them fall away from my hand as I turned and touched my forehead to my mate's chest.

He heaved a sigh of relief, wrapping his arms around me.

He faced the people in the spring. "If you value your lives, you will get dressed and get the fuck out, *now,*" he growled, and the Fae Marked, Imelda, and Fallon hurried out of the water. Their chains vanished as Holt moved to follow at their side, and I watched as Caldris commanded the skeleton out of the water. The skeletons guided the shivering human toward the path down the mountain, herding them away as they fought to tug on their clothing as quickly as possible.

"Not you," Caldris said, the order snapping out like a whip. It struck Holt in the back, making him turn slowly toward Caldris. "The dead will guide them to your riders. *You* will stay right here."

"I didn't even realize she was beneath the water. I was trying not to look at her. We both know you'd be furious if you thought I was peeking at her while she was fucking naked," Holt protested.

"And yet she somehow ended up standing naked in front of you anyway," Caldris said, placing a hand to the small of my back. Sleepiness settled over me as he guided me right up to the edge of the water, quickly stripping off his clothing as soon as the Marked were gone from sight.

He jumped down into the water, standing at the edge and running his hands over my ankles. I shivered, the cold air making me long for my clothes, but I couldn't seem to muster up the energy to make my way toward them.

"I want to go to sleep," I murmured softly, staring down into his dark eyes.

He smirked up at me, running those soothing thumbs over my skin. "Do you remember when I fucked you in the bathing chamber with everyone watching? You were shocked that I would want them to watch me fuck you into oblivion, when I don't even like men staring at you for too long."

"I remember," I murmured, letting my eyes drift closed.

"Now Holt has seen you, min asteren. He's seen you naked and not stuffed full of my cock. Worse yet, I *lost* you. For one fleeting moment, I felt the pain of this world without you in it," Caldris said, his voice dropping low with his jealousy. "I need to be inside of you, and I need him to see it."

I felt that need course through him; I couldn't understand it, but I felt how genuine it was to him. I didn't know that I had the energy to fight him, but I wasn't certain I was capable of sex at the moment, either.

I just wanted to sleep.

"She was fucking *dead*," Holt protested, rolling his eyes to the sky as he dropped down onto the stone, propping his elbow on his knee and cradling his head in his hands. "That was the last thing on my mind."

"If you had a mate, you'd understand, but you don't," Caldris said harshly, his glare settling on his friend's face as his nostrils flared. "Take off her cloak, Huntsman. Show me what's mine."

My eyes widened, my gaze snapping to Holt in shock. "Caelum," I murmured,.

My mate smirked, his dark eyes shining with amusement as he trailed his hands higher up my legs. "He knows if he touches any part of you, I will remove that part of his body. As it stands, he's fortunate I'm not carving out his eyes for seeing you this way."

"I would have anyway, when you finally convince her to let you fuck her in front of the fire," Holt said with a grimace, making his way over. He stepped up behind me, the coolness of his translucent body washing over me in a way that made me shiver.

"We both know that's different," Caldris said, his eyes narrowing on the place where Holt carefully reached around me. He didn't touch me at all, his fingers grasping the clasp delicately and tugging it open until the fabric pooled at my feet.

Caldris reached up, grasping me around the thighs and pulling me forward. Wrapping his arms around me fully, he carried me and turned until we were in the center of the hot spring and he lowered my body down, sliding it against the length of his.

His cock was hard and ready by the time I settled with my feet on the stone bottom of the hot spring, a moment of panic sending me reeling.

I ran a hand over my arm and the tiny scratches along my body from where I'd thrashed and fought for breath. "You're alright," Caldris said, cupping my cheek in his hand. It brought me a small measure of comfort, knowing he was here to support me.

He waved a hand over my shackles, letting them fall away and drop into the hot spring where they clanked to the bottom. "You will never wear those again," he murmured, the words sounding an echo of the anger he tried to hide from me. It was the worst of his rage, all that he hadn't allowed himself to feel in the moments when I'd been a fury on the path of vengeance.

I nodded, not bothering to argue against the special treatment I hadn't thought I wanted. It hadn't made a damn bit of difference in their pursuit to kill me. I'd take the special treatment from my mate any day.

"I can't believe I wanted to defend them. I wanted them to accept me so much that I didn't care if the cost of if that was you." I sighed, enjoying the moment of tenderness he showed me.

"They aren't worth your loyalty," Caldris said, touching his chin to the top of my head. He ran his hands over my skin, soothing the aches in my arms with warm water as he covered me in it. Washing any traces of dirt from my skin, he let me settle into the comfort of his embrace for a few moments. What he wanted to do in front of Holt never left the forefront of my mind, but I sank into my exhaustion and the need I felt to just feel loved for a moment.

This was my mate I knew, not the estranged male who didn't seem to know what to do with the possible repercussions of my lineage.

I ran my hands over his skin, picking up a piece of linen from the ledge and using it to wash away the dirt. He did the same, offering me the care and affection I needed in that moment more than anything.

There had to be a purpose to all of this, and if Caldris and I couldn't come out united on the other side...it would have all been for nothing.

Holt sat on the stone, his head held in his hands and watching the moment stretch between us. I tried not to think about what Caldris wanted him to watch—the coming sex that felt almost like a punishment.

I knew I hadn't been the one to commit the crime, and that Caldris blamed Holt entirely for my near death experience. "The sooner we get to Alfheimr and complete the bond, the better. I don't know how much longer I can stand the dangers that come with your humanity," Caldris murmured, setting the linen on the edge of the spring when he'd finished cleaning my body. He took the strip of cloth from my hand as well, ringing it out and discarding it beside the other.

He studied me carefully, running a thumb over my cheek

for a moment, then he lifted his other wrist from the water, letting the fluid drip off his gleaming, golden skin. Raising a finger, he allowed one black talon to replace the more human-like nails he donned in his less violent moments.

Slashing that nail across his wrist, he watched me as I watched his blood dripping into the spring, tinting the water between us pink. He raised his wrist to my mouth, pressing it against my lips as the warmth of him spread through me. I opened, letting the thick fluid coat my tongue before he pulled it away. That familiar feeling of him sank inside me, strengthening the mate bond that pulled between us, wrapping us in the threads of gold, consuming us entirely. I had to imagine the moments we shared like this were as close as we could come to being fully bonded before that event finally occurred.

Something in his gaze glinted with mischief, and he maneuvered himself to the edge of the spring. Putting his back to the ledge, he placed a hand on each side and lifted himself out. Water sluiced down his body, accentuating every line of muscle in his rigid frame. He spread his legs, his cock jutting up to the sky above.

"I want your mouth, min asteren," he said, and something in the position reminded me of the rock carving not far away. Of the human women centuries ago who had shared his cock in the same way, in the same place.

There was none of the aloofness on his face that was depicted in that carving as I prowled toward him, jealousy burning in my veins. He smirked at me as if he knew it, and he probably felt what that possessiveness did to me.

In the same way he wanted Holt to watch me pleasure him, he knew that I wanted to stake my claim against the visual memory of those humans. Their faces were carved into the stone identical and somehow vague, as if their likenesses weren't worth immortalizing. They were replaceable, and the God of the Dead had probably fucked so many he'd never remembered their names.

But I was his mate. I was the one whose face would be recorded in the books where I stood by his side; the one who would bear his name if we ever managed to complete the bond.

His wife.

I stopped between his spread legs, touching a hand to each of his thighs as I stared at him. "Given that I nearly died, I should think you'd be showing me how grateful you are to see me alive. Not making demands." I watched as he chuckled with amusement.

"You sound as if you're convinced I don't have plans for your pussy after," he said, his chuckle trailing off as he reached out to touch my cheek. He stroked a thumb over my lower lip, sinking the tip into my mouth. "The woman I saw was not victimized by what was done to her. She was an angry, vengeful goddess, hell-bent on the destruction of those who'd wronged her. She bit back, and now I want to feel those vicious little lips wrapped around my fucking cock."

His thumb left my mouth, sliding around to the back of my head and guiding me forward. I bent slightly, rubbing my mouth against his shaft as he groaned. "How do you know I won't bite again?" I asked, cocking my head to the side as I wrapped a hand around the base of his shaft and guided him to the angle I needed.

My lips pressed a single kiss against his head, smiling when he twitched in my grip.

"You like my cock far too much for that, Little One," he said with a chuckle. "The faster you suck it, the faster I can get my tongue between your legs."

I grinned at his impatience, shaking my head once before I

spread my lips around the head of his cock and took him into my mouth. I was far too aware of our audience of one, the Huntsman, watching with his heavy stare on the side of my face.

I opened wider, keeping my eyes on Caelum's as he wrapped a hand into the back of my wet hair, gathering it into his fist as he pushed me further down on his cock. I took a deep breath in, swallowing around him and allowing him to thrust deep. He groaned, tossing his head back as he used the hand at the back of my head to guide me onto him at the exact pace he wanted.

He moved quickly, driving himself closer to the edge of an orgasm within the confines of my mouth. He released me suddenly, allowing me to pull free and breathe as air returned to my lungs. It was almost too much, too close to the reality of drowning in the water below the surface.

But whereas that moment had been marked by fear, and fear alone, this was fear mingled with desire, dancing in an eternal waltz that felt rooted in time itself. As if the combination of fear and desire were always created to intertwine, coming together to create a symphony inside of me.

Caldris watched as I leaned forward, licking him from root to tip and then taking him into my mouth again. I worked him with slower, teasing swallows, flattening my tongue over his skin as I pulled back each time. "Good girl," he murmured, petting my hair sweetly. "Remind Holt that there is only one male you will ever worship with that pretty mouth."

I resisted the urge to glare at Caldris, knowing damn well he fully intended on worshiping me in the same way. I could live with that label being assigned to what I did to him, so long as it went both ways.

So long as he treated me like the Goddess I would never be.

He guided me away from his cock with a ragged groan, finally sliding down into the water between me and the ledge as he captured my face in his hands and crashed his mouth down onto mine. He devoured me, letting his tongue tangle with mine and seeming not to care about where my mouth had been.

Spinning me so my back was to the wall of the pool, he guided my elbows onto the stone face and lifted my waist up. Stepping back to allow me to float, my breasts and stomach emerging from the surface, he curled my knees high and rested my legs on his shoulders.

Staring into the apex of my thighs, he used his hands at my hips and beneath my ass to lift me and guide my pussy to his mouth. I gasped the moment he touched me, his mouth hot even compared to the water of the hot spring. The cold air that kissed my breasts and pebbled my nipples was a stark contrast to the heat he built in me quickly, leaving me squirming as he buried his face between my thighs and ate, like a man starved.

I slipped, my elbow coming out from under me and almost plunging my upper body back into the water. Catching myself at the last minute, I propped myself back up with a ragged breath. "Better hold on tight, Beasty. It looks like you're about to go for a ride," Holt drawled, drawing my eyes over to where he watched. He held my gaze, the shocking white of his stare pinning me in place as Caldris slid his tongue inside of me and curled one of his hands around the top of my thigh. Touching a probing finger to my clit, he circled it firmly enough that my legs trembled on his shoulders.

My attention shifted back to him, and to the way he raised his eyebrows. Even with half his face hidden from view and consumed with licking my pussy, I felt his irritation.

I was not to acknowledge the Hunstman. Even if it did

turn me on to imagine him enjoying the sight, enjoying watching his friend devour me. "Caelum," I murmured, watching as something snapped in the dark gaze of my mate.

He spun me carefully so my breasts were pinned between my body and the stone ledge, the roughness scraping gently against my skin. He kept me lifted up, raising my body out of the water with his arms wrapped around the thighs that he pinned together.

His mouth came back to my pussy, licking through me even though he had me ass-up. The change in angle made me see stars, his tongue stroking my clit in a different way that sent me tumbling into the edge of an orgasm.

I screamed out my release, dropping my cheek to the stone as I came on Caelum's face. He rewarded me by licking me through it, only pulling back when my breathing calmed and then lowering my ass into the water. His cock pressed against my entrance, thrusting inside as he wrapped a hand around the front of my throat and pulled my back into his chest. He held me tight, suspended in the water as he moved his hips, driving inside of me and retreating in a punishing, brutal rhythm that I shouldn't have enjoyed but somehow thrived on.

"Do you want to fuck him?" Caelum asked harshly, using his grip to maneuver me so that I stared at Holt.

"No," I answered, shaking my head. There wasn't a part of me that was at all attracted to Holt; I only desired the mate who moved inside of me.

"But you like knowing he's watching. Your pussy is so fucking wet wrapped around me," Caelum said, thrusting deep to prove his point. "Though it will be even wetter when I fill it with cum."

"Yes, I like knowing he's watching," I said, hating that the admission felt like a weakness. It felt like I was doing something wrong because of the way I'd been raised, and maybe that contributed to my desire to do it more.

Or maybe it was the nature of whatever existed inside of me. Fae or something else, craving the animalistic need to claim my mate. That was *my* mate's cock pushing through my pussy and battering into me as if it was his pussy to use.

And it was.

"That's my star," Caldris said with a chuckle. "*Never* pretend to be something you're not. Never dull how bright you burn so that others may feel comfortable in your presence."

He dropped a hand to my breast, squeezing the flesh as he pinned me by the throat. A woman gasped back at the entry to the path that led below, and I turned to find Imelda's mismatched eyes wide with shock.

She wasn't horrified, and I was certain she'd probably seen similar acts with the Resistance if not engaged in them herself. But her lips pursed, her cheeks hollowing as her mouth dropped open. "I wanted to be sure you were alright," she said awkwardly. She didn't move to leave, even though she clearly had the answer she'd come for.

"If you'd like to join in on the festivities," Holt called, tearing Imelda's gaze off of our bodies moving in the water. "I have a perfectly good cock you can sit on, witch."

Imelda glared at him, holding his stare while Caldris moved inside of me. He seemed riveted by their interaction, gazing back and forth between them. "Would I even be able to find it, Ghost Man?" she asked, crossing her arms over her chest. She tilted her head to the side, glancing down his body as he stood and took a step toward her.

I followed her gaze, trailing it down his body until...

Oh. She'd definitely be able to find it.

I chuckled, feeling Caldris's grip on my throat tighten as he pressed his mouth to his ears. "They need to fuck already," he murmured, lowering his other hand from my breast to stroke my clit beneath the water.

"You may be able to see through it, but I promise you'll feel it," Holt said, taking another step toward her. Imelda stumbled back a step, glaring at him as if she might issue another challenge. But she shook her head, her gaze dropping to the ground before she spun on her heel and retreated back down the path.

Holt grinned at her retreat, looking like he might have followed after her had it not been for Caldris's command that he stay to observe our tryst. "Just go," Caldris said, laughing as he touched his mouth to my neck. The humor in his voice caressed my skin, wrapping me in a warm embrace as Holt disappeared.

And Caldris continued to fuck me, taking what was his regardless of what happened between the Huntsman and the witch. Later, I'd ask. But for now, I had more important things to worry about.

Like the orgasm Caelum's circling fingers brought crashing through me.

allon walked at my side, chattering happily with Imelda. She seemed completely content to avoid the other Fae Marked, even though she must have grown up alongside some of them for the entirety of her life.

"They knew what I was. Or rather what I might be," she said, her voice dropping low as she tipped her head forward. She'd braided my hair away from my face beside the fire the night before, her fingers moving against my head bringing me a strange comfort. It had been welcome after the events of the hot spring. I never wanted to look at the others again after what they'd done, knowing that I would be just as likely to kill them as I would to understand the hatred.

It was a hard place to be, knowing that only a few weeks prior I would have hated the woman I'd become and the choices I'd made. How many of those decisions were made of my free will, with the bond convoluting my free thought and making me question everything I'd been raised to believe?

"Did they treat you poorly?" I asked, trying to ignore the way I felt the heated stare of my mate on my back. He hadn't been pleased when I'd asked to walk alongside Fallon and Imelda for a while, but he didn't question it, either.

As much as I was learning to accept the love that echoed between us no matter what the circumstances, he needed to learn to allow me to have other relationships and bonds that I could cherish. My relationship with Imelda and Fallon was new, but that thread of fate danced between Fallon and I all the same.

I didn't get the impression she could see it, and it didn't flare as brightly as the bond between Caldris and I, but it was there nonetheless, ever since the moment Imelda had revealed the crescent moon burned into the side of my palm.

"Not particularly," Fallon said, shrugging her shoulders. "Some of them were very kind, obviously, but others kept their distance more than anything. I spent most of my time with my family and Imelda."

"It's a shame there wasn't a way to train her to channel any magic she might possess with the Veil up. With the amount of time she spent chasing after me as a girl, she might have been an expert at witchcraft if nothing else at this point," Imelda said, knocking her hip into Fallon's side. The human-looking girl grinned, reaching out to grasp the witch's hand affectionately.

The bond between them was so familial, so recognizable and similar to what I might have had with Brann, that my heart throbbed in my chest. The knowledge that he'd been a witch, and that he'd been a guardian to watch over Fallon and I; the relationship was even more similar than it might seem at a glance.

"Are you alright?" Fallon asked, releasing Imelda's hand and curling her fingers around mine. I nodded, swallowing past the tears burning my throat and trying to ignore the surge of emotion. If Caldris felt it through the bond, he'd pick me up and put me on that horse whether I liked it or not.

"It's been difficult to come to terms with who Brann was and all that he did. I just don't understand how the boy I grew up with was centuries old, and killed to take me away from the Resistance. *Why?* How is that even possible?"

"Anything is possible through magic. Brann's magic was stronger than I could ever dream of. It would have taken everything he had, but he could have maintained an illusion —sort of a witch form of Faerie glamour—if he was determined enough. When it comes to the *why*, the Veil was never meant to be permanent," Imelda admitted, looking at me over the top of Fallon's head. Fallon was similar to me in height, and her hair had the same blue undertones as mine. Where my skin was bronze-toned and darker, she was fair and unblemished from the sun.

In another life, we could have been sisters in truth to match the crescent moons that marked us, connecting us through lifetimes with a magical bond, which I felt as much as saw, shimmering in the sun.

"What do you mean?" Fallon asked, her brows drawing together as she spun away from me to face Imelda. Fenrir stepped up beside me, nuzzling my shoulder and pressing his wet nose into my neck as I patted the top of his head impatiently.

"I don't know all the details. I might have served as your guardian in the absence of the elders, but I was never *meant* to be a guardian. All I know is that Veil was supposed to come down when the first of you entered your thirteenth life. But when Brander took you from us, I lost track of your lives. Fallon is only on her twelfth life," Imelda explained.

"I'm surprised she's an entire life behind me," I said, reaching up to scratch at the side of my nose.

"At least the timing is right then. You both die relatively young. Whatever your souls are, they are not meant to be trapped within human vessels in this way. You eat through your bodies at a faster rate than a human soul would and your life spans display that, but some lifespans were shorter than others. It would make sense that perhaps one of you died younger than the other. Without knowing what the other one of you is, there's no way to speculate if it has something to do with the potency of your soul because of that lineage," she explained.

I nodded, pacing forward steadily even though it felt like my life had been uprooted and turned on its head over and over again in a very short period of time. Why could I not seem to reach the end of the revelations? Of the ways my life had changed and the hints that I might be Mab's daughter?

It would make sense for the daughter of a Goddess to be a more potent soul. To burn through her human bodies at a faster rate.

Fallon squeezed my hand tighter, the mark on hers feeling like fire against my skin. She turned her hazel eyes toward mine, the scar I didn't dare to ask about gleaming against her skin as the sun touched it. "Whatever comes, we face it together," she said, and I felt the pulse of heat that radiated off her mark. Turning sideways to face her, I pulled my left hand out of hers and gave her my right, the crescent moon of my mark pressing into her skin.

Golden threads wrapped around the joining, tugging our hands tighter to one another. "Together," I agreed, sinking into the warmth that wrapped around us. Imelda stepped forward, lifting the knife she kept tucked into the pocket of her cloak and unsheathing it. She ignored my shocked gasp as she pressed the tip into my finger, blood welling as she repeated the process on Fallon's finger quickly. The moon carved into the witch's forehead glowed brightly as Fallon and I met each other's stares. Her finger was just a breath from mine, blood dripping down her skin as the supernatural pull of the blood magic bound us together.

The moment our fingers touched, my head flew back with a strangled gasp. It was undeniable, the way the blood oath sank into me, striking me in the chest. It wrapped around my heart, the golden threads tightening until they became painful. Fallon jolted back from the contact, clutching her finger to her chest as my lungs heaved.

I turned my hand over, staring at the white teardrop that had formed on my fingertip. The mark glowed like the moon, shining brightly as if it could capture the hope that rang true in the night and place it upon my skin. "All magic has a price," Imelda said, her eyes meeting mine when I looked up from the mark.

"What will this cost?" I asked, staring down at it.

"You will not know until you pay it," she said, reaching out to take my finger. She did the same with Fallon, holding the two mirror images beside one another as I heard the sound of a horse's frantic gallop coming from behind us. "You will protect one another. In some moments, it may benefit you; in others it may cost you. But you will stand together, to face what is coming, as you were always meant to be."

"But you don't know what one of us is," Fallon protested, looking toward me. She had felt the pull to me as I did her, and the mark on my finger changed nothing. I wouldn't have been able to abandon her without it, anyway.

"No, but I do know that you'll both be relevant. The guardians wouldn't have placed you in the same hideaway if you weren't meant to know one another. There is a method to all that they do, even if it seems to go against their life's purpose," she said, reaching out to cup my cheek. "Brander did what he believed to be right."

"What the fuck were you thinking?" Caldris demanded, dismounting Azra and coming between Imelda and I. He severed the contact of her skin on mine, taking my finger in his grasp and swiping at the new mark as if he could sever it from my skin.

"We took an oath to face what's coming together. We'll protect each other," Fallon answered, holding her chin high. She stared down the God of the Dead as if she didn't need to fear him, and I supposed she didn't.

I would never allow him to hurt her.

She was as much mine as he was, even if it was in an entirely different way. *Sisters*, united in the magic that brought us together.

"And did the witch perhaps explain what happens if one of you fails to protect the other? If there are circumstances beyond your control and one of you is faced with the choice between death and escape?" he demanded, leveling Imelda with a glare that was strong enough to make me shrink back.

"The cost of failure to fulfill your oath is death," Imelda said, holding his stare before turning it to each of us briefly. "So long as you have the *intent* to uphold the blood oath, the magic will not demand that price."

"Matters of life and death are rarely black and white. Sometimes they require hard choices and exceptions to promises such as this. Your magic does not recognize *circumstances*, Imelda," he said, turning that rage-filled stare to me. "What if she is Mab's daughter? You've just put yourself at risk for nothing."

"It is not nothing to protect a friend," I said, raising my chin in defiance. I yanked my hand out of his grasp. "If you truly believe that, then I am *sorry* for the life you've lived that you would so willingly sacrifice someone you love to save yourself."

"I wouldn't," he said, his tone dropping low. "But I would sacrifice *everyone* I have ever met to save *you*. This was a foolish risk."

"What if it's me? We're all thinking about it, right?" I asked, staring back at him in challenge. "If I am Mab's daughter, I should think it would benefit me to have as many allies outside her influence as possible. Whatever Fallon may be, perhaps she is meant to aid me in dealing with the consequences of my *mother*."

"She is not your mother," he growled, the fury in his voice taking my breath away. "Do not *ever* say such a thing again."

"How could you possibly know that? Even you have kept your distance since I started showing signs of her power. You know as well as anyone that the similarities are undeniable, Caelum," I said, my voice gentling as I trailed off. The broken expression on his face, the outright denial to accept what I was.

He couldn't.

"I would know if that bitch's blood ran through your veins. I would *feel* it. I am far too familiar with all aspects of my fucking step-mother, so I would recognize the way her daughter felt on the inside," he said, the brutal twist of his features knocking me back a step.

Bile rose to my throat—hot and scorching.

Burning a path up and into my mouth as I resisted the urge to bend over and retch. He...

Oh Gods.

Imelda hung her head forward, her face a grimace as she refused to meet my stare. The horror of realization washed over me, watching as Caldris squeezed his eyes closed. When he opened them, they burned with regret.

He took a step toward me, wincing when I stumbled back to avoid him.

"I didn't mean it like that," he said, his voice gentle. "I've never had sex with Mab."

"Then what exactly did you mean?" I asked, letting Fallon step up beside me. She wrapped her arms around me, leaning her head onto my shoulder and offering a small measure of comfort against the pain lacing through my body. The thought that he might have been intimate with my mother had been enough to break me.

How else could he have meant that?

"I meant you. I know what you feel like inside, your emotions. I know your soul, Little One, and I have felt hers. I've felt the twisted mess of it inside of me because of this cursed bond. Estrella, you are nothing like her; do you understand me? You are good and kind and so fucking stubborn, but you would turn the world over for those you love. She is incapable of caring about anyone but herself," he said, and I heaved a sigh of relief.

"So you've never touched Mab sexually?" I asked, wanting a step further. There was more to sex than just sex. I wouldn't fall prey to another Faerie play on words.

"Not directly, no," he said. He sighed when I jerked back, hanging his head forward. "She had friends who were intrigued by me. They treat all her children like their personal playthings. It's just her way."

"But you said you were celibate for centuries…" I said, my voice trailing off. There was no way for me to wrap my head around that deception. Unless it was because he'd been unwilling.

Rape was not sex.

My heart broke. He felt it, tilting his head to the side. "She used her influence over us to make us participate, but we were rarely willing. I stopped reacting centuries ago. It took the fun out of it for them and eventually they left me be, once they'd all had a turn. I meant it when I said I haven't touched anyone. Please, believe that," he pleaded, taking another step toward me. The first warm tear slid down my cheek, but I didn't retreat from the touch when he reached out to wipe it away.

"You always wanted me to have a choice," I said, realization dawning as I connected the dots. Because he hadn't, because they'd forced him to touch people that he didn't want, and he knew that pain deeply.

"You always will," he said, sliding his hand around the back of my neck. He pulled me into his chest, pressing his chin down on the top of my head.

"What about you? Will Mab make you do that again? To hurt me?" I asked, horror dawning over me. If I was her daughter, there was no telling what she would do. If that was how she treated her children...

"Even her magic has limits and it cannot defy a mate bond. If she had tried to force me to respond to someone after you were born, she wouldn't have been able to, and then she would have known that you exist. She cannot force me to be with someone now," he said, pulling back to stare at me. "But there is a reason she cannot know about you until I'm strong enough to fight her. Why she can never have you in her clutches. She may not be able to force you to touch someone in the way she did me, but she could still use your body to punish me. Do you understand what I'm saying?"

"She could tear the skin from my bones," I said, nodding my head.

"She could allow her men to rape you to punish me for keeping you a secret all these years. I knew I had a mate and never allowed her to have that information. I protected you, and she will hate that in ways you cannot understand."

"She would do that even if I'm her daughter?" I asked, looking at Fallon. She exchanged my worried gaze, that bond thrumming between us. Whichever one of us it was, one of us was the daughter of *that.*

"Mab would only reproduce to benefit herself. It has absolutely nothing to do with any sort of love she has for her child," he said, pulling back to look between Fallon and I. "Whoever it is, you will serve a purpose to her one way or another."

"*I*f all magic has a price, how do the witches pay it?" I asked, refusing to raise my hands to play with the swirling winter storm Caldris created in his hands.

He sighed, cocking his head to the side and flicking his fingers. The storm vanished into thin air, and I realized how desensitized I'd become to the sight of such displays. What had seemed impossible to me only a few weeks prior was now ordinary, almost unimpressive compared to the grand magic I'd seen him use. "They channel the nature around them, specifically the element or physical body of the very thing that they draw power from. In Imelda's case, her power is very limited during the day because it is far harder to pull magic from something that you cannot see than if she tries to channel at night."

"But how is that a cost?" I asked. The way she'd bound Fallon and I in our blood oath to each other, that magic had a very real cost. We were duty-sworn to uphold it or face the consequences of our betrayal.

"All magic is finite. If the Lunar Witches were to just take and take and take from the moon without giving, the power within it would eventually subside. Without giving back, the price in that case would be the depletion of the very magic they rely on, and they do not want that," he explained, stepping around my side. I followed him from the corner of my eye, something about his relaxed posture and easy smirk raising the hair on my arms.

"So what do they give?" I asked. I'd never seen Imelda give anything in the rare moments she muttered an incantation. She didn't do it often, using her magic sparingly and only when there was a moment that warranted it. Traveling alongside the Wild Hunt meant that most of her needs were seen to, even if she did still want to stab the Huntsman through the heart every time he looked at her wrong.

"It depends on the spell. As far as I understand, the witches' magic is more like a barter. A life for a life, an eye for an eye. *Someone* has to pay the price. In an ideal negotiation, the witch is able to have her enemy be the one to pay that cost to the magic, which is why Imelda rarely uses it except to protect herself. Then at the end of a witch's life, her soul returns to the power from which it came. It gives strength to the next generation of witches." he explained, circling around my back slowly. I didn't turn, allowing him to complete his rotation and emerge to the side of my other shoulder.

"When she revealed the mark on my arm, what did she have to sacrifice for that?" I asked.

"You paid that cost," Caldris said, glancing down at the burn mark on my hand. I recalled the searing pain, and the way I'd wanted to weep as my flesh sizzled away. I nodded, running my fingers over the mark.

The Fae had a different kind of cost, exhaustion and the risk of over-pulling on the magic in the fabric of the universe. I didn't want to think of what would happen if I pulled too much power before I was ready.

Would it burn me from the inside, scorching my soul the way Imelda's magic had my flesh?

I swallowed, shoving the thought away and shaking my head. Caldris continued his leisurely walk around me, stopping in front of me and regarding me. "Are you ready to begin?"

I nodded as I positioned my hands before me. Cupping them and tipping them up to the sky, I sucked back a deep breath and met his inquisitive stare.

"Good," he grunted, nodding slowly. He moved too quickly, pulling back his arm so suddenly that I barely had time to flinch away from the ball of snow that came barreling toward my face. It hit me in the side of the neck, the snow sliding down to sink into the neckline of my shirt.

"What is wrong with you?" I gasped, grasping my tunic around the collar and shaking it until the snow fell out the bottom, lighting a trail of icy fire down my stomach in the process.

"You aren't responding to slow methods, so we're going to take it up a notch," he said, curling his fingers up toward the sky. The storm that gathered in his hand swelled, building momentum with every dance of his fingers that drew more power into it.

"Don't you fucking dare," I said, taking a step back as he formed another snowball. His fingers continued to work around it, freezing it into a sphere of solid ice as my eyes widened in shock. "Caelum—"

He sent it spiraling toward me, spinning through the air as I ducked to avoid it. The next came quickly, and there wasn't time for me to even think about drawing his power through the *Viniculum*.

"When Mab and her allies come for us, do you intend to duck and weave for the rest of your life?" Caldris asked as I darted behind one of the trees surrounding our little clearing. I pressed my back into the trunk, my lungs heaving. It was ridiculous to be so frightened of a few balls of ice, but something in the intent trickling through the bond was different.

Caldris was done playing games, and if I didn't figure something out soon, he'd find other ways to force me to channel his power.

"I thought you were braver than that," he mused, knowing damn well how the words would grate against my pride and my desire to be independent. I didn't want to hide behind him and his men, lurking in the shadows while he fought for our freedom. "I thought you wanted to stand at my side as my equal, min asteren?" His voice was teasing as I pushed away from the tree trunk slightly. Clenching my fists at my side, I raised them and stared down at them. Willing the snow to come, channeling the cold and trying to sink into that golden thread that connected us.

I pulled on it sharply, grinning when I felt Caldris stumble forward, but it wasn't enough. I couldn't pull his magic toward me while he was using it, the single pathway of our bond blocked by his command over it.

I glanced at the icy teardrops hanging off the tree branches, feeling Caldris's snowballs thump against the other side of the tree trunk. They grew in cadence, their pressure increasing as I peeked around the corner. His ice balls grew in size, his eyes gleaming as he raised the stakes.

He was done with waiting for me to channel what should have been mine to command.

I touched a bare finger to one of the icy drops, letting the cold sink into my skin. A golden halo of frayed threads appeared around it, weaker than what I sensed from the bond, as if it was faded and the image of it only came from Caldris.

But he'd never spoken of being able to see those threads.

I stroked them, twisting them around my finger hastily and letting the cold sink farther into me. Ice flooded my veins as the threads grew, wrapping around my hand and forearm, clinging to me as I fed them with the limited power that came from Caldris's bond.

I felt his smirk as he realized what I was doing, as he could feel me channeling in a bigger way than I'd been capable before.

"Are you planning to come out and play with me, Little One?" he asked, his footfalls crunching quietly as the snow padded his steps. He stepped closer, coming around the other side of the tree as I made myself small and slunk away.

"That depends on what your definition of play is right now," I said, sneaking up behind him. I moved quietly, setting my feet into the snow lightly with the ease that came from being smaller.

Wrapping those golden tendrils around my arm tighter, I focused my attention on the patch of snow just beneath his next step. Lowering my hand to the ground beside my feet, I touched my palm to the snow and willed the cold into it, channeling those golden threads of ice from the tree and sent them spreading across the ground.

My fingers froze, the black tips tinting with frost as it flowed over my skin, but I didn't feel the sting of cold that should have accompanied it. When the snow beneath his feet turned to ice, Caldris spun to look at me, his feet slipping in his haste. I reached out my other hand, hooking it toward me as a chill winter wind spread through the clearing. It caught him around the backs of his knees, and I yanked it toward myself. His legs came out from under him and he fell, thudding against the ice and making it vibrate against the hand that I removed to stand to full height.

"Was that what you had in mind?" I asked, glaring down at

him as he grinned back at me. I darted behind the tree as he vaulted to his feet, slipping on the ice briefly before he caught his balance.

He chased after me as I curled around the tree trunk, sliding over the ice that I'd created and using it to gain speed. I looked over my shoulder, twining my hand to create a snowball that I threw at his face as he ran.

It crashed into his nose, his eyes widening comically disbelief as he laughed and wiped it away to flick back at me. "You're in so much trouble, my star."

I glanced at him as I paused, turning to face him fully. "You'll have to catch me first," I murmured.

He flung four snowballs at me quickly, the formation happening far faster than I could manage. I squeaked, pressing the palms of my hands together in front of me and stretching them out as I winced back with a grimace and waited for the burst of cold against my skin.

It never came.

I held a sheet of ice in my hands, spread between my palms with the splatter of his snowballs against the other side. "Looks like I found the cold," I said, shrugging my shoulders as I flung the ice to the side.

Caldris chuckled, taking a few careful steps toward me. They were slow, his gait controlled as he navigated the frozen terrain. When he reached me, he wrapped a palm around my cheek and leaned down to kiss me.

"Looks like you did," he agreed, dropping his mouth to mine. I didn't tell him about the golden threads, feeling in my soul that they weren't what he'd had in mind when he'd asked me to draw from him. There was something different about those tendrils that wrapped around me and gave me access to the winter.

I kissed him back, allowing him to distract me from that

all-too-familiar warning that rang in my head. The voice that told me I wasn't normal, even for a Fae Marked mate. That something else existed within me, allowing me to reach out and touch the magic around me.

Maybe it was just my mind's way of visualizing it; maybe it was more in my head than real.

His head jerked back suddenly, his gaze darkening as he looked through the clearing. "Get back to camp," he ordered, pushing me away from him gently and sending me a few steps toward where we'd left the others. He grasped the hood of my cloak, pulling it up over my head, and started frantically tearing my hair from the braids Fallon had done. "Leave your hair down and keep your mark covered."

"What's going on?"

"Get to fucking camp. I'll be alright, but you need to go *now*. Tell Holt that Octavian is here," he answered, pushing me forward. I moved, that compulsion striking me in the chest. Whereas before I hadn't recognized it, I felt it pulsing along the bond, knowing that I could stop it and suffocate it if I chose to grasp that thread and send it spiraling back toward him.

I did just that, taking the golden thread into my hands and wrapping fingers around it tightly. The compulsion stopped, severing from me as I slid my hand along it firmly. It collided with Caldris as his eyes narrowed, his gaze turning pleading for just a moment before I turned my back on him and made my way to camp.

I would go back because he asked me to, because I could see the seriousness of it in his face. I would not do it because he'd compelled me to obey.

I was not his pet, and I would not behave like one.

I finished pulling my braids free as I walked, returning to camp. The Wild Hunt lingered around the space, Holt leaning against a tree trunk they'd placed beside the fire. His head rested on it, his eyes barely cracking open when I stopped in front of him.

Imelda and Fallon looked at me, their gazes confused as they took me in. "Where's Caldris?" Imelda asked, raising her nose as if she could scent the air.

"He said to tell you Octavian is here," I said, nudging Holt with my boot. His eyes flung open and he hurried to his feet, looking out toward the woods.

He turned to Imelda, her panicked stare meeting his for a moment. Whatever they felt for one another or didn't feel was irrelevant in this moment. "Take her to your tent and stay there," he instructed her, grasping me gently around the fore-arm. He pushed me toward her, leaving me to stumble forward into her. She pulled my hood tighter around my head. "Cover those marks, witch."

Fenrir rose from his place by the fire, a growl rumbling in his chest. He moved to follow as Imelda guided me toward the tent she shared with Fallon, but Imelda's words stopped him short. "The best protection you can give for now is to stay away," she said, standing straight as the wolf bared his teeth.

Imelda swallowed, nodding as she guided me toward the tent she shared with Fallon. Fenrir sat back on his haunches, obeying the order Imelda had given him and remaining beside the fire. He didn't often demand my attention aside from a few pats by the fire at night, but he was always close by. Without him, I suddenly felt stripped naked for all to see.

Imelda, Fallon, and I ducked inside, but she left the tent fabric open so that the moonlight could stream inside. She tore down my hood, shrugging the cloak back to reveal all of my skin. Turning me into the moonlight, she let it touch my skin. "*Silism na camhorren sin,*" she murmured, the Old Tongue rolling out of her mouth. She ran her palm over every spot where the mark stained my skin, and I watched as the part that covered my hand faded to the color of my skin and blended in seamlessly. "Try not to speak in Octavian's presence. The magic will demand a price. To hide one truth, you must give another. Do your best to make sure you are with people you can trust, because you will have very little control over what is given."

"I can't pick the truth?" I asked, looking at her in horror. I didn't even want to think about the consequence for my reveal. Imelda shook her head sadly and I heaved a sigh. "Who is Octavian?" I asked.

"One of Mab's favorite children," she said, shaking her head with disgust. "He was taken from the Autumn Court a few centuries ago. The Autumn Court has always had an ax to grind with the Winter Court, and that alone was enough to make Caldris and Octavian enemies from the beginning. But Octavian came out differently than the others. He *enjoys* being indebted to Mab, and thrives off the power he feels in being loyal to the Queen of Air and Darkness. She would have sent him here only to spy on Caldris and make sure he is living up to the duty he was tasked with, because she knows just how much Octavian hates that Caldris was chosen for it at all."

"Why was he? If Octavian is such a faithful servant, why not send him?" I asked, watching as she drew the opening to the tent closed. She knotted it tight, pulling me over to share the two bedrolls, pressed between the two of them and hidden away from anything that might expose me.

"As loyal as Octavian might be, he is only a Sidhe. He cannot inflict the kind of damage Caldris can, and that has always made him lesser in Mab's eyes. If Caldris so much as batted an eye at her and served her as she thinks she deserves, he would be her favorite child, because he could be a true weapon to use against her enemies. He already is, even if his loyalty has to be demanded rather than freely given," Imelda explained, lying on her side to accommodate the lack of space with a third person crammed in. She closed her eyes as if she meant to get to sleep, and I stared at her incredulously in the dark.

"You can't be serious. Caldris is out there—"

"He can handle himself," she whispered, touching a single finger to my lips. "But Octavian cannot know you are Caldris's mate. If Mab knows you exist, she can order Caldris to bring you back to her. You must remain a secret for now, Estrella. That means you can no longer share a tent with him until they devise a way to get rid of Octavian. Now go to sleep. I have a feeling we'll all need the rest tomorrow."

I sighed, snuggling back into Fallon. She draped her arm over my stomach supportively for a moment, that sisterly bond flooding through me.

I closed my eyes, and I wished for sleep that didn't come.

"*R*ise and shine!" an unfamiliar voice shouted from the camp the next morning. It was too cheery, the pleasure in it hyperactive and false in every way. I sat up with a start, my eyes heavy and the skin raw underneath them as if I'd spent the majority of my night rubbing at them incessantly.

Imelda touched a hand to my shoulder, keeping me still as she glided to her feet. She stood, carefully keeping her shoes off the bedroll as she did, and turned to look back at me with a finger pressed to her lips.

She slowly pulled back the curtain of the tent, peeking out through the gap she created. Fallon and I leaned into one another, finding the right angle to peer outside through the small hole. People moved in every direction, the Wild Hunt shuffling the half-asleep Fae Marked toward the center where the fire had been the night before. They'd already put out the flames despite the fact that the sun hadn't even fully risen yet.

Imelda turned back toward me, shifting my cloak to the side to glance at the disguise on my skin. I could feel the magic coating me, and worry flashed through me that the Fae might feel it as well. "Make sure to keep your hair covering it and your cloak up as much as possible. We cannot risk the Fae Marked realizing that you're hiding something," she said, turning to look at Fallon briefly. The other girl nodded, agreeing with whatever silent sentiment passed between the two of them.

"They hate you enough to tell him what you are out of spite," Fallon said, as if I needed the reminder. Nearly drowning in a hot spring was all the proof I needed of what they desired for my fate.

"Just keep your distance. Stay with Fallon and I, and don't seek attention from Caldris in any way. He and Holt will determine how we proceed from here," Imelda said, finally unknotting the curtain on the tent and pulling it back. The early morning light flooded the little sanctuary we'd had from the Sidhe patrolling the camp, and Fallon and I hurried to our feet to follow at Imelda's back.

The Marked hurried to form a line next to the fire as a strange male shook the fabric of tents in his hands as he passed them. Stragglers hurried out of their makeshift homes, scurrying to the fireside as Imelda moved at a slow, leisurely pace.

This was the witch who would not be rushed by anyone. She was the witch who commanded the respect she deserved, even by just strolling unconcerned through the chaos and stopping at the edge of the fray. Fallon took the side closest to the group, leaving me to stand as far away from them as possible.

I clasped my hands together in front of me, trying to quell the nervous tremble as I kept my eyes pinned to the ashes that remained of our fire. Channeling Imelda's indifference, I sank into the hollow inside me.

Letting my face shift to that carefully-crafted mask I'd

worn far too often in the confines of Byron's library, I felt all the emotion drain from me, leaving me a husk, a soulless entity who existed within a bubble. The parts of me that made me into the person I was were far away, irrelevant to my survival that mattered in that moment.

Still, that golden thread that linked me to Caldris shone brightly in my peripheral as he stepped out of his tent. His armor and leather had been polished in the night, his figure striking as the crown he so rarely tolerated sat upon his head. The wolves paced at his heels, following behind their master as if they were as under his command as the dead he reanimated.

It had become easy to forget what the rest of the world saw when they looked at him. I spent most of my time experiencing the other side of him, the loving side of Caelum compared to the terrifying figure others saw—the brutal God of the Dead, the Fae male who could bring an entire city to its knees. His steps crackled through the snow, the silence I was used to him moving with gone with the show he put on for Octavian.

Everywhere the other Fae male was, everything about our journey to Alfheimr had changed. The easy camaraderie was gone, the casual pace as we maneuvered through the Kingdom shifted in favor of haste.

Caldris stopped in front of us, his attention going directly to Imelda. She held his gaze, standing flanked by Fallon and me as one would have expected of a guardian. "I trust the three of you slept well," he said, the words a statement and not a question. I looked up at the side of his face, my heart panging within my chest when he did not turn his attention to me. He did not glance my way, giving me none of his focus in a way that I had never experienced.

I'd become so used to being the center of his world that anything less felt like a heartbreak.

"We did, your highness," Imelda said, bowing her head forward respectfully. I quickly averted my gaze, staring at the ground next to my feet to follow suit. I didn't know how to play these games of politics.

I was fucked.

"Good," Caldris said simply, moving down the line. He stopped in front of the Fae Marked as the Sidhe male finally abandoned his pursuit of searching the tents. He strolled up beside Caldris, laying a heavy hand on his shoulder. The move was so familiar, so like a friend, that I grimaced. Knowing Octavian hated Caldris for being favored by the Queen they served, I saw it for what it was—a blatant disrespect meant to grate against Caldris's nerves. But my mate only regarded Octavian impassively, showing not a hint of emotion as the other male was left with no choice but to abandon his useless endeavor to irritate him.

Octavian's hair hung below his shoulders, an almost human-like shade of chestnut that I wouldn't have been surprised to find in Nothrek—had it not been for the bright copper strands that gleamed in the early sun. His features were refined, his cheeks hollow against the sharpness of his bone structure. His ethereal nature was all-encompassing, lacking the rugged beauty of Caldris. The red of his Mark twined up the side of his neck.

His clothing was all black, the stark coloring striking against his sepia skin. Imelda elbowed me in the side subtly, forcing me to turn away from my peripheral watching. It was painful not to look as he made his way down the line, his hands clasped behind his back. His posture was at ease, as if he possessed not a single care about the fear he created in others.

If the others hadn't proven to me that they deserved none of my compassion, I might have felt bad for them. They were unaware of the serpent that had slithered into their company, taking what they would have described as Tartarus and turning it into the pits of torment.

His footsteps continued, his easy swagger stopping when he laid eyes on Imelda. "Hello, Little Witch," he said, and it took everything within me to remain still. When Holt called her witch, it felt like banter. It felt like something playful, resembling foreplay, but this reeked of insult, the disrespect practically dripping from his tongue.

Imelda didn't move her body at my side, but I felt the moment she tilted her gaze up to meet his. "Hello, Pet," she returned, her voice frosty and disinterested all at once. "Such a shame these last centuries did not get rid of you."

"I am not so easy to kill," Octavian said with a scoff, leaning forward to touch his lips to the corner of Imelda's mouth. She didn't flinch back, allowing him the contact with nothing but boredom on her face. Holt took a step toward the scene from where he watched at the edge, but seemed to catch himself with a confused, disgruntled look on his face that brought me far too much amusement under the current circumstances. When Octavian finally straightened to full height, he grinned down at Imelda.

She tilted her head to the side, her brow furrowing in confusion. "Aren't you really?" she asked. No part of her moved, not her mouth or her hands at her sides, but a strangled sound bubbled up Octavian's throat in response. His hands flew to his throat, nails digging in on either side as he dropped to his knees. I watched in horror as his face turned red. "What's that? Witch got your tongue?" Imelda stared down at him, turning her head to the side and leaning forward as if she would be able to understand the babbles coming from him.

He coughed suddenly, the color returning to his face as he gasped for breath. "You fucking bitch—" he started.

"I would say that you've forgotten how to spell from lack of oxygen getting to your brain, but let's be honest. You never really had one of those to begin with," she murmured and looking down at him as if he was a sad little puppy.

"Mab will kill you. You cannot get rid of me so easily without facing the consequences from her," he protested, beginning to push to his feet.

Imelda put a single finger on his forehead, pressing him down softly, yet his body collapsed beneath him anyway. "She'll want you alive, but I highly doubt she'll care if I take a few pieces from you along the way, hmm?" she asked, twisting that finger against his skin. Her nail cut into him, leaving blood to well in response. It dissolved as soon as it touched the air. "A Sidhe will always be a Sidhe. You do not change or evolve, but we witches do. I am not so little anymore, Octavian. You would do well to remember that."

"Why are you here? Shouldn't you be holed up with the rest of your kind, hiding from the wrath of the Queen of Air and Darkness for the role you and your kin played in stealing her daughter? She'll kill you all if she finds you," he said, finally pushing to his feet. He swept a one thumb over the injury Imelda had made on his forehead, his gaze shifting from Fallon to me.

She'd lifted her cloak up in the same way as me, making us a matching pair even though she had no Fae Mark to hide.

Something passed over Imelda's expression briefly, and not for the first time I wondered what had happened to the rest of the Lunar Witches. She'd been the only one I'd seen at the Resistance in my time spent with them, but I knew a majority of the clan had come to this side of the Veil when they'd erected it. "I am precisely where I was always destined to be," she returned simply.

Octavian grunted his frustration, turning back toward where Caldris watched with a bored expression. "Can we continue our journey now, Octavian? Surely you've seen what you must and can understand how anxious we are to return to Alfheimr," my mate said, the words carefully crafted to avoid an outright lie.

"So where is the darling Princess then?" Octavian asked, staring around at the group of us. He reached forward, tugging Fallon's hood back to reveal her face as she slowly lifted her gaze from the ground to meet his eye. My breath caught, feeling the intent behind her boldness. Fallon was entirely capable of making herself small—blending into the background and nearly disappearing in a crowd. I'd seen her use those skills often in our limited time together, as if she could slip into the shadows themselves.

She challenged him because she wanted to, and because she knew that I would not be able to remain small for long. I was not willing to be put into a corner and left to wilt forever, and the longer we spent in Octavian's presence, the more likely I was to draw attention to myself. To put my foot in my mouth and make him look too closely.

If she and Imelda were both a challenge to him, it would be easier for me to blend in amongst them.

Fuck. I hated that oath already.

"It's one of those two," Caldris said, waving an impatient hand toward where Fallon and I flanked Imelda. "The witch can't be certain, so I've brought them both. Does that meet your approval? I would hate for Mab's messenger boy to disapprove of my methods."

Octavian tore his eyes away from Fallon's challenging

stare, stepping to the side and carefully passing Imelda without touching her. He reached up with both hands, tugging the hood back off my face as I raised my eyes to glare at him the way that Fallon had.

He studied me, his eyes, which were the green of leaves just before they turned to brown, roaming over my face. He raised a hand, lifting the underside of my chin to tip it higher before he glanced back toward Fallon. "They could be sisters," he said, his lips pursing as if it greatly displeased him that we looked similar.

"Need I remind you that whoever Mab's daughter is has been reincarnated twelve to thirteen times since her initial life and could look like anyone? It is purely coincidental that the girls have similar attributes in this life, because the vessels they inhabit right now are not of Mab's making at all. Only their soul belongs to her," Imelda corrected, heaving a sigh. Her frustration seemed to grow, confirming that she genuinely believed her earlier words to be true.

Octavian wasn't the brightest.

He flushed with anger. "I knew that," he said, turning his back on us and striding toward the horses in his embarrassment. "Pack up. We leave within the hour."

34

ESTRELLA

"**Y**ou're with me," Holt told Imelda, grasping her firmly around the forearm as he guided her away from the crowd. The Hunters finished packing up the tents and loaded the Fae Marked onto the carts so that they wouldn't need to walk. Not that they'd have been allowed to in Octavian's presence at any rate, even Imelda and Fallon and I would clearly have an escort for the time being.

He lifted her up by the waist, depositing her on top of his skeletal steed while she glared daggers at the ground. "I am perfectly capable of mounting a horse by myself, Horseman," she said, her lips twisting with a snarl.

"I'd like to see you reach the stirrups, Witch," Holt said, placing a foot in one pointedly and lifting himself up onto the back of the saddle. He settled himself against her ass, pressing closer than was probably necessary as she froze solid. "I did warn you that you would feel it," he added with a chuckle, reaching around her to grasp the reins in one hand.

"Brute," Imelda said, her voice shifting back to that tone of disinterest that she feigned, but I watched the flush creep up her neck all the same.

"You take Fallon today," Caldris said to Aramis. The other rider heaved a sigh of relief, looking like he might just stab himself if he had to ride with me. I smiled at him sweetly, tilting my head to wave goodbye to him as Caldris strode off to Azra without a word for me. Following behind him, I let him place me in the saddle and settled into the feeling of him at my spine. He pressed closer than necessary for just a moment, satisfaction trickling down the bond as we reunited physically —even for only a few precious breaths.

He straightened quickly, but regardless of his intent, the proximity of the saddle forced my ass to nestle into his lap. I took comfort in it where it made Imelda squirm with discomfort. She might find the same if she could see past her own denial of what was brewing between her and the leader of the Wild Hunt.

Fallon settled in with Aramis, her eyes wide as she met mine for a brief moment. He was awkwardly trying to create distance between them, as if she'd bite him for touching her. I couldn't be sure if it was because I'd made him distrust anyone who associated with me or if it had more to do with the fact that Fallon just might be the daughter of the Queen of Air and Darkness. I sincerely hoped it was the former, but suspected that Mab's wrath was more intimidating than mine.

I'd have to work on that.

Caldris squeezed his legs, motioning Azra into a steady walk forward as the Wild Hunt was set into motion. Things were quiet, far less jovial than they'd been even the day before. The tension of who I might be had been sitting heavily between my mate and I since the discovery of the moon burned into my hand, but this was new.

This was a horrifying silence that existed out of necessity. All too aware that Caldris was probably being watched at every turn, I couldn't help the instinct to lean into him and his embrace. I fought it, knowing that making us appear as if we were close would not work to my advantage.

"Why do these two and the witch not ride in the carts?" Octavian asked, steering his horse right up alongside Azra. He was close enough that my feet nearly brushed against his horse's flank, his attention feeling heavy on the side of my face where my cloak failed to hide my profile.

"The Fae Marked are not fond of them," Caldris answered simply, not bothering to turn and deem Octavian worthy of his attention as he rode forward.

"Since when do we care about the opinion of the rabble, brother?" Octavian asked, his laugh grating against my ears. I shifted my shoulders, trying to shrug my hood forward to cover more of my face, and my expression in the face of something so smugly classist.

I had always been the rabble, and until the day I died, part of me would cling to that memory.

"I don't, but what I do care about is seeing to the welfare of Mab's daughter. The Marked have tried to harm one of them already. I will not be responsible for the suffering of the Princess of the Shadow Court after all she has already been forced to endure just being on this side of the Veil for centuries," Caldris said, shifting his reins into both hands. The motion put me further into his embrace, offering me a small measure of comfort against the reminder of just how far those humans were willing to go to rid the world of me.

How far even my brother had been willing to go.

She cannot have you.

The words were an unbidden memory, bursting free inside of me and drawing a shocked gasp from my lips. He'd given me the answer, all but the name of who he needed to keep me from, in his last confession before he'd tried to plunge the knife into my heart.

Caldris's arms tightened around me as he felt my moment of panic and the anguish that consumed me for all to see. I'd thought I would need to give a truth to pay for the one I wanted to hide, but I suspected that Imelda's magic wasn't quite so cut and dried.

I'd recognized the truth I already owned, and the debt was paid. The magic swirled around on my skin contentedly, settling against the mark more fully and guarding my secret with the clinging of a desperate lover. "The Princess of the Shadow Court," Octavian murmured, his gaze looking into the distance as I watched from the corner of my eye. "She's been missing for so long. Sometimes I find it difficult to remember that she will be Mab's sole heir."

"She will," Caldris agreed, and there wasn't a single mention of the fact that he was already an heir because of his father. It didn't seem likely that Mab would give her throne to anyone at all, from what I'd learned of her in my short time of knowing she even existed, but she most definitely wouldn't give it to the son of the husband she'd killed.

"It would be wise for us to remember the opportunity this could present for us. Mab will undoubtedly need to choose a husband to rule beside her daughter. We both know how little stake she puts in mates, aside from the purpose of breeding," Octavian mused thoughtfully. "She wouldn't allow something as insipid as fate to determine such a thing. Have either of the girls showed signs of their markings? What court do they favor?"

"Did you see markings on either of them?" Caldris asked, avoiding answering the question. We both knew I had been marked, because I had a mate waiting. I tried to listen, searching for answers to my own burning questions. The Fae must have been marked from birth if no one thought it odd that Caldris had a *Viniculum* on his neck, otherwise they'd have known he had a mate somewhere.

"No," Octavian said, reaching over the gap between our horses. He tugged my hood down to reveal my face and my neck that was bare of a *Viniculum*. "Surely if they were Fae they would have them?"

"We believe their Fae forms will reveal themselves when they reach Alfheimr. That is the way the witch believes the magic that placed them inside human vessels and trapped them there will work," Caldris answered, glancing toward Imelda.

"You put too much faith in witches," Octavian said, a grimace twisting his features. I tried to keep my eyes forward, to avoid attracting too much interest, but I felt the weight of his gaze on the side of my face. Felt it glide down to observe what he could beneath my cloak. "Will their faces or bodies change?"

"They'll become Fae," Caldris said, his body stiffening at my back.

"Oh you know what I mean. Will they change besides better skin and pointed ears? Neither of them look like they'd be a punishment to bed for an eternity. I'm hoping it stays that way," Octavian said, touching a single finger to the top of my knee.

"We won't know until we arrive," Caldris said through gritted teeth, and the tension in his body made me want to reach out and touch him. To comfort him against the swelling jealousy that pulsed down our bond.

"I should like to spend some time with them, I think," Octavian mused, completely oblivious to the hatred coursing through Caldris's veins. How close was he to death, for daring to think of me in such a way?

What a fucking idiot.

"What good will that do you? Mab will choose who she pleases for her daughter, regardless of anything so insignificant as feelings," Caldris said, dancing around the subject he really wanted to discuss.

Like the fact that he would kill Octavian before he allowed him to touch me.

"You wound me, brother. I merely wish to get to know the woman I will be willing to service in the same way I service Mab herself. Should she require my attention, I would be more than happy to please the Princess."

"If Mab is my mother," I said, unable to stifle the disgust that rolled through me at his words. "I would sooner die than fuck anyone who has been with her. That is a boundary I will not cross."

Octavian smirked as I met his steely glare. "You'll severely limit your options in bed partners. Why would you do such a thing when true freedom is nearly at your fingertips? As a Princess of Faerie, you could have any male you wanted to keep you company at night, regardless of whatever political marriage your mother arranged."

"My dignity is worth far more than the freedom to fuck anyone I please," I said, turning my face forward to look in the direction that we rode. "I can understand if you do not have any, but do not project that onto me."

There was silence between us for a few moments as Octavian studied the side of my face. "I *like* her," he said suddenly, his laughter filling the air as he tossed his head back. "She has spent far too much time with the witch to be anything but amusing."

"If I have spent too much time with the witch, I find it necessary to remind you that I may be your Princess soon. I do not look favorably on men who call me 'amusing.' I am far more than a source of entertainment for you, *Sidhe.* Perhaps one day soon, I'll make you entertain me, and I promise you, my idea of entertainment involves spilling blood. Not sex," I declared, ignoring the way Caldris tightened his arms around me slightly.

A warning: to back off, to retreat back into the shelter of not attracting Octavian's attention. But to do so now would only make him think I had something to hide. I'd dug my hole.

Now I would have to lie in it.

"My sweet, sheltered Princess," Octavian chuckled, holding my startled glare. "You can take my blood anytime. There are plenty of us who enjoy having a royal bleed us."

"That's disgusting," I said, shaking my head and turning away finally. Let him think I was horrified by his confession, by the weight of it. I didn't care, so long as everything they did was consensual, as much as I might not understand the desire for such things.

He leaned over the side of his horse, his breath fanning across the side of my face. "Blood eases the way for some of life's more forbidden pleasures."

Caldris growled in warning as Octavian rode forward, turning his horse around and using the reins to guide him to take careful steps backward as he faced us. "It would seem my brother has already grown attached to this potential Princess," he said, dropping his gaze to where Caldris's hands clenched the reins tightly. "I'll take my chances with the other, instead."

He rode off, shrugging. I think it was meant to hurt that I was so replaceable. That I did not matter in the slightest aside from the possibility of being Mab's daughter.

Soon rage swelled within me as he rode up beside Aramis, protectiveness for Fallon flooding my veins. "Push it down," Caldris murmured softly, brushing the back of his knuckles across my cheek. "Fallon is a big girl, and Imelda has had years to teach her to play this game. She's prepared her for this, unlike you." He nodded his head forward, pointing out the way that Fallon smiled even though I knew it was fake.

Even though I knew she wanted nothing more than to hide beneath her hood and kick the male accosting her in the balls, she played the game that I was too inept to even know. She behaved like a Princess.

But we both knew she wasn't.

*O*ctavian stared at Fallon as she moved away from the fire the next morning, his eyes sweeping over her as if he could take in everything that made her with just a single glance. I had no doubt he intended to exploit her for his own purposes, and he'd practically eat her alive.

"You're with me today, menace," Aramis said, surprising me as he stepped up beside me. He lifted me off my feet and onto his skeletal horse, the rib bones digging into my calves as I settled on top of it. "Try not to stab me."

"I make no promises," I said, smiling at him sweetly as I shrank back into my hood. From across the camp, Caldris guided Fallon toward Azra. The wolves followed at his heels, Fenrir's nervous glance coming back to me as he let out a little whimper.

"Those damn beasts are going to fuck everything up if they keep looking at you like you're their mother," Aramis said, his tone scolding.

"Like I have any control over them. They're giant wolves," I protested, shrinking away from the scathing glare he settled on me. He swung his leg up, mounting the horse behind me and squirming away from my body uncomfortably.

"My teeth aren't attached to my ass, you know," I said, facing forward and biting my bottom lip to control my amusement.

"No, but I'm fairly certain Cal's are," Aramis whispered, keeping his voice low as Octavian approached where Caldris and Fallon patted Azra's mane.

I watched in horror as Octavian grasped Fallon around the waist, depositing her onto his own horse with a smug grin. "Can't let you have all the fun, brother," he said, glancing back toward me briefly.

I clenched my fists, tucking them safely within my cloak to hide my frustration. I hadn't been particularly fond of the idea of Fallon riding with my mate's groin pressed into her ass, but I'd been willing to tolerate it over this.

I realized with a shock that the pulsing jealousy I felt over other women didn't exist with Fallon. I'd never questioned what might come if she and Caldris spent too much time together, as if my soul recognized her on a level that knew she could never do that to me, or maybe it had been the bond between us and the emotional connection I'd formed with Caldris.

I shook off those thoughts, glaring at Octavian as he mounted his horse behind her and pressed entirely too close to her back. She kept her face carefully neutral, not giving way to any of the disgust I knew she felt having him touch her. "Don't worry, Princess," Octavian said, staring at me briefly before he winked. "I can give you a ride later, too, if you like."

He kicked his horse into a walk, his heels digging in far more harshly than necessary. He took off at a fast trot, jostling Fallon in her seat so that she bounced into his lap.

Caldris mounted his own horse, walking up alongside us

as we moved forward. "Behave," he ordered, not even glancing toward me. I glared back, knowing without a doubt that the fucking ass could feel it even if he couldn't see it.

"Is he really just meant to be allowed to violate her like that? What of her right to not be touched like that?" I asked.

"She hasn't protested once, Little One. Unless she does, I cannot interfere," Caldris admitted.

"But we both know she doesn't like him touching her. She's only tolerating it..."

"To protect you from yourself, yes. I am quite aware. Unfortunately, you are looking in the wrong place if you think I will try to dissuade her from doing so. Let's not even discuss how you might as well get something out of your foolish blood oath to one another."

Fenrir maneuvered himself between us, and I greatly wished I could forgo the horses entirely and snuggle into the warmth of his fur.

I kind of thought riding the wolf would draw some attention though.

Fuckers.

> ●

*F*allon stood from her place by the fire after she'd finished eating the dried meat and bread that made up most of our diet. There were too many of us to feed with the traps Caldris could set, even with the Wild Hunt being, well... Dead.

One of the shades who wanted to haunt the camp for the night popped up in front of Fallon, making her squeal in surprise. She stumbled back and two firm hands grasped her around the waist before pulling her back and settling her on top of a distinctly male lap.

A Fae male.

One who needed his hands fucking removed. After watching him torment her for the entirety of the day, I had just about had it with the violation of his hands upon her body when she so clearly didn't like it. She smoothed out her expression each time before he could notice her discomfort, but it did nothing to stop the anger that formed low in my belly.

This brought my temper simmering to the surface. "We should get to bed," Imelda said, standing smoothly and taking my hand. She squeezed it tightly, grounding me with the pain of her nails digging into my skin. I let her bleed me; let her take that part of me and use it to make me behave. Because I could not be trusted.

One more day with this fucker would be too much, but he showed no signs of leaving our group until we'd made our way across the boundary to Alfheimr. No doubt he wanted to be part of the procession to deliver Mab her daughter and reap those rewards.

"Come, Fallon," Imelda said as we approached, holding out a hand to take the other girl's. She clasped her fingers in hers to pull her free from Octavian's lap as Caldris watched from the sidelines with Holt. Observing the interaction, but doing nothing to stop or reprimand the male for the way he tightened his hands on her waist and held her pinned in place.

She squirmed against his hold on her, the first sign of her outright refusal to tolerate his behavior. "Take your hands off of her," I snapped, drawing his surprised stare to myself. He dug his fingers deeper, and I could practically feel the way her skin bruised beneath the harshness of it.

"No thank you, Princess," he said, rolling his eyes at the

bark to my tone. "Fallon and I are enjoying getting to know one another."

"She doesn't look like she's enjoying it to me," I said, dropping my eyes to the pained expression on her face. I recognized it all too well, the pain that brought the grimace was nothing compared to the fear of what had yet to come. "She's coming to bed."

"Shouldn't you be going to bed with your mate?" one of the Fae Marked men asked, and the air around us went still. Octavian studied me curiously, peering beneath my hood to inspect the neck I knew was empty of all signs of Caldris's markings. Yet my neck buzzed with warmth, as if the secret being out in the open meant the magic wouldn't be able to sustain the disguise for long. Imelda stilled as if she knew the same, her body at my side going taut before she backed away slowly.

Caldris moved from across the fire, moving toward us hurriedly, but his steps were far too slow to prevent me from doing what I'd longed to do since the moment Octavian had first placed his slimy fingers on my friend.

I bent forward, grasping his wrists and wrapping my fingers around his bare skin. "Are you fond of the cold, Octavian?" I asked, summoning the golden tendrils from the snow on the ground beneath him. They reached up, wrapping around his wrists where I grasped him. Ice crept over his flesh, frost rising in delicate patterns to curl up his forearms as he stared down in shock.

I shrugged out of my hood, feeling the cold extend from my hand all the way up my arm, until the frost licked the side of my neck and my Fae Mark blazed to life in blinding white. "What the fuck?" Octavian asked when I flung his arms away, letting Fallon get to her feet quickly as Caldris finally closed the distance between us. He stayed back ever so slightly, observing the interaction with something painful crossing his face.

This was an impossible situation. Mab would not be pleased if he never returned to her, and with the secret out in the open, there was no undoing it. There was no backtracking from what I'd done.

"Your mate?" Octavian asked suddenly, pushing to his feet. His frozen hands slipped against the ground as he fought to shake off the ice clinging to him, threatening to freeze him solid entirely. His fingers looked like glass, or the first tint of blue sheen atop the lake in the beginning of winter.

"That would be me," Caldris answered, closing the distance. He touched a hand to my cheek, turning my gaze to his. The black of my Fae Mark came to life as he trailed the back of his knuckles down my neck, awakening the darkest parts of me.

For the first time in my rage, golden threads sprouted from the ground. I twined one around my fingers, watching the way Caldris narrowed his eyes on the movement. I realized how wrong I'd been when I'd thought that my price had been a truth I gave to myself.

This was my truth. The one that I gave to Caldris as he watched me summon the golden threads. I pulled up, raising my hand toward the sky with my palm open as a bony hand lifted out of the dirt beside Octavian's feet. The skeleton clawed at the earth, yanking itself up slowly until the second hand emerged.

Its head followed, rolling to the side as it shook the dirt off and turned to face Octavian. "Put your pet back in the ground, Caldris!" Octavian yelled, taking a step away. The terror on his face was far more than I would have expected, leading me to believe that he'd likely already had a negative experience or two with Caldris's dead.

"This pet isn't mine," Caldris said, his voice laced with amusement. He turned to me, a smug smile on his face as I twirled that thread within my hand.

"Bring me his heart," I said, murmuring the words softly as the skeleton stepped forward with awkward steps. Octavian drew the sword from his scabbard, holding it out in front of himself as he sliced at the bones of his attacker.

My skeleton split down the middle, his torso toppling over and falling to the ground in a stack. "You'll have to raise more than one to kill me!" Octavian roared.

I tilted my head to the side as I stacked my fingers on top of one another. The power within me pulsed in recognition, driving me forward on instinct alone as I took a single step. I watched in awe as the bones of the skeleton stacked upon each other once again, forming the lone figure that could not be cut down so easily.

"Holy fuck," Holt said, stepping up and grabbing Fallon. He pulled her and Imelda away from the fray as golden threads wrapped around the waist of my skeleton, holding its body together temporarily.

"I-what?" Octavian said, glancing toward Caldris.

"Never seen that before," my mate muttered, his lips pursing in thought. The skeleton charged forward, taking Octavian's sword through its torso, but its fingers continued to grapple at Octavian's chest, its bones clawing through the leather of his armor until they sank into the flesh beneath it. They toppled to the ground, my skeleton landing on top while Octavian struggled to draw his sword free from the mess of bones that had trapped it.

Fenrir came to my side as I laid my free hand atop his head, settling into the comfort of his fur for a moment. He took a step forward along with me, moving in tandem as he and Lupa each grabbed one of Octavian's wrists in their mouths and held him still. His skin burst open as their teeth broke through, digging deep as the Fae wailed.

I stepped toward them, leaning over Octavian and staring down into his panicked face. "Is this what you had in mind when you said you enjoyed being bled by royals?" I asked, watching as the skeleton struggled to break through the rib bones protecting Octavian's heart. I turned away, leaving them to the fight, confident that my skeleton wouldn't stop until it delivered me what I'd asked.

I made my way back to Caldris, letting my bloodthirsty mate lean down to touch his mouth to mine. Octavian screamed in the background. "Caldris! She'll kill you for this!"

Bones cracked as I turned back to face them, my skeleton having dug its fingers through the skin on Octavian's chest. It grasped a second rib bone, breaking it free and tossing it to the side to get to the heart hidden within his breast.

"Ah, but you see; I can claim I had nothing to do with your death. You just pissed off the wrong woman," Caldris said, grinning as a heartbeat echoed through the clearing. My skeleton stood with the still-beating heart finally in its hands. It carried it to me, blood pumping free to stain its bones.

Octavian watched, his eyes glazing over as I accepted the heart into my extended palms. My fingers wrapped around it, and I watched as the frost spread over the surface of it. As it sank into the flesh of it and froze it solid, and the beating stopped altogether.

When I was confident it was frozen clear through, I spread my hands and let it fall to the ground. It descended as if in slow motion, crashing against the ground at my feet and shattering into thousands of red pieces across the snow.

I felt the moment Octavian's soul fled his body, leaving to wander until he found his way to the Void.

Caldris wrapped his arm around my shoulder, tucking me into his side as I breathed a sigh of relief.

At least that was taken care of.

"Will you require anything else, my Lady?" the skeleton asked in a baritone, rotating his head around so that it spun to face his back.

I squealed, thrusting my hands forward in my panic. The threads released his torso as they flung off my hand, letting his bones collapse in a pile as the animation left him. I stared at him, waiting to see if he would rise once again, but there was nothing left as I released the golden thread I'd used to reanimate him.

Caldris raised his brow as he turned to regard me with an inquisitive stare. The moment of reckoning had come. "Well, that was new."

36

*F*uck.

Caelum glared at me, running his tongue along the underside of his top teeth. Holding my stare, he waited for the moment I would open my mouth and give him the answers his gleaming, dark gaze demanded.

"Estrella..." he said, his voice trailing off. The shock of my real name on his lips in that irritated tone made everything inside of me clench. Not with desire, or with anything even close to resembling it, but with the realization that I was in trouble.

I was in a lot of fucking trouble.

"Caelum," I murmured, keeping my tone soft as I took a step backward. I looked to where Fallon and Imelda had stood only a few moments before, finding their spot empty. Even Holt and the rest of the riders had retreated to the side of the camp where the Fae Marked would sleep in their tents. Making themselves inconspicuous, fading into the background as if we were not aware of their presence.

"Would you, perhaps, care to explain to your mate what the fuck that was exactly?" he asked, glancing down to where my hands were clenched at my sides. I flexed my fingers, following his gaze down to the dark tips and the nails that seemed to sharpen with each day.

I swallowed, lifting my eyes back to his. He quirked a brow, watching me, waiting for my answer. "Not particularly, no," I said, smiling to soften the blow.

He clenched his jaw, gritting his teeth as he took a step toward me. I circled back slowly, narrowly evading the way he prowled after me. Circling around the fire, I glanced over my shoulder to meet Holt's evasive glare as he peeked out from the shadows. His stare was full of judgment, a condemnation for the secrets I'd chosen to keep from my mate.

Who could hardly complain, seeing as he'd done far worse.

"Why did it look as though you were playing the skeleton like a puppet on a string?" he asked, reaching out to grasp my hand in his. He pulled me into his body, guiding me around the edge of the fire so the flames barely avoided catching the hem of my coat.

He stared down at my hand, turning it over and studying it as if my palms could give him the answers he wanted. "I see threads," I admitted.

His brow furrowed. "Like the one you said you visualize between us?" he asked, watching as I lifted my other hand. I stroked the thread that existed between us, giving it a sharp tug in confirmation. His mouth dropped open for a brief moment, the shock of it rolling over him all over again.

"I don't think I visualize it," I said, stepping away from him. "I think they're there. I think I can see them when others can't." I dropped lower to the ground, stopping with my hand just far enough above the surface of the snow that I could brush my fingers over the frayed edges of the threads. I lifted them, dancing fingers over the surface of them and encouraging them to grow. Rising to my feet slowly, guiding those lines to come with me, I grasped Caldris's hand and touched them to his skin.

He didn't react; there was no sign that he could feel them tickling against his skin as I moved them. "You truly cannot feel them?" I asked, allowing the cold of them to wash over my skin. I pressed that coldness into his open palm, watching as the frost danced over his hand. It slid up to his wrist, like the first markings of cold on the glass window in my bedroom. I moved my fingers, watching as the image of a serpent slithered up through that frost and stuck its tongue out at him.

Laying my palm flat against the side of his forearm, I watched in fascination as the serpent slithered off his skin and onto mine, solidifying and growing until the white creature had the density of a real snake, winding itself around my arm and nestling into the layers of my cloak for warmth.

"I've never heard of such a thing," he said, swallowing as he tore his eyes off the snake, glancing over my shoulder. I turned to watch as Holt approached. He stared at the snake crafted from snow and ice as I lowered myself to the ground, watching as it dispersed back into the snow and ceased to exist entirely. "Can you do it with anything other than the dead and the winter? Are there any other threads that have made themselves available to you other than the powers that come from the *Viniculum*?" he asked, his brow furrowing.

"I hadn't thought to look for them," I admitted, because he'd told me to ignore the part of me that was too dangerous to explore. The part of me that was impossible to control and unleashed something like a monster.

"Try it now. I'll pull you back if you wander too far into the darkness, min asteren," Caelum said softly, reaching out to take my hand in his once more. I squeezed him back, nodding as I let my eyes close for a moment, shutting him out and the presence of Holt watching at my side, eerily silent.

He knew more than he wanted to admit, I suspected.

I opened my eyes, turning my gaze to the moon and stars in the sky—the twinkling of lights that ruined the complete darkness. Raising my hands, I waited for the golden threads to make themselves known to me.

They dropped from the moon, hanging from the stars and stretching toward me like the loose threads of a dress, straining to reach the ground. I grasped them in my hands, twining them around my fingers and my palms until I held a ball of them in loose fingers.

I closed my eyes, tightening those fingers into a fist and squeezing. When I opened my eyes, I watched as the light of the moon dimmed, disappearing beyond the clouds that suddenly formed. Darkness descended upon the clearing, leaving us in a void of all natural light. Only the fire at our sides illuminated the shock on Caldris's face as his eyes met mine.

He stepped forward, tipping my face down and studying me curiously. "Your eyes, Little One," he said, running a thumb beneath them.

"What's wrong with them?" I asked, flinching back as Holt stepped up beside me. He, too, stared down into my face, his shock giving way to something that resembled horror.

"They look as if you've trapped the night sky within them. Like you hold the universe within you," Caldris said, dropping his hand away. "What is she?"

His attention shifted to Holt, the friend who was even older than he, who had seen the rise and fall of Gods and men alike.

"I think we both know who can control the darkness and

who has an affinity for snakes," Holt said, crossing his arms over his chest.

"Mab doesn't see golden threads," Caldris protested, raising my hands. "She doesn't touch them with her hands." Even though he couldn't see the way I'd wrapped the shimmering golden lines around my fingers, he held them as if they were sacred.

As if my hands were something to be revered, not feared.

"Perhaps Mab is more skilled and doesn't need to use her hands in such a way. Would you know if she touched them with her mind? Estrella is a novice, and this is what she is capable of. Think of what centuries of knowledge and practice could do for a female like Mab," he said, dropping his head low as he took a step back. "All the answers are right in front of you. You just do not want to admit the truth to yourself."

"I refuse to accept that," Caldris said, shaking his head and shrugging off his friend.

"Exactly!" Holt said, raising his arms in anger. "You cannot expect to see the truth if you have blinded yourself to it! Your mate is the reincarnation of Princess Maev. Do us all a favor and acknowledge it so you can prepare for what's coming."

"Until I know for certain that she is Maev, I cannot and will not accept that. If I do, then I must take her to Mab at once. Let us live in ambiguity for as long as we can, Huntsman. Or would you like to dance with your own truth so soon?" Caldris asked, tilting his gaze toward where Imelda had gone. I didn't understand what truth he spoke of, but the weight of Holt's admission was far more important than whatever secrets Holt was keeping.

If my name was Maev, then why did that feel so wrong?

37

CALDRIS

*S*he left my side in the middle of the night. Her nighttime wanderings had become more and more common, the restlessness that consumed her driving her to the fire where she could stare at the stars in the heavens above. The riders of the Wild Hunt had always given her a wide berth, but after watching what she'd done to Octavian, I could just imagine how they would avoid being near her.

They'd treat her like something to be feared, when she'd only done what I already could. Mostly, anyway. The dead I raised had never been sentient. They'd never once spoken, in all my centuries of animating them to do my bidding. They'd never moved of their own free will, asking questions as if they had a mind.

She hadn't brought him back to life, not with the fact that he was again nothing more than a pile of bones, but he hadn't really been dead, either. He'd existed in the in-between, as if Estrella had reached out and grasped one of the souls wandering the spiritual plane.

I sat up, reaching over to grab my boots and tug them onto

my feet. She hadn't bothered to tie the flaps of the tent shut, leaving them to billow in the wind. She knew how pointless it would be, because I always followed shortly after her.

Where she went, I belonged—in this life or the next.

I stepped out of the tent, making my way toward the place where she lay on the blanket we'd occupied for a few short moments the night before. A deep, cloying sadness had clung to her in the aftermath of Octavian's death, as if she couldn't quite let go of Holt's haunting accusations. He'd put a name to the very thing she already believed herself to be, giving her the name she might have had if she'd never been taken to Nothrek.

I refused to believe it. There was so much goodness in my mate, so much kindness and drive for what was just and fair. She couldn't possibly be the child of the tyrannical queen who ruled through pain and suffering.

"Caldris," Imelda said, stepping up in front of me. She halted my progress, stopping me from reaching my mate and the intense waves of grief that pulsed off of her.

"What is it?" I asked, crossing my arms over my chest. I couldn't feel the cold winter air on the bare skin of my torso, but the intent expression on Imelda's face made me uncomfortable. If she was ready to tell me that my mate was the daughter of Mab, I would lose control over the rage trapped within me.

"I need you to make me a promise," she said, hesitating as she looked back toward the fire.

"I don't make promises to anyone but her," I said, nodding my head to my mate. Her arms were raised toward the sky, her hands and fingers dancing as if she was playing with the very threads that hung from the constellations above her head.

"Promise me you'll protect her. Keep her safe; not only

from harm but from those who would seek to use her for her power," she said, and I raised an eyebrow at her when she paused. She had to have known that such a promise was a given. I would do anything to protect Estrella, at the cost of the very world itself. "But if you fail to do that, if Estrella is lost to the darkness, promise me you'll help me end it."

"What?" I asked, certain I hadn't heard her right.

Imelda's face twisted, her nostrils flaring as she worried her bottom lip and sniffled. The first tear fell, and she shook her head. "You didn't feel it, did you?"

"Feel what?"

"When she hid the moon and stars from view. They weren't just hidden behind the clouds; it was like they ceased to exist," Imelda said, crossing her arms over her chest to mirror my posture. The witch's face twisted with pain, as if the memory of that loss was so great she couldn't allow herself to think of it.

"Don't be ridiculous," I said, stepping around her to approach Estrella.

Imelda grabbed my forearm, halting me once more as my gaze dropped to the contact. "I mean it, Caldris. I don't know if she is Mab's daughter or something else, but that kind of magic could change the world. The two of you could rebuild Alfheimr to be a haven for all, or you could drag it deeper into the darkness Mab created. If Estrella cannot control the magic trapped inside of her, think of the damage she could cause."

"She thinks you care about her. She thinks you and Fallon are her friends, and I would be entirely comfortable saying she loves you like family, even though she barely knows you. You repay that by coming to me and asking me to kill my mate?" I asked, my brow furrowing as she stared up at me with tears in her mismatched eyes.

"I love her. I have adored that girl in every one of her lives, and I know her well enough to know that she would want someone to stop her from becoming the monster she would hate. I'm not asking you to kill her just in case. I'm asking you to do what needs to be done if the Estrella we know is ever lost to us," the witch said, her bottom lip trembling as she glanced up at the moon.

"I would gladly sacrifice this world and everyone in it for her. What do I care of your desire to have a moon in the sky to draw power from?" I asked, my eyes hardening into a glare.

"That's not what this is—"

"Don't ever come to me with this again, and if you ever try to harm her, I will put you down myself, witch," I growled, striding past her to approach my mate.

"Are you going to tell her?" Imelda asked, swallowing as I turned to look back at her over my shoulder.

I studied her, contemplating it and knowing that I could have more time with my mate if she lost the sense of loyalty she felt for Imelda. It would drive a wedge between Fallon and her, leaving Estrella with no one but me to rely on. It shouldn't have appealed as much as it did, but after centuries without her, I wasn't just possessive over her body. I was possessive over her attention, and wanted to be the only one she spent time with.

"No," I said finally, watching as the witch's shoulders sagged in relief. "I would do anything to protect her. Even shelter her from the truth of your betrayal." I turned, leaving Imelda behind me as she closed her eyes slowly.

Drawing cool air into my lungs, I willed my body to relax, pushing the stress and rage away as I watched Estrella's fingers dance over the threads I couldn't see. They must have been quite the sight, hanging from the sky and shimmering in the light of the moon. I raised a hand, looking down at my fingers and wondering what it was in my mate that she could see such things when I could not.

"I miss you every single day," she whispered, the sadness in her voice cracking something inside my chest. "But fuck if I don't hate you too. I hate you for not telling me the truth, for lying to me all my life. What *am* I? Am I her daughter? Is that why you were so desperate to keep me from the Fae?" she asked, and it took me only a moment to realize that she was speaking to her brother.

I paused, waiting for a lull in her one-sided conversation before I would approach. I didn't want to encroach on her private moment or the ways she needed to grieve. "I can feel you watching me," she said, her voice louder. It sank inside me, and I knew she was speaking to me; she sensed me the same way I felt her when she was near or far.

I strode toward her, dropping down onto the blanket beside her, but I kept my gaze off her face, staring up at the stars and wishing I could see what she saw. I wished we could share the glimmering threads that filled her vision.

Maybe seeing would help me understand better, and to grasp why she could see them when the Gods I knew could not. If she was a second-generation God like me, why was there such a variance in the way our powers manifested?

What would reveal itself when she stepped on Faerie soil?

She sat up finally, staring into the flames as she crossed her arms over her chest. "Was there ever a time when you felt guilt for the lives you took?" she asked, finally turning her stare to me. It was filled with the glimmering lights of the stars, the black tinted with purple and specked with gold.

"Yes," I said, nodding as I reached out and touched her hand with mine. "When Mab first started treating me like an executioner, I felt more guilt than you could possibly imagine over the lives I took."

"What about lives you took willingly? Did those weigh on you too?" she asked.

"Do you feel guilty? For killing Octavian?" I asked, reading through the questions she asked. She wanted another creature who'd had a similar experience to commiserate with, but I'd never taken a life without knowing the cost until I'd leveled Calfalls. Not on my own terms; not of my own free will.

That was one massacre that guilt couldn't begin to cover. Some of the people of Calfalls had deserved the death I'd given them, but there'd been innocent bystanders lost to the destruction as well.

"No. What does that say about me?" she asked, her breath expelling in a disbelieving huff. "Surely I'm some kind of monster. I don't feel guilt for killing someone."

"He doesn't deserve your guilt. You know that," I said, turning toward her. I shifted my body into hers, touching my forehead to hers and staring into those eyes that felt as old as eternity staring back at me.

"I know he doesn't. The guilt wouldn't be for him; it would be for me. To tell me I'm still human," she said, her voice catching on a sob as she cast her eyes down.

We'd reached the real point of the conversation. Estrella's belief in her own humanity faded more with every day that passed, and with every time she did something that was distinctly *other*. She couldn't be human if she possessed magic outside of our bond, and for a woman who had been human all her life, that must have been a bitter plant to swallow. "Min asteren," I said, my voice gentle as she pursed her lips and tried to stem her tears.

For the rest of us, her humanity mattered little. She was still the same woman I'd come to love, no matter what shell housed her soul. She was still the same person she'd been a fortnight prior, years prior.

Now, she was just more. More than human, more than a harvester, more than a poor girl in a dirty village trying to find a way to survive. She was the kind of female The Fates knitted threads to create, crafting her from visions of potential futures that no one else knew of. She felt the sudden weight of that, and of how the world rested, awaiting the choices she would make and how they would alter life as we knew it.

"You aren't human, but that doesn't mean you aren't still *you*," I said, leaning forward to touch my mouth to hers. It started as a gentle caress, the light press of my lips meant to comfort her. She took it, deepening it and leaning into my body until she pressed a hand to each of my shoulders, guiding me to my back upon the blanket.

"My star," I murmured as she took her lips from mine. She swung a leg over my hips, straddling me as she laid her weight down upon my torso and brought her lips to the side of my neck. She caressed the *Viniculum* with her mouth, her tongue darting out to taste my skin and drawing a ragged groan from my throat. Her hips ground against mine, seeking the friction of my cock against the heat of her pussy, which seared through both our trousers like a brand.

"Make me forget," she whispered when I settled a hand on each of her hips. I stilled her motions, trying to use the self-control I suspected she would appreciate come morning. The Wild Hunt had been willing to give her space because of their fear of her, but even they would not be able to resist the lure of our sex beside the fire.

They'd engage with one another, pairing off amongst themselves where they could, but all eyes would be on Estrella and I. On the novelty of bodies they hadn't yet seen in the throes of ecstasy.

An eternity was a long time to be confined to certain bed

partners, with only the other members of the Wild Hunt to keep them company.

"Stop being so noble," Estrella pushed, grasping my hands and pinning them to the ground beside my head. "For a single night, I want to forget that I am anything but your mate. I want to quiet the raging questions in my head," she said.

"We should move to the tent if you'd like to avoid an audience," I said, pointedly nodding toward where riders of the Wild Hunt had already begun to trickle toward the fire. They could sense Estrella's need, scent it in the air as well as I could. I rolled her beneath me, feeling protective and sheltering her from their view. With her will lost to her grief and the sadness that had consumed her, I didn't want her to be caught unaware.

She surprised me, reaching up to catch me around the back of my head and dragging my lips toward hers as she cocked a leg out to the side. She spread for me, wrapping it around my back and hooking it over my ass as she lifted herself to rub against me. "Then I suppose you had better get inside me. We both know you don't want them to see me unless I am filled with your cock." She dropped her hands to her tunic laces, untying them quickly as I watched the line of cleavage she revealed.

"Estrella," I warned, rising onto my knees between her legs. She pushed up onto her elbows, grasping the hem of her shirt and then maneuvering her body so that she could tug it over her head. She kept herself suspended for a moment with the muscles of her stomach, lowering back down to lie on her back once more. Her breasts were free from their confines, her nipples pebbled in the cold winter air. "You're playing a dangerous game." I felt the eyes of the Riders of the Wild Hunt on her breasts, felt the way they admired her form.

Because of my friendship with Holt, I knew that they could

feel. I knew they could touch one another and bring pleasure, but was it ever the same as a real, solid figure in your arms? Estrella had flesh and bone; she had skin that was the color of liquid bronze. She had dusky pink nipples that begged for attention until she lifted a hand to pinch one of them after she'd felt my gaze shift lower. She slid her other hand into the waistband of her leggings, reaching into the heat between her thighs to stroke her fingers over her clit. She worked them in small circles, playing with herself more than pleasuring.

The show was for me alone, meant to drive me to the ledge of a possessive claiming. I wouldn't be gentle when I finally touched her, not after daring to reveal herself without my permission.

I bent forward suddenly, wrapping my lips around the breast she didn't already torment and using my hands to lift her ass into the air. I tore her leggings down her thighs and over her knees before I finally had to release her breast to pull off her boots and finish taking her pants off the rest of the way.

She spread for me when I lowered her back to the blanket, showing me the pretty pink color of her pussy as she lifted her legs high and bent her knees. She had to be aware of the eyes on her body, of the members around the fire as they moved and watched the show she put on for them. Her hand went back to the spot between her legs, careful not to block her slit from my view as she toyed with her clit.

"I want your mouth, *God*," she said, her lips twisting with mischief. She was playful as she waited for me to obey her demand, and I knew her words hadn't been an accident. That part inside of her that craved dominance over others, that craved revenge and the power that came with it, wanted to see a God kneeling between her legs. She wanted to be serviced, driven to pleasure, and then fucked by a God for all to see.

She wanted the female members of the Wild Hunt to see me pleasure my mate, and to show them that I was hers and hers alone. None would dare to go against a mate bond, but that didn't change the possessiveness radiating off her naked body as I shifted lower to lie on my stomach and pushed her hand away. I wrapped my arms around behind her thighs, kissing her belly button before lowering my face. "Is this what you wanted, my mate?" I asked, touching my lips to her clit in a slow, teasing kiss.

"More," she whispered.

"Tell me *exactly* what you want, Estrella, or I will not give it to you," I said, licking her clit lightly as she stared down at me.

"I want you to show them you're mine," she growled, that jealousy pulsing down the bond between us. "I want them to see how you worship me, and not just the other way around."

I pressed my mouth more tightly into her flesh, wrapping my lips around her clit and sucking as I slid a finger through her slit and worked it inside. She groaned as I finally gave her what she wanted, savoring the taste of her with long, frenzied thrusts of my tongue against her flesh. Her hand came down to grasp my hair at the back of my head, tugging me where she wanted as I drove her higher.

She resisted the urge to come, trying to prolong the time I spent with my mouth between her legs. I didn't know if it was her need to possess me that drove her to see me devour her pussy for longer or something else entirely, but I watched her possessiveness war with the desire for an orgasm.

"Do you intend to come for me, my star? Or is it that you wish to see my mouth between your legs for the rest of the night?" I asked, staring up at her as I drew my mouth away from her sensitive flesh.

She whimpered in response to the loss of contact, reaching

down between her legs to guide my hand. She encouraged me to add a second finger, holding my wrist as she pumped my fingers in and out of her swollen, greedy little pussy.

"I want to come on your cock," she said finally, her lips tipping up into a smile. I shook my head as I rose between her legs, thrusting my fingers deep and drawing them back slowly as she reached for the laces on my trousers. She unknotted them quickly, shoving them down over my ass until cool air touched my bare skin. She drew her pussy away from my fingers suddenly, leaning forward to wrap her lips around the head of my cock and suck.

The stars above us filled my vision as I dropped my head back, staring at the sky as she slowly worked my shaft into her throat. "Fuck," I grunted, burying my hand in the hair at her nape as she took me as deep as she could. I held her close, stealing the breath from her lungs as I filled her throat.

When I tore her off my cock, I shoved her to her back and covered her body with my weight. Driving inside her without hesitation, I filled her pussy as she arched her back beneath me. *"Gods!"* she screamed, the sound of her voice filling the air around us. I was certain it would wake the Fae Marked who slept, certain it would wake any within an hour's ride of our camp.

She didn't seem to care.

I drew back, thrusting back inside of her as her arms wrapped around my torso and she raked her nails down my back. She accepted my kiss as I united our mouths, joining our bodies in every way. Her pleasure coursed through the bond as her orgasm crashed over her, a tiny whimper escaping her mouth as I swallowed the sound. I fucked her through it, gliding through her soft tissue slowly and filling her.

When her eyes finally opened, I rolled her until her body braced atop mine. I knew the Wild Hunt would have an unobstructed view of my cock in her pussy, of the way she stretched around me. "Take what you need, my star," I said, grasping a cheek of her ass in each hand. She pressed her hands to my chest, letting me guide her movements for the first few strokes of my cock inside her. Her eyes went hesitant, her vulnerability showing. She undoubtedly realized just how much the new position put on display as she glanced over her shoulder to look back at the riders of the Wild Hunt. "You worry about the mate waiting for you to fuck him."

Her gaze snapped back to mine, the barest hint of a smile tipping her lips up. She picked up her pace, the rolls of her hips turning frenzied as she raised and lowered herself on my cock. She shifted her body forward, rubbing her clit against my pubic bone as she rode me, seeking the second orgasm that I knew wasn't far from the way her pussy fluttered around me.

"Caelum," she whimpered, her nails digging into the bare skin of my chest.

"That's it, Little One. Just like that," I said, squeezing her ass in my hands. One day, I'd be able to fuck that too, if we found a safe place to explore such pleasures safely.

"I'm going to—"Her voice broke off into a shuddering breath. Her eyes drifted closed as she prepared for the orgasm that would consume her, the one that would pull me over the edge with her.

"Eyes on me," I snapped, making her reveal her star-filled gaze quickly. She dropped down hard onto my cock, her body all but collapsing with the force of her orgasm as her pussy squeezed me. I thrust up into her, stroking once, twice, three times until I came with a shout and fell into the eternity of her eyes.

Her hands stayed planted on my chest as she smiled, then she rolled her hips once more, demanding more from me, shifting her body to get me deeper. "Again," she ordered, her deep gaze commanding as she leaned forward and touched her lips to mine.

I laughed, seeking a moment to stall the monster I'd created. She'd be the death of me, but it was the greatest end I could ever imagine.

38

ESTRELLA

I awoke slowly, the first trickle of sunshine gleaming off the snowy ground. My lashes fluttered open, and I snuggled my very nude body back into the warmth at my spine. There was a thick blanket draped over us, and I had no recollection of how it'd gotten there. I'd been lost to the throes of passion, demanding Caldris pleasure me two more times before I collapsed beneath him and finally fell asleep.

I had never been like this. Sex with Loris had been limited because of the fear of being caught, admittedly. But even still, after our few minutes of frenzied pleasure, I'd gone on my way and felt satisfied. I probably wouldn't have gone back for a second toss in the hay if it hadn't been for my desire to rebel against the society that wanted me virginal.

Why would I need a man, when my fingers were so much more capable of bringing me pleasure? Why did I need the actual flesh of another person, when the vague images in my head were so much more appealing?

Even then, it had been the image of blue eyes gleaming in the darkness that brought me to orgasm, imagining my fingers as the bigger, more callused version of the male I now knew to be my mate. Imagining the curve of his claws when he sank deep into his feral form, the long black nails gleaming as he trailed them over my flesh and left a thin red line in his wake.

I startled with the realization, rolling in Caldris's arms to look back at his face.

All this time.

He'd been with me always, existing within me even when I couldn't be with him. Even when I couldn't feel those arms wrapped around me. He shifted, folding me into his embrace once again as he slowly opened his eyes. That same blue stared back at me, the color of the thickest ice on the ice floes that lingered out at sea in the deepest part of winter. His expression was carefully blank as he slid a hand over my arm and settled it against the side of my neck, sliding it beneath the curtain of my hair.

"It was always you," I murmured, feeling the ridiculous sting of tears in my eyes. I'd known I loved him. I'd already agreed to accept the mate bond, but something about the realization that it had always been him I saw when I pleasured myself in my bed at night struck deep into my chest. It warmed from the inside in a way I hadn't thought possible, as if the sun itself was shining down into that hollow within me that I'd been so certain would always remain empty.

"Always," he said, and he didn't ask any questions. He didn't need to know the details of what was going on in my head, not when he could feel the surge of love within my heart. I had no doubt he could feel it wash through me, spreading to all the parts of me he hadn't yet claimed. It felt like liquid gold, scalding and searing me alive, but it was an exquisite pleasure to burn for this.

For him.

He touched his lips to mine gently, coaxing me to open for him as I raised a leg and wrapped it around his hips. I pulled him closer, pressing my breasts into his chest as he rolled me beneath him. I spared only a moment to consider who might witness our act, but whereas the night before it had been a turn-on to know they were watching, in the light of day they simply didn't matter.

All that mattered was his weight between my thighs as he settled against me. All that mattered was his cock as he slid it inside of me with a tilt of his hips, joining our bodies as my soul hummed with the first true acceptance of the fact that I'd known him for centuries before I ever met him.

I welcomed him, spreading my legs wider so he could push deeper. His chest met my breasts, his mouth sealing over mine as he kissed me sweetly. The slow rolls of his hips against me were gentle, his pace languid as he made love to me beside the coals of the campfire. I whimpered into his mouth as a different kind of pleasure built, a slowly budding hint of something profound deep within my belly. This was not the all-consuming orgasm that came when he fucked me into oblivion, but something that fed the emptiness inside of me.

Whoever it was that lurked beneath my skin, she craved it. She wanted it more than she wanted her next breath. She drove my motions as I curled my legs around the back of Caldris's waist, clinging to him with his mouth on mine. For once, the monster and I were in unison, driving toward a single, cohesive goal. I wanted to come. She wanted to consume Caldris's pleasure.

My mate drove me higher, building that climax within me both painfully slowly and exquisitely sweetly. It was with nothing but his cock inside of me that he brought me to orgasm finally.

Nothing but his body held tightly within mine, our souls

nearly united as he opened his mouth and swallowed the whimper that escaped as I finally came.

He groaned as he followed, filling me with his essence while the monster inside of me purred in pleasure. She coiled within my stomach as Caldris pulled back from my lips to stare down at me, his face alight with pleasure as he came back from his own orgasm.

She struck against the inside of my chest, making my body jolt with the force of it as she drank down his pleasure. His eyes widened for a moment, staring into my eyes as if he could see the monster lurking within.

But he wasn't afraid. He leaned forward, touching his mouth to mine as he stared into what I suspected was the stare he described as the night sky. "Take whatever you need, min asteren," he said, soothing the frayed parts of me that were terrified of that thing inside of me.

She was so hungry, so demanding. She wanted to feed on his body, from his pleasure.

She wanted to take everything he had to give and leave him nothing but a husk, as if in awakening her I'd roused a being who needed more food than I could ever provide. She wanted me to flip Caldris to his back and ride him until his cock was raw, to take his pleasure inside of me until there was nothing left.

I shoved her down, ignoring the way she seemed to pout. She stretched within me, extending her muscles before she settled. There was no form to her, only the vague sense that she existed. She was me, but somehow not, all at once.

"I see my warning was useless in the end. I knew you were a lot of things, but I never pegged you for a fucking whore," a male voice said, interrupting the moment, and I jolted as I snapped back to reality. Caldris pulled his mouth off of mine, slowly turning to glare at whoever had spoken with a deadly steadiness that I knew meant the male was soon to die.

"Fuck," my mate grunted, hanging his head forward until it touched mine.

I looked toward the ghostly figure lingering nearby, his arms crossed over his chest. The flesh was torn from his bones, and I might not have even recognized the horror he'd become if I hadn't seen his corpse hanging from the fortress walls at Tradesholme.

"Jensen?" I asked, trying to focus on what remained of his face. Only a single eye remained, as if the other had been torn from its socket when the claw of whatever had torn him to shreds sliced across the right side of his face. It was settled into a hard, icy glare that he leveled on me, on my position beneath the man that he'd tried to warn me was Fae.

"Did you miss me, pretty?" he asked, what remained of his lips curving up into a cruel smirk.

Fuck.

39

ESTRELLA

*W*hat would it take for him to go away?

He lingered alongside us, floating above the ground as he followed us through the woods. "Is there really no way to get rid of him?" Imelda asked, perched atop her own horse.

"You wound me, Imelda. You didn't seem to be in such a hurry to get rid of me when you welcomed me to your bed," Jensen said, the insufferable sound of his voice grating against my ears. I was ready to rip out his tongue myself, if it had been at all possible, but every time I tried to wrap my hands around the miserable spirit's throat, I met empty air. He was nothing but the lingering presence of a soul, traveling alongside the Wild Hunt in the hopes they would lead him to the Void eventually.

I was certain Caldris had never regretted not burying a body so much as he did this day.

"You fucked him?" Holt asked, eying what remained of Jensen with distaste. "I suppose there's no accounting for standards." He sneered, turning the cruelty of his gaze to Imelda and letting her know just what he thought about her choice in bed partners.

"There are far better ways to communicate your raging jealousy, Huntsman," Imelda said, her voice cool and detached as ever. She barely spared a glance for Holt, her lips tipping up in that smug way of hers. I knew the words that came out of her mouth next would be brutal. "My options in the tunnels were rather limited, so I learned to be less discerning with who I took to bed. Please keep in mind, I may have fucked him, but I still would sooner die than fuck the likes of you. So I hardly think you are in any place to speak to me of standards."

Aramis guided his horse close, his lips tipped up in genuine amusement. I was certain he enjoyed the torment of having Jensen back, enjoyed the way the dead man was determined to torment me for all my choices. Since we'd departed that morning, all he'd done was nag and grate on me. Reminding me I was a traitor to my kind, that I'd turned my back on the humans in favor of the life Caldris could give me.

Gold digger. Whore. Faerie Fucker.

There wasn't a single thing Caldris or I could do to stop it, and the tension in my mate's body was all the confirmation I needed that he was just as infuriated as I was.

I yanked the dagger from the sheath strapped to Caldris's thigh, pulling the blade free and extending my arm as Aramis came up beside us. "No wonder you killed him—" he said, his voice cutting off when I sank the blade into the flesh of his upper thigh.

"What the fuck was that for?" he asked, his voice wheezing in pain as I pulled the blade free and returned it to the sheath it called home.

"You looked at me," I snarled, the monster feeling closer to the surface than ever before. The complete aggravation that was Jensen would drive me to do far worse before the day was up.

Caldris chuckled at my spine, his amusement washing over me. But my anger made everything feel tight, made even that pleasant feeling bitter. "What's wrong, my star?" Caldris asked, not daring to touch me, lest I strike.

It felt like the barest of touches would bring that monster surging back to the surface. "I think I need to walk for a while," I said, the restlessness in my body stirring in response to my words.

"Alright," Caldris said hesitantly. "Don't go too far with him lurking about." He pulled Azra to a halt and I swung my leg over his withers, jumping down to land in the snow as I sought out Fallon. She lingered farther back than normal, walking alone as if she needed the distance from Jensen just as much as I did.

The hairs on my arms stood up, defying logic as I felt something shift in the air as I approached her. My monster reared her ugly head, as if she herself could search through the trees in the distance to find whatever had disturbed her from the slumber before her attack.

The scream tore through the air, cutting through the trees surrounding us and making me snap my head toward the direction it came from. Fenrir's head snapped toward me, his eyes connecting with mine as I stopped in my tracks.

Holt signaled two of his riders on, staying with the majority of the procession as they stepped forward, but something in Fenrir's gaze as it held mine drew me forward, beckoning me toward the wolf where he waited, lowering himself to the ground.

I didn't know why it was me he turned to and not his master, but I stepped forward quickly as if drawn to him like a moth to the flame. Grabbing onto his back and hauling myself up, I sank into the comfort of his white fur, leaning forward to wrap my arms around his neck and lay my chest against his back as he leaped forward.

"Estrella!" Caldris protested, trying unsuccessfully to guide Azra through the group surrounding him before he dropped behind from my sight.

Another scream ripped through the air, and something in the sky shuddered. I *knew* that sound. I knew that torment. Even if I didn't recognize the voice itself, I recognized the fear.

I'd screamed like that the first time Lord Byron had ordered me caned, standing by to watch my punishment as a child so he could be confident it was appropriately harsh. So he could make sure I bled for my insolence.

The murmur of male voices grew louder as Fenrir followed it through the forest, winding his way around the trees with his long, loping gait. I knew Caldris followed behind us, but we'd long since passed the riders who'd proceeded with far too much caution.

They'd never make it in time. They were already too late to save the woman from the worst pain she'd ever known.

She screamed again, and this time I was close enough that the sound of a whip cracking through the air struck into my chest. That hollow inside of me grew, expanding outward as if it wanted to feed off that pain. As if it needed it to survive, to *breathe.*

Fenrir burst into the clearing, vaulting over the shrubs that lined the space. All eyes turned to us as he prowled forward, stopping in the center so I could swing a leg over and stand beside him. The woman was bound, her hands tied together and suspended from the tree branch in front of her. They'd torn her dress open in the back, revealing the expanse of what should have been smooth skin, if not for the blood flowing down her back and the lash marks that tore her open. Her head hung forward, the faded light of a Fae Mark on her neck.

"Estrella!" Caldris called from far behind us—even once he'd extricated himself from the group, Azra hadn't been able to keep up with the speed of Fenrir weaving through the trees. I stepped forward, tilting my head to the side as four members of the Mist Guard turned to face me. The one with the whip in his hand dropped his eyes to my own glowing mark.

"Looks like we found ourselves another toy," he said, a smug grin twisting his face. He cracked the whip at his side once in warning as I stepped closer, bringing myself directly into his reach. I wouldn't stop—couldn't stop—until I reached the woman and cut her down.

The whip cracked whistling straight toward my face. I twisted back, pulling my face out of danger as I raised a forearm.

The whip caught me there, wrapping around my forearm and sinking into the flesh beneath my clothes. Fire lit my skin, burning through me as the leather sank deep. I grabbed the tail of the whip in my hand, winding it around my palm and pulling so suddenly that the Mist released it.

It stayed wound around my arm, the length of it twisting and coiling, changing into something new and eager. The newly-formed snake slithered along my skin before it lowered itself to the ground in silence.

The Mist Guard's eyes widened, his expression one of horror as I stepped toward him. The forest floor seemed to come to life beneath my feet, the brush and dead leaves covering it moving from side to side as the three Guards who stood farther from the woman turned their attention to the serpents slithering toward them, mostly unseen.

"That's impossible," the one who'd held the whip said as I

moved closer. He drew his sword, the iron carving a path through the air as he focused on me.

"Have you ever wondered what waits for you in the pits of Tartarus?" I asked, continuing to move toward him. I kicked out a leg, catching the knuckles of the hand that clutched his sword. He didn't drop it, clinging to it as though he realized just how tightly his life depended on that weapon.

The snake that had shifted from the whip slithered up my legs, winding herself around my waist until she could place her head into my hand. I pulled my arm back then snapped it toward the Guard, watching in rapt fascination as the snake changed back into a whip. The leather wrapped around the blade of the sword, catching it and allowing me to yank it back and toss it into the trees at the side of the clearing.

It landed a few feet from where Caldris had lowered himself from Azra's back, and paused to take in the destruction around me. A Guard screamed to my right, the sound echoing through the woods in a way that fed the growing storm inside of me. It was the only just thing in this world, that their screams would fill the night sky after what they'd done to the Fae Marked girl hung from the tree.

"Cut her down," I said to Caldris, nodding my head toward the woman. He paused, stepping toward me slowly as if he might help me with the fight, but I wanted their deaths. I wanted to feed them to the Void.

I craved the music of their screams—craved the chaos of their fear.

The serpents dragged one of the Mist Guard into the woods, disappearing into the underbrush as something massive moved through it.

I felt connected to it; felt its soul as it moved to obey my call.

Basilisk.

I turned back to the Guard who'd wielded the whip. The one who'd committed the worst horror. He shrank back from whatever he saw in my gaze as I stepped forward, thrusting a hand out suddenly and grabbing him by the chin.

The darkness welled within me, looming to the surface as his terrified face angled over mine. He raised his hands, clawing at the raw marks on my arm where his whip had torn ribbons of flesh from my bones.

My dress hung off it in scraps, but I twisted his head to look at the mangled back of the woman he'd harmed one last time. "You wish to behave as if you do not have a soul?" I asked, turning his frightened stare back to me. He shook his head, his mouth unable to move beneath the force of my grip. "Your wish is my command."

I summoned those golden ribbons that swirled around him, grasping them with my free hand and pulling them from his body one by one. When they were all gathered into my palm, I tore them free, severing the connection with his body at the same moment I released his chin and drew in a breath.

The light left his eyes as he fell to the forest floor, staring at the sky above him with an unblinking gaze. His chest rose and fell, his lungs moving as I lowered my stare to the golden ball of light held in my hand.

"Min asteren," Caldris said, his voice soft as he stepped forward. "What have you done?" He stared down at the golden ball, the threads gone and blended together so seamlessly that it was as if I held a miniature sun in my grasp. I wrapped my fingers around it, around the warmth of it.

Squeezing them shut, I watched the light fade slowly until only snowflakes remained, falling to the ground like winter snow.

"Gave him a far more peaceful passage to the Void than he deserved," I said, staring at the empty, breathing husk of a man. Nothing remained inside him, and yet his chest rose with each breath.

"Animate him," I said, tilting my head to the side when I couldn't force him to rise. There were no golden tendrils surrounding him in the way I'd gotten used to summoning Caldris's power.

"I cannot. He isn't dead, Little One," he said, stepping over the body and staring down at it.

Caldris spun suddenly, drawing his sword in a fluid motion and thrusting it into the gut of the Mist Guard who remained. He made to stab my mate, but his sword never reached its target as he stopped and gaped at the God of the Dead.

At his friend lying lifelessly on the forest floor, but somehow alive all the same. He wouldn't be for long.

As the last body crumpled to the ground, the brush in the woods moved as something large slithered through it. The basilisk emerged. Covering its body, its scales were dark as midnight but gleaming in the fading light of the sun as it slithered into the clearing.

Caldris grabbed my hand, pulling me behind him and raising his sword to face the creature. Shaking him off, I stepped around him and felt the way my chest vibrated in response to it. It wasn't quite words, yet wasn't quite the way a snake would sound either, but the blind thing heard it anyway.

Turning its head to where I walked over to the warm body of the man I'd sent to the Void, I crouched down beside him. "Are you hungry?" I asked, reaching out to touch the snake's nose. It leaned into the touch, almost nuzzling into my skin before it dropped against the ground once more.

It opened its jaw.

And the basilisk ate.

40

CALDRIS

I hated snakes, so of course by the force of her nature my mate had to treat them like pets. Her gentle care as she watched the basilisk swallow her enemies whole both delighted me and horrified me.

Why did it have to be snakes? She couldn't have had an affinity for puppies?

She stood as the basilisk finished its meal, swallowing heavily as it devoured the last of the bodies she'd left behind. Without another acknowledgement for the woman who had summoned it, the basilisk disappeared into the woods once more.

"Help me cut her down." She moved toward the woman whose head hung forward. She was limp when my mate wrapped her arms around her waist, the woman's head resting against her shoulder. I swung my sword at the ropes tying her to the tree branch, letting her fall against Estrella's braced form.

The prisoner was far too thin, life on the run from the Mist Guard hunting her had not been kind. My mate lowered her to the ground, pressing the burning wounds on her back into the snow as the woman jerked in her grasp.

"You're safe now," Estrella murmured, cupping the woman's face as her lashes fluttered against her cheek. She didn't open them, her body far too drained of all energy from the ordeal she'd suffered.

The riders of the Wild Hunt stepped out from the tree line, their gazes meeting mine in silent question. They'd seen too much of what Estrella had done to deny what she most likely was, but I would remain foolhardy in my willful ignorance.

My mate was not the daughter of Mab.

She couldn't be; not when she only woke the monster that slept within her to protect rather than harm.

One of the riders stepped over, standing over Estrella as she looked up at him. "Let me get her back to the carts. Imelda can tend to her wounds," he said, his voice soft as he studied her. Respectful.

Reverent.

I wasn't the only one who saw what lived inside her, and the potential of what was waiting to be let out. Mab's daughter or not, my mate was no Sidhe.

She was no Fae Marked female who could only draw power from me. She was something almost unheard of in a bonded pair. A match for me. Something in perfect harmony for my soul. She would have helped my ability to fight Mab when I'd thought she was a human. Now, I couldn't even think of what might happen when we completed the bond.

There had only been two pairs who'd both been Gods in the past: my parents and the King and Queen of the Spring Court. Their daughter and I were the only second-generation Gods in existence to my knowledge. Our bond being fulfilled would be nearly unprecedented, and there was no telling what our heritage would do to such a thing. I still couldn't wait to find out.

Estrella nodded, allowing the rider to take the woman into his arms and lift her up to the other rider who sat upon his horse, waiting.

"We'll join you when we're ready. I need to have a discussion with my mate," I said, and the male nodded before mounting his skeletal steed. They disappeared into the woods, and I looked around the clearing. It had been wiped clean of any sign of what'd happened here, the bodies devoured by my mate's pet.

"You were supposed to stay with the Wild Hunt. Not ride off into the danger," I said, gesturing toward where Fenrir watched. He sat on his haunches, licking his paws clean as if he cared very little for the conversation that was coming.

The fucker was a terrible influence. Unruly bastard was too bloodthirsty for his own good.

"Fuck that," Estrella said, crossing her arms. She scoffed at me, looking around as if to say that she'd handled herself well enough.

She had. It was harder to justify wanting to protect her when she so clearly didn't need my protection; she could fight her own battles. But that didn't mean there wouldn't come a day when she wasn't able to handle whatever she foolishly walked into.

The memory of a man standing over her, her neck shackled in iron chains and a sword pressed against her heart, was never far away.

"That could have been you!" I swept a hand out to the tree where the rope still dangled from the branch, a haunting reminder of the games the Mist Guard liked to play once they made the Fae Marked vulnerable, guaranteeing they couldn't fight back.

In the days before the Veil, it had become a game to fuck the Fae Marked. The Mist Guard loved to rape them, knowing their mates felt their anguish and using that to lure them into traps.

I would die before I allowed that to happen to my star.

I sighed, hanging my head forward as her glare met mine. She was too trapped by the magic coursing through her veins and the price it demanded of her for such untrained use. Her humanity was at risk, and only the blood flowing from her arm would serve as a payment for the death she'd caused.

Her sacrifice.

"I cannot protect you if you're reckless," I said, trying to keep my voice soft.

She raised her chin, ever the bright-burning star as she glared up at me. "I never asked you to protect me," she said.

I chuckled, unable to stop myself as amusement filled me. She was a nightmare to control, impossibly defiant until the end. "Be very careful, Little One," I warned, reaching out to cup her cheek as I slid my sword back into its sheath with the other one. "You just might need a reminder that you are not the all-powerful creature you seem to think you are."

She scoffed, her eyes lighting with the challenge. The darkness in her faded slightly, amused by the way Estrella's human vessel enjoyed the games we could play. "And who will show me that?" she asked, lifting her chin with a taunt that reeked of false bravado. "You?"

I swept her legs out from under her in a single motion, watching as she fell. Her back thudded against the ground, the breath knocked from her lungs as the snow seemed to thicken. It wrapped around her wrists, grabbing her arms and yanking them up above her head. She struggled to sit, but the snow hardened to ice, pinching her tightly and holding her firm.

I watched her eyes darken as she tried to grasp the threads

she claimed to see and twist her fingers around them. Her face fell when she realized she couldn't; the ice holding her was mine to command.

She may be able to visualize it differently than I could, but she was not the heir to the Winter Court. That title and responsibility rested with me alone.

"Winter is mine. I think you've forgotten that," I said, standing over her and staring down at the way her legs grappled for purchase.

"I could bring back the snakes," she said, a cruel smile lighting her face. The little monster knew just how much I despised them.

"That would take away my chance to play with you," I said, dropping to my knees beside her. She stilled, staring up at me with interest. "And I think we both know just how much you want that."

I touched a hand to her stomach, gliding it lower to cup her pussy through her pants. Her hips rose in response, seeking more as I ground the heel of my palm against her. "*Gods*," she rasped.

"Yes. We are," I said, offering her the truth I knew she wasn't ready for. Estrella shut out the facts she wasn't prepared to deal with, deceiving herself into believing the information that was right in front of her and easier to accept.

She'd done it with the truth of what I was, and she would do it with her truth until she could no longer deny the overwhelming evidence that she was different.

"What do you want?" I asked, watching as her cheeks flushed. So far from innocent, she might as well have bathed in the blood of her enemies for all the brutality she showed them. Yet somehow, my mate was still a blend of shy and starved when it came to sex. "You're restrained. I need the words."

"I want you to fuck me," she said, raising her hips into my hand once more.

I lifted it from her pussy, grabbing the waistband of her pants and tearing them down her thighs. She gasped as her bare ass pressed into the snow, the cold sinking into her skin as I left her boots on and kept the pants trapped around her ankles.

Yanking open the laces of my trousers, I pulled myself free and used my other hand to lift her legs up. Draping them both over one shoulder, I lined myself up with her greedy little pussy.

When I glided my head through her flesh, she whimpered and raised her hips, fighting against the icy bonds that held her hands pinned to the ground. She was already wet, her body responding to the touch of my cock against her and preparing for what she wanted. Sliding through her, I pressed into her entrance and stared down at where we joined.

Her body spread around mine, accepting me inside of her like she'd been born to do. *This* was her place, beneath me with her body sprawled out. Taking me and meeting me thrust for thrust. She knew it as well as I did, greedy and desperate, a hunger like I'd never seen existing inside of her.

She groaned as I pressed farther into her and touched a hand between her legs to wrap my fingers around my cock, feeling her body open for me as I pushed in. When my groin touched my hand finally, I pulled it away, shifting my gaze to her face.

"Nice of you to notice I'm here too," she said, an amused smile lighting it and drawing a laugh from me.

"Trust me, my star. I know *exactly* who I'm fucking," I said, pulling my hips back and driving into her. She gasped as I rolled them, sliding the head of my cock over that part inside her that drove her absolutely wild. Her fingers clawed at the ice restraining her hands, her sharp nails scratching against the surface.

"Who am I, then?" she asked, and despite the challenge apparent in the set to her lips, there was a tiny insecurity in her eyes. It haunted her, not knowing for sure who or what she was. Her entire identity had been stolen from her, along with the family that she couldn't really claim to own in the same way she'd always believed.

"You're my fucking mate. Nothing matters outside of that, min asteren," I said, growling the words as I set a slow, hard rhythm. I wanted to move faster, craved the release that her body provided in ways I'd never imagined.

The animalistic need to fill her with my cum at all times of the day was maddening, pushing me closer to the edge than I'd thought possible. If we had a safe space to spend our time, if we'd been able to spend our days in the palace at Catancia, she'd spend most of them impaled on my cock with her eyes on mine.

And she'd already begun to want that, even though she wasn't yet Fae.

Her eyes stung with tears, but her hips still raised to take more of me. To unite us in all the ways that were possible. Knowing that we would cross the boundary and be mated in truth, and I would be as one with her as I was with myself, I pressed her legs to the side and forward.

Bending her in half, pressing her knees against her arms so I could lean down and capture her lips with mine for a brief moment. "Soon, Little One. Soon you'll understand," I said, because no matter how much she read the book Holt had given her, nothing could prepare her for the Fae side of the mate bond.

Nothing could prepare her for the all-consuming need that would soon take her over.

She breathed deeply, sinking into the earth under her as I shoved through her tender tissue, stroking myself into her more fully, chasing the orgasm that loomed at the edges of my mind. She sank her teeth into her bottom lip, pinching the flesh so tightly I thought she might bleed.

I leaned forward, licking the seam of her mouth and almost wishing she would. I wanted all the parts of me to be inside of her, and to take what I could of her essence inside of me. But the first time we shared blood during sex had to be when we completed our bond, because I wouldn't take my cock out of her until our blood faded from one another's systems.

"*Es to un caoin asteren en min awyr,*" I murmured, watching as her eyes lit with the words that she tried to translate in her mind, attempting to focus on them beyond the slow drag of my cock through her flesh. "You are the only star in my sky."

She smiled sweetly, chasing away the shadows that lingered in her eyes. The green of them shone back at me, blinking back the tears that made her eyes burn. "And you are the only light in my darkness," she said, sending a shock of awareness running through me. I'd spent so much of my life looking at her as the only thing good in my bleak existence, the thought of her surrounded by the darkness that wanted to consume her sent rage spiking in me.

I fucked her slowly, holding her gaze with mine as my soul burned with the weight of her confession.

I'd never been something good. I'd never had someone look at me as if I was the sun shining on a dark day. Our bond was her way of pulling back from whatever was inside of her, and I would never let go.

I lowered a thumb to her clit, circling it slowly and taking what I wanted. Her pussy clenched down on my cock, squeezing me for all she was worth as she fluttered inside. "I love you, Little One," I murmured, leaning forward to touch my mouth to hers as she came around me. "Until chaos reigns."

"Until chaos reigns," she whispered as she breathed through her orgasm. I released her hands finally, letting the ice melt back into snow. She wrapped them behind my head, holding me so that my breath mingled with hers. "I will love you long after."

I came, filling her with my release as I dropped my forehead to hers. We'd cross the boundary by the next day if all went well.

And then she'd be mine in truth.

41

I made my way to Imelda's side, staring down at the woman who lay on her stomach in one of the carts. The other Fae Marked had cleared out of it so the witch could tend to her, and the Riders were setting up camp for the night. The sunset hadn't yet arrived, but it wasn't far enough away to be worth risking the girl's safety by forcing her to travel before Imelda could stem the bleeding.

"How is she?" I asked, watching as Imelda ground herbs into a paste. She muttered an incantation over the rocks she'd gathered for smashing them, stabbing the tip of her dagger into her finger. Blood welled, dripping down onto the rocks but never touching the paste itself.

A payment for her magic, rather than an ingredient. She sucked her finger into her mouth as she continued grinding the herbs. "She'll live. She'd heal faster if I had turmeric," she answered, and I looked around the woods surrounding us. The odds of finding the plants that grew the tunnel-shaped flowers would be nonexistent with the cold surrounding us. Even the bigger, stronger plants were preparing for the winter. The roots would survive to see the next year, but the plant itself would have withered and died already.

I stood anyway, prepared to go in search of the plant. If anyone had any chance of recognizing it in the woods, it would be me. Imelda placed a hand on my arm, pulling me back down as she shook her head. "It would be a waste of time," she said sadly, dipping her fingers into the poultice and carefully applying it to the fresh wounds on the girl's back.

Her back twitched, a whimper escaping her as I moved toward her head. I sat next to her, making sure she had soft cloth under her cheek and running tender fingers through her hair. Trying to offer her a touch of kindness in the moments of pain when Imelda did what needed to be done.

"She'll need another dress," I said to Caldris as he watched from beside the cart. I didn't know that we had any spare clothes we could give her. Holt shrugged out of his cloak at the corner of my eye, draping the fur-lined warmth of it over his forearm. His chest was entirely bare without it, his pale gray skin gleaming in the sunlight that trickled through his corporeal form.

"It will have to do for now. We'll find her something when we reach Mistfell," he said, stepping forward and laying the cloak across the railing on the edge of the cart. Fallon picked it up, draping it over the girl's legs to offer her both warmth and privacy from prying eyes.

Imelda didn't glance up from her task, her attention fixed solely on the girl and her wounds, but the Huntsman watched her intently, observing her motions and the calm set to her features with something that felt like admiration. Imelda's fingers paused, lingering just off the girl's skin as if she could feel his attention fixed on her face.

She turned her eyes up to look at him, never shifting her face toward him as their gazes connected. Something passed between them, a brief moment of understanding when Imelda's chest filled with air and she never released it. I felt like an intruder on a moment that should have been private as my eyes darted back and forth between them.

Finally, Imelda turned her attention back to the girl's wounds, the flush staining her cheeks the only sign that anything had happened. Holt clenched his jaw, turning and storming off to help with the assembly of the tents.

"What was that?" I asked, staring at the side of her face.

"Nothing. That was nothing at all," she said, her voice a low murmur. I wasn't certain if she was trying to convince herself or me, but it was clear there was more to the story than Fallon and I knew.

I ran my fingers through the girl's hair, wishing I could do more than offer her comfort as she slept, and that she would have a familiar face to wake up to, instead of the fear that would come from being surrounded by strangers and the Wild Hunt.

"Look at you pretending you care about what happens to her," Jensen said, the sneer tipping the unruined side of his mouth up. He bared his teeth as I watched, that monster trapped within me coiling and tensing her body.

I slid away from the girl's head as I stood, lowering myself down from the cart. "He isn't worth your energy," Imelda said, never taking her eyes off the girl's back as she worked.

I stalked forward, my gaze snagged on Jensen and the gleaming golden thread that pulsed through the center of his filmy, ghostly figure. His sneer hardened into a glare as I approached, the condescending expression on his face only fueling my determination.

"What are you going to do? Glare at me? I'm already dead, you dumb bitch," he taunted, a laugh making his chest shake.

I stepped forward, stopping when I was only a breath from

him and the energy of his soul kissed my skin. Raising a single hand, I grasped him by the front of the throat. His entire frame jolted when my touch landed and I squeezed against what would have been the muscles of his neck if he'd been alive. He wheezed, his chest rattling when I pinched my fingers together. My right hand reached into the transparent mass of his chest, grasping the golden threads that ran from his head to his feet.

Catching them with my fingers, I yanked them free from his ethereal body. "Estrella," he gasped, staring down at me as I felt the coldness within me rush forth. The darkness within me filled my eyes, taking me back to the place where the monster had control.

She controlled my movements as I released his throat, pinching the top of a thread where it pulled taut away from his body. I held an end in each hand, pulling them in opposite directions until I felt the exact moment the threads snapped, cleaving his soul in two as the ruined threads fell to the ground. The golden light from them faded to gray as they fell, landing upon the snow.

A look of shock filled Jensen's face as he looked down at his feet. They melted away, fading from view, caught in the wind that blew though the clearing in the woods. Bit by bit, the wind took what remained of his essence and scattered it across the ground.

His ruined face faded from view last, leaving me to stare at Caldris where he stood on the other side of what was now an empty space between us. He looked down at the gray threads on the ground, stepping forward as he lifted one touched the fine length of it. "Threads," he said, and I realized that he could see them. He could see the gray, destroyed threads that had been Jensen's tether to this world. "Where is he? Where did you send him?"

"He's no longer here. Isn't that all that matters?" I asked, staring back at the mate who looked at me as if I was both a monster and a savior in a single breath. As if he himself couldn't tell the difference between the two.

In truth, neither could I.

42

ESTRELLA

The forest surrounding us became familiar, the same paths I'd walked regularly in the lifetime I'd spent in this village. All the years, I'd wandered in the woods at night, drawn to the Veil I wasn't supposed to stray too close to; They'd all led me to Caldris, and to the moment we met in the barn that night, even without me knowing fate had wrapped its golden threads around us centuries before.

Caldris looked around warily. I imagined him trying to see the forest through my eyes and to think of how they must have felt to a young girl who was stifled by the village and the Lord determined to force her into a mold that didn't fit.

I would never be the Lady of the Manor. I would never again be docile and complicit in my own suffering; not when I'd once chosen death over that fate already.

When the end of my time came, I would walk willingly into the Void to await the judgment of The Father and The Mother. Holding my head high in the knowledge that, come whatever may, my choices had led me to this path.

Caldris's arms tightened around me as we rode with the

Wild Hunt and the procession of his dead army at our backs. I stretched out an arm to point at a clearing to the side of us. The snow fluffed against the ground as I reached out with my senses to tickle those golden threads that floated off of it. Adelphia stepped out of the procession, moving to lay a hand on the log where we'd all sat that day that seemed so far away. "This is where we celebrated Samhain," I said, turning to look at Caldris over my shoulder.

Adelphia stepped away from the log, coming up beside me as she reached into the bag strapped across her shoulder. She pulled the skull free, the gleaming off-white of the bone catching the light from the sun filtering down through the canopy of trees and reflecting off the snow.

I reached down, allowing my mate to hold my hips steady. "Jonab," I said, feeling Caldris's body go still at the mention of the God of Changing Seasons. He'd been killed during the First Fae War between the Seelie and Unseelie Courts, when Mab fought against her brother Rheaghan.

Caldris looked down at the woman standing beside the horse, holding the reins in one hand so that he could take the skull from me. He stared at it as if he'd never seen a skull before; as if it was as foreign to the God of the Dead as it might have been to the Goddess of Light.

"It has been passed down through generations of my family for centuries," Adelphia said, turning her stare to me so suddenly that my breath caught. Something lingered in that stare that I hadn't seen before, something ancient and knowing. "Every year, without fail, we've used it on the night of Samhain to draw the Fae souls who may have been trapped inside human vessels when the witches erected the Veil. When the child was stolen from the tunnels, a group of our ancestors set out to find her, seeking to protect her through the lifetimes until her final life when the Veil would fall."

"When the Veil would fall?" I asked, turning my stare to Imelda who watched as realization dawned on her face. I'd known it was destined to fall; it had only been meant to be temporary. Imelda had said as much, but even still....

"I did not possess enough of the magic of my ancestors to tear it down myself. The magic of my mother has been lost to time, but with all of us combined, we were able to weaken it. We were able to pour what remained of our magic into you, Estrella. You and your mate did the rest," she said with a sad smile, leaving the skull in our possession as I stared down at it.

"I touched the Veil," I whispered, the words coming from the deepest recesses of my mind. That day had been pure chaos; it had plunged the world into the darkness.

In the moments before the Veil fell, I'd had one half of my soul partway to the Void, and the other had reached out to the Veil itself, stroking the magic for the briefest of moments. Caldris had been on the other side, the impossibility of blue eyes shining back at me as I'd let my eyes drift closed and welcomed my true death.

"You're a witch?" I asked, turning my confused stare to Adelphia. She'd disappeared, the rest of her group fading along with her as if they blended into the trees themselves.

"She's not a witch," Imelda said, stepping forward to take Jonab's skull from Caldris. She tucked it into her own pack, cradling it gently as if it was sacred to her. "She's the child of a witch and a human. They all are."

"Where are the rest of the Lunar Witches, Imelda?" I asked, studying her as she sank her teeth into her dark bottom lip.

"They left. Looking for you," Imelda admitted with a sad smile. "I remained to guard Fallon through her lives and to seek her out each time she was born. We thought she would be safe within the tunnels, but you were out in the open, exposed to whatever may come for you. They never returned from their search."

I tried not to let the knowledge that my life had been responsible for the loss of so many sink deep inside me. It hadn't been my choice to leave the Resistance.

At least I didn't think it had.

We rode on through the main streets of the village. The homes were empty as we passed, and it was obvious that whatever had happened to my mother, she wasn't living in the shack we'd called home. My heart sank as we rode past.

"Is that your home?" Caldris asked, and something in his voice was tight. He knew logically that I'd come from nothing, but that meant something very different in the abstract than seeing it for himself.

"It is," I said, pointing a finger to the window I'd snuck out of on far too many nights. "Brann always threatened to bar the window shut, but he couldn't afford the iron." A bitter laugh came up from my throat, knowing he'd probably avoided the iron because of my heritage.

Because of what he'd known about me, never sharing it.

"Your mother can come with us," he said, and he nodded to Aramis. "Search the house. Kindly."

"She's not there," I said, and I could feel it in my bones. This house hadn't been occupied since Brann and I left, and why would it have been? She wouldn't have been able to get herself here in her chair. "She uses a wheeled chair to get around. Her legs aren't strong enough to support her for long, not since she had me."

"Humans were not meant to bear Fae children," Caldris said, and the statement made me turn a curious stare toward Fallon. I'd seen who I had to presume were her parents, and they'd been fine at a glance. "Are you certain you don't want to go in? To take one last look?"

I shook my head. The last thing I wanted was to be reminded of the family I would probably never see again. I'd probably never know what had become of my mother, and my brother was already gone.

There was nothing left in that house but the pain of memories better left in the past, and it wouldn't give me the answers I sought about my mother. Even if it did by some miracle, what good would it do me? She never would have left that house of her own free will.

We rode on as Aramis emerged from the dwelling, word-lessly confirming what I'd already known. My mother was gone. We passed the gallows, passed the village proper and Mistfell Manor. All bore the signs of war; all the homes were shuttered and appeared empty, as if the entire town had simply disappeared without a trace.

The air changed as we approached the empty gardens where I'd spent the majority of my life toiling, caring for the plants held within it and burdened with the task of feeding the Kingdom and the Court in Ineburn City. The scent of magic filled the air, and the thick, salty fluid of the sea was suffocating as we approached.

In all the times I'd met the ocean before, never had I felt like I would drown in it before I even touched the water. "Stay here," Caldris instructed, lowering himself from Azra. He unsheathed his sword, striding forward as the army of the dead surrounded us. The Fae Marked remained in the carts, slumping low and practically lying down to avoid being seen. The girl from the day before still hadn't awoken, and I looked down at her sleeping face as Fallon sat with her.

The Wild Hunt and Imelda followed after Caldris, stepping

toward the boundary at the edge of the gardens. The wolves and hounds remained with us, forming a protective circle around the army of the dead as we hid in the streets of the village and beneath the copse of trees that hung over the buildings lining the road.

Fallon glanced at me as I dismounted Azra. Metal clashed through the fading light in the distance, the sky darkening above our heads far too quickly to be natural. I peered around the edge of the buildings, watching as a force of the Mist Guard emerged from the barracks to fight one last stand and keep us from crossing over the boundary.

There were so many of them—far more than I'd ever realized. They had to be reinforcements sent by the King in Ineburn City, and they wielded iron blades and traps against the Wild Hunt as Fallon and I watched on helplessly.

Taking a single step forward, I flinched back when the bodies of the dead closed ranks in front of me and kept me locked away. I fumbled for the golden threads trailing off him, but they refused to respond to my touch, or to slide around my skin and do as I commanded.

"I guess we know Caldris meant it this time," Fallon said, forcing an uncomfortable smile to her face. I grimaced, looking back toward the boundary where the Veil had once shimmered, and to the man who stood there as if he had any right to still be breathing. The Guards at Lord Byron's side wheeled a woman toward the boundary, her brown hair plastered to her head as rain pelted down on them. Her chair bumped over the uneven surface of the ground, jarring her from side to side as she fought to hold on to the armrests in the crude chair he'd had crafted for her as a favor to me after my father's death.

"That's my mother," I told Fallon, ignoring her touch as she reached down to take my hand in hers. Between my mother and I, a battle raged. The sounds of death and fighting wrought the air, and the tang of blood filled my nostrils.

Fallon hurried out of the cart, gripping my forearm tightly. Her nails dug into the bare skin there as she peered toward the witches gathered at the edge of the Veil, and she realized who they had taken with them. Caldris, the Wild Hunt, Imelda: all of them were fighting except for the small group of the dead left behind to guard the group of us.

There was no one around to summon to my side. No one I could shout to without risking their life as they battled with the Mist Guard. The Guard that Brann had stabbed that day in the woods hadn't been unique. There were dozens of them fighting in the gardens, larger than life and almost inhuman in the way they functioned.

"You can't," Fallon said, shaking her head from side to side with an urgent warning. I gritted my teeth as I turned back to the Guards who wheeled my mother's chair up to the Veil, where the witches waited beside Lord Byron. Caldris was too busy with his fight, splitting his power between controlling the dead who guarded us and fighting four of the unnaturally large guards who shouldn't have existed.

"I have to. I'm sorry," I said, darting forward suddenly. I slid in the mud, dropping onto my ass and pushing through the spread leg bones of a skeleton. Its head spun in a full circle on the vertebrae of its neck, those hollow, empty eye-sockets following me as I jumped to my feet on the other side and ran forward.

Caldris spun quickly, as if he felt the moment I broke free from the circle of protection he'd created. I focused my attention on my mother, ignoring the heavy weight of his stare as he cut down the man he fought with.

The tinge of iron coated the air, the weaponry of the Mist Guard making the hair raise on my arms. If I was so affected by the proximity of it, it was no wonder why Caldris seemed subdued from his usual overpowering presence. The threads around me felt hazy, as if my fingers might slip through them should I try to reach out and grasp at them.

I bent down as I ran, grabbing a sword from one of the fallen corpses. My skin sizzled against the iron, burning my flesh. "Estrella!" Caelum growled, the warning of his deep voice sinking inside me.

I shook my head, warding off the thoughts that plagued me. The instinct to turn back to the safety of the circle of the dead, a command that pulsed down the bond between us.

I severed the thought, picturing my bedroom window slamming shut in his face. I glanced over to watch as he stumbled back as if he'd been struck, nearly taking a sword to the chest. He turned at the last moment, narrowly avoiding the blow as the iron blade cut through the flesh of his arm. Blood flowed freely from the wound, spraying into the air and mixing with the rain pelting down around us.

Closing myself off from the stabbing wound of guilt that threatened to consume me, I strode forward toward the edge of the Veil. I ignored the burning of my palm, and the way that I didn't think I'd be able to remove my hand from the sword intact. My skin melted against the iron in a way that would peel the flesh from my bones when I tried to let it go. The growl of the wolves and hounds sounded behind me, mixing with the sounds of the battle. I knew Fenrir had to be occupied for him to not come to my side, and my heart throbbed with the realization that I'd left Fallon behind. I didn't know if she had any ability to defend herself, but I couldn't turn back to find out.

Something slithered along through the grass beneath my feet as I forced myself to move forward with steady steps. The ebony lines of serpents traveling through the snow emerged from the woods behind me to follow as I walked, and I swallowed back the impending sense of doom I felt with every pace that brought me closer to the boundary between Nothrek and Alfheimr.

The magic of Mab coursed through my veins.

I approached the witches, ignoring my mother's wide-eyed stare as she twisted the best she could to look at me over her shoulder. One of the witches stepped forward, deep blue hair hanging down to her waist in loose waves. Her hand glowed with a blue swirl of magic, a ripple of energy radiating from her as she narrowed her glowing sea green stare on me.

She flung the magic at me, a leading wave of sea water tearing through the air between us as I thrust the sword in my hand up to block the attack. It struck the iron of the blade, making it vibrate in my grip painfully, but the magic broke, the wave bursting into droplets of water that parted around me and further soaked the ground.

I glared at her from behind my iron blade, wishing I didn't have to choose between the power in my *Viniculum* and the comfort of a weapon in my hand. The snakes slithered forward, closing the distance between the sea witch and I. She screamed as they approached and wrapped around her ankles, pulling her down to the ground along with them.

I dropped the tip of the sword to the ground beside me as I watched in horror, the twisting, writhing shapes of their mass covering her as she struggled. Pinning her arms to her sides, they encased her in a tomb of serpents and *squeezed.*

Her eyes bulged in her face, the sea green light of them fading slowly as she fought for breath.

My sword moved at my side, one of the midsize serpents winding around the blade itself until the scales of its face touched the tips of my fingers. A forked tongue slithered out of its mouth, licking my hand and the blood that dripped free from my melted skin. It wound around my hand, up over my wrist and twirled its body around my forearm and bicep.

Finally, it draped the heavy weight of its body over my shoulders, its face pressed against my cheek. I swallowed back the surge of fear, closing my eyes as the sea-witch died and breathing in the comfort of the presence of the snake resting on me.

Its tail wound around my sword arm, thrumming as one of the others sank its fangs into the sea witch's corpse. As if it had devoured her soul itself, it transferred her life energy through them and into me. The skin of my hand healed enough that I was able to pry my fingers free, burning red flesh sticking to the hilt of the blade as new skin formed to cover my bones. The snake wound its tail around the hilt, wrapping it in its entirety and giving me something to grip that wasn't poisonous.

At least not to me.

His scaled flesh formed a barrier for me to grip onto as I hefted the heavy blade once more and strode forward. I passed by Holt on my way, striding right by him and the Mist Guards he fought with. "*Gods,*" he muttered, his shocked eyes meeting mine for a moment as I walked by.

By the time the serpents abandoned their previous meal and slithered on ahead of me, the other two witches were ready for them, casting water toward them. I left the witches to their battle with the snakes, narrowing my eyes on where Lord Byron waited beside my mother with two Guards at his side. One of them pressed the tip of his sword to my mother's throat, his act the only thing that kept me from attacking outright.

"Drop the sword, Estrella," Lord Byron ordered, glancing out the corner of his eye to where one of the sea witches approached. Her body was drenched from the rain, her navy hair plastered against her face as she flung the body of one of the snakes off her arm.

"Do not deceive yourself into thinking we are on a first-name basis just because I have seen you fuck women who looked like me," I snapped back, raising my sword to point it at him. "You haven't got the first clue who I am now, but there is one thing you can know with absolute certainty. Any chance you had of walking away alive vanished the moment your men put their hands on her. Now you can spend your last moments knowing that my face will be the last thing you see before I send you to The Father for final judgment."

"You think you can fight two Guards before they kill your pathetic mother *and* you? They've instilled you with an inflated sense of self-worth. You are nothing but a Fae male's whore," Lord Byron spat, the ground absorbing the spittle that sprayed from his mouth.

In spite of the iron humming beneath the snake in my hand, my *Viniculum* darkened, the swirling lines of shadows writhing around as I stroked the fuzzy golden threads around me. They shuddered, acting as if they too would reject my call before they finally allowed me to wrap them around my fingers and pull. Behind me, the magic touched the closest body. It rose from the ground, its presence behind me noticed as the dead sea witch rose from what would have become her very wet, watery grave. "You would be wise to be careful how you speak to me. The God of the Dead is not fond of people insulting his mate," I said.

The sea witch's body stepped forward, feeling far too familiar as some twisted part of me danced within her. It replaced the soul that had moved on, the part of her that lingered in the air around us, waiting for burial or burning.

Waiting for the ferryman to take her to the Void.

There was a hole where her heart should have been,

devoured by the snakes that had claimed her. Even a witch couldn't survive the loss of a heart. I felt the emptiness and I filled it with myself instead—with my purpose and my determination. She stepped forward slowly, approaching her sister witches with sluggish steps as they stared at her in horror. Killing someone we loved, even while knowing they were already gone, was not a task most were familiar with.

It was a dilemma that threatened to impair anyone who did not spend time with the dead. Those moments of doubt, of questioning their instincts, were the moments that would lead to the end of all they loved.

Because the dead cared not for the living, reanimated woman only served my demand for blood. For vengeance.

She served my desire to watch the world burn.

She attacked the one witch who remained standing, the other still grappling with the remaining snakes in what had once been the gardens I'd toiled in for the entirety of my life. I took a step forward toward Lord Byron, knowing the witches were handled for the moment.

"Drop the sword, or I'll slit her throat," the Mist Guard said, pressing the blade deeper into my mother's neck. Blood welled at the tip, staining the iron blade with the viscous fluid. I uncurled my fingers from the hilt of the sword, feeling the serpent around my shoulders unwind her body from the weapon until it dropped to the ground at my side with a heavy thud.

The magic of Alfheimr rolled through the boundary, dancing across my skin. It awakened the part of me lingering beneath the mark, the darkness that stained my soul. My fingers burned with ice, my eyes bled to black as I tilted my head to the side. "Step away from her. We both know you need something far stronger than a human woman to reform the Veil." I glanced toward where the witch fought against her dead sister. The body dropped to the ground with a twist of my hand, crumpling into a pile of flesh. The remaining witch breathed deeply, leaning forward to place her hands on her knees as she glared at me. Her fingers twitched at her sides, ripples of water forming as she began to chant beneath her breath. "Use me instead," I said, turning my attention back to Lord Byron.

I would die at the Veil. Give my life to the formation of the a one to save my mother. The villain of my story might have changed, shifting Lord Byron from my worst nightmare to someone barely worth a thought, but some fates were written in stone.

All the threads of my fate led me here.

"Use you?" Byron asked, taking a cautious step toward me. "Why would you agree to such a thing?"

"Because I love my mother. I love in ways that we both know you will never understand. Not with your own self-hatred and the way you've become the portrait of everything you hated as a boy," I said, the answer resonating inside of me. Part of me wondered if it wasn't for the best, if I needed to stay on this side of that boundary in spite of my promise to my mate. The reality that waited for me on the other side meant that my death might be a blessing to the world.

I was Mab's lost daughter. There was no other explanation for the monstrous thing that existed inside my chest.

The Princess of Air and Darkness.

Byron nodded toward the Guard, watching as the man released my mother and stepped away from her chair. She heaved a sigh of relief, but her face shone with tears. "Estrella, don't do this. You must let me go."

The snake that had draped over me retreated when I glanced toward it, winding its way down my left arm and brushing against the mark on the back of my palm as it lowered itself to the ground. It slithered toward my mother, wrapping around her legs and settling on her lap as if it were a pet. The others abandoned the witch they fought with on the ground, grappling to steal her life the way they had the other.

They followed the larger snake, forming a barrier around her that even the Mist Guard would hesitate to cross. I stood alone, glaring at the man who'd tried to take everything that made me who I was, and who had tried to bury me under the weight of his expectations.

The man who'd replaced the love I'd had for my father with something hideous and loathsome.

The sea witch at his side stepped forward, rage stamped into her features as her sister rose to her feet beside her. Byron held out an arm to stop them both, his head nodding as he held out his other hand. The Guard placed an iron blade into his open palm, and Byron stepped back to gesture me forward toward where the sand at the very edge of the garden met the sea. "Come, Estrella. It is time for The Mother to cast her final judgment upon you. You understand you cannot be allowed to have the gift of another life. Not with a mate waiting for you."

"The Father will take me to Valhalla," I said, stepping forward slowly. I forced myself to ignore my mate's shouts behind me and the slaughter of the men he killed in his effort to get to me.

I stepped up to the edge of the ocean, the icy water lapping against the toes of my boots. Byron grabbed a handful of my hair, yanking my head back to expose my throat as I stared up at him. My only regret in my death was that it would be at his hand. That I wouldn't have the satisfaction of watching the life bleed from his eyes. "But I suggest you hurry. My mate seems quite angry."

Byron narrowed his eyes, turning back to watch where

Caldris fought with the Mist Guard's elite army. I couldn't see him fighting to get to me, but I could feel the rage in his bones.

I felt his anguish, his desperation, in spite of the way I'd cut off our bond, and my eyes burned with tears as the wave of his grief crashed into me, shattering the window I'd closed between us. His pain was a deep anguish, the surge of emotions overriding the burn of iron in his arm where he'd been injured. My own arm throbbed with pain, feeling heavy at my side as it connected again with his injury.

Please, don't leave me alone again.

I squeezed my eyes closed, shoving back the burn of grief in my throat.

Where you go, I will follow.

Byron spun me around so suddenly that I stumbled over my own feet, that grip on my hair tipping my head back sharply. The iron of his blade pressed into the column of my throat, searing the flesh as I recoiled. Caelum fought to close the distance between us. With a few more moments of effort, he'd be able to reach us.

"Say his name," Byron commanded, something curious in his voice making me clamp my mouth shut. He raised the knife from my throat, slashing a white-hot line across my cheekbone. Fire burned through the wound, setting my face ablaze as the blood dripped down. "Say it!"

"Caldris," I said, his name echoing through the gardens of Mistfell. Something drummed between us as my mate cut down the last opponent standing in his way, a thick spray of blood arcing from the other man's chest as the Fae tore his sword from the place where the Guard's heart had once been.

"So this is the legendary God of the Dead," Byron murmured, his voice soft against my ear. "What do you think the King will give me when I bring him the head of a God?"

I stilled suddenly, giving away far too much in the agony of the thought. I'd only wanted to save my mother, not condemn my mate to death. "You don't like that. Don't tell me you have feelings for this beast?"

"You are far greater a monster than he could ever dream to be," I said vehemently, the conviction in those words shocking even me.

Caelum's dark stare met mine as he wielded a sword in each hand, stepping as close as he dared before Byron adjusted the blade at my throat. My skin sizzled all over again as Caelum's eyes dropped to where the blade touched me. His glare trailed over the cut on my cheek, his nostrils flaring as he clenched his jaw.

"It takes a truly pathetic excuse of a male to toy with a woman and to mark her flesh," Caldris said, his glare honing in on where Byron loomed over my shoulder.

The Lord's breath washed over my face when he leaned forward, saying the perfectly wrong thing in his absolute arrogance. "Estrella is well-acquainted with wearing the marks I leave on her skin." His next words turned the earth of his own grave. "Aren't you, sweetheart?"

Everything in Caldris froze, his entire being and soul pausing as the meaning beyond those words penetrated him. His eyes narrowed, bleeding to complete and utter black. "Byron," he growled, and the memory of revealing my tormenter's name to Caelum in the hot spring washed over me.

"How sweet of you to tell him about me," Byron said smugly as he leaned forward into my back. "Did you tell him all the things I made you feel that he never could?"

"I told him you were so weak a man you couldn't even beat me yourself most of the time," I said, trying to shift his attention back to me. The tip of the blade cut into my throat and Caldris's gaze snagged on the blood.

"I see he has done nothing to make you behave appropriately," Byron complained.

"He likes it when I stab things. Call it a character flaw," I said, smirking in spite of my death staring me in the face. The fact that Caldris himself paused meant he knew exactly how quickly Byron could drag the blade across my throat. He knew even he couldn't cross that distance in time to get to me.

"She's just a mate," Caldris said, tossing Byron one of his trademark smirks. "But it's cute that you think her soul will be powerful enough to form a Veil. The last male who gave his life to it was a God, but sure. She should do the trick."

I jerked against Byron's grip, knowing exactly what Caldris was doing. Whether his words were true or not, I wouldn't allow him to give his life when I felt the ominous energy rolling off the boundary. I felt it in my flesh, whatever came when I crossed the barrier would be horrible. It would be a fate worse than death—all the things Brann had promised.

"Don't listen to him. He's just toying with you," I said.

"Perhaps, but a Veil formed from his soul would be a lovely trophy, and then you would still be alive. *Without a mate,*" he said, leaving little doubt as to where that would leave me exactly.

"And I would still choose death over you."

"Lay down your swords," Byron said, his order going straight over me and to Caldris. My mate dropped his swords at his side, not flinching in the slightest when the two men stepped up to him. He held my gaze as he placed his hands in front of him, allowing them to shackle his wrists in iron while he grimaced. His skin sizzled inside them, nearly dropping him to his knees as the force of it weakened him.

The chain that connected the two shackles hung between his arms, swaying as he stood. "Now let her go."

"Don't do this. I'm ready to die," I said.

"If you're gone, then so am I," he returned, smiling slightly. The Guards brought him closer to the boundary, until he stood beside me but out of reach. Byron spun me to face him, watching as the Mist Guard forced him to his knees in the sand.

"Stop," I ordered, wincing when the protest fell on deaf ears. One of the witches stepped up, chanting at the edge of the boundary. The waters of the ocean receded from my feet, sucked into the vortex as she created a wall from the very seawater itself.

"*O' dromneacht en farroile,*" she said, drawing her hand up from where it lay beside her thigh. "*Go ti en sparath thas.*" The Guard pressed his blade to Caldris's throat in preparation for whatever was about to come.

"No!" I shrieked, the sound blasting from within me. It echoed through the space, cracking into the wall of water the witch worked to build. She flew back into it, the wall bursting back into the ocean like a popped bubble.

Time stood still as she broke through the wall, falling to the ocean below. The water was shallow, her head smacking against the sand as she landed. Darkness descended, crashing through the twilight with the force of a midnight sky.

I twisted my head, ignoring the fiery path the blade drew across my throat, and grabbed Byron's arm with both hands. Pushing the knife away from my neck while I turned, I elbowed him in the side as I spun free from his grip. In the same moment, Caldris rose to his feet, smashing his shackled hands into the face of the first Guard and disarming him with a fluidity that still took my breath away.

He tossed me the sword he'd stolen, not pausing to see if I caught it before he turned his attention to the other Mist Guard. I spun again, catching the sword out of mid-air as I twirled. I wrapped my fingers around the hilt, swinging in an upward arc. The Lord's stared at me in horror as I faced him, something shining off his pale skin. The light of a million stars twinkled over his flesh as I sliced the sword toward his neck. He opened his mouth as if to speak, but he never managed to say the words.

The edge of the blade cut deep into his throat, blood splattering against my face and chest as I closed my eyes. My stomach heaved as fire lit me from the inside. My shoulders slumped forward as I staggered backward two steps, folding in on myself and watching Byron's hand fall away from the hilt of his dagger. His eyes were glossy, his mouth parted in shock as he raised both hands to his throat and tried to hold the flow of blood within his neck. It stained his skin, spilling through his fingers and onto his wrists in a heavy stream.

The hilt of his dagger burned my hand as I grasped it, pulling it free from my stomach carefully and tossing it to the ground. Time slowed, my vision going hazy at the edges. I swayed but managed to stay on my feet long enough to watch Byron crumple to the ground before me. His blank, unseeing eyes stared up at the raining, night sky, and the Void pressed in on me.

Caldris hurried to my side, thrusting his hand into Byron's chest. He wrapped his fingers around Byron's still heart, yanking it free and tossing it to the serpents that guarded my mother. They devoured it as if it was their only meal for the day, destroying Byron's soul before it could have time to leave his body.

"Not all men are worthy of reincarnation," Caldris said, rising to his full height. His hand was stained with blood, his armor coated in the thick, cloying scent of death. I raised a hand to my stomach, concealing the wound I didn't want him to see.

Even as exhaustion claimed my limbs, I forced myself to

remain standing. Caldris yanked his shackles apart, snapping the chain that connected them as he closed the distance between us. Reaching up to touch my cheek, his nostrils flared as he scented the air. His brow furrowed as his gaze darted over my face and my neck.

My bottom lip trembled as his focus finally settled on the hand covered in blood. He pulled it away, eyeing the stab wound as my knees buckled beneath me. "*Fuck,*" he grunted, catching my weight as we dropped to the ground. "Imelda!" he shouted, wrapping an arm behind me and shifting me so that my head rested in his lap.

The witches stepping toward us told me everything I needed to know, why he'd summoned Imelda to his side. She moved between us and them, holding up her hands to placate them. "The Veil was never meant to be anything but temporary. One of these girls needs to get to Alfheimr," she murmured, the words sounding all too distant as she spoke them.

Caldris pulled the dagger from his sheath, lifting it to his wrist. I reached up, grasping his hand and pulling it down. "Take Fallon to Alfheimr. Whatever is waiting for her, help her however you can," I said, swallowing back the surge of white hot nausea creeping up my throat. "Imelda thinks she needs to get there."

"What are you talking about?" he asked, staring down at where I gripped his wrist and refused to let it go.

"We both know the odds of me not being Mab's daughter are almost nil. The Veil was created to keep me from her. Maybe this is how it was supposed to be, Caldris," I said, touching his cheek with my other hand. "This is where my life was always meant to end."

"Don't you dare ask that of me," he growled, the rumble crawling up his chest and his throat.

"I don't have a choice," I rasped, watching as he cut his wrist with the blade against my wishes. I closed my mouth, turning my face away from him when he tried to guide it to my lips.

"I will not sit here and watch you die," he said, leaning his face over mine. Staring into the shock of his blue eyes, I felt the rain around us turn to snow as his magic took over and pushed away the witches' magic.

"I would go anywhere else with you. Anywhere but Alfheimr. Remember when you told me that her daughter was better off for having been stolen?" I said, reaching up to guide the hand that held his dagger down to my heart. I touched the tip to it, staring up at him as the first of my tears fell free. "I wanted to spend eternity with you."

"Don't."

"I love you," I said, admitting the truth in my heart; he still owned me as if I could never claw him out.

"We will have our eternity," he said, pressing his wrist to my lips. I struggled against his grip, silently pleading with my eyes for him to stop. He pushed hard enough that my lips parted, the sweetness of him touching my teeth and gums. He slid inside me, coating my tongue with his essence.

My wound healed, my flesh knitting itself back together as he stared down at my stomach, watching it seal shut as he dropped his forehead to mine.

My gaze fell to the dagger at his side, the horror of what I would need to do to escape the fate that waited for me rushing through me.

I choked back a sob, lunging to my feet as my stomach twinged with the pain of my still healing wound. I wrapped my fingers around the handle, turning to face my mate where he stood before me with raised hands.

As if he were a victim, and not the male who wanted to

take me to the one place I couldn't go. "I don't want to go," I said, spinning the weapon in my grip to point toward him. His eyes fell on it, a sad sort of smile consuming his face before he raised them back to me.

"I know."

43

*H*e didn't make a move for either of his swords that lay just a short distance away. He just stared at me with those sad, understanding eyes as I lifted the sword at my side. "I'll do anything to keep you safe," he said, taking a single step toward me.

He paused, watching me warily to see if I would move to strike. My brow furrowed as I willed my arm to move, trying to convince it that killing the male in front of me was my only chance not to face the woman I believed to be my mother. "How can you protect me? You can't even protect yourself!" I accused, my voice trailing higher as I became too aware of the audience watching our drama play out. With Lord Byron dead and the witches convinced to stop their fight, the Wild Hunt picked off any of the remaining Mist Guard who'd stayed behind to fight. Most of them fled, darting into the same woods I'd escaped in only a few weeks before.

It seemed impossible, for so much to have changed in such a short time.

"Estrella?" my mother asked. Her voice hitched, and I

glanced toward her where she sat, in mystified, staring at the sword clutched in my hand. "Where is your brother?"

I didn't answer; couldn't keep my attention on her long enough to find the words to tell her that her only son was dead. "Gone," Caldris answered, his voice short and ill-tempered at the reminder of what my brother had tried to do. "The Wild Hunt killed him when he tried to stab Estrella."

"He failed," my mother breathed, her voice and face dropping with what I had to assume was grief. Her words washed over me, the meaning behind them striking me in the chest so harshly that I stumbled back a step. She held my eyes. "Then you have to be the one to do it."

"You knew?" I asked, feeling tears well in my eyes.

"He was only a boy when your father found him. At least he came to us as one," she said, her voice strangled as she swallowed past the burn of the tears making her eyes glisten. "He swore the day would come when you needed his protection. Your father would have sworn he was half-delirious from starvation, if he hadn't changed before our eyes to prove what he said was true."

"He was the missing Lunar Witch," I said, the words feeling torn from me. It was such a startling confession to make out loud, to voice it to someone who could confirm it.

My mother nodded in agreement. "He said he was your guardian, and that he would allow us to raise you so long as we took him in and told everyone he was your father's son from an affair on the road. Nobody questioned it, because nobody cares when people like us have illegitimate heirs."

"Could he be alive?" I asked, twisting to look at Caldris in shock.

"It's possible," he agreed, nodding. But if Brann had survived that day on the cliff, why hadn't he found me in the weeks that had passed since?

"Whatever happened to your brother, you have to consider what he wanted for you. I don't understand what's waiting for you in Alfheimr or why he swore everything would change the moment you stepped foot on Faerie soil, but I know that he loved you more than *anything*. For him to make a choice that your death was necessary, I truly fear what will happen if you cross that boundary, Estrella," my mother said, and I knew it pained her to admit it. I'd seen the anguish in her eyes the day they'd tried to sacrifice me to the Veil, and I knew my mother loved me.

I nodded back to her, tightening my grip on the sword before I turned my gaze back to the God of the Dead. "I know," I said, sinking my teeth into my bottom lip and trying to push back the cloying sadness that threatened to draw me under. I'd never be able to do what needed to be done, not with him alive to heal me.

Caldris smiled, stepping toward me as he unlaced the ties on the leather and metal covering his chest. He dropped it to the ground as he took another step, moving closer until the tip of my sword pressed into the fabric of his shirt. "I told you once before, I would rather die than go on without you."

I swallowed, the lump of sorrow in my throat making it hard to breathe. "Caldris," I murmured, the anguish in my voice palpable in the air. We were too far past the point where I could pretend I didn't care for him, that he didn't own my soul. Even if I hated him for putting me in this position, for saving me when I hadn't wanted it. Death would have been far more convenient than the horror that was coming for me.

That part of me that was his continued to reach across the gap between us, wanting nothing more than to stare into his blue eyes until my last breath. "Just promise me that your face will be the last thing I see before the darkness claims me."

"You aren't supposed to accept it," I said, barely resisting the urge to drop the sword so I could punch him. "You're supposed to fight me."

He reached out, wrapping his palm around the sharp edge of the blade. His blood slid free as he cut himself, mixing with the blood of all the men he'd killed in his attempt to get to me.

To save me.

"Why would I want to fight with you, my star?" he asked sadly. "I just want to love you until my last breath. You were worth every century I waited, even if I only had you for a short time."

I squeezed the hilt more firmly, clinging to it even though I already knew the answer to the question in my soul.

It was him. Always him.

I released it as soon as the thought solidified in my mind, letting the dagger clutter to the ground. It dropped as if in slow motion, as if fate itself recognized the descent for what it was.

The beginning of the end.

Caldris closed the distance between us before it clattered against the ground, stepping over the blade as he slid a hand beneath the curtain of my hair. His hand cupped my neck, my face, my mark and everything he could reach. Staring into my eyes for a moment, he lowered his mouth to mine and kissed me with the slow, consuming passion that we didn't have time for.

Time we'd been robbed of, no matter what the outcome of crossing the boundary would be. He pulled back, staring down at me. "Let me take you to Catancia," he murmured.

"But you have to bring Mab's daughter to her. We both know—"

"We know nothing," Caldris said, touching my lips with

his to silence me. "I have to bring you and Fallon there to present you to her, but there's no reason we cannot make a stop along the way. Let me take you to the frozen falls of Lumen. Accept me as your mate as you already agreed to do. We'll stand a chance of breaking the bond she placed on me as a child. If she can no longer command me, then I won't need to bring you to her at all. We could be *free*."

His words built an ache inside of me, a longing I hadn't wanted to admit I possessed. I wanted nothing more than to be free, except to be with him. The promise of having both seemed completely unattainable, with his possessiveness and the way he thought to protect me from all the horrors of the world.

Could I ever really be free with a male like Caldris at my side?

"Okay," I whispered, slumping my shoulders forward as I gave my answer. If there was even the slightest chance that we could find a place that offered us peace, I had to take it.

The smile that lit his face would hold in my memory for the rest of my days, the shock of relief crashing into my chest making my heart skip a beat. He crushed me to his chest, wrapping his free arm around the small of my back tightly and dropping his mouth to mine.

His gaze held mine as his lips teased the flesh of my mouth. He murmured against them, the intensity and intimacy of his smoldering stare raising the hair on my arms. The words felt significant, pulsing through the silence of the gardens as the Fae Marked moved from their hiding place. "I am going to love you until the stars disappear from the night sky and the sun ceases to shine. Until the world returns to the void from whence it was born and chaos reigns once again."

He touched his lips to mine as he dropped his hands to

grab my own. Raising them at our sides, he pressed his palms against mine and aligned our fingers the best he could. My skin hummed with warmth as I closed my eyes, breathing in the deep scent of lotus flowers on the lake in the summer with a hint of sandalwood as the winter breeze washed over my face.

When he pulled his mouth away, I blinked up at him, the golden light radiating from our hands. Something in the magic required an answer, a calling I couldn't ignore. "Until chaos reigns and eternity begins anew, and for every moment after," I said, turning my attention to our laced fingers. Golden threads twined around the backs, squeezing them together until I gasped in pain. The threads cut into my skin, the red stain of blood trailing down Caldris's skin in the same way.

"My soul, my heart, my flesh, and my sword are yours, and if ever there should come a day when your heart ceases to beat, I will follow you into the Void." He twisted our bound hands, letting my blood glide across my flesh to touch the edges of his. The moment the first drop touched his blood, the golden threads tightened suddenly and then burst out in a sudden wave of light.

He lowered our hands to our sides, releasing mine so that I could raise it and stare at the crisscrossing marks the threads had left. The blood was gone, and if it hadn't been for the golden lines shimmering from under my skin, I might have thought it had all been a figment of my imagination.

"What have you done?" Imelda asked, stepping forward through the hush in the group that had gathered to watch. She took my hand in hers, running her fingers over the faint gold lines and turning a wide, white-eyed stare to me finally. She stepped back, dropping her hands to her sides slowly.

"What is it?" I asked, looking back and forth between her

and Caldris. He raised his chin high in defiance, glaring down at her.

"Your mate swore a blood oath, and The Fates accepted it," she said, glaring back at him. "Do you have any idea how foolish this was? You have no idea what awaits her on the other side of the boundary! You are the sole heir to the Winter Court. You cannot gamble with your life when chaos will be the only result of your death."

"I don't understand," I said, staring at him as I tried to understand the words he'd spoken.

"Your lives are now one. The mate bond will tie your mortal life, assuming you *are* mortal, to his immortal one, enabling you to live longer. He's made it so that whether you are mated or not, whether you are mortal or immortal, he will die alongside you. If we lose one of you, we will lose you both. It was a fool's bargain," Imelda said, looking toward Holt as if she expected him to back her up.

"I think it's quite romantic," Holt returned, crossing his arms over his chest with a smirk.

"If codependence is your thing, sure," Imelda said, her lips forming a cruel smile. "It isn't mine, and you'll doom us all for yours," she added, turning her attention back to Caldris. She pinned him with all the judgment of her all-seeing stare, and I knew that if the force of it had been focused on me, I'd have withered on the spot.

She took Fallon by the hand, guiding the other girl away as they murmured between themselves. There was little doubt they needed to strategize for what they would do when we learned what Fallon was. I'd all but proven to everyone except my mate that I was the lost daughter of Mab.

The same power flowed through my veins.

"Why would you do that?" I asked, staring up at him as he leaned into my space once again. His fingers toyed with the lock of hair that hung around my shoulders, my body seeming to recognize the drum of fate that pulsed off of his hand and echoed off of my body.

"You may not be able to kill me, but that does not mean that you wouldn't take your own life if you became desperate enough. You will not be a martyr, min asteren. Not unless you're willing to take me with you," he said, the confirmation of his outright willingness driving a stake into my heart. While I didn't doubt the emotion behind his profession, the blood oath had been a very conscious decision.

Tying my life to his, knowing that it would prevent me from doing the one thing I still had any sort of control over. Keeping me from fulfilling my promise to Brann.

My brother. My guardian. I didn't know what to call him anymore.

"That shouldn't have been your choice to make," I said, raising a brow. I wanted to be furious with him, but I was so tired of fighting. So exhausted with pretending he didn't make my entire world spin and believing that I should hate him simply because it was what I'd always been taught. I couldn't hold him to human conventions, because he wasn't human.

And neither was I.

"It is my life, Little One. I get to choose how or when I live it. I choose to do it with you for eternity."

"We should go," Fallon said, glancing back toward the woods where we all knew there could be more Mist Guard gathering forces, waiting for back up. Mistfell wouldn't hold in the long run, but it was the place where all the battles between the humans and the Fae would occur.

I released Caldris's hand, stepping toward my mother. The serpents finally slithered away, retreating into the woods and back to where they belonged. Only the one who had draped herself over my shoulders remained, coming toward me so that she could wrap around my leg and coil her way up my body to settle on on her perch once more.

"Come with us," I said to my mother, ignoring the look of shock on her face. "His mother will give you a safe haven in Catancia, and you'll have a comfortable life. They'll kill you if you stay here." I knew without a doubt it was true, that they would take one look at the only remaining survivor and know without a doubt she wasn't entirely on their side.

Particularly with Lord Byron lying dead at the boundary, his face covered in sand as the tide washed over him.

"I never wanted to go to Faerie," she said, looking out over the water. A single ship sailed where the waters deepened, barely visible through the cloud of mist on the water. "But I don't suppose I have any choice but to follow you now." There was nothing left to tie her to Mistfell. They'd killed her husband, tried to kill her only daughter. "I knew you were special from the moment I fell pregnant. I felt it within me, whatever you were stronger than any babe should be. You took everything from me, and still it wasn't enough." She touched her legs, the part of her I'd been told started to pain her during her pregnancy with me. "But I would give all of that and more all over again to see you grow into the woman you've become, Estrella."

"What?" I asked. My mouth dropped open in shock. I'd expected her to pass judgment for the fact that I'd fallen in love with a Fae, that I'd disobeyed what Brann wished for me to have him at my side.

"Sometimes, it is far braver to love the man the world has tried to convince us is a monster. You have always wanted to carve your own path, write your own future. Now you can," she said, patting the top of my hand with hers. Holt took up his place behind her, shifting her chair to the edge of the sea.

"How do we get to the boat?" Fallon asked, staring out at

the ocean. Imelda tilted her face up to the sky and the moon shining above her head, murmuring words in the Old Tongue. The water parted, the waves shifting to the side as a channel appeared in the middle of the ocean. The Wild Hunt went first, guiding their skeletal horses through the corridor she'd created.

We followed.

*M*ist floated through my fingers. The land of Alfheimr appeared slowly, the sandy beach leading up to a grass-covered hill. Atop it, a golden gate shone in the moonlight, a fence taller than anything I'd ever seen extending to either side of the gate itself. It traveled farther than I could see to both sides, fading into the distance.

Beyond the shimmering gold, snow kissed the ground, as if what existed on one side of the barrier was one season, and what lay within another entirely.

The Winter Court.

Rocking from side to side on the waves, the boat pulled up to the enormous pier jutting out from the land and two members of the Wild Hunt grabbed onto the rope and anchor. Hooking it over the dock itself, the nearly translucent figures jumped down onto the deck. The wood creaked beneath their feet, as if it hadn't been touched in years. "Where did the Veil fall on this side?" I asked, looking around for a place where they might have been able to reach it.

"It extended to just outside the gates," Caldris answered, a shadow moving his face as he stared at the gleaming gold. As if he was seeing the barrier that had once existed between us.

"But that means that the Veil was thick. It always seemed to sway in the wind," I answered, thinking of all the nights I'd wandered too close. Of all the times I'd barely been able to refrain from touching the shimmering magic.

"We believe the Veil was actually two separate barriers. One was crafted from the flesh, the other from the bone," Holt answered, stepping away as he helped lay down the gangplank that would allow us to walk off the ship.

"The Veils of Flesh and Bone," Caldris echoed, placing a hand on the small of my back. Imelda took Fallon's hand, guiding the more hesitant woman toward the plank.

"But who's flesh and bone was it?" I asked, trying not to think of the implications beyond such magic.

"My mother's husband's," Caldris answered as he ground his teeth in thought. "He gave his life to the Lunar Witches so they could form the Veil. That's all we know, and my mother has never spoken a word of what she might know about the purpose."

"Does she know anything?" I asked, wondering if he would even know her well enough to guess.

"I doubt it. Mab tortured her for more information. If she'd known anything, she'd have told her, I think he purposefully kept it from her so she couldn't reveal whatever it was that he knew," he said, watching as Imelda guided Fallon down the gangplank.

The dock waited for them, and I watched as they stepped onto the structure with shaky feet. We followed, the slope of the crossing tripping me up as I tried to function past the overwhelming dread in my body.

Something was wrong. Something in me was missing.

That hollow part of me lit aflame, flickering through the void as he guided me onto the boards of the dock.

Imelda's words about not knowing what to expect when we touched the magic of Faerie for the first time rang in my ears while I watched as Fallon paused at the edge of the dock. Imelda stepped down onto the soil of Alfheimr, her body going rigid as she sighed in what looked like relief, reunited with her home and the source of her power.

Two moons nestled in a sky full of stars above our heads, radiating light down onto the land before us. "Take me back," I said suddenly, the words spilling from the depths of my soul.

"What?" Caldris asked, looking down at me in shock.

"I can't go to Alfheimr. I can't," I said. I couldn't explain the feeling inside of me, the absolute revulsion that I would be here, when I wasn't meant to be here yet. Holt wheeled my mother down the gangplank behind us, the pier creaking under the weight of her chair and the horses who stepped onto the dock behind her.

"You have to. We cannot go back to Nothrek," Caldris said, watching as Imelda struggled to pull Fallon down from the dock. She was frozen in fear, her face pale and a mirror of my own.

"Fallon feels it too," I said, nodding my head toward her. "We aren't supposed to be here."

"Whichever one of you is Mab's daughter, this is just as much your home as it is mine. This is exactly where you belong. Not in the human realm with people who would kill you if they knew what you were. You are *Fae*," he said, using his hand on the small of my back to guide me further toward the land of Faerie.

"No! Caelum please!" I begged, turning back to the ship. I'd fight my way through him if I had to—anything to avoid that sinking numbness that grew inside me with every step I took closer.

"We don't have a choice, min asteren," he said, grasping me around the waist. He lifted me onto his shoulder, tossing me over it like a sack of potatoes as he strode for Alfheimr.

With his free arm, he wrapped it around Fallon and lifted as she struggled against Imelda's grip. Her eyes met mine from behind his back, her gray eyes wide and terrified. I reached behind Caldris's back, taking her hand in mine and squeezing.

Caldris stepped down off the docks, our bodies suspended in the air as he carried us. The entrance of Alfheimr loomed, buzzing with the odd vibration of magic. I heard rather than saw the massive golden gates swing open as he approached, the creaking of the hinges making something inside of me split.

The part of me that belonged to Caldris and the part of me that needed to escape. Split down the middle as if lightning had struck, a terrifying chasm in the center, where there was just *nothing.*

He lowered Fallon to her feet once we were inside the gates of Alfheimr, her boots touching the soil for only a moment before she collapsed with a silent scream. "Fallon!" I shrieked, struggling on Caldris's shoulder. He set me to my feet as he turned to her, his brow furrowed in pure confusion and attempting to understand exactly what had happened.

Imelda had hinted at it in the moments when Caldris wasn't within earshot, that we would never know what might happen when an immortal soul touched the land of Faerie for the first time after centuries of human existence.

My knees caved under me. The breath expelled from my lungs.

They writhed inside my body, moving around as if everything inside of me was unmade. I fell to my hands and knees on the soil and grasped the heady earth in my hands as I clawed at it.

I couldn't breathe.

Couldn't begin to fathom what was happening to my body. I'd thought the pain of being Fae Marked was painful, but it was nothing compared to the complete and utter burning inside of me now. It could never compare to suffering as my intestines unraveled and rearranged, my bones breaking and reknitting to build a new form.

My fingers felt so cold they might fall off, contrasting with the agony of each of them breaking. "Estrella!" Caldris's roar came to me as if it was on the other side of a window. Muffled, separated.

As if he couldn't reach me. He turned me to my back, settling me gently on the snow as his face filled my view. He hovered in and out of sight, my vision going white with the blinding pain consuming me. He dropped a finger to touch my ear, the light caress scalding against my skin.

I turned my head to face Fallon, seeing her hair darker than normal. Her ears were pointed and tipped slightly in the same way all the Fae had. A fiery path extended across my neck, lighting it on fire as Caldris flinched back. He touched a hand to his own neck and chest, as if he felt the way the fire coiled and curled around my unmarked shoulder. My fingers burned and I looked down to find them gleaming blacker, as if dipped in the night sky itself with the scattering of stars shimmering against my darkened skin.

Caldris tore the collar of my shirt, staring at the place where I burned from the inside out. "Fuck," he cursed, releasing the blouse as quickly as he'd grabbed it.

"Fallon," Imelda whispered in a hush voice. She covered her mouth with her hand as I forced myself to sit up through the pain, looking over at where her hair turned to the blackest night. Her neck twined with the perfect image of a black Fae Mark, disappearing into the fabric of her dress.

She looked like herself, the same girl I'd met in the tunnels when we began our journey to Mistfell, but somehow...*more*. With her pointed ears, black hair, and shining hazel eyes, there was nothing that stood out to signal what she might be.

Except for the color of the Shadow Court inked upon her skin.

"What is she?" I asked, looking at her and trying to decide as the pain in my soul eased off. It seemed impossible to think of her being anything else, any creature from the depths of the Shadow Court and written into nightmares.

"She's my daughter," a woman's smoky voice said. I looked around, finding not a soul looking back at me, aside from those who'd made the journey with us. It all changed so quickly, a wave of shadow and the scattering of blight upon the sky as she appeared from the inky darkness she commanded.

She stepped onto the snow, using whatever magical passage she'd been granted. She studied her daughter, a gleaming smile transforming her face as she stared at Fallon. It wasn't the affection I'd have expected from any normal mother, but ownership at having property returned to her finally.

She leveled a stare at me next, glancing up and down my body and grinning maliciously when her focus narrowed on the Fae Mark that matched my mate's.

"You've been a very naughty boy, Caldris. You never told me you had a mate," Mab said, tilting her head to the side as she stared down at me. I backed into Caldris's legs, letting him place his hands beneath my arms and haul me to my feet. "I'm not certain what you've brought home," she said, stepping forward until she stood just before us. She reached out with a hand, the black talon-tipped finger brushing the collar of my tunic aside. My skin throbbed where her nail touched me, an ache spreading through my body as everything in me seemed to revolt against her touch. "But I'm most interested in finding out."

She twisted her hand, and I watched in horror as a lash struck against my mother's cheek. *"No!"* I screamed, rushing forward and putting my body between Mab's and hers.

The Goddess's eyes were so dark they were black as she studied me. They gleamed with satisfaction as she snapped her fingers. An army of armed Fae soldiers appeared behind her, their armor gleaming in black with red leather surrounding it.

Caldris stepped forward, pushing my mother and I behind him and standing between us and Mab. "I brought you your daughter. I did as you required. According to the Accords, you cannot touch my human mate."

"Interestingly enough, she doesn't look human at all. Whatever she was moments ago hardly matters now. You know I do not suffer secrets, my sweet. *Kneel*," she said, a cruel smile lighting her face with absolute glee. She turned to the male who stepped up beside her. "Take the girl and have your men remind Caldris what happens when he displeases his Queen."

"Yes, my Queen," the male said, wrapping an arm around my bicep as Caldris fell to his knees. His grimaced, a roar erupting from his chest as he tried to force himself to his feet. But each time, his legs stopped working, even as the other male pulled me away from him, yanking me despite my struggles.

"Caelum!" I screamed, trying to pry the male's fingers off of me as the army stepped up to my mate where he knelt. Mab

spoke to one of her other males, sending him after Fallon. Imelda cried as the male took her ward off the ground and lifted her into his arms, but something in me settled seeing the gentle way he carried her.

As if she mattered to him.

I kicked the male holding me between the legs, finding satisfaction when he crumpled forward. His face twisted with pain, the great and terrible beauty of the Fae evident in every line stamped on his features. Stomping on his foot, I bolted away from him and made my way back to Caldris.

He knelt on the ground, his face already battered as Mab's men took turns pummeling into the features I loved so dearly. Grabbing one of the Fae bastards by the hair, I yanked back until he had no choice but to bend his neck backward to alleviate some of the pressure. Slamming the side of my hand down onto the cord of his throat, I reveled in the way he sputtered for breath under his crushed windpipe.

He wouldn't die, but it would hurt like a bitch anyway.

I swiped the dagger from his sheath as he fell to the ground beside me, spinning to the side and swiping for the male next to him. The blade planted into his chest, stabbing him through the heart, and I wished for once that the blade had been iron.

"Enough," Mab said, demanding I turn my attention back to her. She raised a single hand, turning it so that her palm faced up. With a look of pure disdain on her face, she curled her fingers into her palm and squeezed.

It was Caldris who groaned, his face twisting as he dropped forward to his hands. "One good pull, and you will find yourself as mateless as you were with the Veil between you, girl. Except this time the situation will be permanent."

"Stop," I said, curling my fingers tighter around the knife.

"Greater women than you have tried," Mab said, arching

her brow as she studied me with an amused smile, making me want to challenge her. I released the knife where it protruded from the Fae male's chest, dropping my arm to my side. "I'm going to enjoy breaking you," she murmured, that cruel twist of her lips coming before the blow to the side of my head.

"No!" Caldris yelled, but there was no movement in his body.

The male I'd hit in the balls stepped up, grabbing my swaying body even as I fought to shove his touch off. "Be a good girl and hold still," he said, his voice as condescending as his words. He draped me over his shoulder, leaving me with one last glimpse of Caldris bleeding on the snow before everything went black.

There was only one thought spinning in my mind as I was lost to the nothingness within me. If Fallon was Mab's daughter...

What was I?

*B*ook three in the *Of Flesh & Bone* series, *What Lurks Between the Fates*, is coming March 28th. Pre-order now.

ALSO BY ADELAIDE FORREST

Adelaide Forrest writing fantasy romance as

Harper L. Woods:

What Lies Beyond the Veil

What Hunts Inside the Shadows

What Rules Beneath the Surface

Adelaide Forrest writing dark romance:

Please heed the trigger warnings for each book.

BELLANDI WORLD SYNDICATE UNIVERSE

Bellandi Crime Syndicate Series

Bloodied Hands

Forgivable Sins

Grieved Loss

Shielded Wrongs

Scarred Regrets

Settled Scores - Coming Soon

Bellandi Crime Syndicate Volume One

Massacred Dreams Series

Dreams of the Vengeful

Dreams of the Deadly

Dreams of the Wicked